From the very beginning, there had been some intangible bond, something that drew Zack to Katie.

It was as if her heart were transparent and he could see right into it and it was a safe place. She made him feel things he'd never felt with anyone else—understood and accepted and whole.

His hands landed on her waist.

A hot shock ricocheted through him; his groin was against her bottom, his nose in her hair. She smelled like herbal shampoo and Katie—a scent that smelled like summer and desire and a nameless longing—a scent that made him so hard, so fast, that he could have been seventeen again.

Neither one of them moved for long seconds. And then his fingers tightened around her waist as if they had a will of their own. His mouth moved against her hair.

She inhaled sharply, then gave a little moan. He dipped his head and kissed her neck, right where her pulse beat, right on the little brown birthmark. He felt her pulse flutter under his lips.

"Turn around, Katie," he whispered. "Turn around and kiss me."

Praise for Robin Wells

"4 Stars! A delightful romance [and] wonderful tale."
—*RT Book Reviews* on *How to Score*

more . . .

How to Score

"Wells's contemporary romance . . . hits the mark."
—**Publishers Weekly**

"Sweet . . . and absolutely perfect!"
—**RomanceNovel.tv**

"Sexy and enjoyable."
—**Bookloons.com**

"[A] character-driven romance full of wonderful subplots . . . Perfect."
—**Daily Advertiser** (Lafayette, LA)

"A good way to spend a summer afternoon."
—**BellaOnline.com**

Between the Sheets

Still the One

ROBIN WELLS

FOREVER

NEW YORK   BOSTON

Copyright © 2010 by Robin Wells
All rights reserved. Except as permitted under the U.S. Copyright Act of 1976, no part of this publication may be reproduced, distributed, or transmitted in any form or by any means, or stored in a database or retrieval system, without the prior written permission of the publisher.

Cover design by Claire Brown
Book design by Giorgetta Bell McRee

Forever
Hachette Book Group
237 Park Avenue
New York, NY 10017
Visit our website at www.HachetteBookGroup.com.

Forever is an imprint of Grand Central Publishing.
The Forever name and logo is a trademark of Hachette Book Group, Inc.

Printed in the United States of America

First Printing: May 2010

10 9 8 7 6 5 4 3 2

To Ken, who will always be
Still the One!

Acknowledgments

Special thanks to the world's best parents, Roscoe and Charlie Lou Rouse; the world's best daughters, Taylor and Arden; the world's best cowboy lawyer brother, Dick Rouse; and the world's—make that the universe's—best husband, Ken.

I'd also like to thank my dear friend Lisa Bourgeois for helping with the many family health issues that occurred during the writing of this book. Lisa, you are beyond a jewel; you are the Hope Diamond of friends!

Last but not least, I want to thank my amazing editor, Selina McLemore, for her insight, wisdom, and guidance. Selina, you are the greatest!

Still the One

CHAPTER ONE

"What are you doing Saturday night?" Lulu's protuberant green eyes, magnified by her round horn-rimmed eyeglasses, met Katie Charmaine's light brown ones in the salon mirror.

The question set off Katie's internal cupid alarm. Lulu had promised to quit playing matchmaker, but that was three fix-ups ago. "I'm not sure," Katie hedged as she towel-dried Lulu's red curls. "Why?"

"Well, I was wondering if you want to come over for dinner."

Katie blotted Lulu's hair, aware that the four other women in her kitschy pink-and-black beauty shop were actively listening over the drum of rain on the salon's slanted roof. Not that they could help it; the Acadian-style Curl Up 'N Dye beauty salon was only slightly larger than the space shuttle. The two stylist's chairs, the manicure station, and the window-seat waiting area were within such close proximity that all conversations were public property.

But then, most conversations in Chartreuse were like

that, anyway. The close-knit nature of the community was both the blessing and the curse of living in the small Louisiana town.

Katie put down the towel, picked up a wide-toothed comb, and eyed Lulu sternly in the mirror—or, at least, as sternly as she could manage. Katie's late husband used to say that her face was half angel, half pixie, and that she couldn't muster a stern look if her life depended on it. "When we have kids, they're going to walk all over you," Paul used to tease.

The fact he'd died before she'd been able to prove him wrong was the tragedy of Katie's life. Pushing aside the thought, Katie slid the comb into Lulu's hair. "You're not trying to fix me up again, are you, Lulu?"

"Oh, no!" Lulu's eyes rounded in faux innocence.

Bev, the tall, angular stylist dabbing a shade called Brown Sugar onto the retired librarian's gray roots in the next chair, let out a disbelieving snort. One of Katie's closest friends, the forty-something blonde winked at Katie in the mirror. "Lulu would never do that. How could you even think such a thing?"

Katie opted to ignore Bev's sarcasm. "So it would just be dinner with you and your family?" Katie pressed.

"Well…" Lulu fiddled with the edge of the pink-and-black polka-dotted styling cape draped around her like a giant bib. "Not exactly."

Just as Katie suspected. She worked the comb through Lulu's short curls. "So who else, *exactly*, will be there?"

"Well…" Lulu blinked earnestly. "My Robby just put porcelain veneers on a new patient from Hammond."

"A male patient?" Rachel the manicurist looked up

from Josie Pringle's hangnail, her straight black bob swinging.

Lulu nodded, nearly jerking the comb out of Katie's hand. "He's single and he's really nice and now he has a beautiful smile, so I thought I'd invite him over, too."

"And you don't call that a fix-up?" Katie demanded.

"Oh, no!" Lulu said. "The thought never occurred to me."

Bev snorted again.

"You're a terrible liar, Lulu," Rachel said.

"Not to mention incorrigible," Katie added.

"I don't know what you mean." Lulu turned up her palms and attempted to look baffled. Since it wasn't far from her usual expression, it wasn't much of a stretch. "I'm just inviting a couple of friends to dinner."

"A couple of friends you happen to be fixing up on a blind date," Bev said.

Rachel giggled.

"Nice try, Lulu," called Josie, an attractive thirty-nine-year-old brunette who was rocking her sleeping eight-month-old daughter's stroller with her foot as she got her nails done.

"I think you should go, Katie," said Mrs. Street, the elderly librarian.

"Yeah," called Josie. "It never hurts to meet new people."

Katie stifled a sigh. She knew her friends meant well, she really did, but she wished they'd quit trying to meddle in her life. "Thanks, but no thanks."

"He's got beautiful teeth now," Lulu said earnestly. "You know what good work my Robby does." She flashed her own shockingly white veneers, which slanted out like a row of venetian blinds. Robby really should have sent Lulu for some orthodontic work before slapping those puppies on her overbite, Katie thought for the umpteenth time.

She ran the comb down Lulu's scalp, sectioning off the front from the back. "I really appreciate the thought, Lulu, but I'm not interested."

"Still?"

"Still." *And probably not ever*, she thought, tackling a snarl in Lulu's hair.

"Katie, honey," Mrs. Street said gently from the next chair, "it's been two years."

Two years, six months, and four days, to be exact—and if she turned and looked at the clock, she could pinpoint exactly how many hours and minutes had gone by as well. Her life was divided into before and after 6:10 that fateful Tuesday morning. That was the time glowing on her bedside alarm clock when she'd awakened from a dream of Paul—a dream so real, she'd thought the pillow against her back was her husband spooning her—to realize the doorbell was ringing. She'd gotten up and padded to the door, the dream still wrapped around her like a blanket, expecting to see the UPS delivery man with the new chair she'd ordered as a welcome-home surprise for Paul.

Instead, she'd peered out the sidelight window and seen two Marines in full-dress uniform standing on her porch. A scream had started in her soul, pumped through her veins, and burst out her throat. She remembered covering her ears—from her screams? From the doorbell? From reality? She still didn't know—and running into the kitchen. She would probably still be there, rocking back and forth on the floor, her fingers plugged in her ears, chanting, *No! No! No!* if Sue Greenley across the street hadn't seen the military van parked at the curb. Guessing the awful reason, she'd come over, let herself in with the key Katie kept under the potted fern by the back door, and sat beside her on the kitchen floor while the Marines delivered the awful news.

"It's time you got back out there, Katie," Josie was saying now.

What was the point? A man like Paul didn't come along twice in a lifetime. For most women, he didn't even come along once. Paul had been The One. Everyone else was destined to be second-rate, second-choice, second-best.

She was relieved to have the conversation interrupted by the jangle of the bells on the beveled-glass door. She looked up to see Eula, the local real-estate agent, step inside, bringing the scent of rain and a blast of humid July air with her.

Eula thought ladybugs brought good luck and always wore at least one ladybug accessory. Today's ensemble featured a blue ladybug-emblazoned scarf tied amid the wattles of her chinless neck.

"Hi, Eula," Katie called, glad for the distraction. "Any news on who's moving into the Ashton house?"

The whole town had been buzzing about the sale of an elderly couple's home to a large Las Vegas consortium days earlier.

"No, but we'll know soon enough." The heavyset woman shook out her ladybug-printed umbrella. "I had to unlock the place for a fancy interior designer from New Orleans a couple of days ago, and she's had painters and carpenters working through the night. I saw a Hur-witz Mintz Furniture truck outside the house on my way here. Apparently the new owner is moving in today or tomorrow."

A murmur arose among the women. "Why would someone buy a house they hadn't even seen?" Rachel wondered.

"Maybe they just plan to use it as a vacation home," Josie suggested.

"Why would anyone want to vacation here?" Lulu asked.

It was a good question. Chartreuse, Louisiana, was not exactly a tourist mecca.

"I think it's someone in the witness protection pro-gram," Bev said, wiping a blob of hair color off Mrs. Street's neck.

"Or maybe a mobster," Josie said. "It's obviously someone with money, and Nellie says all the businesses in Vegas are connected to the mafia."

Lulu rolled her bobble eyes. "Nellie thinks she knows everything."

"That's because she usually does," Rachel said. "At least about what's going on in town, anyway."

It was true. As the clerk at the town's only drugstore, Nellie had insider information on practically everyone. Unfortunately, she also had one of the biggest mouths in town.

"Speaking of Nellie..." Eula closed her umbrella and turned to Josie, who was peering in the stroller at her baby. "I was in the drugstore this morning, and I heard you might have some news to share."

Josie looked up. "Oh, yeah?"

"Nellie says you bought a pregnancy test yesterday."

Josie's mouth curved in dismay. "Nellie wasn't even there! I made sure she was on her lunch break."

"Nellie counts the EPTs and condoms before she leaves the store, and if any are missing when she comes back, she looks back through the security tapes to see who bought them," Bev volunteered.

"Good heavens. Is that even legal?" Mrs. Street asked.

Rachel shrugged. "As long as her dad owns the place, I guess she can do what she wants."

"So...are you expecting again?" Lulu asked eagerly.

"Mercy, no!" Josie protested. "I didn't buy the test for myself."

"If it wasn't for you, then who..." Lulu stopped midsentence. Her eyes rounded. "Oh, Lord—*Madeline*?" she asked in a choked whisper.

Madeline was Josie's seventeen-year-old daughter— exactly the same age that Katie had been when she'd...

The comb slipped through Katie's fingers and clattered to the floor.

"Oh, no!" Josie's eyebrows shot up in horror. She waved her hands back and forth and vigorously shook her head. "No, no, *no*! She's barely seventeen. Are you crazy?"

Katie hadn't even realized she'd been holding her breath until she exhaled.

"Well, then, who'd you buy the test for?" Lulu demanded.

"Fifi."

"Your *dog*?"

Josie sheepishly nodded. "She got outside before I

knew she was in heat, and I wanted to make sure that she wasn't already in a family way before I paid the ridiculous fee at the poodle stud farm."

Laughter filled the room. "There's a poodle stud farm?" Eula asked.

Josie nodded. "Just outside New Orleans. It's called Who's Your Daddy."

The women laughed again.

"Pregnancy tests work on dogs?" Mrs. Street asked.

"I sure hope so," Josie said. "It came out negative."

Lulu's forehead crinkled thoughtfully. "How did you get her to pee on the little stick?"

"I didn't," Josie said when the howls of laughter died down. "I took her for a walk and dipped it in the grass afterward." Her brow pulled into a worried frown. "You don't think other people will think I bought that test for Maddie, do you?"

"Oh, no," Bev said. "Not the way you and Marcus go at it."

The whole salon roared. Josie had a total of six children—the youngest of whom began to squall in the stroller.

"I'll have to skip the polish, Rachel." Josie sighed, pulling her hands out of the water bowl and wiping them on the towel. "The baby's not going to give me time to let it dry."

As Josie bent to pick up her baby, Katie knelt to retrieve the comb, which had slid underneath the counter. The bells on the salon door jangled again as she extended her arm and reached under the bottom shelf, her butt in the air, her short khaki skirt riding up her thighs.

"Is Katie here?" asked a deep male voice.

Oh, great. That was probably Derwin, the pompous, beer-bellied hair product salesman. Thanks to Lulu's not-so-subtle hints that Katie was single, he stopped by in his pink panel van every week, even though Katie only placed an order every other month or so.

"She's, uh, right over there," Rachel said in an oddly breathy voice.

Terrific. He was getting a good look at her airborne backside—which would probably encourage him to stop by even more frequently. Katie grabbed the comb and started to rise, only to bang her head on the countertop. Wincing, she scrambled to her feet, turned around, and stared directly into a blast from the past.

No. No way. It couldn't be.

But it was. The shiver of attraction skittering up her spine confirmed it. Standing in the entryway was not the bald-headed sales rep she'd expected, but Zack Ferguson—the boy who'd stolen her heart and broken it into a million pieces the summer after her junior year in high school.

Except he wasn't a boy any longer. He'd been at least six feet tall when she'd known him, but he seemed to have gained another inch or two in height, and his once-lanky frame had filled out into the kind of broad-shouldered, muscular build that women fantasized about. His face had matured into a study of planes and angles, with a strong nose, a cleft in his chin, and a five-o'clock shadow, even though it was only two in the afternoon. He'd been cute as a teenager, but now he was devastatingly handsome—the kind of handsome that should come with a warning label, the kind that any sensible female would steer clear of, because he was no doubt accustomed to getting whatever he wanted from women.

He'd certainly gotten it from Katie eighteen years ago. The thought made her stomach tighten.

"Hello, Kate," he said now.

Kate, not Katie. He'd been the first person to call her that, and at seventeen, it had been a heady experience. It had made her feel grown-up and worldly, as if she were an adult whose thoughts and opinions counted.

It had been a seriously bad delusion.

Still, the sound of her name on his lips made her heart patter like the rain on the salon roof, and it took a moment before she could make her mouth move. "Wh-what are you doing here?"

"I'm moving to Chartreuse, so I thought I'd come by and say hello."

Katie felt as if the room had suddenly tilted. The women in the salon all murmured.

"So you're the person moving into the old Ashton house?" Bev ventured.

"That's right."

Eula scrambled to her feet and thrust out her hand. "I'm Eula Belle Johnson—the Realtor who handled the property sale."

Zack shook her hand. "Nice to meet you. Thank you for doing such an excellent job."

"Oh, it was my pleasure." The older woman gazed up at him as if in a trance. She must have realized she'd been pumping his hand as if it were a tire jack, because she blushed and abruptly pulled it away. "So you're associated with Winning Strategies, Incorporated?"

Zack nodded. "I'm the CEO."

Lulu whirled around in her stylist chair and flashed an overly white, bucktoothed grin. "Well, welcome to

Chartreuse! I'm Lulu." She swept her hand around at the other women. "And this is Mrs. Street and Bev and Josie and Eula and Rachel. And apparently you already know Katie."

Avoiding looking at Katie, he nodded and smiled at each of the other women. "Nice to meet you. I'm Zack Ferguson."

Oh, God—how had Katie forgotten about his smile? He hadn't even turned it on her, yet she felt it like a heat lamp. The appeal of Zack's smile was more than the physical components of straight white teeth, deep-set dimples, and devastating crinkles at the corner of his blue, blue eyes; it was a force of nature, a lightning bolt of testosterone, a shot of pure sex appeal, and she wasn't the only woman affected by it. Rachel spastically licked her lips, Josie looked as if she'd dived headfirst into a bucket of blush, and Eula was tugging on the ladybug scarf around her throat as if it was suddenly too tight. Even the retired librarian was fanning off a hot flash, and she was a good fifteen years past menopause.

A murmur of "Nice to meet yous" sounded around the room.

The librarian regarded him thoughtfully. "Zack Ferguson, the poker champion?"

He inclined his head. "I used to be. I no longer compete."

"Oh, my husband idolizes you!" Mrs. Street gushed. "He has the whole series of your *Play to Win* CDs."

The last time Katie had looked Zack up on the Internet—which had been about seven years ago, before she married Paul—he'd been the top-rated poker player in the world, living a jet-set lifestyle and dating a Victoria's

Secret model. She hadn't been all that surprised at his success; he'd been an amazing card shark even at seventeen. He'd spent most of his evenings that summer hustling cards in the back room of the roadhouse the next town over, and he'd made a small fortune.

"So what brings you to Chartreuse?" Rachel asked.

He stuck his hand in the pocket of his jeans. "Well, actually, Katie does."

The women collectively gasped.

No one gasped louder than Katie. "Me?"

He dipped his head in a curt, all-business nod, his eyes giving away nothing. "Is there someplace we can go to talk?"

Panic shot through her veins. "I—I'm sorry, but I'm with a client."

"Oh, honey, don't you worry about me." Lulu's bug eyes were fixed on Zack as if he were a double serving of mile-high pie.

"But your hair's wet and I haven't cut it yet, and..."

Lulu wafted her hand in a dismissive wave. "That's just fine. I'll come back later."

"But—but..." Panic narrowed Katie's throat.

"Oh, dear! Silly old me." Lulu jumped out of the chair and pulled the polka-dotted cape off her neck. "I think I left my oven on!" Her wet hair dripped onto her white linen shirt, creating transparent spots. "I better head home right now and turn it off."

She gave Zack a broad wink as she reached for her enormous orange leather purse and black umbrella on the counter. He rewarded her with another smile, causing Lulu to flush like a smitten groupie. She teetered to the door on her high-heeled orange mules, her eyes never leaving his face. Zack stepped forward and opened the door for her, then took her umbrella, stuck it out the door, and opened it as well.

"Oh, my," Lulu murmured, placing one hand against her chest and shooting Katie a look that clearly said, *Don't let this one get away.* "How gentlemanly. Thank you!"

"My pleasure." The wind blew his thick dark hair as he closed the door behind Lulu and turned to Katie.

He had gorgeous hair—thick and wavy, so deep a brown it was almost black. It looked overdue for a trim, but it had been cut by someone who knew what they were doing. Katie could usually tell a lot about a person by their hair, but she wasn't sure exactly what Zack's hair was telling her.

She wasn't at all sure about his face, either. It must be all that poker playing, because his expression was inscrutable.

"Guess this means you're free for a few minutes," he said. "Is there someplace around here where we can get a cup of coffee?"

"The Chartreuse Café is right around the corner," Rachel volunteered.

Zack's eyebrows quirked up. "That old place is still in business?"

"Oh, yeah. It's like sharks and cockroaches—it'll still be here, unchanged, long after everything else is extinct and gone," Eula said.

"So you've been to Chartreuse before?" Bev prompted.

Zack nodded. "I spent the summer here with my aunt's family eighteen years ago."

"Really? Is that when you met Katie?" Josie asked.

"As a matter of fact, it is."

The memories of that summer flooded her mind. Katie had been seventeen, working at the bait-and-tackle shop down at the lake. When Zack had walked through the door one hot afternoon, his gray T-shirt clinging to his lean frame, her lungs had felt as if they'd forgotten how to work.

"How do you breathe in here?" he'd asked.

For a moment, she thought he'd read her mind. "What?"

"The sign on the door says live bait, but it smells like it's been dead for days."

"Oh." He was talking about the odor rising from the cooler of day-old shrimp by the door—of course. She lifted her shoulders. "After a while, you get used to it."

"You mean it doesn't bother you?"

"No. I mean I'm used to being bothered."

He'd laughed, a hearty, appreciative laugh, and the sound made her heart feel like it was tied to a hot-air balloon. He hooked a thumb toward the cooler at the back of the store. "Let me grab a Coke and I'll come bother you some more."

The door opened as he sauntered to the rear of the store, and two men in orange hunting vests ambled in. The stench of stale beer clung to them like sweat. Their bloodshot eyes ran over her in a way that had made her skin crawl. "Oo-ee. Lookee what we got here," said the taller one.

The shorter, chubbier one, who had a stubbled chin and a scar by his eye, stared at her chest. Apparently the cretin could read, because when his gaze eventually made its way to her nametag—*Katie Landers*—his contiguous eyebrow rose. "Hey—are you Mona's girl?"

Her stomach had clenched. She didn't want to say yes, but it would be disloyal to deny her own mother. She nodded her head.

"I knew it. My, my, my. The apple sure don't fall far from the tree." He gazed pointedly at her breasts.

The taller one chortled, revealing two missing bottom teeth. "How old are you, honey?"

Katie decided to ignore the question. "May I help you with something?"

"Well, now, that just depends," the shorter one said. "You ever party with your old lady?"

The other one gave a phlegmy cackle. Katie felt her face flame.

"Your mama, she sure knows how to party."

Oh, God. Her mother had a drinking problem, and when she drank, she didn't always remember what she did.

"Know what I hear? I hear she's hot and heavy with the mayor now," the taller one said.

Katie's mouth went dry. She'd known the news was all over town, but being confronted with it head-on made her want to barf.

"Yes, sir, you're your mama's daughter, all right. The family resemblance is right there for all to see." His eyes locked on her breasts in a way that had made her feel as if he could see through her shirt. "Yesirree. Your mama's mighty fine, but I do believe you've got an even nicer pair of…"

"Leave her alone," said an authoritative voice from the back of the store.

The men turned as Zack strode up. The shorter one squinted at him. "Who the hell are you?"

"The mayor's nephew. And he's not going to like hearing that you two are spreading nasty rumors about him."

The short one spat in the trash can. "We don't care what he likes and don't like."

"Yeah, well, maybe you'll care to know that when folks tick him off, he gets the police to follow them. Before they know it, they're being stopped for speeding or reckless driving or worse, and it's their word against the cop's."

The two men looked at each other.

"We were just havin' some fun," the tall one said. They both edged toward the door.

"You picked on the wrong girl." Zack's brow lowered into a badass scowl. "Now get the hell out of here and don't bother her again."

The door banged behind them after they scurried outside. The tires of their dirty red pickup threw up a rooster tail of gravel as they squealed out of the parking lot.

Zack plopped the can of Coke on the counter. "When you said you were used to being bothered, you weren't kidding, were you?"

"No." To Katie's chagrin, tears sprang to her eyes.

Zack's eyes went all warm and sympathetic, which made a lump the size of a bullfrog form in her throat.

"Hey—don't let them get to you. They're just a couple of losers."

"But what they said about my mom…" A tear snaked down her cheek. She scrubbed it away with her fist.

"They're full of bull."

"No." Katie drew in a ragged breath. "It's true."

He just kept looking at her with that same warm,

nonjudgmental gaze. "So? Your mom's not you. None of us get to pick our relatives." His mouth curved in a wry smile. "If we did, I'd sure ask for another set."

"Yeah?"

"Yeah. Mine parked me here for the summer because neither one wanted me around."

The frankness of the remark disarmed her. "Where are you from?"

"Chicago." He'd grinned at her, and his smile had worked its magic.

She wiped her face with the back of her hand. "Are you really the mayor's nephew?"

He'd given a rueful nod. "He's married to my mom's sister, sad to say. He's another relative I'd disown if I could."

She'd given a tremulous grin, and his smile had widened. In the heat of it, she'd forgotten how to breathe.

She had to remind herself to take a breath now.

Rachel's gaze darted from Zack to Katie, then back to Zack. "Have you and Katie stayed in touch all this time?"

"No." Zack turned his blue eyes on her, and a flame of heat licked her neck. "We have some catching up to do."

Yeah, thought Katie. *Maybe you'd care to explain why you left town without a word, phone number, or forwarding address the day after we first made love.* Katie's spine stiffened against the old hurt.

"Well, you two run along—and take your time." Bev flapped her wrist at them. "After Eula, I'm free for the rest of the afternoon, so I can take your next appointment. You're going out to the retirement home later anyway, right?"

"Um...right." Katie felt an irrational urge to dash out the back door.

"Ready?" Zack asked.

No. But if he was moving here, she'd have to talk to him sooner or later. Might as well get it over with.

Besides, he could no longer hurt her. Everything between them had happened nearly two decades ago. She'd handled things then, and she could certainly handle them now.

Couldn't she?

She forced herself to smile. "Sure." Grabbing her purse and umbrella, she followed Zack to the door.

CHAPTER TWO

The lunch rush was over, but the quaint Main Street café painted in the town's namesake color was still half full as Katie stepped through the door with Zack. The three men in coveralls perched at the yellowish-green Formica counter looked up, as did most of the other patrons seated at the green tables in the gumbo-and-fried-seafood-scented restaurant. Katie wondered how long it would take before her mother-in-law, Annette Charmaine, heard that she'd come here with an unfamiliar man.

Not long at all, Katie thought with chagrin as she spotted Nellie from the drugstore at the front table. Oh, and wouldn't you know it—the long-nosed, horse-faced woman was seated with three elderly ladies who lived at the Sunnyside Assisted-Living Villa, where Annette was staying while recovering from knee surgery and multiple fractures after a bad fall. *Great, just great*, Katie thought, giving the women a feeble wave and a feebler smile.

The waitress, a busty blonde named Cindy, looked Zack over with frank curiosity, then raised an eyebrow at Katie. "Hi, Katie. Who's your friend?"

"This is Zack Ferguson. Zack, this is Cindy."

"Pleased to meet you." Zack's dimple flashed.

Like all women, the waitress seemed to melt under his smile. "Not from these parts, are you?"

"Not until now," Zack replied.

Cindy's painted-on eyebrows rose higher.

"Zack just bought the old Ashton house," Katie felt compelled to explain.

"Oh, my! We all wondered who was moving into that place." Cindy set the pitcher of water in her hand down on the counter and sank down on a barstool, as if she were settling in for a long chat. "So what brings you to Chartreuse?"

Katie cut in, not wanting to risk him giving the same response he'd given at the salon. "Actually, Cindy, Zack and I are in something of a hurry. Could you bring us a couple of cups of coffee?"

"Uh—oh, sure. Sit wherever you all want. Would you like a piece of pie to go with your coffee?"

"No, thank you," Katie said. Whatever Zack had to say to her, he could say it quickly and be done with it.

"Looks to me like she's already found something sweet," murmured a blue-haired lady at Nellie's table. The other women giggled.

Katie felt her skin color. She decided to take the high road and pretend she hadn't heard the remark.

"Let's go over by the window," Zack suggested.

Katie had forgotten how he'd always been a take-charge kind of guy. She used to like that about him, but now it seemed like a liability. This time, she wouldn't surrender any control.

"The back is quieter." Decisively heading in that

direction, she selected the seat facing the wall so she wouldn't have to wave greetings to everyone who walked through the door.

Zack sat down across from her and folded his hands on the plastic chartreuse place mat. The sight of his hands sent a rush of fresh adrenaline pumping through her. Oh, God, those hands—large, tan, and long-fingered. She'd watched his big, masculine hands that summer—watched them pop the tops on Coke cans; watched them steer his car as he drove her home after work; watched them shuffle and deal cards as he taught her to play poker. She'd spent most of the summer watching his hands and fantasizing about what they'd feel like on her body.

When she'd finally felt them, they'd exceeded anything she'd ever imagined.

And then he'd disappeared. Just up and left. Not a word, not a phone call, not a note. Nada.

She closed her eyes for a moment and pushed down the memories. Why the heck was she thinking about all that, anyway? She was no longer a starry-eyed girl with a fatal attraction to bad boys. She was a grown woman who'd known the love of a good man.

She straightened her spine and leveled a cool gaze at him. "So... what really brings you back to Chartreuse?"

Cindy flitted up, bearing two green ceramic coffee mugs. She set them down and fussily adjusted them, then fished a fistful of Moo-Cow creamers out of the pocket of her chartreuse apron and put them in the small bowl on the table. "Here you go."

"Thanks, Cindy," Katie said, hoping to send her on her way.

But Cindy didn't budge. She put a hand on her hip,

cocked her head, and gazed at Zack. "You know, you look really familiar."

"I hear that all the time," Zack said. "Guess I just have one of those faces." He flashed that disarming smile. In the face of it, Cindy retreated, a goofy grin plastered on her face.

Zack's smile faded as he looked at Katie. His eyes held something she couldn't quite place. Before she could figure it out, it was gone, replaced by his inscrutable poker face.

"She's probably seen you on the cover of the tabloids with a model or an actress," Katie said.

"That's one reason I don't travel in those circles anymore." He reached for his coffee. "Too much of a hassle."

"Yeah, I hear it's really tough work, lying on the beach with Kirsten Dunst," she said dryly. She immediately regretted letting him know she'd seen the tabloid stories. She didn't want him to think she'd deliberately followed his activities.

Zack grinned. "That whole Hollywood scene looks like a lot more fun than it is."

"I'll bet."

"And I'll raise you a hundred."

She felt like she'd gotten sucked into a time warp. He'd said the same thing that summer, every time she'd used the familiar figure of speech. Her usual response had been, "You're on."

Well, he wasn't on. Not anymore. She wasn't interested in playing games with him—word-wise or any other wise. She reached for a container of creamer. "I forgot I'm talking to a professional gambler."

"Actually, I'm not playing professionally anymore."

"Oh, no? Have a run of bad luck?"

Zack took a sip of coffee. "You know I never believed in luck."

Yeah, she did. He'd explained the complex system of card counting he used, based on some higher math formula she'd never fully grasped. "I figured Winning Strategies, Incorporated, was just some kind of tax shelter. It's a real company?"

He nodded. "It's a risk-management consulting firm. Companies hire us to figure out the statistical odds of business ventures. We try to come up with all possible scenarios and calculate the chances of each one occurring."

"So you're still playing the odds, huh?"

"Pretty much." His mouth curved into a grin.

It was weird, sitting across from him, getting zapped by that megawatt smile. It stirred up all kinds of old warm feelings. It was just emotional déjà vu, though. She couldn't genuinely be harboring feelings for someone she didn't know, and she no longer knew Zack at all.

Not that she'd ever really known him. She couldn't have. The Zack she'd thought she'd known never would have dumped her the night after they'd shared the most intimate experience two people could share.

He set down his mug and leaned forward. "I read about your husband. I'm so sorry."

The mention of Paul jolted her. "How did you find out about that?"

"I googled you."

She turned her wedding-ring set on her finger, aligning the solitaire over the simple gold band. "When?"

"The first time was years ago," he admitted. "I saw your wedding announcement in the *Chartreuse Gazette,* and I figured...Well, you'd been married about a month, and I figured you wouldn't want to hear from me."

She tried to imagine how she would have reacted to a call from Zack at that point, and couldn't.

He looked down at his coffee cup. "I googled you every now and then through the years, then again last week." He looked up, his eyes blue pools of sympathy. "I'm really sorry for your loss."

Katie poured creamer into her cup and watched it spread through the dark liquid, lightening it, wishing her thoughts would do the same in her head. Was that why he was here now? Because he'd just learned that she was a widow? Why would that matter to him? Did he think they'd pick up where they left off? That made no sense. He hadn't wanted to be with her then, so he wasn't likely to want to be with her now.

"From what I read, he was a helluva guy," Zack said.

Yeah, and she had the posthumous Medal of Honor to prove it. Paul had tackled a suicide bomber in Baghdad and saved the lives of four troops and several civilians.

Her reaction had been considerably less heroic. For months she'd burned with anger. Why hadn't he saved himself? Why had he put strangers ahead of her? Hadn't he thought about their future, about the family they'd planned? It had taken her a long while to work her way toward acceptance. The truth had slowly taken root and grown within her: Paul wouldn't have been the man she loved if he'd saved himself and left other people to die. He would have come home broken in spirit, which would have left him more dead than he was now.

"He was the best," Katie murmured.

"You deserved the best."

"Funny," she bit out before she could stop herself. "You didn't used to think so."

"I always thought so."

"Is that why you left?"

He blew out a sigh and leaned forward, his forearms on the table. "Katie, I feel really bad about the way we ended things."

She jerked her head up. "*We* didn't end things. *You* left. Without a word, I might add."

"That wasn't my idea."

"Oh, no? Whose idea was it? Your girlfriend's?"

"I didn't have a girlfriend."

"What?" He'd told her he had a girlfriend in Chicago. All summer, she'd been jealous of the girl with the prior claim on Zack's heart.

"I didn't have a girlfriend," he said again. "I made that up so we wouldn't get involved."

She stared at him.

"You were the kind of girl who took relationships seriously, and I wasn't a relationship kind of guy. With your mother's situation and all, I was trying to protect you."

Her mother's "situation" was that she'd been the town skank. Katie had told Zack all about how her mother's nonstop partying had made her childhood a living hell. "Protect me from what?"

"From me, I guess." He took a sip of coffee. "I figured that if you thought I had a girlfriend, it'd make it easier to keep things platonic."

Katie glared at him. How dare he paint himself as some kind of teenage Dudley Do-Right? It took two to tango. "You didn't seem too interested in keeping things platonic that night on the boat."

He shifted his weight on the chair. "The truth is, my feelings about you were never really platonic."

A jolt of shock shot through her. He was admitting he'd had the hots for her?

"I tried to keep a lid on things, but that night..." His blue gaze locked on hers. "That night I just lost it. I'm sorry, Kate. It was never my intention to hurt you."

"So leaving the next day without so much as a 'So long, nice knowing you' was your way of not hurting me?"

He dropped his eyes to his coffee cup. "I need to explain that."

"Please do." She folded her arms across her chest and stared at him, her body language telegraphing, *This should be good*.

"Kate... after I drove you home, I went to pick up my cousin in Lacombe."

His cousin, Bruce, had lost his driver's license for a year—he'd seriously injured a woman while driving drunk during spring break in Florida, too far away from Chartreuse for his daddy's influence to get him off scot-free—so Zack had been his designated driver for the summer. It was a good thing Zack was chauffeuring him around, because Bruce spent every night getting stoned and smashed.

"As usual, Bruce was totally wasted; he spilled a beer in the car and it got all over everything, making my car smell like a brewery. And then I was stopped by a highway patrolman on the way home."

"Should have been no problem, with your uncle's connections."

"This was a state trooper, not a Chartreuse policeman.

And it turns out I'd played poker with him earlier in the week. He was mad as hell when he saw my ID and realized a seventeen-year-old had taken him for most of his paycheck."

Zack paused and leaned forward. "The next thing I knew, he'd clinked a set of cuffs on me and called for backup, claiming I tried to assault him—which was a total lie. To make a bad situation worse, Bruce had stashed a bag of pot under the seat while I was talking to the cop."

She could believe it. Bruce had been a total pothead.

"We were both arrested, but only I was charged. My uncle had enough influence to keep our names out of the paper and get me tried as a minor, but I had to spend four months at juvie." He sat back. "I wanted to call you, but I couldn't."

"You could have written."

"Yeah, I could have." He ran a hand down his face. "But, Kate—I knew I wasn't any good for you. I was going to leave at the end of the summer anyway, and I didn't see any point in leading you on. I figured the best thing I could do for you was to just stay out of your life."

"It was a little late for that decision."

"I know." Zack pulled a piece of folded looseleaf paper from his back pocket. It crinkled loudly as his large hands unfolded it and flattened it on the table. "Kate—I ran across something of yours." He turned the paper around and slid it in front of her.

She stared down at her own handwriting. It was written when she was much younger, back when she made circles for dots and formed her letters with fat, round loops, but it was her handwriting all the same.

Her heart faltered, then thundered in her chest. She knew what it was even before she read it.

To my baby's adopting parents:

I know I'm not supposed to have any contact with you, but I couldn't let Grace go without leaving you a note. If you're reading this, I guess you found it in the lining of the diaper bag. Please please please love Grace and take good care of her! When she's old enough to understand that she's adopted, tell her that I love her with all my heart, but I can't give her the kind of home she needs.

I know this is a closed adoption, but if she ever wants to know who her parents are and you decide to tell her, my name is Katie Anne Landers, and I'm from Chartreuse, Louisiana. Her father's name is Zachary Gage Ferguson. He's from Chicago, and he doesn't know about the baby.

Please love her and take good care of her and give her the good kind of life she deserves.

Sincerely,
Katie Landers

The room felt like it was spinning. "What…how… who…" She stared at Zack, her mouth dry. "Who gave this to you?"

A voice sounded behind her chair. "I did, Momzilla."

• • •

Zack looked up to see a teenage girl with a nose piercing, spiky black-and-blue hair, and an angry scowl slouching behind Katie's back. His heart sank. This was not going as he'd planned. "Gracie, I asked you to wait until I called you."

The girl lifted her shoulders and adjusted her enormous macramé purse over her stomach. "I got tired of waiting."

He glanced at Katie. She'd twisted around in her chair and was staring at Gracie with eyes the size of the coffee mugs, her face Moo-Cow Creamer white. A round of tangled emotions shot through him, sharper than physical pain, the same acute emotions he'd felt when he'd first seen Katie at the salon. He'd known that seeing her again would be hard. He'd expected to feel remorse and guilt, and he'd been prepared for a flare-up of the anger that had been simmering in his gut ever since he'd found out about Gracie.

What he hadn't counted on feeling, damn it, was attraction. He'd thought he'd be immune to Katie by now, but she still pushed all his buttons. He could still remember the first time he'd set eyes on her in that bait shop, her honey-colored hair rioting on her shoulders, her pert, lively face brightening into a smile. Light brown and long lashed, her eyes had crackled with warmth and life and energy.

When those two creeps had walked in and started in on her, he hadn't been able to stand the way her bright eyes had dimmed. Her whole bearing had changed, as if she were trying to make herself smaller. She'd looked ashamed and cowed and worst of all, resigned, as if she had to endure that kind of thing all the time.

He'd never played the white knight role before, and he liked the way it made him feel. Hell, he just flat-out liked the way Kate made him feel—as if he could do anything, as if he could tell her anything. He'd talked to her until she'd locked up the bait shop for the night, talked as she waited for her mother in the parking lot, talked as he'd driven her home when her mother never showed. He'd continued talking to her every day throughout the long, hot summer. Something about Kate's big whiskey-colored eyes loosened his lips like hundred-proof bourbon.

He'd told her things he'd never told anyone—about his parents' screaming matches and accusations, interrupted by the occasional tearful plea for forgiveness and saccharine pronouncements of love. He'd told her about eighty-year-old Mr. Jenkins next door, who'd taught him how to play poker on the afternoons after school when no one was home. He'd told her how he'd figured out a system for counting cards and beating the odds. He'd told her his plan to go to Vegas as soon as he was old enough to legally gamble, where he intended to make a fortune.

Katie hadn't laughed at him or told him he was crazy. She'd listened and asked him questions and encouraged him to weave his dreams into a plan. She'd believed in him before he'd believed in himself.

And how had he paid her back? By knocking her up, then disappearing without a word. He'd acted like a stupid, callous, insensitive A-hole, turning what should have been a wonderful experience into a painful ordeal.

Judging from the ashen look on her face, he'd just done it again. "I meant to break this to you more gently," he said apologetically.

Gracie snorted. "Yeah. Having me show up after you

thought you were rid of me must be your worst nightmare."

"That's not what I meant," Zack said irritably. Gracie had a real knack for taking words and turning the meaning upside down. But then, she'd turned his whole world upside down the moment she'd walked into it. "I meant it's a shock. I wanted to prepare her to meet you."

"Grace?" Katie's voice came out cracked and low, barely more than a whisper. "You're my Grace?"

"No. I'm not *your* anything." Her voice held a barely reined-in fury. "And it's Grac—*ee*. With an *i-e*. You can call me G-girl. Or just G. But never, ever just Grace." She glared at Katie across the table. "If you'd stuck around long enough to get to know me, you'd know how badly the name fits me."

Katie drew back as if the girl had struck her.

Zack rubbed his hand across his jaw. There was no way to make this easy, but Gracie was making it harder than it had to be. From what he'd seen, that was Gracie's whole approach to life.

Katie, on the other hand, approached life with her arms wide open. He'd known how Katie would react to seeing her daughter again. He'd known she'd want to offer the girl her heart, just as she'd offered it to Zack all those years ago.

And Gracie would crush it, just as he had.

Zack pulled out a chair. "Have a seat, Gracie."

"I'd rather stand."

"H-how...," Katie stuttered. "Wh-when..."

"Let me lay it all out for you." Despite her earlier words, Gracie plopped into the chair, her enormous macramé bag in her lap. "My adoptive parents died a year and a half ago in a car crash, and I had to go live with my aunt, who's a total nazi. One day I was going through a box of my parents' belongings in her attic—the old bat had just stashed their stuff up there like it was garbage! Can you believe it?—and I found that letter." She gestured toward the paper that lay on the table.

Katie sat stock-still, as if she'd turned to stone.

Gracie blew an unkempt lock of dark hair away from her eyes. "So I googled Zack and learned that he's this rich poker dude. I figured he owed me for not having to pay child support or anything all these years, and I'm going to need some money for when the baby comes."

"The—the *baby*?"

"Yeah. I'm pregnant." Moving her purse, she rested her hands over her belly. The chipped black nail polish on her bitten-down nails stood out in stark contrast to the white, stretched-out T-shirt covering her small but unmistakable baby bump.

Katie's jaw dropped. Gracie fixed her with a venomous glare. "Unlike you, I'm not giving my baby away."

The waitress returned, coffeepot held aloft. She looked at Gracie, then at Katie, then back at Gracie again, her eyes huge. The family resemblance was nothing short of remarkable, Zack realized. Gracie had his blue eyes— the color and shape were identical—but her pert nose, full lips, and heart-shaped face were the spitting image of her mother's. He hadn't needed a DNA test to confirm Gracie's story, although he'd gotten one anyway.

"Oh, my!" the waitress gasped.

Gracie shot her an angry look and tightened her grip on her belly, apparently thinking the waitress was shocked by her pregnancy. Well, it *was* pretty shocking, considering that Gracie looked three or four years younger than her seventeen years.

"Can I get you anything, sugar?" the waitress asked.

"Yeah. I'll have a Coke to go."

The waitress hesitated a moment. "Are you sure you don't want milk instead?"

Gracie glared at her. "Did I ask for milk?"

"I just thought..." Gracie's glower made the waitress abruptly shut her mouth mid-sentence and She mercifully trot away.

"So how...when...why..." Katie tried again to form the words, her eyes locked on Gracie as if she was afraid to blink.

"Why am I here?" She fixed Katie with a hateful stare. "Well, God knows it's not my idea. You didn't want to have anything to do with me, and I sure as hell don't want to have anything to do with you, but the Zack-ster here and my aunt cooked up this lame-assed plan, and I really didn't have any choice but to go along with it."

Katie pulled her gaze from Gracie to Zack. Before he could open his mouth to explain, Gracie continued.

"See, my Frankenstein of an aunt said she'd put up a huge legal battle to get me back unless you and Zack share joint custody. She says I need"—she rolled her eyes, made air quotes with her fingers, and raised her voice in a derisive falsetto—"*a woman's influence,* at least until the baby's born and I turn eighteen. So we're all going to live in this hellhole town for the next four months. After that, Zack will advance me my parents' life insurance money—they made this stupid trust where I don't inherit anything until I turn twenty-one—and then my baby and I can go get a life."

"That part hasn't been decided," Zack told her.

The waitress returned with a Styrofoam cup covered with a lid. Gracie picked it up and rose from the chair. "I saw a bookstore down on the corner. I'm gonna go hang out there." The chair squawked on the green linoleum floor as she shoved it back against the table. Her lip curved into a smirk. "Oh, and Momzilla—better close your mouth before you catch a fly."

CHAPTER THREE

Katie turned and stared as the girl flounced out of the café. *My daughter. That's my daughter.* The thought reverberated in her head as the door closed behind Gracie.

The daughter who had been in her prayers every day for the last seventeen years, the daughter she thought about every time she passed a young girl on the street, the daughter she'd mourned and missed like a lost piece of her soul. Katie rose from her chair to go after her, her pulse thudding in her ears.

Zack laid a hand on her wrist. His palm seemed wired with electrodes.

"Let her be," he said gently. "She needs to cool down."

"But..." He had no idea how Katie had yearned to see her child, how she'd ached to hold her, how she'd wondered if she'd ever get to meet her. Now that she had, she couldn't just let her walk away. "I need to go talk to her." She pulled her hand out from under his.

Zack gently took it again. "Later. Give her a little space."

A little space? She hadn't seen Grace since the nurse had taken her from her arms in the delivery room. Seventeen years was more than enough space.

"She'll be a lot more receptive in a few minutes," Zack said.

How the hell did he know so much about Grace? Irritation tumbled into the twisted stream of emotion roaring through her veins.

"Sit back down, Kate." His fingers caressed the back of her hand, sending disturbing prickles up her skin. "We need to talk."

Katie sank back into the chair, her stomach feeling like she was riding a roller coaster. Oh, they needed to talk, all right. Irritation flared into outrage. She welcomed its heat, welcomed the way it burned some clarity through the fog of shock.

She looked over to see Cindy watching her, her eyes rapt. The men at the counter were watching, too, the bills of their caps pointed toward them, looking for all the world like a gaggle of big-eared geese. Katie twisted around to view the rest of the café. Nellie and the gray-haired ladies were craned forward, primed to catch every word.

Katie turned back to Zack. "Not here," she said tersely.

"Okay." He pulled a ten-dollar bill out of his wallet, placed it on the table, then picked up Katie's umbrella. "In my car, then."

Katie headed to the door, her back stiff, her legs wobbly, her thoughts flailing about like a kite tail in the wind.

"Good-bye, y'all!" Cindy called gaily. "Have a nice day."

Katie couldn't even muster the wherewithal to respond as Zack opened the door. The warm, humid air enshrouded her. He opened the umbrella and held it over her head, then took her arm and led her across the street to a black Volvo parked at the curb. Something about his touch left her feeling raw and unsettled. He opened the car door, holding the umbrella over her as she ducked and slid into the passenger seat. He rounded the car, closed the umbrella, and climbed into the driver's seat. Water dripped from his hair as he slammed the door. He'd made sure she was dry, but he hadn't used the umbrella himself.

He should have been so concerned with her protection seventeen years ago. The thought shot through her, hot as a flaming arrow—and then, just as quickly, another thought followed: If he had, the beautiful, vibrant young girl she'd just met wouldn't be here.

Katie's stomach got that loop-de-loop roller-coaster feeling again. Questions raced up and down hills and valleys of her mind so fast they blurred together. The words coming out of her mouth were the same weird litany of questions she'd recited when she'd first met Gracie. "Where...how...when..."

Zack drew a deep breath, swiped a raindrop off his forehead, and decided to start with the easiest question. "I met her about two weeks ago. I was participating in a Monte Carlo–themed charity benefit in Dallas, and she just showed up."

Katie's eyes were dark in her pale face, like coals in snow. "How did she find you?"

"She googled me and found an article in the *Dallas*

Morning News. The charity was auctioning off the opportunity to play poker with me, so my name was in the prepublicity." It never ceased to amaze him that people would pony up three thousand dollars for the privilege of playing a hand of poker with him, but he got requests from charities all the time. He'd agreed to do the one in Dallas because an old friend had asked him to.

"What do you mean, 'She just showed up'?"

"She ran away from her aunt's, bought a Greyhound bus ticket, and rode twenty-seven hours to Dallas. A woman she met on the bus gave her a ride to the Four Seasons Hotel."

"And she just walked up and said, 'Hello, I'm your daughter'?"

"More or less."

Gracie being Gracie, of course, she'd done it in a far more dramatic fashion. He'd been playing a boring game of Texas Hold'em with three rank amateurs—and holding a straight flush, jack high—when a scuffle had drawn his attention. He'd looked up to see a scruffy young girl straddling the burgundy velvet rope that cordoned off the poker section of the casino-decorated ballroom.

A thick-waisted matron in pink chiffon held the edge of her shirt, trying to restrain her. "Where do you think you're going?"

"I need to talk to Zack Ferguson," he'd heard the girl say, brushing the old woman's hand off her clothes. The girl looked straight at him, a determined expression on her heart-shaped face. Something about her looked oddly familiar, but then Zack was used to seeing familiar faces in the crowds around him. Thanks to televised poker, the popularity of his poker-playing CDs, and the fact he used to date movie stars, Zack was accustomed to fans and groupies. They usually weren't this young, though. The girl looked barely old enough to have cut her twelve-year molars.

"He's in the middle of a game," the older woman said, "and he's our special guest. You can't bother him."

Gracie continued to climb over the red velvet rope, a crocheted purse dangling in front of her. The pink-clad woman grabbed her arm.

Gracie wrested away from her grip. "Get your hands off me, you pervert!"

The woman's mouth formed a shocked "O." Zack grinned. The evening had just gotten a lot more interesting.

The matron's face reddened like a boiled lobster's. "Who are you, and what are you doing here? This is a private event."

The girl's chin tilted up to a combative angle. Something about the set of it gave him a strange sense of déjà vu. "Yeah, well, I'm a private citizen."

"You clearly don't belong here."

"How do you know?"

"You're too young, and you're not even dressed."

Gracie looked down at her baggy top and jeans in mock horror. "Don't tell me I'm wearing my invisible clothes again."

Zack laughed. The woman's face grew even redder. "Do you have a ticket?"

"I got one for jaywalking once."

If the woman were a cartoon character, steam would have blown out her ears. "I'm going to get Security." She whipped around and stormed off.

The girl wasted no time scrambling over the rope and heading straight to Zack. He set his cards facedown on the table as she approached.

She stopped in front of him, clutching that monstrous bag in front of her stomach. "You're Zack Ferguson, right?"

"Right."

A gold stud glinted in her nose as she stuck out her hand. "Well, I'm Gracie Whitstone, and I'm your daughter."

Katie's lips, so similar to Gracie's, pressed into an angry line now as he finished relating the story. "You met her two weeks ago, and you didn't call me?"

A nerve twitched in Zack's jaw. "That's kind of the pot calling the kettle black, don't you think? Nine months of pregnancy and seventeen intervening years, and you couldn't let me know you'd had my child?"

Katie's chin tilted up in exactly the same way Gracie's had. No wonder Gracie had looked so familiar. "How was I supposed to do that? *You* disappeared." The heat in her eyes practically scorched him. She turned and stared out the windshield. "Besides, I did try to contact you."

"You did?"

She nodded. "When I found out I was pregnant, I went to your cousin. He just blew me off. He said you'd gotten bored in Chartreuse and decided to go back to Chicago— that you didn't want anything to do with a small-town skank like me. He refused to give me your address or your phone number." The rain drummed down harder. "I tried to find you on my own. I called every Ferguson in Chicago."

Self-loathing, bitter as bile, balled in his throat. "We didn't live in Chicago proper. We lived in Berwyn—a suburb about ten miles out."

"It would have been nice to know that." Her brown eyes flashed. "Do you have any idea how much long-distance cost back then?"

Hell. Could he possibly feel any worse? "Kate—I'm sorry. For leaving, and for…"

For losing control. He prided himself on his self-discipline, but he'd completely lost it that night. The hell of it was, he'd known better. All summer long, he'd been fighting his attraction to her, but he liked her too much to do what he should have done, which was just leave her the hell alone.

He'd told himself that taking her for a nighttime sail in his uncle's boat would be harmless. After all, he sometimes saw her at night—he often drove her home from work—and they'd sailed together a few afternoons when they'd both been off work. They would just be combining two things they'd already done. He was sure he handle it.

Yeah, right. It had been like sitting in a pool of lighter fluid and playing with matches.

It was a gorgeous summer evening, clear and bright. The sky was heavy with stars, like a fruit-laden branch bending toward the earth. Katie wore cutoffs and a blue T-shirt that the wind molded against her body, outlining her breasts in a way that made it hard for him to breathe. The breeze was soft but steady, and they were a couple of miles from shore in no time at all.

She stretched out on the deck and gazed up. "Look at that sky!"

Zack dropped anchor, then stretched out on the deck beside her. The varnished wood was warm against his shirtless back. The boat rocked beneath them. He was careful not to touch her, but his hand was milimeters from hers, and he swore that her body heat jumped the space between them.

"The light from those stars is millions of years old by the time it reaches the earth," she said. "They might not even still be there."

"That's kind of a sad thought."

"Yeah. Makes you want to seize the day, doesn't it? Carpe diem and all that."

The movie Dead Poets Society *had come out the preceding year.* "Yeah. What part would you want to seize?"

She turned her head and looked at him. Her eyes held everything he was feeling—all the tenderness, all the yearning, all the emotion, all the need. "You," she whispered. "I'd seize you."

"Kate..." He meant to say her name in a cautionary way, but it came out as more of a groan.

She raised up on her elbows and leaned over him, her eyes brighter than any of the stars behind her. His last conscious thought was that he shouldn't kiss her, but when she lowered her lips to his, God help him, he kissed her back—and then he was kissing every inch of her, and doing all the things he'd dreamed about all summer, and she was doing them to him, and they were adrift on a sea of fire.

He realized he'd closed his eyes. He opened them and glanced over at her. "I'm sorry, Kate. I'm totally to blame."

She glanced away. "No, you're not."

"What?"

"Well, you're to blame for not contacting me afterward, but I don't blame you for what happened between us." She knotted her hands in her lap and stared down at them. "I mean, *I* kissed *you*."

"I sure didn't put up a fight." The wind blew an oak leaf against the windshield, plastering it to the wet glass. "I'd been dying to kiss you all summer."

"So why didn't you?"

He glanced at her, and the air inside the car suddenly seemed charged with enough electricity to generate a lightning strike. He broke eye contact and studied the oak leaf. "Because you'd told me how you believed in love and all that white knight, Prince Charming stuff. I was afraid that if we started something, you'd think I was the love of your life."

"I already did."

"Yeah, well, that's exactly why I didn't make a move. Until that night, I mean."

He heard her inhale and blow out a deep breath. A silver SUV sloshed by, slinging water against his car. He saw a "Baby on Board" triangle in the back window. "How long was it before you found out you were pregnant?"

"About a month later. I was two weeks late, so I bought a test. I told my mother, and . . ." Her throat moved as she swallowed. "She wanted me to end the pregnancy. I couldn't. But I couldn't stay here and face things, either. It was already bad enough, just being my mother's daughter."

She told him how hard it was—how she'd been ostracized and taunted and lied about at school. How she didn't have any friends, because no one wanted their child associating with the daughter of the town trollop. How everyone thought she was just like her mother. Being pregnant under those circumstances would have been a nightmare.

"I didn't want my baby growing up like I did. I wanted her to have a real home. A minister at a local church referred me to a place in Wichita where I could live and take classes, and they said they'd make sure my baby was adopted by good parents." She stared out the passenger window. "Putting her up for adoption was the hardest thing I ever did, but I thought..." Her voice broke. "I really thought it was for the best."

A tear dribbled from the corner of her eye. His throat grew tight as she wiped it away. "From everything I've heard, Gracie had a great home. She adored her parents."

"They died last year?"

"Actually, sixteen months ago. In a car accident."

"Oh, the poor girl."

"Yeah. Her aunt said it really hit her hard."

"Well, of course it would!"

"After Gracie moved to Pittsburgh to live with her aunt, she really went off the rails. She started cutting class and sneaking out at night and drinking and just generally acting out."

Katie turned her eyes to him. "You met the aunt?"

Zack nodded. "She flew out to Dallas. She'd had the police looking everywhere for Gracie.

"What's she like? The aunt, I mean."

"She means well, but she's pretty clueless about how to deal with a teenager."

"Gracie called her a nazi."

"I wouldn't go that far, but she does seem to subscribe to the rule-with-an-iron-hand philosophy, which didn't go over too well with Gracie." Zack watched the oak leaf slide down the windshield, pushed by a rivulet of water. "When Gracie ended up pregnant, well, the aunt just didn't know how to deal."

"Poor kid."

"Poor aunt." He gave a rueful smile. "Gracie's a handful." He stared back out at the rain. "Gracie had a scheme all worked out. She wanted me to get custody of her, have her declared an emancipated minor, and give her a big wad of cash."

"She's too young to be on her own."

"She's too young to be a mother. She's just seventeen." Which was the same age Katie had been when she'd had Gracie. The realization made him swallow.

"She sounded pretty adamant about not wanting to give up her baby."

"Yeah. But she's going to need some help caring for it." Zack turned to her. "She's going to need a mother."

The rain softened. So did Katie's eyes. "The baby, or Gracie?"

"Both."

She worried her bottom lip. "She didn't sound like she wanted anything to do with me."

"We can change that."

"We?"

"Yeah. The aunt will give us joint custody of Gracie."

Katie stared at him. "I can't believe you made all these arrangements without even talking to me."

"It wasn't a conversation I wanted to have over the phone. And I couldn't leave Gracie by herself while I came down here to talk to you." *Besides, I had to see you.* He squelched the words before they came out of his mouth. When he'd set out on this course of action, he'd promised himself that he wouldn't say anything or do anything that could be misinterpreted. The last thing he wanted was to hurt her again. "It just seemed more expedient."

"You must have been awfully sure of my answer if you bought a house before you even got here."

"I was pretty sure the girl who wrote that letter wouldn't turn away her own daughter."

Katie dropped her gaze, but not before her eyes verified that he was right. "So how do you envision this working?"

"I'll temporarily work out of Chartreuse. My job involves some travel, but I'll try to schedule things for your convenience. She'll live half the time with you, the other half with me."

"How long do you see this arrrangement lasting?"

"Until she has the baby and turns eighteen."

"And afterward?"

He lifted his shoulders. "We'll see how things go and what she wants to do. Hopefully you two will have bonded by then, and you can figure out where you want to take things from there."

"Why are you doing this?"

The question made him freeze. "What do you mean?"

"Well, you never wanted any attachments or strings or

commitment. You could have just sent Gracie back home with her aunt."

I had to give you a chance to get to know your daughter. But Zack couldn't tell Katie that. If he did, she'd think there was more to him than met the eye. She'd think he was sensitive and caring, and she'd probably end up getting hurt all over again.

"No, I couldn't. You've met Gracie. She's like a force of nature."

"But you never wanted children. Or any kind of commitment, for that matter."

"I believe in doing the honorable thing." Actually, he believed in being the exact opposite of his own father, who had been a liar and a cheater and who'd never shown the slightest interest in him as a child. "How about you? Are you in?"

"Of course I'm in! You already knew it would never be a question."

He did. But it was good to hear it, all the same.

She stared out at the rain. "I hope Gracie will warm up to me."

Zack studied Katie's profile, taking in her small straight nose and the freckles dusted over it, and felt an old tenderness waft through him. He steeled himself against it. Getting close to her would just end badly, like before. She was a vine-covered-cottage, white-picket-fence kind of girl, and he didn't believe in happily-ever-afters. From what he'd seen, the phrase "I love you" was just a manipulative tool, a way to get someone to do something for you. Love was nothing more than a gussied-up word for lust. It didn't last. Attraction faded and degenerated into insecurities and bickering. Romance happened, fell apart, and dissolved.

Love was like heaven—if it really existed, it wasn't for people like him. He didn't even believe in it. But Katie did, and he hoped she could find it with Gracie.

"Of course she will," he told her.

After all, who could help but warm up to Katie?

CHAPTER FOUR

The balding man at the front of the bookstore peered over the wire-rimmed reading glasses low on his nose when Gracie stepped inside. "Can I help you find anything?"

"No. I just want to look around."

Gracie made her way down the narrow aisle of book-shelves, her stomach churning, her thoughts spinning about the woman she'd just left in the café. So that was her birth mom—her B.M. Appropriate initials, Gracie thought dourly, considering the shitty way Katie had discarded her.

That letter made it sound like Katie had loved her and cared about her, but Gracie didn't believe it. Katie had probably written it to relieve her own conscience. Well, Gracie wasn't buying it. She'd spent a lifetime wonder-ing why her B.M. had given her up, and one tearjerker of an I'm-so-noble, I'm-giving-you-away-for-your-own-good letter wasn't going to make everything all right. She'd spent too many years thinking she was somehow secretly flawed, that something about her just wasn't good enough.

Her mom—her real mom—had told her that being adopted meant she was special—that she was chosen and wanted and prayed for and loved more than other kids. Gracie had never really bought that bull, either. It was just a bunch of empty words meant to make her feel less pathetic. What she really believed, deep down, was that she was unlovable. Why else would her birth mother give her away?

The rejection had always gnawed at her. Whenever Gracie asked her parents why her bio mom hadn't kept her, her real mom's mouth would get all pinched and tight, and she'd say something like, "I don't know. There's certainly no way under heaven that *I* could ever give you away. As far as I'm concerned, you're my daughter, and that other woman was just a vessel."

Gracie had spent an awful lot of time thinking about her vessel—wondering what she looked like, what she did, if she had any other kids. After her real parents had died, though, her curiosity had made her feel ashamed. Wondering about her birth parents—especially her B.M.—seemed like a betrayal or something.

Well, one thing was for certain: She wasn't going to get all close and friendly with Katie. How could she cozy up to someone who'd basically said, "I don't want you in my life"? She intended to treat her with the contempt she deserved.

Meeting her had been weird—beyond weird. Gracie had been unprepared for how much they looked alike. Looking at Katie had kinda been like looking at an older version of herself. They had the same widow's peak and small chin, the same tipped-up nose, the same wide mouth.

The thought made her lips press together hard. Yeah, well, she couldn't help it if she looked like her B.M., but she damn sure wasn't going to be anything like her otherwise. Gracie would never make the choices Katie had made. She'd never willingly live in a podunk town, she'd never have a lame-ass career like running a beauty salon, and, most important, she'd never give away a baby like old clothes to the Salvation Army. Gracie was more like her real mother—the mother who had chosen her and wanted her and loved her and cared for her.

Tears stung the insides of her eyelids as the image of her mother's face, round and smiling, filled her mind. Her father's face floated into the picture beside her, his dark eyes twinkling like they used to when he teased her. Why hadn't she told Mom and Dad how much they meant to her when she'd had the chance? That was the thing about death—there were no more second chances. It was final, permanent, forever. Whatever she'd said or hadn't said, done or hadn't done, that was the way things were from now on.

Come to think of it, that was how life pretty much worked, too. No taking things back once they were done. Like having this baby.

Gracie blinked back her tears and realized the man behind the bookstore counter was watching her. She drew her purse protectively over her stomach and ducked down another aisle. Ever since she'd started showing, people stared at her. Some of them got all prune-faced, as if they had a right to judge her. Some acted as if her big belly were public property and reached out to touch it. Just about everyone seemed to think it entitled them to ask personal questions like, *When is the baby due?* and *How old are you?*

Her purse did a pretty good job of hiding things. She didn't have much stuff in it—just some orange Tic Tacs, a black eyeliner pencil, a tube of ChapStick, and a grand total of about ten dollars, tops, counting the change. The value of the bag was purely sentimental.

Her mother—her *real* mother—had macraméd the bag for her.

Gracie felt the old familiar lump rise in her throat, the lump that had lurked there in varying sizes ever since she'd been called to the principal's office, where a police officer, her mom's best friend, and the school counselor had dropped the bomb.

The lump was getting big now, big enough to clog her throat, big and hot and coated with guilt.

"Are you looking for anything in particular?" the man called out.

She swallowed down the lump so she could speak. "Do you have any comic books?"

"No, but we have some of those graphic novels. They're all the way in the back on the right, at the end of the aisle."

Gracie headed that direction and found a selection of books with manga covers. She picked up one showing a big-eyed girl in a short skirt kicking serious ass with high-heeled, thigh-high boots. She'd just started reading it when the front door creaked open. Gracie peered around the corner and saw Katie and Zack walk in. Her stomach tightened, and she ducked back where she could watch them without being seen herself.

The older man beamed at Katie, gave her a warm hug, and kissed her cheek. "Hi there, sweetie! Great to see you."

Katie hugged him back. "You, too, Dave."

A moment of silence beat between them as the man looked at Zack, apparently expecting an introduction. "Dave, this is Zack Ferguson. Zack, this is my father-in-law, Dave Charmaine."

Father-in-law? Oh, this must be the dad of that dude she'd married—the Marine who'd died in Iraq. She'd read about it on Google. Gracie watched Zack and the older man shake hands, while Katie stood awkwardly beside them. Silence circled in the air like a buzzard.

"Are you okay, Katie?" Dave asked. "You look kind of pale."

"I'm—I'm fine. It's just...well, actually, Dave, I've just had some startling news."

"Oh?"

She bobbed her head. "It would probably be better if you and I sat down and talked about it in private later."

Gracie's lips pressed together. *Yeah, right. Break the bad news to him easy.* What was it about her very existence that made people need to sit down and reach for the smelling salts, like something out of a bad Jane Austen movie? Apparently Dave didn't know what kind of a coldhearted bitch his son had married.

"Well...okay." The old man looked at Zack curiously, as if he was trying to size up the situation, then turned back to Katie. "Brad is taking a coffee break. When he comes back, maybe you and I can go for a walk."

Momzilla looked like she was about to puke. "Sure."

The man turned back to Zack, his eyes frankly curious, and made another stab at extracting information. "So...how do you and Katie know each other?"

Katie twisted her purse handle. "We were, uh, friends. A long time ago."

Friends. *Yeah, right.* The old guy didn't seem to be buying it, either, from the expression on his face. He looked at Zack. "Can I help you find a book?"

Zack pulled his hands out of his pockets. "Actually, I came in looking for my daughter."

"Must be the gal in the back of the store."

"My daughter"—not "our daughter." So Zack was going to just grab her and leave, without telling the old dude that Katie was her mom. Oh, sure, Katie was going to break it to him later—she had to, since she and Zack were moving to town. But why should she let B.M. do things her way? She'd had things her way for seventeen years.

Seventeen years of pretending she didn't have a daughter was long enough. She wasn't going to get away with it a moment longer.

Gracie stepped into the aisle, clutching the manga book. A perverse pleasure coursed through her as she sauntered up the aisle, her boots clunking on the hardwood floor.

"Hey—while everyone is introducing themselves, I ought to, too. I'm Gracie." She treated Dave to a toothy grin. "Katie and Zack are my birth parents."

Katie's face grew as white as a roll of toilet paper. The old man gaped like one of those wall-mounted singing bass.

"Guess you're my grandpop-in-law. Or maybe it's step-grandpop-in-law. I don't know a lot about complicated blended family arrangements."

"You're...you're...," the old man stammered, then

cast a wide-eyed glance at Katie. "Did you say that you're Katie's...?"

"Birth daughter," Gracie filled in helpfully. "As in, she gave birth to me, then she gave me away. Guess you didn't know I existed, huh?"

The old man's Adam's apple bobbed as he gulped.

"Well, don't feel bad. She didn't bother to tell me about you, either." She plunked the book on the counter. "What's your name?"

"I'm—I'm Dave Charmaine."

"Nice to meet you." She pulled aside her macramé bag. "Guess you're going to be my baby's great-granddad-in-law or whatever."

"Your—baby?" The old man sounded like he needed to cough up a phlegm ball or something.

"Yeah. Heck of a deal, isn't it? You're getting a new grandkid and a great-grandkid all in one package."

The old man's face turned the color of Silly Putty. He gripped the countertop. Katie jumped forward, her eyes wide and alarmed. "Dave—are you all right?"

"Yeah."

Katie's forehead scrunched in concern. "You sure?"

"Yeah. Just a little angina, is all."

Angina? That was pain from heart trouble. She learned that watching *Grey's Anatomy* on TV—and then she'd looked it up in *Gray's Anatomy*, the book. Gracie's own heart raced as the man dug in the back pocket of his khaki Dockers, pulled out a pill container, and opened the lid with trembling hands. He popped a pill into his mouth.

Oh, jeez—she hadn't meant to give the old dude a heart attack. She hadn't meant to hurt him at all. She'd meant... Oh, hell. Guilt snaked through her. She'd meant to cause trouble, and this was the result. *Nothing good ever comes from bad intentions,* her mother used to say. Remorse flushed through her veins. She was always screwing things up. Why did she always have to screw things up?

"You should sit down." Katie took the man by the arm and edged him two feet back, to the barstool behind the counter. The wooden stool squeaked on the hardwood floor as he sat down.

"I'm fine," Dave said. "Really. It's already better."

"Does this happen often?"

"Nah. Just every now and then, if I get upset or excited or"—he looked at Gracie—"surprised. It's no big deal."

"Heart trouble certainly is a big deal," Katie said. "How long have you had it?"

"Awhile. But it's all under control." He straightened on the stool and looked through the window. "Here comes Brad. We can go in the back and talk, if you like."

"Are you sure you're okay?"

"I'm fine," the man said. "The pain's already gone."

A thin young man a year or two older than Gracie walked through the door. Katie looked at Zack. "You two can run along."

Zack touched Katie on the shoulder. "I'll catch up with you this evening."

The man gave Gracie a weak smile. "And I'll talk to you later, Gracie."

"O-okay." She looked at him. Her chin trembled. "I didn't mean...," she started. "I mean, I'm...I'm..."

Sorry. The word stuck in her throat like a chicken bone. Dear God, she was sorry about so many things,

things that she could barely stand to think about, things that woke her up in the night sobbing and covered with sweat, things that she would never be able to apologize for. How could she say she was sorry for this, when she'd never be able to apologize for the things that possessed her like a demon, stank up the air she breathed, and tainted her every thought?

Sorry. Yeah, she was, but what good did it do? It was just a word—a stupid, meaningless word that didn't change anything.

Nothing could ever change all the things she was sorry for.

"It's okay, Gracie," Dave said. His weathered face creased in a smile, and he said the words she needed to hear but didn't believe. "It's not your fault."

Zack opened the door, punched open the umbrella, and held it over her. She moved away from him, stepping off the sidewalk and into the gutter. Raindrops plopped down on her head. The sky was weeping, she thought as she wiped her face. No one needed to know that she was, too.

CHAPTER FIVE

The sun rode low in the sky as Dave steered his sedan into the parking lot of the Sunnyside Assisted-Living Villa. He turned off the engine, picked up the bouquet of roses he'd bought at the grocery store, and climbed out of the car. As he walked toward the large, French-country-style building, he thought again how the place looked more like a resort than a place for the elderly or disabled.

Disabled. It was hard to think of Annette that way. Of course, she was just temporarily in that condition—a nasty fall down the stairs at her home in New Orleans had broken her leg in three places and required a total knee replacement—but it was still hard, because in his mind's eye, she'd always be the girl he'd fallen in love with in high school. Annette had been his first kiss, his first lover, his first wife.

Hell. She'd been his only real wife. That thing with his secretary didn't count. That had been nothing but a stupid, alcohol-fueled, midlife crisis—a way of denying the fact he was getting older, of trying to feel better about himself. It was no excuse, but if he hadn't been drinking so heavily, it never would have happened. It sure as hell never would have escalated into a wedding. He'd been planning on breaking off the affair when Annette caught him in the act.

The memory made his face heat with shame. Linda had been bent over his desk, her skirt up to her waist, and his pants had been around his ankles. A loud gasp had sounded behind him. He'd twisted his head to see Annette standing in the doorway, both hands over her mouth. His heart and his dick had both headed south.

"Annette," he'd blurted.

She'd turned on her heel, walked out of his office, and kept right on walking—out of his life, into a divorce attorney's office, out of Chartreuse, and into a new career as a substitute teacher in New Orleans. He'd married Linda on the rebound, but it had never really been a marriage. She'd sure wasted no time bailing when he'd started having health problems.

He pulled open the tall arched French door and stepped inside the assisted-living center. Music tinkled from the parlor, where about twenty elderly people mingled and chattered gaily, as if they were at a cocktail party.

Some of them weren't all that much older than Dave. At fifty-seven, he was only a decade or so shy of fitting right in. The realization burned. He'd tried to deny the realities of aging, but his recent heart diagnosis had made it all too real. He was getting old, and he was a fool. What was the saying? There's no fool like an old fool. Yeah, well, there he was—Exhibit A. The only thing worse than an old fool was an old fool with a drinking problem.

The thought made him wince as he headed toward

the elevator. At least he'd finally put the plug in the jug.
Thanks to AA, he'd been sober a year and a half now. He
was working his way through the twelve steps, and now
he was on step nine, trying to make amends and clear up
the wreckage of his past.

Most of that wreckage involved his family. It was too
late to make amends to his son; Paul had died not speaking to him. The guilt over that had driven him back to
the bottle during three earlier attempts to quit drinking. It
was hell, having to accept the things he couldn't change.
He didn't know that he'd ever be able to forgive himself
for all the mistakes he'd made as a father. Those were just
things he had to live with, one day at a time.

He couldn't live without making amends to Annette,
though. He needed to set things right, because the shame
and remorse were eating him up. If he didn't do his best
to make amends, he was afraid it was going to drive him
back to the bottle.

He'd avoided Annette for years, but when he'd heard
about her fall, he'd rushed to the hospital in New Orleans.
She hadn't been pleased to see him. She'd been pretty
doped up on painkillers, though, so hopefully he'd get a
better reception now.

He wondered if Annette would be as shocked to learn
that Katie had a child as he'd been. He'd had no idea, but
then, Annette had always been closer to Katie than he
had. His son had cut him out of his life after the affair.
Katie, bless her heart, had been more forgiving, but she'd
never really confided in him.

The elevator opened, and he stepped out into the
medical-care wing on the second floor. If you had to be
someplace besides home while recovering from a big-dog

surgery, this was a good place to do it, he thought. The rooms looked like hotel suites, an RN was constantly on staff, and the best doctors and physical therapists in the area made daily rounds. It was as good as, if not better than, a hospital.

He knocked on the casing of the partially opened door that had her name on it. "Annette?" He pushed the door open.

She was sitting up in bed, wearing teal satin pajamas. She always used to wear flannel ones, the kind with long sleeves and high necks. She was pale and kind of peaked, as if she'd been through an ordeal, but she looked better than she had any right to, considering her accident and surgery had been just five days ago. Her hair was different from the way she'd worn it when they were married. It was longer, and a lighter shade of blonde.

She was lovely. It had always amazed him that a woman so beautiful had ever had anything to do with the likes of him.

The way she stiffened against the pillow as he stepped closer made his heart squeeze. So did the wariness in her usually soft gray eyes. "Dave. What are you doing here?"

The faint scent of his Aramis aftershave stirred up a hornet's nest of emotions in Annette's chest. Damn it—despite the fact he'd yanked out her heart and stomped all over it, Dave still made it skip. She tilted up her chin, determined not to let him know it.

"I thought I'd come see how you're doing," he said.

He hadn't cared in years, Annette thought. Why should he care now? Probably because he was lonely now that the tramp he'd married had left him. It had been all over town when Linda had run off with the owner of that bar in Hammond a year ago. Annette had been living in New Orleans then, but she'd gotten eleven phone calls within four hours of Dave's new wife picking up and moving on.

She shouldn't have cared. She'd told herself that she was over him and she was better off without him. She liked to think that she was the kind of person who didn't harbor grudges or hold ill will, but God help her, she'd been glad. *Good*, she'd thought. *Let him find out what it feels like to be left.* Turnabout, after all, was fair play.

"How are you feeling?" Dave asked.

"Just fine," she said stiffly.

"I'm mighty glad to hear it." He stretched his hand out and laid the bouquet on the tray. "I brought you roses."

Too little, too late. She could count on one hand the number of times he'd brought her flowers during their thirty-two years of marriage. Four times the first year, then once again after she'd given birth to Paul two years later. Of course, he'd deluged her with flowers after she'd caught him with his pants down, but those times didn't count, because as far as she was concerned, the marriage had been already over.

Still, she was a Southern lady, and her upbringing insisted that politeness be observed. "Thank you," she said stiffly.

"Do you want me to put them in water?" he asked.

"I don't have a vase."

His face fell. He rubbed his jaw. "I should have thought of that."

You should have thought of a lot of things. Why was

he here, tormenting her? She'd moved on. She was over him. She didn't want him coming around, picking at scabs she'd thought had healed. She didn't want him to know he still had the ability to affect her in any way. Her grandmother's soft Southern drawl replayed in her mind: *A lady kills her foes with kindness.* Determined to follow the advice, she forced her voice into a modulated tone. "Maybe the staff has something."

Dave nodded. "I'll check at the nurse's desk when I leave."

Which couldn't happen too soon, Annette thought darkly. Instead of heading for the door, though, Dave sat down in the faux-leather recliner beside the bed. "You look good, Annette."

Her hand flew to her hair before she could stop herself. Katie had washed and styled her hair yesterday, but Annette hadn't combed it since this morning, and she wasn't wearing any makeup. It annoyed her that Dave had caught her at less than her best, then it annoyed her even more that she cared. She lowered her hand and smoothed the sheet. "I'm sure I'm a vision of loveliness," she said dryly.

"Actually, you are."

"A little old for your tastes, apparently." The words flew out before she could stop them. Damn it—she hated the bitterness in her voice, but she couldn't help it. Aging wasn't an option she'd selected. It was something happening to her without her permission. How could she compete with a woman twenty years younger? She couldn't. It had hurt like hell that she'd been traded in on a younger model, like a car that had too much mileage. She tried to take good care of herself, but gravity inevitably took a toll.

It had taken a toll on Dave, too. He looked like he'd aged ten years in the four since they divorced. For some irritating reason, though, it hadn't detracted from his attractiveness. Why was that? Why did men seem to age with impunity? It wasn't fair.

"Annette..." Dave's brown eyes held a disconcerting amount of pain. "I can't begin to tell you how sorry I am for my behavior. I was a fool."

She picked at an invisible piece of lint on the sheet. What did he expect her to say? That it was all right? It wasn't. It never would be. Besides, this wasn't the first time he'd apologized. He'd started begging for forgiveness before he'd even gotten his pants zipped that awful afternoon. He'd apologized when he'd picked up the belongings she'd tossed on the lawn, he'd apologized on her voice machine when she wouldn't take his calls, he'd sent her flowers and candy and—unforgivably, she thought—a teddy bear that had made her cry, because it reminded her of the one their son had dragged everywhere when he was little. Dave had finally, thankfully, quit badgering her to take him back when the divorce papers were finalized.

He leaned forward, his head down. "I know it's no excuse, Annette, but I had a drinking problem."

"No joke."

A nerve twitched in his jaw. "I know, I know. I should have listened to you. You'd been telling me that for years. But I didn't listen, and, well, I guess it takes what it takes. Anyway, I joined AA, and I've been continuously sober for a year and a half now."

"Congratulations." She hadn't meant for the word to carry a derisive tone, but it did anyway. Why the hell couldn't he have done that back when they were married, back when she'd begged him to, back when she'd started going to Al-Anon?

His Adam's apple bobbed. "I'm working my way through the steps. I'm at the ninth one now." He paused and swallowed again. "I want to make amends to you, Annette."

Make amends? How the hell did he think he was going to make amends for ripping her world apart? "Just how do you intend to do that?"

"I—I don't know. By being here for you, I guess."

Annette pulled herself higher on her pillow. Her leg throbbed. Her heart throbbed harder. Anger pulsed through her, hot and sharp and acute. Who the heck did he think he was, that she would want or need him, after the way he'd treated her? He'd betrayed her. Why should she do anything that would make him feel better? She fixed him with a hard glare. "Quite frankly, Dave, I don't want you here."

"I can understand that, but..."

"No buts about it, Dave. The best thing you can do for me is stay away."

He dropped his head and rested his forearms on his thighs, his hands clasped together. From her position above him on the hospital bed, she saw the balding spot on his crown. An unwanted ache of tenderness squeezed her heart. He'd hated his thinning hair, but she'd secretly loved the widening patch of skin on his head. It made him look somehow...vulnerable. It reminded her of the head of their child when he'd first been born.

He blew out a long sigh. "Okay. I'll go for now, but before I go, there's some news I need to tell you."

The somber note in his voice made her stomach tense.

"Have you seen Katie today?" he asked.

"She came by this morning." Alarm shot through her. "Why? Has something happened to her?"

"No, no. She's fine. But she came into the bookstore this afternoon, and..." She knew that expression, knew that pause of silence. He was about to tell her something she wouldn't like hearing. "Annette, she wasn't alone."

Oh, Lord. She'd known that someday Katie was likely to find someone new—after all, she was only thirty-five, young enough to remarry and maybe even have a family—but the thought of another man replacing Paul in her life made her chest tighten. Katie was her living tie to Paul, the daughter she'd always wanted. If Katie moved on, the memory of Paul would grow fainter and more distant. She wasn't ready for it. "Who was she with?"

Dave looked away, as if the topic made him uncomfortable, then looked back at her. "A couple of people."

So maybe it wasn't a man, after all. Still, Dave had that bad-news look about him. "Who were they?"

"Did you know Katie has a child?" he blurted.

Annette stared at him, trying to make sense of his words. They were so bizarre they held no meaning. She couldn't have been more confused if he'd spoken in Swahili. "A child?" she blankly echoed.

Dave's head bobbed. "A daughter. A teenage daughter. Katie had her out of wedlock when she was seventeen. She gave her up for adoption."

"No," Annette breathed.

"Yes. I met her. Then Katie sat me down and explained it all. The girl—her name is Gracie—looked up her birth parents after her adoptive parents died. She found the father, and he brought her here so he and Katie can share custody of her."

Annette's head swam. "You're kidding." But she knew from the expression on Dave's face that he wasn't. Her fingers tightened on the sheet. "Who—who's the father?"

"A man named Zack Ferguson. He lives in Las Vegas. Apparently he made a name for himself as a professional poker player."

"A poker player! How on earth did Katie know him?" A larger question formed in her mind. "Did—did Paul know?"

Dave nodded. "Katie says she told him about the baby when they were dating."

"So Paul knew."

"Apparently so. And it didn't make a difference to him."

Annette's thoughts bobbed up and down like a fishing cork in high seas. "Why didn't he tell us?"

Dave lifted his shoulders. "Probably because it was none of our business."

"Not our business? Of course it was our business!"

"Think about it, Annette. Most young men don't give their parents a rundown on the sexual history of the woman they decide to marry."

"A child is more than sexual history."

Dave's mouth pulled tight. "Yeah. But Katie gave her up for adoption."

"Still, it's a child."

"Yes, but Katie had no contact with her."

"Still…"

"I was kind of outraged at first, too," Dave said. "It takes some time to get used to the idea. And then, after the shock wore off, I looked at it this way: If she'd had an abortion, would that have been our business, too?"

Annette supposed not. Dave had a point. But still...

Dave fidgeted. "There's more."

Good Lord in heaven. "What more could there be?"

"The daughter—Gracie—well, she's pregnant herself."

It was almost too much to take in at once. Annette stared at him. "My God. How old is she?"

"Seventeen."

"The same age Katie was when she had her?"

"Yeah. But this girl looks more like thirteen."

"Wow." Annette flopped back against her pillow. "How—how is Katie?"

"In shock. This all hit her out of the blue."

"Good heavens."

"She's coming by this evening to tell you, but I thought I'd give you some advance warning."

"A daughter," Annette said wonderingly. "Katie has a daughter."

Dave nodded. "And she's about to have a granddaughter."

"She's going to be a grandmother at thirty-five?" Annette tried to wrap her mind around the concept. Grandmothers were her age. Katie was young enough to be having a baby herself. "Does the girl look like Katie?"

"Yeah. But she kind of looks like her dad, too."

"You've seen him?"

"Yeah."

Anger and something that felt oddly akin to jealousy rushed through Annette. Paul should have been the father of Katie's child. They'd tried for a child; they'd both wanted one so badly. And now it turned out that Katie already had one, and Paul was dead, and...

"It's so unfair! Paul should have been..." The words choked off in her throat.

Dave grasped her hand in both of his. "I know, Annette."

His hands were warm and familiar, and they covered hers like a long-lost glove. She hadn't felt his touch in more than four years—not even when Paul had died.

The days surrounding Paul's death were mostly a blur, but one day stood out. She'd been at the funeral parlor with Katie, in the room with the coffin displays, walking from coffin to coffin, numbly trying to pick one. Dave had walked into the heavily draped room and looked at Annette, his eyes watery, his shoulders hunched, his expression stricken, his eyes reflecting all the agony she'd felt inside.

"Annette," he'd whispered in a tear-choked voice. "Oh, Jesus, Annette." He'd reached out his arms. She'd started to step into them, into the only place she might find comfort, into the embrace of the only other person on the planet who had been there when this child they had lost was created and born and loved into manhood. And then, over his shoulder, she'd seen that tramp he'd married walk into the room and flip her hair. Annette had jerked away.

She hadn't wanted his touch then, and she didn't want it now. She yanked her hand from his.

"Can I get you a Kleenex?" he asked. "Do you want to talk?"

"No." Her throat felt as swollen as the bayou after a rain. "I want you to go."

"Annette, this thing with Katie—we should be glad for her."

Annette tried to swallow.

"She'll need your support. You're like a mother to her."

He was right. Annette jerked her head in a stiff nod.

"That's my girl."

"I'm not your girl," she said curtly.

Dave's voice grew low and soft. "In my heart, you'll always be my girl."

"Please go."

"Okay. On my way out, I'll ask the floor nurse if she has a vase." He headed toward the door, then turned, his hand on the doorknob. "See you tomorrow."

"Don't bother."

"Oh, it's no bother." He gave her a wink as he closed the door. Dave used to wink at her all the time, a silly little you-and-me-are-in-this-together signal that always made her smile.

Despite everything that had happened between them, her foolish heart leaped at the gesture.

CHAPTER SIX

After talking with Dave at the bookstore, Katie hurried to the Sunnyside Assisted-Living Villa, where she rushed through an appointment to perm Mavis Shroeder's thin, gray hair in the tiny, one-sink salon. Unfortunately, she couldn't rush the perm's timing, so it was nearly two hours later before she could make her way up to Annette's room in the rehab wing. She wanted to break the news about Gracie and Zack in person, but gossip spread faster than melted butter on hot toast in the small community. She knocked on the door, wondering if Annette already knew.

"Come in," Annette called.

Katie hesitated, her stomach roiling. She wasn't sure how the older woman would react. Annette was the mother she'd never had, the mother she'd always wanted, and her good opinion meant more to Katie than anything. All of the self-help experts out there would probably say it wasn't healthy to care so much what someone else thought about her, but Katie couldn't help it. She loved Annette, and the last thing she wanted to do was to hurt her or let her down.

Annette clicked off the TV as Katie stepped into the room. An uncharacteristic tension stretched between them.

She knows.

All of the old shame she used to feel about her mother's behavior gorged Katie's throat. Oh, God—did Annette think she was like her mother? Was she repulsed? Did she feel scornful? What if she wanted nothing further to do with her? Even faint disappointment would be unbearable. Katie tried to swallow, but her tongue felt thick and her mouth was too dry. "Annette, I..."

Annette's face broke into a smile. "I heard. You have a daughter! And she's here in Chartreuse. This is so wonderful, sweetheart!" She held out her arms.

Katie stepped up to the bed and into the embrace, tears filling her eyes. Annette wrapped her arms around her and patted her back as tears streamed down Katie's face.

When she finally pulled back, Katie realized that Annette was crying, too. The older woman reached for a box of tissues on the rolling hospital tray beside the bed. She held it out to Katie. "Aren't we a pair of sentimental sisters," Annette said.

Katie nodded and dabbed her eyes. "I was so afraid of what you'd think of me."

"Oh, sweetie, I could never think you were anything but wonderful."

The unconditional acceptance brought fresh tears to Katie's eyes.

"I've got to admit, it was quite a shock. But it's wonderful news." Annette patted the side of her bed. "Now sit down and tell me everything."

• • •

An hour later, Katie went back to the Curl Up 'N Dye to close for the evening. She let herself in the back door and found Bev standing at the shampoo sink, rinsing disinfectant off the day's worth of combs and brushes. Bev looked up and grinned. "Well, if it isn't Little Miss Talk of the Town."

Katie sighed as she set her purse on the counter. "Guess you heard, huh?"

"I've heard an awful lot of things." She turned off the faucet, reached for a towel, and looked at her curiously as she dried her hands. "I don't know which, if any, are true, but I'm dying to find out."

"What did you hear?"

Bev raised her hand and ticked items off on her fingers. "That you have a daughter. That the hunk who came in here is the dad. That the girl is pregnant. That they've moved here so you can share custody."

Katie nodded. "That's about the size of it."

Bev dropped her hand and stared. "Holy mackerel, honey. Why on earth didn't you tell me?"

"Because I didn't know! Well, I knew I had a daughter, of course, but..."

Bev held her hand back up. "That's the part I don't understand. Why on earth didn't you tell me you'd had a baby?" Her eyes held a soft reproach. "That's the kind of thing a friend should know."

"You're right. You're absolutely right." Katie had wanted to tell her, just as she'd wanted to tell Annette. She'd even come close a few times. But each time she'd started to say something, the conversation had changed or someone else had entered the room or the situation had somehow shifted. "It isn't the kind of thing that just comes up in conversation. I never seemed to find the right moment."

Bev gave a get-real look.

Katie threw up her hands in surrender. "Okay. That's no excuse. We've worked together every day for years. But that somehow made it harder. The longer I went without telling you, the worse it seemed that I hadn't told you, so the harder it got. But mostly..." Katie dropped her hands, closed her eyes for a second, and blew out a hard breath. "Oh, God, Bev, when it happened, I was all wrapped up in guilt and shame and secrecy. And that guilt and shame never really went away."

"You've done nothing to be ashamed of. You were just a kid." Bev walked over and gave her a hug. Katie hugged her back, which kind of felt like hugging a scarecrow. Bev pulled away and looked down at her. "Were you afraid I'd think less of you?"

"I suppose." Katie bent down and picked up the laundry basket of used towels. "I've never really settled in my mind what I think of myself. Adoption seemed like the best thing for the baby, but I've second-guessed that decision a lot."

Bev pulled the disinfected brushes out of the sink and laid them out to dry. "I can't believe you kept a thing like that secret this long. Especially in this town!"

Katie stepped through the door to the back room and dumped the towels into the washing machine. "Nobody knew where I'd gone except for the Methodist minister. He told me about the adoption center in Kansas."

"Bless your heart. That had to be so hard!"

"Harder than anyone could know." Katie added detergent, closed the lid on the washer, and turned it on.

"I can't even imagine." Bev watched Katie cross to her styling station and sit in her chair. "And you haven't had any contact with your daughter until today?"

Katie shook her head. "It was a closed adoption. I had no idea where she was or what her last name was. And I certainly had no idea Zack was about to bring her here." Katie gazed at the patch of sunlight shining on Rachel's nail polish collection, illuminating the sparkles in the frosted shades and making the sheer tints glow. The rain had stopped a few hours ago, and since it was July, it wouldn't get dark for another couple of hours. Still, it was weird, having the sun come out at the end of the day.

"I always hoped I'd hear from her someday," Katie found herself saying. "Years ago, I registered with a service that helps reunite children and birth parents if both are looking for each other. But I always wanted the first move to be hers. I didn't want to interfere in her life if she didn't want me to."

"And now she wants you to!"

"Not exactly." Katie explained about the deaths of Gracie's parents, the aunt's requirements for relinquishing custody, and the less-than-warm reception she'd received from her daughter.

"It'll all be fine, honey," Bev said. "You two are going to end up thick as thieves. All you need is a little tincture of time."

"I hope so."

"Just you wait. These things have a way of working out."

"In the movies," Katie said dryly. "Or the soap operas."

"This is like a soap opera, that's for sure."

"Yeah. Especially the way it's being broadcast. Everyone at the retirement center already knew when I got there. Even Annette."

"Annette. Oh, my." Bev's eyes narrowed with concern. "How did she take it?"

"Pretty well. She was shocked, of course, but it turns out Dave had already told her."

"Dave?" Bev's eyes widened. "I thought those two weren't on speaking terms. The last time I saw them together was..."

At Paul's funeral. Bev apparently caught herself before she said the words. Katie pressed her lips together at the memory. They'd sat on opposite sides of the church during the service and stood on opposite sides of the grave at the cemetery.

Bev sank into her chair beside Katie and looked at her in the mirror. "Well, I have to say, Dave's sure changed for the better. Fergie Johnson was saying just last week that he seems like a different man since he started going to AA."

"You're not supposed to be talking about who belongs to that," Katie scolded. "The second *A* stands for Anonymous."

Bev flipped her hand in a dismissive gesture. "Nothing's anonymous in this town. Not when you can drive by the Lutheran church on Thursday nights and see whose car is in the parking lot. I guess I'm not surprised Dave went to see Annette, but I'm pretty surprised Annette let him in the room."

"That's probably because she was in no shape to throw him out."

"Annette and Dave talking, and you with a daughter."

Bev shook her head. "This really is a red-letter day." Bev leaned forward, her elbows on her bony thighs. "So tell me about the hunk."

Katie's heart missed a beat. "There's nothing much to tell."

"Must be something, if you two made a baby together."

Katie lifted her shoulders. "It was a teenage summer thing."

"Ahh. First love, huh?"

On her part, it had been. She'd been completely head over heels. She'd been so smitten, so young, so totally naive. She'd even told him how she felt.

Her face burned at the memory.

She was lying in his arms after their lovemaking, covered with a sheen of sweat, trying to regain the ability to breathe, her heart about to burst.

Zack stroked her hair. "That was amazing," he whispered against her ear.

"You're amazing." The sailboat dipped on a wave—or maybe the earth moved. She gazed up at him, her heart in her eyes. "I love you."

His fingers froze in her hair. His eyes took on a stricken look. "You don't mean that."

He didn't want her to mean that; she caught on to that right away. Her heart felt like it had been stung by a bee.

"You have a crush on me, just like I do on you," Zack said. "It's not love."

"Yes, it is."

Zack ruffled her hair and tried for a light tone. "Yeah,

*well, I'm crazy about you, too." He rolled over and rose
to his feet. "It's late. We'd better get back to shore so I
can go pick up my cousin."*

Bev's voice pulled her back to the present. "How did
he react to the news you were pregnant?"

"He never knew."

"What?"

"We were only together once, then he disappeared. I
didn't know how to contact him."

The front door rattled. Bev cast a glance at the paned
window in it, then threw Katie a sideways grin. "Looks
like he has no problem contacting *you*."

Katie turned to see Zack standing outside the locked
door. Against her will, her heart thudded against her
rib cage. She walked toward the door, her legs feeling
strangely stiff, her fingers awkward as she unfastened the
lock and opened it. "Hi."

"Hi, yourself." His eyes crinkled in that way she
remembered. The lines around his eyes were deeper now,
but they somehow only served to make him more attractive. He stepped into the room, smelling of rain and soap
and that faint undernote she so distinctly remembered,
the scent that was Zack, the scent of pure man. She
stepped back, steeling herself against the disconcerting
pull of it.

He waved at the older woman. "Hi, Bev."

Bev beamed. "You remembered my name!"

He'd always had a way with names. And a way with
women, Katie thought.

"Of course." His smile widened as he regarded the
older woman. "You're unforgettable."

Bev's hand flew to her chest, and a goofy smile spread across her face. Apparently even Bev wasn't immune to his charm. Wiping her hands on her pants, she made a big show of picking up her purse. "Well, I'm calling it a night. See you tomorrow, Katie."

Katie felt a moment of panic at the thought of being alone with Zack. "Hang on, Bev. I, uh, need to talk to you about something before you leave."

Bev looked from Katie to Zack, then back again. She gave that I-know-what-you're-up-to-and-I-won't-be-an-accomplice smile. "Oh, gee—I told George I'd be home twenty minutes ago. Talk to you in the morning!" Bev disappeared out the back of the salon.

The door banged closed behind her. The small salon suddenly seemed more crowded with just the two of them in it. Katie moved to her station, trying to put some distance between them. Zack followed her and stood unnervingly close as she sorted the supplies in her equipment cart.

"Sorry about that scene in the bookstore," Zack said. "Gracie can be difficult."

"She's got a lot of anger toward me."

He rubbed his chin. "Her adoptive mother kind of set that up."

Katie looked up, wondering what he meant.

Zack picked up a silver hairclip and examined it as if it were a foreign object. "According to the aunt, Gracie's adoptive mom had been adopted herself when she was seven. Her parents had a natural child a few years later, and Gracie's mom always felt second-rate to the natural child. She didn't want Gracie to grow up feeling inferior like she had, so she overcompensated."

"How?"

He put down the hairclip and picked up a stray blue curler from the top of her cart. "She made a big deal of telling Gracie how lucky she was to have a mom who loved her and wanted her so very, very much, instead of being stuck with a mom who...." His voice tapered off.

"Didn't love her or want her," Katie finished for him. Her heart felt like somebody had tied a lead weight around it.

Zack toyed with the hair roller. "Long story short, you were painted as the bad guy so the adopted mom could look like a rescuing angel."

Katie's throat grew tight. "I gave her up because I thought it was best for her. It was the hardest thing I ever had to do."

"I'm sure it was." His eyes, warm and sympathetic, met hers in the mirror. "I'm not saying you did anything wrong. I'm just telling you where Gracie's coming from. She's seventeen, and she's stubborn. All her life she's been set up to think that her adoptive mom saved her from a life of neglect."

Plus Gracie was grieving the only mother she ever knew, and was about to become a mom herself. Katie straightened the cans of mousse and hair spray on the counter. "I imagine she decided to keep her baby so she wouldn't be a bad mom like me."

"You weren't a bad mom."

"But in Gracie's mind..." Her voice trailed off.

"She'll warm up to you once she gets to know you," Zack said.

How did Zack know so much about Gracie? An

irrational spurt of anger shot through her. "Did she start out treating you badly, too?"

"She still treats me badly, just in a different way." Zack bent to put the roller with the others on the bottom tray of her cart. "She tolerates me, but just barely. I think she views me as a necessary evil, because I'm the key to her getting what she wants."

"Which is?"

"Money. And independence. At least, independence from her aunt." He straightened and looked at her. "I made a point of telling Gracie that she's got to get along with you, because the whole aunt thing hinges on our sharing joint custody. We have to call the aunt tomorrow, by the way. She wants to talk to you."

"So she can evaluate my suitability?" Katie said dryly.

"Something like that." He leaned against the station counter. "She's relieved to have Gracie out of her house, but she wants a clear conscience about letting her go."

"I'll be happy to talk to her." In the mirror, she could see Zack's back. She took in the way his broad shoulders stretched the fabric of his polo shirt, the way his hair swirled to the right at the top of his crown, the way his jeans outlined his sexy buns.

Whoa. What was she doing, thinking about Zack's buns? She hadn't thought about a guy that way since Paul. Rattled, she moved from her station to the cash register.

Zack followed her. "I came by to see if you wanted to go to dinner with Gracie and me."

The thought of going out and being ogled by everyone in town made Katie's stomach twist, but she was dying to spend more time with Gracie. "I have a better idea. Why don't you and Gracie come to dinner at my place?"

His smile seemed to go right through her. "Great."

"Do you know where I live?"

"Yeah. I deliberately bought a house just a block away."

She should have known the proximity was no accident. Few things escaped Zack's notice.

"I figured it would make it easier for us to share custody if Gracie could just walk back and forth between our places. Do you have a room where she can sleep?"

"Sure." The spare room was set up as a guest room, but Katie thought of it as the nursery, because she and Paul had planned to turn it into one when she had the baby they so desperately wanted. How ironic that it would now be used by the baby she gave away.

"As I said before, half the time Gracie can stay with you, and the other half with me," Zack said.

"How do you want to structure this? Are we going to alternate weeks?"

"We can play that by ear. At first we should probably just alternate nights, because Gracie..." His voice trailed off.

"Won't want to stay with me," Katie filled in.

"She doesn't know what she wants." Zack shifted. "Can she stay with you tonight? The beds weren't delivered, and I don't want to make her sleep on the floor."

"No problem." The thought filled Katie with excitement. She would get her daughter all to herself. They'd spend some time together, Gracie would begin to thaw, and before she knew it, they'd be laughing and talking, and Gracie would be confiding in her, just like a regular mother and daughter.

"So what time do you want us to come over?" Zack asked.

Katie ran a fast mental inventory. She always kept the ingredients of an emergency dinner on hand: pasta and spaghetti sauce in her pantry, plus garlic bread, ground meat, and ice cream in her freezer. She had a fresh bag of mixed lettuce in her fridge. She wouldn't even have to run by the store. "In, say, thirty or forty minutes?"

"Great." He turned toward the door. "We'll see you then."

CHAPTER SEVEN

Katie's house was a taupe-colored cottage with a deep front porch, green-shuttered windows, and white, Victorian-style trim. It looked like Katie, Zack thought—small, pretty, and stylish. Gracie's flip-flops slapped loudly as she climbed the wooden porch stairs beside Zack, her face set in a stubborn sulk.

The scent of cooking garlic and onions wafted out the door as soon as Katie opened it. "Umm. Smells delicious," Zack said as he stepped into the house. He handed Katie the bottle of wine he'd picked up on his way home from her salon.

She took it from him, her eyes surprised. "Thanks."

He looked around. The living room and the connected kitchen were painted a soft golden yellow and decorated with a mix of antiques and Pottery Barn–style furnishings. The overall effect was charming and inviting. "Nice place, isn't it, Gracie?"

The girl tilted up her nose and ignored the question.

He should have known there was no way she'd be conned into saying anything positive.

"Where's my room?" Gracie asked.

Katie gestured toward the back of the house. "Down the hall, to the right."

Without a word, the girl clomped away, her purse slung over one shoulder, a backpack over the other.

"Make yourself at home," Katie called.

A door closed with a hard thud.

"She's not big on manners," Zack said apologetically.

"It's okay." She looked at the wine bottle, then smiled up at him. "You more than made up for it. Come on in."

He followed her into the living room and paused in front of an old black upright piano. "Do you play?"

"No. My husband did."

Husband. The word knotted something in Zack's gut. He glanced at Katie's left hand and noticed that a wedding ring still sparkled there.

"He was teaching me, but I haven't touched it since he"—her eyes darted away—"didn't come back."

"I'm really sorry. That had to be rough."

"Yeah."

That must be her husband in the photo on the piano. He looked like a nice enough guy—sandy hair, ramrod posture, and an easy smile. Zack's gaze drifted to a large urn on the mantel. Oh, God—was that what he thought it was? He swallowed. Yeah, it probably was, because it was surrounded by smaller framed photos, and they all featured the same man.

Zack walked over and looked at them. A large photo in a heavy silver frame showed a man in a tuxedo, standing beside Katie as a radiant bride, beaming at her as if he'd just won the lottery. In the next one he stood with his arm around her in front of a Christmas tree with a bunch of other people. To the right, Katie and the man sat in a buggy drawn by a horse. On the left, they lounged on a white-sand beach.

The knot in Zack's stomach tightened. He picked up a photo of the man in a U.S. Marine Corps Reserve uniform. "So this was Paul."

Katie nodded.

"How long were you married?"

"Four years."

He'd known Katie only a little over six weeks that summer. Funny how much of an impact those six weeks had made on his life. "I understand he died in Iraq."

"Yeah."

"I'm sorry."

Katie's head bobbed in acknowledgment. "He was in Baghdad, on his second tour. He was twenty-nine days away from coming home when a man pulled a bomb out from under his coat in the middle of a crowd. Paul tackled him, and it went off." Her mouth pinched with pain.

"He was a real hero."

"Yeah." She bit her lip as she gazed at the photo. "But then, he'd always been my hero."

It was as it should be. So why did the words sting? "How did you two meet?"

"He was a drug rep before his Reserve Unit was called up. I met him at a local doctor's office the day I had the flu. I was at my absolute worst—runny nose, fever, and a hacking cough—not to mention stringy hair and baggy sweats."

"Baggy sweats," he said dryly. "That's a flu symptom you don't usually hear about."

She laughed. The sound was like a forgotten favorite

melody playing on the car radio, the kind that made him sit in the car to listen after he'd reached his destination.

"When he came back through town the following week," she continued, "he called and asked me to lunch."

Zack carefully set the photo back atop the piano, quashing the childish urge to place it facedown. "Even at your worst, Kate, you always outshone every other woman in the room."

Katie wrapped her arms around her chest and tried to squelch her pleased reaction. It was meaningless flattery, she told herself. He'd dated movie stars and models, so he probably kept a tankful of high-octane compliments at the ready. "Yeah, right."

"I mean it."

It was alarming how much a pathetic part of her wanted to believe he actually did. "Uh-huh."

"Remember that day we got caught in that downpour and you fell down and got covered in mud? And you'd worn eye makeup that day, and it ran all over your face."

"I'm so glad you remembered that."

"It was a memorable sight. You looked like a cross between a raccoon and a melting clown."

"Thanks a lot."

"Don't mention it. The thing is, you looked better messed up than most women look after hours of primping."

He was BS-ing her, but her cheeks heated all the same. "I'm not sure I'm pleased that's your most enduring memory of me, but thanks." She headed for the kitchen.

He followed her. "I didn't say that was my most

enduring memory." He leaned his hip against the counter as she checked to see if the water was boiling in the pasta pot. "I have lots of memories about you."

He was laying it on a little thick. "Really."

"Seriously. Every night at juvie, I'd lie in my bunk and think about you, recalling all the details. I'd picture those silver earrings you always wore, and the way you pinned your hair back and it kept getting loose and falling in your face, and that tiny little beauty mark on the back of your neck." He reached out and touched her neck, just below her ear.

The touch was electric, loaded with the current of a million memories. It buzzed through her, shocking her with its intensity, making it impossible for her to breathe, much less move.

It seemed to paralyze him as well. The steam rising from the simmering water hung in the air between them, as if generated by the heat of their skin. It seemed like forever before he lifted his hand.

She turned away and crossed the room to the built-in oven. "I, uh, need to check the bread." Her face felt so hot that when she opened the door, the blast of heat was almost cooling.

He moved to the sideboard below the window and picked up another picture of Paul, one that Katie had taken of him while he'd been installing the cabinetry in this very kitchen. "So this husband of yours..."

Katie slammed the oven door harder than she'd intended. "Paul," she said sharply. "His name was Paul."

"You were happy with him?"

She strode back to the stove, picked up a wooden spoon from the pewter spoon-rest and stirred the sauce.

"Very happy." She stirred the sauce too vigorously, and some splatted out of the pan, leaving a red blob on her black cooktop. She grabbed a paper towel and wiped it up, feeling his gaze on her. "I was crazy about him, and he felt that way about me. It was one of those even-steven, real-deal marriages. In some relationships, it seems like there's a lover and a lovee, like one person cares more, but we were equally matched." Why was she talking so much?

"How come you never had kids?"

"We wanted to, but..." She put down the spoon and picked up a bag of spaghetti. Her hands shook as she tried to rip the bag. Why the heck was she telling him all this? It was personal information, and she didn't have any intention of getting personally involved with Zack. "I'd rather hear about Gracie."

He took the bag from her, opened it in a single tug, then handed it back. "What do you want to know?"

"Everything. What do you know about her adoptive parents?" Katie had tried to imagine them, time and time again. She'd told herself that they were warm and loving and nurturing, the kind of people who would read to her, kneel by her bed for prayers and tuck her in at night, after a full day of dance lessons and playdates and romping around a large, child-friendly, spotless, beautiful home. She'd idealized them, she knew she had. No one could possibly be as perfect as the parents she'd imagined for her child; no child could possibly have the idyllic life she'd painted in her head. She knew it was unrealistic, but a part of her clung to that, wanting it to be true, even as she asked for the facts.

"Her dad was the personnel manager at a bank, and her mom stayed home with Gracie."

Okay, so the house probably wasn't as large as she'd imagined. But it sounded like a nice, stable family, and the stay-at-home mom fit in with her ideal scenario.

"According to the aunt," Zack continued, "Gracie was the center of their lives."

Even better.

"She was an extremely bright child," he continued. "She grew into a typical teenager—a little rebellious, but not too bad. She thought her parents were too strict. She really loved them, though. When they died, she kind of fell apart."

Katie's heart turned over. "She must have been devastated."

"Yeah. She had to move to Pittsburgh to live with her aunt, and she had a rough time adjusting. She not only lost her parents, but everything else comfortable and familiar—her home, her friends, her school."

Katie's throat thickened, like the sauce on the stove.

"Gracie started acting out—staying out all hours, getting her nose pierced, cutting class. When she turned up pregnant, the aunt was completely overwhelmed."

Katie turned down the heat under the sauce and picked up the pot lid. "Who's the father of the baby?"

"Gracie won't say."

Katie's hand froze, the pot lid in midair, and looked at Zack. "Does she know?" When she'd been at the adoption center in Kansas, she'd known a girl who hadn't. In a sad attempt to feel loved and wanted, the girl had slept with any boy who would have her.

"Gracie says she does, but she doesn't want him involved in the baby's life. She refuses to talk about it.

She said it's none of my business." Zack's lips formed a hard line. "I intend to make it my business."

"How?"

"Electronic snooping. She hasn't posted anything on Facebook in months, but she's got a phone, and I've downloaded her address book. I'm also checking all her recent texts and calls."

"Don't you think that's a little extreme?"

"Maybe, but it's important. I don't want another guy in the situation I'm in."

Katie felt herself bristle. "And exactly what situation is that?"

"Having a child and not knowing about it until she's nearly grown."

There it was again—the implication that knowing would have somehow changed things. Which, by inference, faulted her for not tracking him down and informing him she'd had his baby. She slammed the lid on the pot and whirled toward him. "And exactly what would you have done if you'd known? Raised her yourself? Married me?"

He lifted his shoulders. "Maybe."

Katie blew out a frustrated breath of air. "I can't count how many times that summer you told me how you never wanted to be tied down and end up like your parents." She turned away and stalked to the refrigerator. "Besides, I tried to let you know."

"Did you keep trying to find me after you gave birth?"

"No."

"Why not?"

"She'd already been adopted. What possible good would it have done?"

"I don't know. But knowledge opens options."

How dare he? Her spine went ramrod straight. "You lost all your options when *you* didn't contact *me*. I did what I thought was best for Grace, and I thought it was best for her to grow up in a family that loved her and could care for her."

He turned toward the counter and propped his hands against it, then blew out a long, exasperated breath. She braced herself for a sharp retort.

"You're right," he said instead. "You're right." He pushed against the counter as if he wished he could topple it and muttered a low oath. After a long moment, he straightened, raked a hand through his hair, and turned toward her. "I'm sorry."

As you damn well should be. But his apology took the wind out of her sails.

"Look—I don't really blame you, Kate." He took a step toward her. "The truth is, I blame myself."

"For what?" called a voice from the hallway. "Not doubling up on the condoms?"

Katie and Zack both whipped around to see Gracie standing in the doorway, her arms crossed over her chest, her eyebrows hunkered in a scowl, and her lips pressed together so hard that the skin around them was white. "Sorry my existence is creating such a problem."

"Gracie—that isn't what we're talking about," Zack said.

"Yeah, right." She turned and stalked back down the hall.

"Gracie...," Zack called. The door slammed.

Katie put down the spoon and wiped her hands on a dish towel. "Keep an eye on the spaghetti. I'm going to talk to her."

Gracie flung herself across the white comforter on the queen-sized bed. Not for the first time, she wished she'd been in the car with her parents when they died. Her parents, at least, had wanted her.

She wouldn't cry. She wouldn't. She refused to let anyone get to her, ever again. She was strong. She'd have the baby, and she and the baby would be a family, and they'd love each other and not need anyone else, and everything would be fine.

A knock sounded on the door. "Go away."

The door creaked open anyway. "Gracie," Katie said, "I'd like to talk to you."

"I don't want to talk."

"Well, then, maybe you can just listen."

A sharp retort was on the tip of Gracie's tongue, but for some reason, she held it back.

She lay sprawled on the bed, her head resting on her arms, as Katie moved into the room, closing the door behind her. Gracie felt the bed dip as Katie sat down beside her. She smelled Katie's perfume—something soft and warm and kind of green—and turned her head the other direction.

"You must miss your parents very much."

Gracie said nothing. Against her will, tears pooled in her eyes.

"I know what it's like when someone you love dies," Katie said. "It feels like a part of you has been cut off—like you had an amputation with no anesthetic and you're bleeding and so hurt you can barely draw another breath. And it feels like no one else can even see how hurt you are, much less help. Everyone else is just going on with life and they act like you should, too; like you should just get up and get over it and move on."

Exactly. Gracie turned her face down, so that the comforter caught her tears, not wanting Katie to know how she'd nailed it.

"I know you loved them, and I know that you miss them. And I know that no one will ever take their place."

"Especially not you."

The words were muffled by the comforter, but apparently Katie heard them anyway. "I know, sweetie. Your mom raised you and loved you. She got to see your first step and hear your first word, and..." Katie's voice choked. "Gracie, you have no idea how much I wished I could have been her."

Oh, man. Was Katie crying, too?

"No idea," Katie continued. "When they put you in my arms, I almost couldn't..." Her words broke off into a little sob.

Against her will, the icy knot in Gracie's chest started to melt a little.

Katie sniffled, then started again. "I almost couldn't do what I knew in my heart was best for you. I didn't have a home. I didn't have an education. I didn't have a job. I didn't have a clue. I wanted you to have all the things I never did, to have a better childhood than I'd had."

"What was wrong with yours?" The words came out of Gracie's mouth before she could stop them. It was funny; she'd never really thought about her mother's childhood. She knew nothing about it.

"My mom had me as a teenager, and..." Katie paused. "Well, my dad was never in the picture, and my mom wasn't ready to be a mom."

"Great. So getting knocked up as a teenager is a family tradition?"

"It appears to be so." Katie's voice held a wry note.

"Thanks for the great gene pool."

"You're welcome." Katie plucked at a thread on the comforter. "Gracie, more than anything, I wanted you to have a good home. I wanted you to have two parents, and a nice house where friends could come over, and clothes that didn't come from Goodwill. I didn't want kids to come up to you in grade school and say, 'Hey, you're wearing my old coat,' or 'Why are your lunch tickets different from everyone else's?' I wanted you to have somebody at home to comfort you if you woke up in the middle of the night, someone who'd push you on a swing and read you books and take you to the library and tuck you in at night."

"And you didn't think you could do that?"

"I was afraid I couldn't. I didn't know how to support myself, much less a baby."

"Your mom didn't do any of those things for you?"

"No."

"What was wrong with her? Was she just a total loser or what?"

"My mom..." Katie swallowed. "Well, she drank a lot."

"Great. Grandma was a lush."

Katie drew in a ragged breath. "Gracie, giving you up was the hardest thing I ever did. And the only reason I did it was because I wanted the best for you."

"That is such a cliché."

"Things become clichés because they're true. Parents really want the best for their children."

A thought that had been gnawing on Gracie's insides spilled out. "I guess you think I should give my baby up, too."

"I didn't say that."

"But you're thinking it."

"I don't know what's best for you and your baby. Only you know that. But I do know one thing: I'm glad you're here now, and I'll help you however I can."

Longing, deep as a bone bruise, ached in Gracie's chest. She fought against it. "I don't want your help. I want to be declared an emancipated minor, and I want an advance on the insurance money my parents left. That's all I need and all I want."

"You know your aunt won't agree to that."

"She's a total bitch."

"She's the person your mom and dad entrusted you with, so they must have thought she'd have your best interests at heart."

"She's a freak." And living with her had been the seventh ring of hell. Aunt Jean had thought Gracie needed to be "straightened out," which, in her mind, meant completely controlled. She'd confiscated all of Gracie's "inappropriate" clothing, taken away her phone and iPod as punishment for "back talk," made her come home directly after school, and grounded her. As if telling her she was grounded was going to work, Gracie thought derisively. She'd just sneaked out of the house after Aunt Jean went to sleep.

Still, it had been awful. Beyond awful. She'd felt like

she couldn't breathe, like she was being smothered by a cloud of constant disapproval. And the woman just didn't get that she was in a black hole of grief. She kept saying how much she missed her brother, how awful it was to have lost her last "blood relative"—as if her loss was somehow deeper, as if Gracie's didn't count, because her mom and dad weren't "blood relatives."

"Zack and I can share custody of you, Gracie, or you can move back with your aunt. The choice is yours."

"I'm here, aren't I?"

"Yes." Katie's voice was gentle. "And I'm glad you are."

Yeah, right.

"Is there anything I can do or get for you that would make you more comfortable?"

"There's something you can stop doing. You and Zack can quit talking about me behind my back."

"Well, come join us for dinner and talk to us face-to-face."

"I don't have anything to say."

"Fine. Just come join us."

"I'm not hungry." Her stomach traitorously growled. She pressed her hand against it to muffle the sound.

"You may not be, but your baby probably is," Katie said softly. "When I was pregnant, sometimes I didn't realize I needed to eat, but I felt better after I did."

No way was she buying into the "I can relate to your pregnancy" BS. "Look, I'm not like you."

"Of course not. You're your own person."

"I'm not like you in *any way*," she carefully stated for emphasis, "and I refuse to pretend that we're a family."

Katie lifted her shoulders. "No pretending required."

"Apparently there is, if you expect me to sit down at some kind of faux family dinner."

"It's just a meal, Gracie. Nothing more."

Katie's tone was soft, matter of fact, and nonconfrontational. Hell. How was Gracie supposed to stay mad at her? She wanted to stay mad at her. Needed to, actually. Anger was her one coping skill. She lifted her chin. "I refuse to go through some kind of grand inquisition."

"Okay."

"I mean it. I don't want you asking me any questions."

"Okay. No questions."

"*At all.*"

"Okay." Katie smiled and rose from the bed. "Dinner will be ready in about ten minutes." She walked to the door and opened it. "In case you need it, the bathroom is down the hall and to the left."

The door closed softly behind her. Gracie sat up, sniffed and wiped her eyes, then pulled out her phone. She had a text from Megan, one of the few friends she'd made in Pittsburgh.

Megan: Dying to know—how're things? What's your mom like?

Gracie: She's not my mom.

Megan: OK

Gracie: She weirded out when she met me—then got all over-eager and mushy.

Megan: What does she look like?

Gracie: Sorta like Reese Witherspoon with brownish hair and a less pointy chin.

Megan: Sounds like U.

Gracie rolled her eyes, then rolled off the bed, onto her feet, and into the bathroom.

"If we can't talk about her or ask her questions, I guess we'll have to talk to each other," Zack remarked.

"Or about the weather or politics."

"I'd rather talk about you."

Her cheeks flamed. "Grab the colander from that cabinet, would you?" Katie waved an oven-mittened hand at Zack.

"Sure." Zack opened the indicated cabinet. He had to watch what he said with her. He found himself sliding into flirtation mode without thinking, and that was not his intention. And yet, the attraction was there—as strong and undeniable as it had been that summer.

Especially when he touched her. When he'd put his finger on her birthmark, it was as if he'd pressed some kind of time-warp button. He'd felt seventeen again—overexcited, overeager, and overheated, with a hair-trigger erector set.

"It's on the bottom," she said.

What the hell was a colander? Zack peered at a mystifying assortment of cooking utensils. "What's it look like?"

"It's stainless steel."

All of the pots and pans and cooking gizmos were stainless. "Any other clues?"

"It's the bowl with holes."

"Why didn't you just say so?"

"Because I didn't know you were so domestically impaired."

He saw a stainless-steel contraption that fit the bill and pulled it out. "I don't do a lot of cooking."

"Apparently." She lifted the pot of boiling water from the stove. He stood there, the stupid thing in his hands. "Would you please put it in the sink?"

"Sure." He did as she asked, then stepped out of her way. He didn't think she'd deliberately pour boiling water on him, but he wasn't going to take any chances. Steam curled around her as she dumped the potful of spaghetti and hot water into the colander.

"If you don't cook, what do you do for meals?" she asked.

"Eat out or order in."

"Sounds expensive." She put the pot in the other side of the stainless-steel sink. "But then, I guess that's not an issue for you."

It wasn't. "Do you like to cook?"

"I used to."

When her husband was alive. The unsaid words hung between them. She turned from the sink back to the sauce on the stove. "I eat a lot of Lean Cuisine these days."

His gaze ran over her figure. "You sure don't need to."

He wasn't sure if it was the steam or the compliment, but her face reddened. "Pull the garlic bread out of the oven, would you?"

She pulled off her red pepper–printed oven mitt and handed it to him. He pulled it on, wondering how much of the warmth was from her body heat and how much was from the spaghetti.

Gracie moped into the kitchen, looking uncomfortable.

"Hey, Gracie," Katie called. "Would you please get the Parmesan cheese out of the refrigerator?"

It was smart of Katie to give her something to do. Gracie crossed the room and opened the fridge.

"You can pour yourself some milk while you're at it," Katie said. "The glasses are on the top shelf."

Gracie pulled the half-gallon out of the fridge. "Too bad expectant mothers can't drink wine."

"Too bad seventeen-year-olds can't, either," Zack said.

"Lots of seventeen-year-olds drink." Gracie dumped some milk into a glass.

Jeez. The girl just never let up. "Not in front of me, they don't."

"You are such a hypocrite. Your bio says you started playing poker in bars when you were sixteen."

It was actually fifteen. "That doesn't mean it was a good thing to do."

"You turned out okay."

"Not everyone would agree with that."

"You're rich and famous and get to hang with movie stars."

"That's not all it's cracked up to be. And for the record, I haven't done the Hollywood scene in several years."

"Why not?"

He lifted his shoulders. "It's all phony."

"Yeah, well, life is phony," Gracie said.

"What do you mean?" Katie asked.

Gracie glared at Katie. "You're not allowed to ask questions."

Annoyance flared through Zack. "And you're not allowed to be rude."

"Fine. I'll just sit in silence."

That would be a first.

Gracie carried her milk to the table and plopped down. Zack turned to Katie. "Anything I can help you with?"

"Bring the spaghetti to the table, and then we're all set."

Zack moved to the table, waited to see which chair Katie headed for, then pulled it out for her. Gracie reached for the bowl of spaghetti.

"Hold on, there, buckeroo." Zack said. "Mind your manners."

Gracie glared at him. "You don't get to do the parent thing."

"Yeah, well, I wouldn't have to if you weren't doing the teenager-with-attitude thing."

Katie kicked him under the table. "Have some salad," she said, handing him the bowl with a warning look.

Fine. He'd turn the conversation to her. "So, Kate— when did you move back to Chartreuse?"

"Ten years ago, when my mother got sick."

"Your mother the lush?" Gracie said.

Zack raised his eyebrows. Must have been some talk they'd had in Gracie's bedroom.

"Yes," Katie said, with admirable composure.

"What did she have? Cirrhosis?"

"Terminal cancer. But she did have liver problems, and that made things worse." Katie passed the garlic bread to Gracie.

"You moved back to take care of her?" Zack asked.

Katie nodded.

"I thought she never took care of you," Gracie said.

"She did the best she could. Besides, life isn't a tit-for-tat proposition."

Katie had always covered for her mother. She was too forgiving for her own good.

"Tit proposition. Sounds dirty." Gracie scooped up a forkful of spaghetti.

Zack chose to ignore her and looked back at Katie. "How did you get into the beauty business?"

"The adoption center helped me get into a local beauty college after I finished my GED. Once I started working, I went to night school and earned an associate degree in business."

"Good for you," Zack said.

"You're in an awfully shallow profession," Gracie offered. "All about external appearances."

"When people feel good about how they look, they're more confident," Katie said calmly. "And confident people are more successful and outgoing and happy."

"Whatever." Gracie shoved a meatball into her mouth and chewed. "So, Katie—are you dating any hot guys?"

Katie fixed her gaze on the plate. Gracie didn't give her a chance to reply before she chattered on. "Zack dates some real hotties. Victoria's Secret models and *Sports Illustrated* swimsuit models and actresses. When I met him, he was with a *Playboy* playmate."

Nice, Gracie. Katie's eyebrows quirked up. "Is that so?"

"Yeah. She was hanging all over him. She had these enormous fake boobs, and she kept trying to rest them on his shoulder."

"She was a blind date, and she was really annoying," Zack explained.

Katie lifted an eyebrow. "Is that a fact."

"You weren't acting too annoyed," Gracie said. "She was wearing a blue sparkly gown cut down to her navel, and you kept looking down her dress." She speared a leaf of lettuce and looked at Katie. "You should have seen them."

Zack wasn't sure if Gracie was referring to the woman's boobs or to him and the woman.

Katie shot him an arch smile. "Sorry I missed it."

"If you google Zack, you can see all kinds of photos of him with lots of different women."

"Is that so."

"Yeah. Have you ever googled him?"

Katie moved a piece of lettuce around her plate. "I don't spend a lot of time online."

She had! Otherwise she wouldn't have deliberately avoided the question. Gracie smirked through her spaghetti.

"There's not a lot on Google about you, but I read some stuff about your husband."

Katie's hand stilled.

"Bummer he got killed."

"Yes." Kate ducked her head and picked up her glass of wine. "Thank you."

Gracie forked in another huge mouthful of spaghetti and Zack relaxed, thinking the topic had been exhausted. But Gracie wasn't through. "Why didn't you two have any kids?"

"It just never happened."

"So...did you have any other illegitimate kids besides me?"

A wounded look passed over Kate's face. Her spine

straightened, as if she were bracing herself against another jab of pain. "No. No, I didn't."

"Zack says he didn't, either. Not that he knows of, anyway."

If deliberately getting on their nerves were an Olympic sport, Gracie would get a gold medal. "Since you're so interested in love lives, Gracie, why don't you tell us about yours."

She stiffened, her posture an uncanny duplication of Katie's. "Nothing to tell."

"Apparently there was something."

"Nothing that's any of your..."

A knock sounded at the door. Katie rose, crossed to the foyer, and opened the door to reveal the round-eyed redheaded woman who'd been in Katie's chair at the salon that afternoon.

"Hello, Katie," she said breathlessly. "I dropped by to see if you needed anything or wanted to talk or needed moral support or anything. Is it true? Do you really have a daughter? And is that hunk who came by the salon really the..." Her bug eyes bugged out further as she stepped into the foyer and saw Zack and Gracie seated in the dining room. "Oh, my!" she gasped.

Zack rose to his feet. "Hello, Lulu."

The redhead put her hand on her chest. "You remembered my name!"

Amazing, the effect that always had on people. It was a skill he'd learned from an old blackjack player—associate each person's name with their features. In this case, it was easy; Lulu looked loony.

Katie closed the door and moved into the dining

room. "Lulu, I'd like to introduce you to my daughter, Gracie."

Gracie looked up. "I'm not really her daughter. She just squeezed me out and then gave me away."

"Oh!" Lulu blinked, looked at Katie, then looked back at Gracie. Her baffled expression settled into a befuddled smile. "Well, you look just like Katie anyway. My, oh, my. How do you do?"

Gracie shrugged. "Pretty crappy, but thanks for asking." She shoveled another forkful of spaghetti into her mouth.

"Would you like to join us, Lulu?" Katie offered. "We have plenty."

"Oh, no." Lulu's red curls bobbed as she shook her head. "I don't want to interrupt. I didn't know you had company. I'd just heard the news, and I thought I'd drop by and..." Her gaze rested on Zack. She swallowed hard and seemed to lose her train of thought. "I—I better be going."

"Thanks for stopping by." Katie moved back to the foyer and opened the door. "Give me a call tomorrow and we'll reschedule your haircut."

Lulu nodded and glanced back at Zack. "Nice to see you again." She waggled her fingers at Gracie. "Good to meet you, honey."

Gracie lifted her fork in acknowledgment.

Katie closed the door and returned to the table.

"Guess your secret's out of the bag," Gracie said. "Hope I haven't made things too awkward for you." The little smirk on her face said she really hoped otherwise.

"Not at all, Gracie." Katie sat back down, replaced her

napkin in her lap, and smiled at her. "I'm so glad you're here."

"Yeah, right." Gracie rolled her eyes. "I'll bet."

The funny thing was, Zack was a betting man, and he bet she really was.

CHAPTER EIGHT

The next morning, Katie got up early and made blueberry muffins. Zack had told her that left to her own devices, Gracie would sleep till noon, but Katie wanted to leave her breakfast in case she woke up while Katie was gone.

Katie had agreed to meet Zack at his house at eight-thirty to call Gracie's aunt. She dressed in a floaty navy-and-white top, navy capris, and flat navy sandals, and took more time than usual with her hair and makeup. Not because she cared what Zack thought about her, she told herself as she changed her lip-gloss shade for the third time. It was normal for someone in the beauty business to want to look her best. Zack had absolutely nothing to do with the fact she'd curled, then straightened her hair before deciding to pull it back in a low ponytail.

But she wasn't very good at lying to herself. The truth was, she hadn't been so physically aware of a man since Paul, and the awareness left her feeling unsettled and uneasy and more than a little guilty.

"Well, you need to get over it," she told her reflection in the bathroom mirror as she set the peach gloss back in her makeup bag, then set the bag in the drawer. It was nothing but an old habit. Her memories were stirring up old emotions, that was all. The physical attraction she felt for Zack wasn't anything like the deep, honest emotions she'd felt for Paul. It couldn't be, because her feelings for Paul, right from the beginning, had been based on the mutual desire for love and commitment.

Zack was not relationship material. He was the antithesis of it, in fact. She'd stayed up late googling him last night, and she'd run across several different interviews where his thoughts had been presented in black and white:

"Of course I believe in monogamy—serial monogamy," he'd said in a *Playboy* article about self-made millionaires.

"Maybe some people are cut out for marriage," he'd told a *Cosmo* reporter when he'd been declared one of America's Most Eligible Bachelors, "but I'm not one of them."

"I value my freedom," he told a *BusinessWeek* reporter who'd asked why he was single. "I don't want to have to compromise, and long-term relationships always require compromise."

"Do you ever see yourself settling down and having a family?" an *Entertainment Weekly* reporter had asked him when he was dating Scarlett Johansonn.

"Family isn't a warm and fuzzy concept to everyone," Zack had replied. "To some people, it's something that was survived. Escapees of a prison have no desire to go knock on the door of another prison and say, 'Hey, I'd like to sign up for more time.'"

Katie understood why he felt that way. He'd told her

about his melodrama of a home life—how his parents had put on smiling faces to the world, complete with public I-love-yous and kisses, then fought like cats and dogs at home, calling each other horrible names and cheating behind each other's backs. They'd completely ignored Zack unless they needed to use him as a piece of rope in their angry tug-of-war. Whenever one parent would threaten to leave, the other would mount a big, tearful scene and insist they had to stay together for Zack's sake. They'd been obsessed with keeping up with the Joneses, preserving appearances, and worrying what everyone thought about them—everyone, that was, except their own son.

She understood why Zack had an aversion to commitment; his parents had made it look like a trap. They'd been emotionally unavailable to him, so he'd grown up being emotionally unavailable to others. At seventeen, she'd been too young to understand that; she'd thought he could genuinely return her feelings.

Well, she knew better now. Besides, they had nothing in common, except for two generations of offspring— how ironic was that?—and the memory of a torrid, teenage summer, when they'd been the same age their daughter was now.

It was weird how clear her memories were of Zack at seventeen. In a lot of ways, he hadn't changed. He'd been tall and tan and sure of himself, so loaded with high-test testosterone that he practically gave off sparks, an indisputable alpha male capable of running off two men twice his age with nothing more than a glower.

He'd tried to warn her off that first night. He'd told her that he had a girlfriend back home and that he wouldn't be dating anyone while he was in Chartreuse. He'd made it clear that he'd be playing poker at night, working at his uncle's marine repair shop during the day, and chauffeuring around his stoner cousin whenever he needed a ride, so he wouldn't have time to hang out.

And yet, he'd somehow managed to find time. Every day, while she was working he'd come by the bait shop for a Coke and linger a couple of hours. He'd stop by after her shift and give her a ride home. On her days off, he'd show up at her trailer in the morning, tell her to grab a swimsuit, and take her out on the lake in one of his uncle's boats. One of those outings had crystallized in her mind in vivid detail.

About three weeks after they'd met, they'd taken out a fishing boat one afternoon, anchored it about a mile from shore, then tethered a raft to the boat. They'd stretched out on the raft, just soaking up rays, their bodies mere inches apart, when she'd finally brought up the topic that had been weighing on her mind. "Tell me about your girlfriend."

"What about her?"

"Well, what's she like?"

He threw his arm over his eyes. "She's just a normal girl."

"Blonde, brunette, or redhead?"

"All three."

Katie shot him a puzzled glance.

"Her hair is kind of a reddish-blondish brown," he said.

Katie closed her eyes, trying to imagine this amazing creature. "Blue eyes or brown?"

"Yellow."

She looked over at him.

"Around the center," he added helpfully. "They're actually green, with little golden flecks."

Her stomach balled up. Apparently he'd spent a lot of time gazing into her eyes to be able to describe them so thoroughly.

"Is she pretty?"

"Sure." The sun glistened on his bronzed abs. "Think I'd have an ugly girlfriend?"

Katie immediately pictured a gorgeous woman who was her complete opposite. The ball in her stomach shrank tighter. "Do you love her?"

"Nah. Love is nothing but hype."

"Does she know you think that?"

"Sure. She thinks the same thing."

That was hard to comprehend. "So…you don't love each other, but you kiss and fool around and stuff…"

"Stuff?" Zack shot her an amused glance, his eyebrow arched.

"Yeah." The raft bobbed in the wake of a distant motorboat. "I imagine you do stuff."

They bobbed in silence for a moment. "What kind of stuff are you imagining?"

She tried hard to sound nonchalant and worldly. "Same kind of stuff I did with my boyfriend."

"You had a boyfriend?" He looked at her.

"Sure." It was stupid to lie, especially to someone who was an expert at reading poker faces, but she couldn't seem to stop herself. The jealousy was a living thing, twisting like a snake in her gut.

The problem was, she'd already told him that she'd never been out on a real date. She'd told him about the one time a boy from school had invited her to a dance, *then hadn't taken her to the dance at all, but straight to the town's make-out spot. The memory always made her feel like she needed to take a bath.*

"You told me you'd only been out with one guy," Zack said.

"One guy from Chartreuse," she ad-libbed. "My boyfriend was from out of town."

"When was this?"

"Last summer."

"So you and this out-of-town boyfriend—you got hot and heavy?"

"Yeah." She wanted jealousy to lasso his gut into a pretzel, too. "He couldn't get enough of me, and I couldn't get enough of him."

A corner of Zack's mouth quirked up. "So what did you two do?"

"Everything."

"Everything?" Zack shot her an amused glance. "S and M? Bondage? Back door? Threesomes?"

"You're sick."

"Hey, you're the one who said you did everything."

"I meant everything normal."

"That can cover a lot of ground." She wasn't looking at him, but she was pretty sure he was smiling. "So . . . do you still stay in touch?"

"Sure. But not as much as we used to. He, uh, went to college, and he's busy, and, well . . ."

She turned her head away so he couldn't see her face. He always knew when people were lying. He said he picked up on little micro expressions in their faces and things about their body language, but sometimes it seemed like he could read minds. "You know how it goes."

"Yeah."

She trailed her hand in the water. "So...what's your girlfriend like?"

Zack put an arm over his eyes again, shielding the sun. "Unlike you, she doesn't ask a lot of questions."

"Does she know you're hanging out with me?"

"No. Do you think I should tell her?"

"No."

"Why not?"

"She might not like it, and then you'd have to stop."

He moved his arm and looked at her. "Maybe that would be a good idea."

"It would be a terrible idea."

"Why is that?" Something in his eyes seemed hot and dangerous. She was barely able to breathe. Part of her thought he was about to kiss her. Another part was terrified he was going to tell her they shouldn't see each other anymore. Without knowing how she'd gotten there, Katie was in a minefield.

"Because...then I wouldn't have anyone to race to the buoy." She rolled off the raft, upsetting it, plunging them both into the water, then took off for the distant bobbing buoy.

Katie smiled at the memory as she fastened an earring. Zack had no doubt seen right through her tall tale, but he hadn't embarrassed her by calling her bluff. He'd always been kind. Protective, even. And he'd shown a lot of restraint for a seventeen-year-old boy—especially since she'd seen the way he looked at her when he didn't know she was looking.

But there had been more than chemistry between

them. He'd talked to her as if her opinion counted, as if he was interested in what she had to say, as if her thoughts and ideas were important. Aside from a couple of teachers, he was the first person who made her feel that she mattered.

It was no wonder she'd fallen for him, despite his warnings. But it was not a mistake she was going to make again. She'd been married to a man who'd loved her with his whole heart. She wasn't going to fall for a man who didn't even have a whole heart to give.

She glanced at her watch, then hurried to the kitchen, scrawled a quick note for Gracie, and propped it by the plate of muffins. She grabbed four of them, wrapped them in a plaid cloth napkin and plopped them in a small basket, then headed down the street to Zack's house. It was a large, two-story Craftsman-style home, which had been gutted and completely renovated two years earlier.

She rang the iron doorbell. Zack opened the door, wearing jeans and a blue-and-gray shirt. He filled the doorway, and when he smiled, she felt an unwelcome blast of heat.

"Come in." He held the door wider and stepped back. "I'm making coffee. Want a cup?"

"Sounds great." She handed him the muffins. "I made these for Gracie, and thought you might like some."

"Thanks."

She stepped into a home that looked like it had been staged for a TV show. A mix of modern and Craftsman-style pieces, the living room featured a sage, gray, and blue patterned rug under a large sage sectional and a large mahogany coffee table. A pair of chairs covered in a modern geometric print in the same colors flanked the fireplace. Perfectly scaled and coordinated lamps, pillows, paintings, and accessories completed the room.

"Wow." She followed him to a granite breakfast bar that separated the living room from the enormous restaurant-grade kitchen. "This is beautiful."

Zack nodded. "The designer did a pretty good job on short notice." He set the basket on the counter. "How is Gracie?"

"Still asleep."

"That figures. That kid keeps Vegas hours."

Katie perched on a barstool. "Part of that is being a teenager, and part is probably being pregnant. Has she gotten prenatal care?"

"Not as much as she should. From what she's said, she didn't realize she was pregnant until she was four months along, and then her aunt took her to a quack."

"Any clue what that means?"

"He was near retirement age and very old-school." Zack moved toward the coffeemaker across the room. "He didn't think an ultrasound was necessary."

"I'll make an appointment with my ob-gyn. Dr. Greene is smart and tech-savvy. I'm sure Gracie will like her."

"I wouldn't bet on that. Gracie doesn't seem to like much of anyone."

Probably because she didn't much like herself, Katie thought sadly. "Poor kid. She's really had a tough time of it."

"True. But Gracie could take a good time and turn it into an ordeal."

"Has she talked at all about what she's going to do when she has the baby?"

"She has an unrealistic picture of things." Zack pulled two green ceramic mugs off the shelf, along with matching small plates. "She envisions herself floating around in her own little dollhouse in a cloud of self-sufficient bliss, caring for a beautiful baby who never cries."

Katie grinned. "Where does she intend to live this fantasy?"

"She hasn't thought that far ahead."

"She can live with me, and I can help her care for the baby." Katie had lain awake last night fantasizing about that very thing.

"May I make a suggestion? Don't offer that. At least, not yet. Right now, she's sure to say no—and once she makes up her mind about something, it's hard to change it."

It was an insightful observation. "In other words, tread carefully and don't back her into any corners."

"Exactly." He grinned, and the temperature of the room rose several degrees. "I suggest you use the same game plan on me."

"As if I would want to."

"A guy can dream, can't he?"

And so can a woman. Her face blazed. Where had that thought come from? She wasn't looking to start anything, yet here she was, falling back into the flirtatious banter they'd shared that summer. It wasn't wise. It wasn't wise at all. She needed to keep the conversation focused on Gracie.

She studied the high-end, grind-to-brew coffeemaker as it hissed out the last few drops of coffee. "What are we going to do about Gracie and school?"

Zack brought the two plates to the breakfast bar and

set them down by the basket of muffins. "Well, Gracie's grades were terrific before her parents died, but they plummeted afterward."

"That's not surprising. On top of losing her parents, she was moved to a strange town and a strange school."

"Gracie thinks she can attend one semester before the baby's born and bring up her GPA, then either take the GED test or finish up with some online courses."

She watched Zack move back to the coffeemaker, lift the pot, and fill the two mugs. "One of my clients is a school counselor. I'll talk to her about the options."

"Great. This is just July, though. She's going to need something productive to do for the rest of the summer." He carried the coffee mugs to the counter and handed her one. "I'd like to see her get a part-time job. I talked to her about it, and she didn't seem opposed to the idea."

Katie nodded. "She can work at the beauty shop with me."

"Bad idea." Zack sat on the barstool beside her.

"Why?"

"Because she has attitude issues. She hates authority. If you're her boss as well as her mother, it'll make her push back against you harder."

She stared at him. How had he already figured all this out? "I wouldn't have thought of that."

"I was just like her." Zack pulled back the napkin on the basket and looked at the muffins. "These look delicious. Want one?"

"No thanks. I've already eaten."

He selected one and took a bite. "Mmm. This is great."

An unwelcome curl of pleasure shot through her. "Thanks."

She watched him polish off the muffin, delighting in the pleasure he took in eating it.

"Ready to get this phone call out of the way?" he asked when he'd finished.

"Sure. But maybe you'd better brief me about what I'm getting into."

"The long and the short of it is, the aunt didn't want Gracie living in Vegas—she said the girl finds trouble too easily as it is, without moving her to Sin City. Plus she wants Gracie to have a woman's influence. That's when I got the idea of moving here and sharing custody with you."

Katie's eyebrows rose. "And the aunt went for this, without knowing if I'd agree?"

Zack rose from the barstool, avoiding eye contact. "I might have led her to believe that you were on board with the whole thing."

"You *might* have?"

"Okay. I did." He flashed her one of his heart-stopping smiles. "I knew the odds were in my favor."

And one thing about Zack, he knew how to play the odds. His biceps flexed as he lifted his coffee mug and took a drink. It bothered her that she noticed.

"Want to move into my office and get this call over with?" he asked.

"Sure."

"That was easier than I thought it would be." Katie relaxed in the tan chenille Parsons chair opposite Zack's desk when he turned off his speaker phone. The aunt had wanted reassurance that Gracie would be in good hands and had made them promise to keep her informed, but she hadn't thrown any major obstacles in their path.

"She's relieved more than anything," Zack said. His black leather office chair squeaked as he rose. "She and Gracie were virtually strangers when Gracie moved there. They'd only seen each other a couple of times over the years, and they never really bonded."

"Poor Gracie."

"Yeah. But don't let her hear you say that. If there's one thing that makes her throw up her defenses, it's being pitied."

"Good to know." Katie rose as he rounded his desk and followed him into the kitchen. "When did you become such an astute observer of human nature?"

"Gotta read people to figure out how they're playing their cards." He picked up the coffeepot. "More coffee?"

"No thanks. I need to get to work."

"Me, too." A beep sounded on Zack's BlackBerry. "That's a reminder that I have a conference call in five minutes." He poured some coffee into his cup.

"I left Gracie a note that I'd be home around noon. I'll take her to lunch and talk to her about getting a job."

"Great." His blue eyes settled on her, making her feel distinctly *un*settled. "So... what are you doing this evening?"

Why did he want to know? "Nothing special."

"Do you usually have plans?"

Her pulse skipped crazily. "Why are you asking?"

"Well, you didn't answer Gracie's question last night. I was wondering if you had a beau."

Katie felt her face grow warm. "Beau? Wow. I didn't know people from Las Vegas used such courtly Southern language."

"It's the live oaks and magnolias," he said, grinning

over the rim of his coffee mug. "They make me wax poetic."

"There you go again. I thought the only waxing going on in Vegas was the cosmetic kind."

He laughed. His laugh was even more sensual than his smile. "So do you?"

"Do I what? Wax?"

He grinned again. "Well, that wasn't the question, but I can't say I'm not curious."

Katie's face heated even more.

"I'll put that question aside for another time, but I'd love an answer to the one on the table."

"Which is?"

"Are you seeing anyone?"

"No. I haven't really dated anyone since..." Her mouth went dry. She fiddled with her wedding ring.

His gaze went to it. "Since your husband."

She nodded, stilling her hands.

He finished his coffee with a quick swallow. "He was a lucky guy."

"I was the lucky one." She needed to turn this around. "So what about you?"

"Am I lucky? Always. Although you know I don't really believe in luck."

She remembered. He believed in random chance and personal skill. Zack believed in working the odds. "I was asking if you're in a relationship."

He grinned. "You know better than that."

"Right." He'd explained it all that summer: He didn't believe in emotional involvement. He believed in mutual exchanges of companionship and sex, like some kind of fair-trade barter system.

"So you're still operating on the 'love is like a meal' principle?" He'd said that relationships should be enjoyed like a good dinner; when it's over, just walk away from the table, remembering only how enjoyable it was.

"You know it."

"Well, silly me. I thought maybe you'd experienced some emotional growth in the last eighteen years."

He grinned. "Nope. Not a bit."

His involvement with Gracie indicated otherwise. Still, Katie would be a fool not to take him at his word. She headed toward the door.

He followed her. "Why don't you and Gracie plan on coming here for dinner?" he asked. "At, say, seven? The beds are supposed to be delivered later this morning, so Gracie can stay here if she wants."

"Okay."

He opened the door for her. She brushed against his arm as she walked out, and an unwelcome shock of sexual awareness shot through her. The man was like an electric coil, she thought as she stepped out onto his wide porch.

Well, once burned, twice wary. She was older and wiser, and she knew enough about Zack to keep her distance.

CHAPTER NINE

With Coldplay blaring on her iPod, Gracie danced around Katie's living room. She loved to dance, but she didn't want anyone to see her, because she wasn't very good at it. Besides, if people saw you dancing, they thought you were all bubbly and happy and crap like that.

She'd awakened an hour and a half earlier to find herself alone. She wandered into the kitchen and found Katie's note, along with the muffins. After eating two of them, she chugged a glass of milk and promptly set about snooping through the house.

It was a pretty boring place. The only things of real interest she'd uncovered were a drawer of sexy lingerie in Katie's bedroom and a vibrator in her bedside table. Those were pretty funny.

The rest of the place was just normal stuff, except for one thing: It looked like a guy still lived here. A man's belongings sat on one of the nightstands as well as on top of one of the dressers. Half of Katie's closet was filled with men's clothing, and one of the two dressers in her bedroom was filled with men's underwear and T-shirts and jeans. Fishing stuff sat in the hall closet, along with a man's coat and boots. And pictures of her husband—it was the same guy as in the wedding pictures, so it had to be her husband—were everywhere: in the bedroom, the living room, the kitchen, even the bathroom. It was kinda creepy. Oh, and that urn on the fireplace. If it was what Gracie thought it was, it was beyond ick.

The song was getting to the good part. "You are...," Gracie sang. She twirled around and then stopped short. Damn—Katie was standing in the doorway, smiling at her.

Shit. She yanked out the earpieces. She didn't want Katie to think she was thrilled to be staying with her or anything. She immediately dropped her shoulders into a slouch and eyed Katie warily. "What are you doing here?" Which was totally stupid, because Katie lived here.

Thank God Katie didn't choose to point that out. "I brought you lunch." Katie dropped a white paper bag on the dining table. "I don't have a lot in the fridge, and I thought you might be hungry."

"Oh." Truth was, she was starving, the muffins notwithstanding. "Thanks. I guess."

"No problem." Katie moved into the kitchen, turned on the faucet and washed her hands, then opened a cabinet and took out two glasses. Placing them on the counter, she opened the fridge and pulled out the milk.

Gracie watched her, twirling the lock of hair above her ear. "Do you come home for lunch every day?"

"Not every day." Katie put the milk back in the fridge and closed the door. "Did you sleep okay?"

That was a lame-ass question. The sort of thing a mom

would ask. On the other hand, it probably wasn't worth getting into a snit over. "Not too bad."

Katie carried the glasses to the table. Gracie followed her. "So what is there to do in this podunk town?"

"Well, Zack said you might be interested in finding a part-time job."

Gracie shrugged. She kinda liked the idea. It sounded grown up and independent. Besides, she liked staying busy, and she liked knowing what she was supposed to do. "Maybe."

"Sunnyside Assisted-Living Villa is looking for help," Katie said. "I'm working out there this afternoon, and I thought you might want to come with me."

"Assisted living? You mean a place where old geezers live?"

"Well, I doubt they think of themselves that way." Katie sat down in the same chair she'd sat in at dinner. "But yes, it's mainly for elderly people—although they have a physical-rehab wing for people who are recovering from injuries or surgeries. My mother-in-law broke her leg and needed knee replacement surgery, and she's staying there for a few weeks. When she gets out, she's going to stay here with us until she's well enough to go back home to New Orleans."

"So it's basically a nursing home." The chair squeaked on the hardwood floor as Gracie pulled it out.

"Not exactly. Most of the residents are completely independent and rent small apartments." Katie picked up the white bag. "Others need some help."

"You said you're working there? I thought you were a hairdresser."

"Well, Sunnyside has its own little beauty salon.

Another stylist and I take turns going out there three or four times a week. The residents are some of our most loyal clients."

"What do you do—dye their hair blue?"

Katie grinned. "Not as blue as yours."

Gracie smiled, then abruptly caught herself. She was *not* going to like Katie.

Katie pulled out two wrapped sandwiches and handed one to Gracie. "I hope you like turkey po'boys."

Gracie took a bite. The tang of spicy mustard filled her mouth. She wanted to say something negative to cancel out grinning at Katie's comment, but the sandwich was delicious and she didn't want to stop eating it. She decided to dis the job. "I don't think I want to work at a retirement home. I'm not changing anyone's Depends."

"Why not? It would be good practice for the baby."

Her mouth fell open in horror. She put down the sandwich. "You're not serious."

Katie grinned. "You're right. I'm not." She unwrapped her sandwich. "Actually, I think they're looking for someone to help the recreation director. You could come with me and find out."

Gracie started to say no, just on principle, but the truth was, she didn't want to just stay here all day. "Why not? Anything beats hanging around this shrine to your dearly departed."

A flicker of hurt shot across Katie's face. Aw, hell. Treating Katie badly didn't feel nearly as good as she'd thought it would.

Katie gave one of those I'm-gonna-smile-even-though-I-feel-bad smiles that her mom used to give her when

Gracie turned nasty. "I made an appointment for you to see an obstetrician next week."

"Yeah?"

"Yeah. Her name's Dr. Greene. She's really nice. I hope you'll like her."

Gracie liked the idea that the doctor was a woman. The old dude she'd seen before had been awful. "Does she do ultrasounds?"

Katie nodded. "She has a machine in her office."

Gracie was dying to see her baby. Maybe if she saw it, it would seem real. As it was, it was hard to believe she wasn't just getting fatter and fatter. "So do you think she'll do an ultrasound?"

"I can't say for sure, but I'd imagine so."

Annette had just swung her leg out of the bed when Dave appeared in the doorway. For a moment, the room seemed to spin. Probably the pain meds, she told herself, clutching her pajama shirt across her chest. "What are you doing here? I told you not to come back."

"I needed to see you."

"Well, *I* don't need to see *you*."

"Methink the lady doth protest too much."

Arrogant SOB! How dare he presume to tell her what she needed or wanted? "That was always the problem with you," she spat out. "You never listened to me."

"I didn't?"

"No. You just heard what you wanted to hear."

"Gee." He rubbed the top of his head. "I'm sorry."

The remark was as uncharacteristic as it was unexpected. Annette narrowed her eyes, looking for signs of sarcasm, but didn't find any. Dave always had excuses and explanations and long reasons to justify why he was right and she was wrong. This must be a new tactic, part of a new, clever campaign to get back in her good graces. Well, it wasn't going to work. "It's too late for sorry."

He sank down in the faux-leather recliner and somberly nodded his head. "I understand why you feel that way. I was a total ass, and I want to make it up to you."

"Then go away, and stay away."

His mouth curved into a winsome smile. "I don't think you really mean that."

Annette straightened her spine. "Why on earth would you think that?"

"Because you're all stiff and prickly and angry-looking—the same way you used to get when you gave me the old silent treatment." He grinned. "Remember the time you didn't speak to me for four whole days?"

"It was five."

"Yeah. I had to sleep on the couch, and the springs dug into my back like knives. What had I done that ticked you off so much, anyway?"

"You don't remember?"

"No."

That figured. He never remembered the things he did that made her angry, and Annette could never forget. "You used the money I'd saved for a new washer and dryer for a new set of golf clubs, and you didn't even discuss it with me."

"Oh, yeah." He had the nerve to grin.

"It wasn't funny," Annette said. "It's still not. It was as if I was a junior member of the marriage, and you had all the power."

"I would have sworn it was the other way around," Dave muttered.

Annette wasn't sure she'd heard him correctly. "What?"

"Nothing."

"No. You said something, and I want to know what it was."

Dave sighed. "You always had these lists of chores and jobs—mow the lawn, repair the window, pick up toothpaste."

"I needed help! I was doing all the work in the marriage—all the cleaning, all the cooking, all the grocery shopping and errands—not to mention everything involved in raising our son. And I was holding down a job at the same time!"

"I know, I know." He settled into the chair beside the bed. "But it seemed like there was never any time for fun."

"And that was all my fault?" She put her hand on her chest.

"No." He ran a hand down his jaw and shifted his weight in the chair. "No, it wasn't. Look—I'm sorry. I didn't come here to argue with you or to blame you for anything, Annette. I take full responsibility for screwing things up. I was a jerk."

Dave never apologized. That had always been one of their problems. Hearing him apologize now, when it was too late to make any difference, made her heart throb as badly as her leg.

She turned her head away from him. "Well, I have nothing further to say to you."

"I think you do."

Anger gathered in her chest like steam. "What part of the words 'I have nothing to say to you' don't you understand?"

"It's not the words; it's just—well, I know you. After you'd do one of those silent treatments, you'd let loose a torrent and really let me have it."

"It never made any difference. You always twisted things around and made it seem like I was the one to blame."

"I got mad at you because you were mad at me."

"Exactly. You acted as if I never had a right to be mad!"

"Yeah." He wagged his head in agreement. "I didn't want to be wrong."

His willingness to admit it left her speechless. She realized her jaw had fallen open, and abruptly closed it.

"Anyway," he continued. "I think you have things you need to get off your chest, and if I go, you'll never get to do that."

"I repeat: I have nothing to say to you."

"Okay." He nodded amiably. "Then I'll say it for you: I'm a prick. I'm a worthless bastard. I'm shallow and selfish and ungrateful, and I never fully appreciated you or let you know you were loved. I was a lousy husband."

"You were a pretty crappy father, too."

The guilt on his face made her heart squeeze. Oh, God—she wished she'd kept her mouth shut.

His gaze dropped to his lap and he blew out a sigh. "You're right. Not a day goes by that I don't wish I could do it over. If I could, I'd make every one of Paul's softball games. I'd take him fishing and camping and I'd play catch in the backyard." He looked up at her, his eyes full of pain. "I'd be home every night for dinner."

She hadn't meant to talk to him, but now she couldn't seem to stop. "You spent more time playing golf and drinking with your buddies than you did at home."

He'd called it networking. He used to say that the insurance business was built on relationships, and in order to get and keep business, he needed to court his clients. That might have been true to some extent, but it had gotten out of control. Way out of control.

He nodded. "Yeah, I did. And I turned into an alcoholic along the way."

"That's no excuse." It irritated the hell out of her, how they called alcoholism a disease. Oh, she knew that at some point it became an addiction, a thing beyond an addict's control, but before it reached that point, Dave had had a choice.

"It's not an excuse," Dave said. "It's just a fact. I take total responsibility for my actions. I'm working the steps, Annette, and one of the steps is to make amends to everyone I've hurt."

"Well, you can't make them to me."

"I think I can. I think I can help you vent some of that anger you've been hauling around."

"What if I don't want to?"

"Why wouldn't you?"

Because being angry keeps me from feeling anything else for you. The thought was as unwelcome as the pain in her knee, and just as sharp. At least her knee would get better.

"Get out of here, Dave."

"Okay. But I'll be back." He rose from the chair and grinned. "So start making a list of ways to rip my head off."

"It's not your head I want to rip off."

He shot her a roguish grin—the same one that had made her heart flutter back in 1974, when she'd looked up at a sorority party and seen him across the room. It still had the same effect on her. Electricity sparked through the air, and despite it all, she found herself grinning back.

A knock sounded on the door, then it slowly opened to reveal Katie. "Annette?"

Thank God for the interruption! What was wrong with her, sitting there grinning at Dave like some kind of mindless jack-o'-lantern? "Katie! So nice to see you. Come in, dear."

The door widened, and Katie walked in. A pale, sullen-lipped girl with dyed black-and-blue hair skulked in behind her.

Katie smiled. "Dave! I didn't know you were here."

"He was just leaving," Annette said.

The girl looked at him with interest. "Hey—you're the dude from the bookstore."

"Yeah. Nice to see you again, Gracie."

"Are you feelin' okay?"

"Sure, sure. I'm right as rain." Dave turned to Annette. "Annette, this is Katie's daughter."

The girl scowled. "Don't call me that. Saying I'm her daughter implies she's my mom, and a real mom doesn't give her baby away."

Katie's face flamed with misery. Annette exchanged a look with Dave. Dave had said that the girl had an attitude, and he hadn't been kidding.

"Then we need to come up with a better way to describe your relationship." Dave stroked his chin thoughtfully. "We could call Katie 'the woman who gave you life,' I suppose."

Gracie rolled her eyes.

"No? Well, maybe we could call you 'the DNA product she chose not to abort.'"

Gracie's scowl deepened. Annette suppressed the urge to chuckle.

"I can tell you don't much care for those," Dave said. "I don't, either. Come to think of it, 'mother' and 'daughter' is a whole lot simpler. And there are all kinds of mother–daughter relationships. Why, Annette and Katie have one, and they're only related by marriage." He patted Katie's shoulder, smiled at Gracie, and winked at Annette. "See you all later."

As the door closed behind Dave, Annette turned her attention to the teenage girl. "So, Gracie—it's nice to meet you."

The girl chomped on a wad of gum and ignored the pleasantry. "What's wrong with your leg?"

"I fell down some stairs. I broke my leg in three places, and I had to have my knee completely replaced."

"Replaced with what—plastic or something?"

Annette nodded. "I think it's a combination of plastic, ceramic, and metal."

"Awesome. How did they get your real knee out? Did they saw your leg off or something?"

"Gracie, I don't think...," Katie began.

"It's okay," Annette told Katie. During her years as a high school teacher, Annette had gotten used to the bluntness of teenage curiosity. She smiled at Gracie. "They didn't cut it all the way off, but they did use an electric saw."

"Cool. Guess you're gonna have a pretty gruesome scar, huh?"

"Not too bad."

"Can I see?"

"It's all wrapped up right now. But they're taking the bandages off tomorrow. You're welcome to come back."

"If I get a job here, maybe I will. I like looking at scars."

Katie looked horrified—which was probably just what Gracie intended. Annette decided to put a positive spin on the remark. "Sounds like you might be interested in a career in medicine."

Gracie shrugged. "I've always thought it must be awesome to cut people open and take out parts and replace them and crap."

"It's an amazing skill," Annette agreed. "I can't imagine having the confidence to do it."

"You'd have to be pretty ballsy, all right." She glanced disdainfully at Katie. "It's sure cooler than being a hairdresser."

Annette caught the pained look that flashed across Katie's face. "I've always thought that styling hair is an art form," Annette said. "A very special one, since it uses human canvases."

"Yeah, right." Gracie rolled her eyes.

Annette decided it would probably be best to just change the subject. "So, Gracie—I understand you're expecting."

"Yeah." Her eyes were guarded. Her hand went to her stomach. Annette noticed that she didn't have that eager glow most pregnant women got when talking about their child.

"Do you know if it's a boy or a girl?" Annette asked.

The girl shook her head.

"She's got an appointment to see Dr. Greene next week," Katie volunteered.

"Oh, you're going to love her," Annette said.

"We're hoping she'll be able to tell us the sex of the baby," Katie said.

"Tell *me*." Gracie's chin shot up. "It's none of your business."

Katie shot Annette an apologetic smile. My, my, my. The girl was a real piece of work.

The door squeaked open and a white-haired woman who looked like Santa's wife stepped into the room, closely followed by a tall, thin man. Annette grinned. "Dorothy! And Harold. Come in, come in!"

The elderly couple bustled in and gave Annette loud smacks on the cheek. "You're looking chipper," Dorothy said. She turned to Katie and gave her a hug. "And you're looking beautiful, as usual." Katie hugged both elderly people.

"And this darling girl must be your daughter!" Before Gracie had time to protest, Dorothy had gathered her to her ample bosom.

"I'm not...," Gracie started.

Annette decided to preempt Gracie's not-my-mother speech. "Dorothy, Harold, this is Gracie," she said quickly.

"Gracie, your mom is one of my favorite people in the world," the little old lady said.

Gracie scowled and opened her mouth. Uh-oh. Here it came.

But Dorothy didn't give her a chance to speak. "Katie's the godfairy of my great-grandchild," she continued.

Gracie's brows pulled together. "Godfairy?"

"She means godmother," Annette translated. Dorothy had a knack for mangling the English language. "Dorothy's granddaughter is Emma Jamison."

Gracie's eyes widened. "*The* Emma Jamison? The one on TV?"

Annette nodded. "The one and only." Emma was the star of a nationally syndicated show called *The Butler's Guide to an Organized Home*. She'd first gained notoriety when she'd unwittingly become embroiled in a terrible sex scandal involving the death of the president-elect, but Gracie probably had been too young to have understood much of that.

"Emma and Katie are boffers," Dorothy volunteered.

"*What?*" Gracie's eyes rounded.

"I think she means BFFs," Katie supplied quickly. "We're best friends."

"Oh. Wow." Gracie looked at Katie as if she was revising her opinion upward. "Emma's really famous."

And today's youth equated "famous" with "wonderful." Hopefully, some of Emma's shine would rub off on Katie.

"Emma moved here after that awful scandal," Dorothy volunteered. "Katie was one of the few people who believed in her and stood up for her. And Katie helped her start her own business."

Gracie shrugged, trying hard not to look impressed.

Katie turned to Dorothy and Harold. "I understand you two are going to join Emma and Max in Italy."

Dorothy bobbed her head. "Yes. Harold and I are meeting up with them in Rome in a few months."

"I can't wait to show my bride the Trevi Fountain by moonlight," Harold said, taking Dorothy's hand.

"Bride?" Gracie looked from one to the other. "Did you two just get married or something?"

"Practically." Dorothy batted her eyes at Harold. "We've only been married three years."

"Wow. I never knew old people got married."

"You're never too old for love, sweetie," Dorothy said.

Gracie wrinkled her nose, as if the very concept was disgusting. "Whatever." She shifted her purse over her stomach. "So who do I talk to about maybe getting a job here?"

"Mrs. McCracken. She's in the business office on the first floor. She's so much nicer than that awful old biddy who ran the place when Emma was here." Dorothy linked her arm with Gracie's. "Come on, dear, and we'll show you where she is. Your mom needs to get down to the salon in a few minutes, because that old sourpuss Iris Huckabee is sitting outside the door with her stopwatch, and she'll complain through her entire shampoo and set if Katie is one minute late."

"Thanks, Dorothy—Harold. I'll see you later." Katie waved as the elderly couple escorted Gracie out of the room.

"Gracie's a real firecracker," Annette said.

Katie grinned. "She is, isn't she?"

"She looks just like you."

Katie dropped her eyes, embarrassed.

"It makes me wonder..." Annette stopped herself.

"What?"

"Nothing." Annette picked at a piece of lint on her blanket. Why, oh why, had she opened her big mouth?

Katie gently placed her palm over Annette's hand. "I thought about it, too. If Paul and I had had a child, would she be like Gracie?"

"That's exactly what I was thinking."

"And now you're thinking it's so sad we'll never know."

Annette smiled at her. "When did you become a mind reader?"

"I didn't have to read your mind. I've been thinking the same thing." Katie sat on the side of the bed and took her hand. "I'll tell you something I wouldn't have predicted—seeing Dave here."

"Me, neither." She glanced at the roses he'd brought the day before. He'd conned a nurse into providing an empty pitcher to use as a vase, then popped back in her room to set the flowers on the windowsill. "He says he wants to make amends."

"What did you say?"

"That he's a day late and a dollar short." Annette wanted to steer the conversation away from the uncomfortable topic of her ex-husband. "Gracie is a lovely girl."

"Don't let her hear you say that. She'd probably go pierce her other nostril, her lip, and her tongue just to prove you wrong."

Annette grinned. She'd seen a lot of rebellious teens during her years of teaching high school English, and her heart always went out to them. A lot of pain and confusion hid behind their attitudes of defiance and detachment. "That girl's got a lot to cope with—losing her parents, moving to a strange town, and being pregnant."

"Yeah. It is a lot."

"You've got a lot on your plate, too, Katie. A daughter! And a grandchild on the way."

"That's a hard thought to wrap my head around. I'm going to be a grandma at the ripe old age of thirty-five!"

And Annette would never get to be one, since Paul had been her only child. The thought was a fresh stab of grief.

"So what's Gracie's father like?" she asked to change the subject.

"He's okay, I guess." Katie's cheeks colored and her eyes darted away in very un-Katie-like fashion.

Was she just uncomfortable discussing this man with her, or did Katie have feelings for him? "Is he like you remember him?"

"In some ways, but not in others. I mean, it's been over seventeen years."

"A lot happens in that amount of time." It was only normal that Katie would have had romantic involvements before she'd met Paul—after all, she'd been twenty-nine when she and Paul had married—but the thought still disturbed Annette. Which didn't make sense. Paul had had girlfriends before Katie. "So...did you love this Zack?"

"I thought so at the time. But I was just a kid."

"How do you feel now?"

"About how I felt back then?"

She was more curious about Katie's current feelings, but she didn't want to ask, so she nodded.

Katie lifted her shoulders. "It seemed real at the time."

Which was only natural. The tightness in Annette's chest loosened. "I don't imagine you two have very much in common anymore. Isn't he some kind of jet-setting poker whiz?"

"He was. Zack doesn't play professionally anymore."

Was she imagining things, or did Katie sound defensive?

"He runs a risk-management consulting firm now," Katie said.

Apparently he hadn't evaluated risks too well as a teenager, Annette thought dryly. But then, who did?

An unusual awkwardness filled the air. Katie rose from the bed. "I'd better get down to the salon before Iris has a cow. Do you want me to help you get up or anything before I go?"

"No, dear. The physical therapist will be here in a moment."

"Well, then, I'll see you later." Katie leaned down and kissed Annette's cheek, then headed for the door. She paused, her hand on the doorknob. "You're looking good," Katie said. "When I walked in, I noticed that you had color in your cheeks for the first time since your surgery."

"Thanks, dear." Annette saw no point in telling her that the flush on her face probably had less to do with her improving health than Dave's visit.

She leaned back against her pillow and sighed as Katie closed the door. When had everything in her life gotten so mixed up?

CHAPTER TEN

Zack looked up from his computer as Gracie walked into the house at five-thirty that evening. "How was your day?"

"Okay, I guess." Gracie shrugged. "I filled out an application to work at the old folks home. They have two job openings—as recreation assistant, and as a waitress in the restaurant."

Zack rose and followed her into the kitchen. "Sunnyside has a really nice restaurant."

"Yeah. Apparently Emma Jamison jazzed it up when she worked there. Did you know she lived here?"

"Yeah, I did." Emma's scandal had been all over the papers three years ago. That was actually when Zack had looked up Katie and learned that she was married.

"She and Katie are best friends."

"Is that a fact?"

"Yeah. Katie's godmother to one of her kids." Gracie opened the refrigerator door. "There's nothing to eat in here."

"There's a basket of fruit the real-estate agent left on the counter."

"That's all that's in the house?"

"Yeah. We need to go to the store."

"I can do it if you give me the keys to your car."

"Do you have a license?"

Her eyes shifted away. "Sort of."

"How do you 'sort of' have a license?"

"I have a learner's permit. My dear, sweet, trusting aunt wouldn't let me go get my license on my birthday like all the other kids because she didn't think I was"— she made air quotes with her fingers—"'mature' enough." She rolled her eyes. "But I took driver's ed and I know how to drive, so I can go to the store and back."

Zack shook his head and sat down on a barstool. "Sorry. I believe in obeying the law."

She sighed and moved to the fruit basket on the counter. "Laws are just a bunch of stupid rules."

"They're there for a reason. And there are some awfully bad consequences to getting caught."

She tugged at the red cellophane. "Sounds like you've had personal experience."

Might as well tell her. "I got arrested once, and I ended up in juvenile detention."

"Wow." She froze in mid-rip and looked up. "So you have a record?"

"No. It was sealed when I turned eighteen." At least his uncle had had the decency to see to that. He'd had no compunction about letting Zack take the fall for his son's illegal drug posession, but he'd cleared his record.

Gracie finished tearing off the cellophane, then

looked up suddenly. "Hey, I have an idea. You can take me to the DMV!"

It was the first sign of real enthusiasm that he'd seen on Gracie's face—which made it an enormous bargaining chip. "I'll tell you what. If you get a job and start acting like a decent human being around Kate, I'll let you get your license."

"No shit?"

Her eagerness made Zack grin. "You're going to have to start talking in a more ladylike manner, too."

She picked up an apple. "Yeah, well, I'm not a lady."

"You're not a sailor, either. If you want your license, you'll clean up your language."

"For how long?"

"Forever."

"When I turn eighteen, I can do what I want."

"Work with me on this, and you might get a car out of the deal."

"For real? When?"

How long would be a significant amount of time to demonstrate real behavior modification? "If you treat Kate with respect, get a job, take care of yourself and that baby you're carrying, and watch your mouth, I'll get you a car next month."

"A month! That's way too far away."

He'd forgotten how time seemed to drag to a teenager. He'd been sentenced to juvenile detention for three months, and it had seemed like a lifetime. "That's the deal. Take it or leave it."

"But it sucks."

"At this rate, you're never going to get a car."

"There's nothing wrong with the word *sucks*."

Zack shot her a look.

She blew out a sigh. "All right, all right."

"Okay. The clock starts now." Zack looked at his watch. "At five-thirty on August twenty-fifth, you can be picking out a car, if you abide by the rules. Deal?"

"Deal."

Katie juggled the large, plastic-wrapped bowl of salad in one arm as she pressed the doorbell on Zack's front door, then drew a deep breath, trying to quiet her nerves. Get used to it, she told herself. If she was going to share custody of Gracie, she was going to have to get accustomed to seeing Zack.

She didn't know why, exactly, she felt so on edge around him. No, that wasn't quite true. She knew, all right, but she didn't want to acknowledge it.

She was attracted to him. She straightened her shoulders and lifted her head. Well, so what? Lots of women were attracted to men. That didn't mean anything had to happen between them.

The door squeaked, then Gracie stood in the doorway, backlit by a lantern hanging down in the entryway.

Was it Katie's imagination, or was Gracie's expression a little less sullen than before? Katie smiled. "Hi."

"Hey."

It wasn't her imagination. It was definitely a more cordial hey than she'd gotten before. Gracie pulled the door wide and stepped back to let Katie enter the foyer.

"Hi, Kate." Zack stepped forward and kissed her cheek. It was a friendly greeting, nothing more, but his clean, soapy scent and the rasp of his five-o'clock shadow against her cheek made her feel things that were decidedly more than platonic. She held out the bowl. "I brought salad."

"Great." Gracie took it from her. "I'll put it in the fridge until the pizza arrives."

Zack gestured toward the living room. "Come on in."

Katie stepped into the living area, struck again by the beautiful decor. "I can't get over how lovely this place is."

"Not the bedroom that was supposed to be mine," Gracie said. "I'm in the so-called guest room because the room the designer did for me is a piece of crap."

Zack frowned at her.

Gracie winced. "I meant to say, 'The decor is not to my liking.'"

"Much better," Zack said.

Katie looked curiously from Gracie to Zack. Gracie shot him an anxious look. "That one doesn't count, does it?"

Zack grinned. "I think we can make an allowance for an adjustment period."

"Good." Gracie opened the Sub-Zero refrigerator, stuck the salad bowl inside, then slammed the door.

"Well, I'm going to my noncrappy room. If you two will excuse me, that is," she added with exaggerated politeness.

"Of course," Katie said, not sure what to make of Gracie's behavior.

She watched Gracie head up the stairs, then turned to Zack. "What's going on? Did you perform some kind of personality transplant?"

His mouth curved into a grin. "No transplant. Just a bribe."

"What?"

"I promised her a car if she shaped up." He made it sound offhanded, as if getting a teenager a new car was no big deal.

For some reason, his nonchalant attitude ran all over her. "You should have discussed that with me, don't you think?"

He looked bewildered. "Why?"

Katie put her hands on her hips. "Because if we're going to share custody, we need to discuss major decisions."

"I didn't think it was that major. She's going to need a license and transportation."

"A car is expensive."

"Not a problem."

The answer shot her temper into the red zone. "For you, maybe. I don't have your deep pockets."

"I didn't mean for you to pay for it."

"If we're going to share custody, I should pay half."

"No, Kate. Things aren't going to work like that."

Who was he to say how this was going to work? He didn't have a monopoly on setting the rules. "We haven't discussed how this is going to work."

"Fine. Let's discuss it." He fixed his dark eyes on her. "She'll split her time between your home and mine, and I'll take care of all Gracie's expenses."

"That's not fair."

"Why not? I've got the resources."

And you don't. He didn't say it, but it was implied all the same. She wasn't broke. She made a good living, and she had Paul's life insurance money. But that wasn't really the issue. She wasn't quite sure what the issue was.

"There's no reason to make this complicated," Zack said.

Damn it, it *was* complicated. There were plenty of reasons he shouldn't foot the bill for everything—good reasons, she was sure—but she couldn't come up with any at the moment, so she stated the one that was on the top of her mind. "I don't want to be beholden to you."

"You wouldn't be."

"I would feel as if I were, if you're paying for everything."

"Kate, I have plenty of money."

"This isn't about money. It's about us each handling our fair share."

"You've already more than done your share. You went through the pregnancy. You gave birth. You've worried about her all this time, while I didn't even know she existed. This is the least I can do, and I want to do it."

Why couldn't she just let him? She didn't know, but she shook her head all the same. "It doesn't feel right."

"Why not?"

"Because...It feels as if you have all the control."

"This isn't about control." He stepped closer, close enough that she could see the green facets around the pupils of his blue, blue eyes.

"It feels like it is."

"Why?"

"Because..." *Whenever I'm around you, I feel out of control. I think things and feel things I don't want to think and feel.* She straightened her back, trying to steel herself against the pull she felt toward him. "Because it feels like you've swept in and made all the decisions and moved a block away from me and turned my life upside down and I haven't had a say in anything."

"You have plenty of say, Kate." He blew out a frustrated breath. "Look—if you don't want her to have a car, I won't get her one."

"I can't very well take it away from her if you've promised it."

"She won't have to know you're the one saying no."

Did she really want to force Zack to break his word to their daughter? She looked away. "It just seems like a car is a privilege, something that should be worked for and earned."

"She's going to earn it. She has to shape up her attitude, get a job, and start acting responsibly." He put both hands on her upper arms in what was no doubt meant to be a conciliatory gesture. The touch burned. "Look—I'm sorry I didn't discuss it with you first. The fact is, I'm used to making unilateral decisions."

"Yeah, well, so am I."

"Sounds like we're both going to have to make some adjustments, then." His hands slid down her arms as he grinned at her.

She started to grin back, but something in his eyes made her breath hitch in her throat. A wave of awareness crashed over her. They were standing close, as close as lovers, so close that she could smell the clean scent of him and see his eyes darken. The moment when someone should have stepped away came and passed. His gaze held hers, then it dropped to her lips.

Oh, God. Desire, hot and heavy, flared inside her, so fast that it nearly took her breath away. A hot ache coiled between her legs. His eyes moved back to hers. His eyes were dark and heavy-lidded, a reflection of what she was feeling.

"Kate…" He reached up and smoothed a strand of hair away from her face, his thumb flicking over her chin. He curled his other hand around her head, cupping her face.

Air refused to enter or leave her lungs. A memory of that summer sucked her down into a hot, swirling vortex.

A few days after meeting Zack, Katie trudged home along a deserted road after locking the bait shop for the night. Her mother had promised to pick her up, but as all too frequently happened, she hadn't shown.

It was a dark moonless night, and the air was thick with heat and humidity and mosquitoes. The roar of an approaching car drowned out the hum of tree frogs and cicadas in the cypresses beside the road. To Katie's alarm, the car passed her, ground to a squealing stop, then backed up along the shoulder.

She was considering running into the woods when Zack lowered the electric window. "What are you doing?"

"Going home."

"Are you nuts, walking alone at night?"

She tilted up her chin, her pride injured. "No."

"Get in." His voice had been tight and abrupt. He leaned across the seat and threw open the passenger door.

She scrambled in. He glared at her. "Do you have any idea how dangerous that was? Someone like those two assholes—or worse—could have stopped." He clenched his jaw and shook his head. "It's flat-out stupid."

Her eyes filled with tears. "I didn't have any choice. My mother didn't show up." He let out a low oath.

She thought he was cursing her mother. "She's not that bad. She means well. She just..." A hot tear rolled down Katie's cheek.

"Oh, hey." He reached out and flicked her tear away with his thumb, his eyes instantly remorseful. "I'm sorry. I just...It's just a screwed-up situation." His hand stayed in her hair, and his gaze locked on hers. The air in the car suddenly seemed to crackle and buzz. His thumbs, calloused from working on marine engines and shuffling cards, ran down her cheek. The sandpaper texture of his skin somehow made the gesture all the more tender.

For the first time in her life, she felt cared about and special. Her heart floated out of her chest and over to him, where it made itself at home. She was certain he was going to kiss her. She started to close her eyes, and then he dropped his hands.

"You get off work at what...nine?"

She nodded.

"From here on out, I'll drive you home."

His thumbs moved over her cheeks now. She should say something, she knew she should, but words wouldn't form in her brain, much less in her mouth. The pads of his thumbs stroked her face, the touch soft and insistent as it moved toward her lips. She parted her lips to speak, but nothing came out. The ache in her groin grew deeper, hotter, stronger—a living thing, taking her over.

He dipped his head. His lips touched hers in a soft, barely there kiss. She must have moaned because she heard it, although she wasn't aware of making any sound.

She wasn't aware of anything but the feel of his hands moving down her back, the sweet heat surging between her thighs, the taste of his lips. He pulled her forward and his mouth moved over hers, hot and possessive and hungry and demanding. She fit herself against him and felt the shockingly hard proof of his desire. She moaned again, aching for him. He cupped her bottom, picked her up, and held her against the refrigerator.

She was on fire, ablaze. Her hands roamed down his back to palm his muscular buttocks. She wanted to...

The doorbell rang. She opened her eyes, feeling as if she was coming out of a daze. Oh, God—what was she doing? Her face burning, she dropped her hands and struggled to get her feet on the floor.

Zack pulled back and blew out a reluctant sigh.

"Hey, that's probably the pizza," Gracie called from upstairs. "Aren't you going to get the door?"

Zack cleared his throat, stepped back, and adjusted his jeans. Pulling his shirt down over his fly, he tugged his wallet out of his back pocket and strode toward the door, leaving Katie leaning against the counter, wondering what the hell had just happened.

CHAPTER ELEVEN

"He kissed you?" Bev's painted-on eyebrows flew toward her hairline, which was currently a flattering shade of Warm Sand Dune, thanks to Katie's color application last Wednesday.

"Yeah." Katie pulled a stack of white towels out of the dryer in the back of her salon and set them on top of the washer. She'd lain awake much of the night thinking about it. "It just kind of happened."

"Oh, my!" Bev fanned herself, as if having a hot flash. "What happened next?"

"Nothing."

"Nothing?"

"The pizza arrived, Gracie came into the room, and we sat down and ate." It had been an awkward meal. Katie struggled to act as if nothing had happened. Fortunately, not much had been required of her. Zack and Gracie were busy discussing cars, debating the merits of each brand and model. Katie was grateful that they'd carried the conversational ball. Since the bedroom furniture had arrived, Gracie was staying the night with Zack. Katie left immediately after helping clear the table.

"He just acted as if nothing had happened?" Bev pressed.

"Yeah."

"So—what are you going to do about it?"

"Nothing." Katie picked up one of the towels and folded it lengthwise in thirds. "I'm just going to make sure it doesn't happen again."

"Why on earth not?"

"It just seemed...inappropriate."

"Because of Paul?"

Katie nodded, noticing the gleam of her diamond wedding-ring set on her finger.

"Oh, honey, Paul would want you to be happy again."

"I know, I know. But head knowledge and heart knowledge are two different things." Part of the problem, Katie thought guiltily, was that she'd sometimes thought about Zack when Paul was around. Not often, but there had been moments when he'd crossed her mind. Especially when she'd wondered about their child.

But she couldn't explain that to Bev. Far better to keep things in the realm of the more pragmatic. "It's not just a matter of Paul." Katie pulled out another towel. "It's Zack. He doesn't do long-term relationships."

"Maybe he just hasn't met the right girl." Bev cocked an eyebrow. "Or maybe he met her, but he wasn't at the stage of life where he was ready."

Katie shook her head. "No. His parents had a miserable marriage, and it really soured him on commitment."

"Surely he knows that not all marriages are that way."

She lifted her shoulders. "People know what they've grown up seeing. His aunt and uncle weren't much better. His uncle cheated on his aunt...with my mother, among other women." She folded the towel. "He thinks that people who say they're happily married are deluding themselves or simply settling." She placed the towel on top of the others. "Did you see what he said in the article about America's most eligible bachelors in *Cosmo*?"

She shook her head. "But I'm guessing you did."

"I looked it up on the Internet a couple of days ago," she admitted. At the time it had come out, she'd deliberately avoided reading it—just as she'd avoided watching Zack on TV or reading tabloid articles about him. The truth was, even though she was married to Paul, every time she thought of Zack, she always felt a little twinge of emotion.

Not that she hadn't loved Paul with her heart and soul. She had. But she'd never told Paul the identity of the boy who'd gotten her pregnant. He'd said he didn't need to know, that it wasn't important, but she had still felt, deep in her heart, as if she were keeping something from him.

"So what did Zack say in the article?"

"He said, and I quote, 'Love is just a more socially acceptable word for lust. The new wears off, and it burns itself out. I don't want to live my life trying to fan a flame out of cold ashes.'"

Bev's lips quirked up. "You memorized it?"

Every single word. She lifted her shoulders. "More or less."

"Wow, didn't make too much of an impression, did it?" Bev reached for a towel. "You know, he doesn't have to be Mr. Forever to be good for you."

"What?"

"He's certainly fling-worthy."

"Oh, come on, Bev."

"Think about it. Maybe he's not Mr. Long Term, but he's a heck of a Mr. Right Now." Bev snapped a towel. "I mean, who says every romance has to be forever? Maybe you need a transitional romance."

"A what?"

"A fling between forever-afters."

"I don't think there's going to be another forever-after."

"All the more reason to have a fling, don't you think?"

Katie felt her back stiffen. "I don't do casual sex. I'm not like my mother."

Bev's face flooded with dismay. "Oh, honey—I'm not suggesting you are. There's a huge difference between dating a man for a few months and sleeping with every guy in town." She put her hand on Katie's shoulder. "No disrespect to your mother intended."

"None taken." It was the truth, as painful as it was.

"This could be perfect for you, sweetie. You said he's only here for a few months. And you wouldn't be getting involved with a stranger. In fact, this wouldn't even increase your number."

"My what?"

"Your number. The number of people you've slept with. This is a man you've had a child with, for Pete's sake."

"All the more reason not to get involved. If we're going to be co-parents, we don't need to complicate things."

"It's not like you're going to be raising a young child together. Gracie is nearly grown."

"And about to have a child herself. We'll be co-grandparents."

"So? If he lives in Vegas and you live here, you're not likely to see him all that often." Bev closed the door of the dryer. "I just don't see the harm in it. You need to move on with your life, and a little fling might be just the thing to boost you over the hump and onto the next stage of your life."

The bell over the front door jangled.

Lulu pushed through the door. "Helloo!" She was wearing a leopard-print top and carrying her favorite orange bag. Her face lit up when she saw Katie. "Sweetie, you've got to tell me everything. I can't believe you had a whole secret life and none of us knew it!" Lulu headed toward the chair. "This is so exciting. Start with Zack. Oh my gosh, he is *so* sexy." She put her hands over her chest and rolled her eyes heavenward. "How do you know him? Where did you meet? And what's going on between you now?"

Katie's heart sank. She knew she was going to have to explain the nature of their relationship to her friends, but she wasn't quite sure how, when she didn't even know herself.

Katie sneaked out at noon and headed home. Gracie was still at Zack's, which meant she had the place to herself. Going into the master bedroom, she flipped on the light in the closet and turned to the men's clothing hanging on the left side. A row of pressed shirts, pressed trousers, and jackets stood like soldiers, next to a round electric tie rack that would spin at the touch of a button—a gift Katie had gotten Paul their last Christmas.

Katie tugged her blouse off over her head and reached for one of Paul's shirts. This time she selected an old black-and-gold rugby shirt with the New Orleans Saints logo. She pulled it on, enjoying the feel of the soft fabric against her belly, enjoying the feel of something that had been close to Paul's heart close to her own.

Bending down, Katie reached for an old navy blue T-shirt on the shelf, carefully folded and tucked in a plastic bag. It was the shirt that had been in the laundry basket the day he'd shipped out. She hadn't washed it; instead, she'd pulled it out and wrapped it up to preserve his scent. She'd learned, during his first tour of duty, how comforting it could be to have something that smelled like him—something that would let her close her eyes and pretend, for just a moment, that he was simply away from the house for a little while.

Carefully extracting the shirt from the bag, she lifted it and put it to her nose, inhaling deeply. Nothing. She drew in another breath. The last few times, she could smell only the barest, faintest hint of Paul. Maybe not even that; maybe just the memory of a hint. Now she didn't even have that; now she just had a memory of a memory. The fact was, the shirt was starting to smell like the cedar in the closet.

Oh, God—another loss. Before Paul had died, she'd thought that losing a loved one was a huge, single catastrophe. No one had told her that grief was a series of little, cutting losses that nicked her heart every day. It wasn't just sleeping alone or having an empty chair at dinner; it was buying a quart of milk instead of a half-gallon, making one cup of coffee instead of two, hearing a joke and having no one to share it with. It wasn't just missing him; it was missing the scent of him on the one remaining unwashed shirt.

Maybe her sense of smell was off today. Unwilling to

admit defeat, she carefully refolded the shirt, tucked it back in the plastic bag, and put it in the back of the closet, hoping the smell would be there the next time.

Reaching up to the top shelf, she pulled down a brown leather photo album etched with gold. She knew the pictures by heart: Paul at the beach, buff and tan and smiling; Paul at Mardi Gras, ropes of beads around his neck; Paul at a Saints game, pumping his fist in the air; Paul installing the kitchen cabinets in their house. Usually the photos set off a warm glow in her chest, but today they failed to give her any feeling at all. She put the album back, then reached for his leather bomber jacket. Pulling it off the hanger, she lifted it to her face and breathed deeply. It smelled like leather—not like Paul, exactly, but he'd worn it, and when he'd worn it, he'd smelled leathery. It would have to do. She needed to feel a connection, a solid, here-and-now sensory experience. She needed something that made Paul seem real, because more and more, he seemed like a figment of her imagination.

He was slipping further and further away, more and more into the past. Holding his jacket, she sank to the closet floor.

"Don't go," she whispered. "Please don't go."

But in her heart, she knew that even the last, lingering ghost scent of him was already gone. Like it or not, Paul had left the building.

Annette was up and taking steps with a walker, Dave at her side, when Katie pushed open the door to her room at Sunnyside a little after one.

Katie stopped in the doorway. "Oh—hi."

"Well, hello there, sweetie," Dave said, his voice a shade too hearty.

Annette's cheeks pinkened. "Katie! I didn't expect you until later."

Katie held out a white bag holding a shrimp po'boy from the Chartreuse Café. "I thought you might be hungry."

"Oh!" Annette leaned heavily on the walker. "Oh, thank you, dear—but Dave already brought me something from the China Station." Katie looked at four little Chinese take-out boxes on her bed tray. "He had to go to Hammond for something, so he brought it back."

"Oh. How nice." She drew back her arm. "I'll take this home, then, and Gracie and I will have it later."

"That was very thoughtful of you, dear."

"It was thoughtful of Dave, as well." And quite the surprise. Katie hadn't known that Annette and Dave were on an eating-lunch-together basis.

"Yes, well..." Annette cleared her throat, looking thoroughly flustered. "He brought it, so I figured I might as well eat it."

"Of course."

"Are you ready to get back in bed?" Dave asked.

"Yes, please," Annette said.

He helped her maneuver the walker to the bedside, then took her arm and helped her onto the bed. Annette winced as she tried to swing her leg onto the mattress. Dave bent and lifted her leg for her.

"Thank you." She slid back against the pillow.

"My pleasure." Dave straightened. "Well, I ought to be going." He picked up the containers of Chinese food and carried them to the trash. "See you tomorrow."

Without giving her time to respond, he slipped out the door.

Katie looked at Annette. "What's going on with you two?"

"Nothing. Absolutely nothing."

The vibe didn't feel like nothing. But then, who was she to say? Nothing was going on between her and Zack, either, yet yesterday evening she'd found herself smashed against his refrigerator, her legs wrapped around his thighs, squeezing his buns and playing tonsil hockey for all she was worth.

CHAPTER TWELVE

A week later, Gracie lay across the bed in her room at Zack's house and texted Megan.

Gracie: Got a job at the old folks home.
Megan: OMG! Is it gross?
Gracie: Nah. I'm the recreation assistant. I help them play bingo and shuffleboard and shit.
Megan: Sounds cool.
Gracie: At least it's something 2 do. This town totally sucks.
Megan: Nothing 2 do here either. Got grounded for getting an F on summer school quiz. How's the BB?
Gracie: Going to OB today. Guess I'll find out.

Gracie put a hand on her belly. She didn't feel anything emotional or motherly toward the baby growing inside her. It didn't really seem to be a person; it was more like an alien that had taken over her body without her permission. Most of the time she just tried not to think about it, but it was getting harder and harder, considering she was starting to look like she'd swallowed a beach ball.

The whole thing kind of freaked her out. She sorta liked the idea of having something cute and cuddly to love, something that would love her back, no matter what, but she was scared to death that she wouldn't know how to take care of it. What if she couldn't be a good mother? After all, she wasn't a very good person. She couldn't be, because she'd been a terrible daughter.

Oh, God—how she wished she could do things over! Now it was too late. She'd never get a chance to make things up to her parents or even tell them she was sorry. They were dead, and it was all her fault.

A soft knock sounded at the door. "Gracie?"

It was Katie. Part of her wanted to talk to her. Another part hated that she wanted to. She put a note of annoyance in her voice. "What?"

"It's almost time to go to the doctor."

"I don't want to go."

There was a moment of silence. "Are you okay?"

"I'm just peachy."

Another bout of silence, then Katie's voice sounded, soft and concerned. "Can I come in?"

"I can't keep you out."

"I won't come in if you don't want me to. Is it all right?"

"I guess."

The door squeaked open. Katie stepped through it, bringing the scent of herbs and flowers with her. She looked around at the room, which was all done in shades of taupe, tan, and brown. "This is really pretty."

Gracie lifted her shoulders. "Kinda bland, but beats

the hell out of the room the designer did for me. That one looks like she thought I was seven, not seventeen."

"I'm sure Zack will let you redecorate."

"Nah. I don't plan to be here long enough to bother with that." She didn't know exactly where she was going to be, but once she had some money, it sure wouldn't be here.

"Are you okay?"

"Yeah, I guess."

"You look like you've been crying."

"I never cry." For some stupid reason, just saying that made the waterworks start up again.

She hated herself for being weak, but she couldn't stop the sob from spilling out, a sob that felt like it came from the depths of her soul.

"Oh, sweetie." The bed sagged as Katie sat down beside her. Katie's hand rested on her back, soft and warm and tentative. Gracie wanted to shrug it off, but she couldn't bring herself to do it. She kept her face down and cried, her shoulders heaving.

"Do you want to talk about it?"

Gracie couldn't have gotten any words out around the lump in her throat even if she'd had anything to say. She shook her head.

Katie's hand moved up and down her back. "That's okay." Her hand felt warm and...good. Reassuring, somehow. "It's good to cry. Sometimes you just need to let the pain out."

Wow, this was a switch. Her aunt had made her ashamed to cry. "You need to get ahold of yourself," Aunt Jean had told her when she'd caught her sobbing into her teddy bear, Beary. "Wallowing in self-pity won't bring your parents back."

Even her friends told her not to cry, but Gracie figured that was because it made them uncomfortable. It was funny—being told it was okay to cry made her feel like she didn't need to so much. Her sobs slowed to hiccups.

"If you're not up to going to the doctor this afternoon, I can reschedule the appointment."

Gracie hesitated. "This doctor—is she going to do a, you know, exam?"

"A pelvic? I'm not sure."

Gracie's shoulders tightened. "The last doctor did, and it really hurt." Even worse than the pain was the sheer embarrassment. She'd nearly died a thousand deaths. No one had ever seen her private parts before. Even Kurt—or was it Kirk? It might even have been Dirk—she hadn't been sure—hadn't looked at her down there. He'd just groped her in the dark and then stuck it in.

"Dr. Greene's really gentle," Katie told her. "It'll be okay."

The fact that the doctor was a woman made her feel better. "All right. I'll go."

Thirty minutes later, Gracie found herself in the bright, fluorescent-lit waiting room, her palms sweating, sitting next to a pregnant woman who looked pretty old—probably in her thirties. The door to the inner office opened and a grandmotherly woman in blue-flowered scrubs called her name. Gracie's fingers squeezed together so tightly that they hurt. Her butt felt glued to the chair.

"Do you want me to go with you?" Katie asked.

"Suit yourself." Gracie gave an I-don't-care shrug, but she was relieved when Katie stood and followed her down the hall into the examination room. Katie turned to the wall and pretended to stare at a poster of the female reproductive tract while Gracie changed into a paper gown.

Dr. Greene was surprisingly young and pretty, with shoulder-length dark hair pulled into a ponytail, and she talked to Gracie like an adult. She asked questions about the date of her last period and her medical care, but she didn't push for info about the baby's dad. When the doctor asked her to lie on the table and put her legs in the stirrups, Katie stood by her head and reached for her hand. Gracie let her take it, then wound her fingers tightly around Katie's, squeezing hard while the doctor prodded and poked.

"You can scoot back," Dr. Greene said, rising from the stool and pulling off her latex gloves. "Everything looks fine."

Blowing out a sigh of relief, Gracie released her grip on Katie's fingers—jeez, she'd been gripping them so hard her own fingers were sore—and moved up the table.

"Are you ready to look at the baby on the ultrasound?" the doctor asked.

Gracie's heart pounded. "Sure."

Dr. Greene switched on a machine that looked like a computer, then adjusted the paper blanket to expose Gracie's belly. "This is ultrasound gel. I'm going to put some on your stomach to help the transducer slide over your skin. The image will appear on the screen." She indicated a screen that looked like a computer. Katie kept her eyes locked on it as Dr. Greene squirted on something cold and wet, then ran a thing that looked like a computer mouse over her belly. A bunch of blobs and squiggles appeared on the screen, shifting from dark to light as Dr. Greene moved the mouselike thing around.

"There's the baby—right there," the doctor said.

Gracie lifted her head and craned her neck. "Where?"

Dr. Greene pointed to a light blob on the screen. "That's the head."

Gracie peered at the blob, trying to make it out. And then, all of a sudden, she saw it. *A baby, all curled up like a cat.* Gracie's mouth fell open. "It—it's sucking its thumb!"

Dr. Greene smiled. "That's right."

"Oh my God." Gracie's gaze was glued to the screen. A baby. Her baby. Right there, on the ultrasound. A sense of awe swelled around her, large and engulfing and speech-stealing. "It can suck its thumb?"

"Sure can."

"Can you tell if it's a boy or a girl?" Katie's voice sounded as breathless as Gracie felt.

The doctor moved around the ultrasound mouse or whatever it was. "Not today. The baby's torso is turned away."

"But—wow. That's my baby!"

"Yeah. Wow," Katie echoed.

"This is really happening!" Gracie exclaimed. "There's really a baby in there." The moment she said it, she felt ridiculous. "I mean, I knew there was, of course...but seeing it—it makes it so real."

"Having a baby, Gracie, is as real as it gets." Dr. Greene smiled. Katie beamed, her eyes so warm and caring that Gracie almost liked her in spite of herself.

"The baby's okay?" Gracie asked.

"The baby looks wonderful, and the heartbeat is perfect. Have you felt it move yet?"

"No. Not really." Not that she'd noticed, anyway.

Dr. Greene nodded. "With a first pregnancy, it can be hard to tell. You've probably felt something and thought it was just gas."

Now that she thought about it, her stomach had felt awfully grumbly lately.

"Look—the baby's kicking." The doctor pointed at the screen. "Do you feel that?"

Oh, God—something was happening in her belly. It was very faint, like an air bubble popping. She felt it again as the baby's foot kicked on the screen. "Yeah!" Her insides suddenly felt all lit up, as if a bulb of joy had flashed on. "I feel it!" She put her hands on her stomach, right over the slimy gel, hoping to feel the baby kick again, wanting to feel it from the outside as well as the inside. To her disappointment, the baby's legs stilled.

Dr. Greene pressed some buttons. Little green markers showed up on the screen. She pressed another button. The image froze for a moment, as if she were taking a picture.

"What are you doing?" Gracie asked.

"Taking measurements." She took a few more pictures. "Looking at the size of the baby, I'd say our due date is right on the money. You're about twenty-four weeks along. You'll have this baby in about sixteen weeks—right around Thanksgiving."

That seemed like forever.

Dr. Greene moved the mouse thing some more. "There's one thing I'm not liking."

Gracie's heart nearly stopped. "What?"

"The placenta is attached awfully low." Dr. Greene pointed to a large mass of squiggles. "It's partially covering your cervix, which could be a problem. Hopefully, the placenta will move upward as the baby grows. Ninety percent of the time, it grows toward the top of your uterus, and all will be well."

"And if it doesn't grow upward?" Katie asked.

"Yeah. What if it doesn't?" Gracie echoed.

"Well, as you get closer to delivery, your cervix will start to dilate and thin, and if the placenta is covering it, you could start bleeding. If you have any bleeding at all, Gracie, I want you to lie down and call me immediately. Better yet, just go to the hospital."

"It's that serious?" Katie said.

"Yes. It can be a life-threatening condition for both the mother and the baby. But as I said, ninety percent of the time, partial placenta previa resolves itself."

Katie's brow wrinkled. "What will you do if she starts bleeding?"

"It depends. If it's close to her due date, we'll deliver by C-section. If the bleeding isn't too severe, we'll put her on bedrest for the remainder of her pregnancy, but we'll still need to deliver by cesarean, probably a week or so early."

"So I'll have a scar?" Gracie asked. The thought of having one wasn't quite as intriguing as looking at them on other people.

"Yes, but it would be low enough you can still wear a bikini." Dr. Greene clicked some more buttons on the console. "In the meantime, don't worry. But as a precaution, I don't want you having sex or putting anything in your vagina."

As if! Gracie felt her face heat.

"She's just gotten a job as the recreation assistant at Sunnyside. Is it okay for her to work?"

"Sure. She can do anything she normally does." Dr. Greene smiled. "Congratulations, Gracie. Your baby looks beautiful and completely healthy."

A grin started deep inside her and radiated out, a grin so big it hurt her face.

"I'll make a disk for you to take with you."

"Awesome," Gracie said. She couldn't wait to send it to Megan. "Thanks!"

"Zack will want to see it," Katie said.

"Yeah," Gracie said. "He'll be blown away." If she wanted to keep up the screw-you attitude, she shouldn't be so freaking agreeable, but she was too excited to care. That was her baby, right there on the screen. Holy shit—this was for real! "How big is my baby right now?"

"About the size of an eggplant." Dr. Greene shut off the ultrasound machine and opened a cabinet on the far wall. She pulled out a model of a fetus. "Your baby is just a little smaller than this."

The plastic baby was a little bigger than the doctor's hand. A baby like that, perfectly formed with little eyes and ears and everything, was moving and alive inside her! Wow. It was totally awesome—scary and wonderful and amazing, all at the same time. A sense of pride and importance surged through her. For the first time in her life, she felt as if she mattered, as if she had a purpose.

She was going to be a mother!

Oh, God. A mother! The pride was chased by panic. She was just a kid herself. She didn't know anything about how to be an adult—how to pay bills or get insurance or any of those other mysterious things that grown-ups knew how to do. How was she going to take care of a baby by herself?

Dr. Greene handed her some paper towels to wipe the gel off her belly. "You can get dressed, Gracie. Considering the position of your placenta, I'd like to see you in two weeks."

"Okay."

Katie handed her her clothes, her eyes tender and warm, and a traitorous thought crossed Gracie's mind: She might want Katie's help after all.

CHAPTER THIRTEEN

Zack squinted at the screen of his laptop open on the kitchen table. It was like looking at a moving Rorschach test. He saw lots of things that looked like bubbles and spilled cola, but nothing remotely humanoid. "I still don't see it."

"Right there." Gracie leaned over and pointed to a blob. "That's the head. Do you see it now?"

Zack still didn't, but he didn't want to disappoint Gracie. She and Katie had burst through the door after the doctor's visit, happy and hyper and talking a mile a minute, and Gracie was obviously eager for Zack to share her excitement. He didn't want to let her down.

"That's a foot right there, " Katie said, bending over his other shoulder. The scent of her shampoo made it hard to concentrate.

Something on the screen moved—and all of a sudden, he made out a tiny form. His pulse kicked up as if he'd drawn the last ace in a straight. "Well, I'll be damned." Holy smokes—it looked so—so *human*! In an abstract kind of way, like it had been run through a special-effects machine or something.

Still, it was definitely a baby.

"The doctor said it looks perfect," Gracie said. "The heartbeat is strong and the head size is right and everything looks great."

"That's terrific."

"Yeah." Gracie smiled. For the first time, she had that glow that people talked about pregnant women having. "The placenta is kinda low, though, and that might be a problem, but the doctor thinks it'll be okay."

"Why would that be a problem?"

"The placenta is the part that implants in the uterus and feeds the baby. It's supposed to come out after the baby, not before," Katie explained. "If it's over the cervix, she might start bleeding and have the baby too early."

Zack's stomach tightened.

"The doctor says it usually corrects itself as the pregnancy progresses. She thinks it'll be all right."

The screen went blank. Gracie headed for the refrigerator and lifted out a carton of milk. "The doctor said my diet is really important, so we're going to need to get lots of fruits and vegetables and healthy crap." She cut a guilty glance at Zack. "I mean stuff."

She was trying to clean up her language. She got an A for effort. "Sure thing."

"What's for dinner, anyway? I'm starved."

"I, uh, don't know." Zack usually didn't think about dinner until he was hungry. "We can go out, or we can order pizza."

"Again?"

There weren't a lot of culinary options in Chartreuse.

"I've got frozen veggies and some cooked chicken,"

Katie offered. "You can come home with me and we'll make stir-fry."

"Sounds great," Gracie said. "I'll cook."

Katie gave Zack a polite smile. "You're welcome to join us."

She didn't really want his company; she was inviting him out of her ingrained sense of Southern hospitality. She'd been stiff and distant ever since he'd kissed her, sending off prickly vibes.

Well, hell. He deserved stiff and prickly. He deserved a whole porcupine, shoved squarely where the sun didn't shine. What had he been thinking? He'd told himself before he came to Chartreuse that he wasn't going to get anything started with Katie. He wasn't even sure how it had happened. One minute they were arguing about getting Gracie a car, and the next...

Hell. What had happened next had melted his brain, and he hadn't thought straight since. He shouldn't have touched Katie. That had been his downfall. Touching her had set off some kind of weird chemical reaction that had short-circuited his prefrontal cortex. His reptilian brain had taken over, and it had held only one thought: *Get closer*. It hadn't helped that Katie had seemed awfully amenable to the idea at the time.

He hadn't been able to get rid of that reptilian thought, either. It kept nagging at him, making him take long showers and use excessive amounts of soap, which only resulted in an unsatisfactory, temporary abatement of what seemed like a chronic condition.

From her reserved, overly polite behavior, it was pretty clear that Katie regretted the moment of regressive behavior and wanted to keep her distance. If he was any kind of gentleman, he'd refuse the dinner invitation and let her off the hook.

Unfortunately for her, he wasn't. "Thanks. That sounds great."

The summer air steamed around them as the three of them traipsed down the block to Katie's house, past an elderly couple sitting on a front porch swing. The man wore an orange plaid shirt, olive khakis, and bright green suspenders. The woman wore a flowered button-up dress like his great-aunt used to wear, a thing she called a housecoat.

"Hello, there, Katie," the man called.

"Hello, Mr. Gantor—Mrs. Gantor."

"We sure enjoyed that casserole," the man said.

"I'm so glad."

"If you have a moment, I'll fetch the dish for you," the old woman called.

Gracie blew out an impatient sigh. "I'm starving."

Katie glanced at her anxiously, then smiled at the elderly couple. He could see that she was torn between making the elderly couple happy and appeasing Gracie. Apparently Gracie won out. "We're kind of in a hurry. I'll stop by for it tomorrow."

"I couldn't quite hear you, dear. Did you say there's something you want to borrow?"

"She said she'll stop by tomorrow," Mr. Gantor said loudly.

"Oh. Okay, dear." The woman smiled at Katie. "Who's that with you?"

"This is my daughter, Gracie."

"Racy? Oh, I wouldn't say that, dear. All the girls wear their clothes tight these days."

"She said it's her daughter, Gracie," Mr. Gantor said.

"I'm not her...," Gracie began.

"Stuff it," Zack warned her under his breath.

"And this is Zack Ferguson," Katie continued. "He's moved into the old Ashton house."

"Well, I'll be."

Mrs. Gantor pulled on his sleeve. "What did she say?"

"That Nellie was right after all."

"I'll come see you tomorrow and we'll catch up," Katie promised.

"Ketchup? That's sweet, dear, but we have a full bottle." The woman wiggled her fingers in a little wave. "Nice meeting you."

"Nice meeting you, too," Zack called. He glanced down at Gracie and gave her a nudge. "Likewise," she muttered.

Katie strode quickly past the next house, where a curtain parted as they walked past. She opened her front door.

"Don't you lock your place?" Zack asked.

"I do at night, and when I'm gone long, but not when I'm just going down the street. My neighbors keep an eye on things for me."

A louvered window opened across the street. This place took neighborhood watch to a whole new level. "Apparently so. But you should lock up anyway. Someone could sneak in when your neighbors aren't looking."

Katie looked like she was about to protest, then glanced at Gracie. He could see the thought rolling through her head. She had to set a good example. "You're right. Gracie, I'll have a key made for you in the morning."

She strode into the kitchen, opened the fridge, and pulled out a green pepper and a stalk of celery. She handed them to Gracie and indicated the cutting board. "Would you please dice these?" She went to the cupboard and pulled out an onion and two cloves of garlic. "And you can cut these."

"I can see where I rank," he commented. "I get the stinky work."

From the corner of his eye, he saw Gracie almost crack a smile. Katie opened the freezer and pulled out a bag of frozen vegetables, then opened the refrigerator and pulled out a package of precooked chicken breasts. As Katie made rice, she gave Gracie directions on preparing the stir-fry. Zack set the table, and twenty minutes later, they sat down at the dining table to steaming bowls of stir-fry and rice, fragrant with lemongrass and garlic.

"I think we should say grace," Katie said.

"Grace," Gracie quickly said. "Although I prefer to be called Gracie."

Katie grinned at her. "I meant a blessing."

Gracie rolled her eyes. "What for? That's just superstition."

"Not to me."

Gracie huffed out an exasperated sigh. "You didn't insist on praying last time we all ate together here."

"You were upset."

"I can get upset again."

Apparently the baby high was wearing off and she was reverting to ticked-off teenager mode. Zack decided to try to head things off. "It's Kate's house, so let's do things her way."

Katie held out her hands. Zack folded his fingers

tightly around hers, enjoying the sensation of her warm palm in his. He extended his other hand to Gracie. The girl rolled her eyes again, blew out another long-suffering sigh, then took each adult's hand.

The moment struck him as surreal. There they were, gathered around the table, holding hands, just like one big happy family. The concept should have alarmed him, but oddly enough, it didn't. Katie bowed her head and closed her eyes. "Thank you, God, for this food and all our many blessings. Help us to remember how loving and kind you are toward us, and help us to be loving and kind to others. Amen."

"Amen," Zack echoed.

Gracie remained silent. He squeezed her hand.

"A men," Gracie said, jerking her hand back. "A women, too." She picked up her fork.

"Napkin, Gracie," Zack said.

She huffed out a sigh. "What are you, the etiquette police?"

"Yeah. And I'm citing you for a moving violation." Zack grinned and picked up a pair of chopsticks. "You're going to have to set a good example for your child, you know."

"Oh, like you did?"

The kid really knew how to kick him where it hurt. He forced a smile. "I'm trying to make up for lost time."

"Yeah, well, don't bother." Ignoring the chopsticks Katie had put out, Gracie scooped a pile of food on her fork. "I had a dad, and you're not him."

"I couldn't believe how clearly the baby showed up on the ultrasound," Katie said in a transparent attempt to change the subject.

Gracie's face softened. "Yeah. That was way cool."

"You ought to send a copy of the ultrasound to your baby's father," Zack remarked.

Gracie's hand went still. "My baby doesn't have a father."

"You're saying it was an immaculate conception?"

Gracie's face turned stony. "I'm saying it's none of your business."

A nerve ticked in Zack's jaw. He'd meant to try to cajole her into a conversation about her baby's father, but if she wouldn't cooperate, he had no problem forcing the issue. Seeing that ultrasound had made the baby's arrival seem imminent. The fact that there might be a problem made it seem all the more urgent that they waste no time notifying the baby's father.

If he had seen a picture of Gracie in Katie's womb, it could have changed his whole life. He was sure of it. He wasn't sure what he would have done, but he liked to think he would have given Katie the option of keeping her baby if she'd wanted to. "I beg your pardon, Gracie, but you made it my business when you showed up and asked me to take you in."

"Zack, I really don't think...," Katie began.

"I never asked you to take me in." Gracie's eyes flashed. "I asked you to make me an emancipated minor."

"Which I'm not going to do."

"Well, there are some things I'm not going to do, either." Gracie stabbed a spear of broccoli. "Including having this conversation."

"Drop it, Zack," Katie urged.

But Zack wasn't about to. "Your baby's father needs to know."

"He's not a father. He's a sperm donor." She stuck

the forkful of food in her mouth, and continued talking. "Like you were."

She shoots, she scores. She'd wanted to hurt him, and she had. He leaned forward. "Is it Justin?"

Gracie's mouth fell open, inelegantly exposing her partially chewed broccoli, then abruptly closed. He watched an array of emotions play across her face: surprise, then disbelief, then amusement. "Justin? No way!" Her expression morphed again—this time into anger. "How'd you get his name, anyway?"

"I called your old high school in Pittsburgh and talked to some of your teachers."

"Jesus." Her jaw stiffened. "Is there no such thing as privacy?"

"This isn't just about you, Gracie."

"Well, it sure as hell isn't about you." She glared at him. "You're way off base, anyway. Justin's gay."

"So who's the father?"

"No one."

He leaned back in the chair. "Look, if you're not sure who it is, just give me a list of the suspects, and we'll get a blood test after the baby's born."

Her face went scarlet. "Holy crap. You think I'm a *slut*?"

"I didn't say that."

"You might as well have."

"Gracie, sweetie, he didn't mean anything," Kate said. "There's no need to get upset."

"He accused me of sleeping with a whole list of guys, and you don't think I should be *upset*?" Her voice was shrill and loud.

Zack scowled. "I'm not judging you. I just believe that

the father's right to know trumps any embarrassment you might have about who you've slept with."

"My baby has no father. I'm a single parent. Got that? A single parent." Her chair squawked as she pushed it back from the table and rose. "Stay the fuck out of my business." Her glower encompassed Katie. "Both of you!"

"Gracie...," Katie began.

But she wasn't listening. She stormed out of the room and into the bedroom, slamming the door behind her.

Zack blew out a sigh. "Well, that went well."

Gracie wasn't the only one upset with him. Katie's eyes threw daggers. "She was just starting to warm up to us. She was excited about the baby and starting to talk. Why did you have to start railroading her about the baby's father?"

"That wasn't railroading. That was straight talk, which is just what that girl needs. You're not doing her any favors, tiptoeing around her as if she's a prison guard with a new stun gun she's just waiting to try out."

"I'm trying build a relationship with her."

"Yeah, well, letting her walk all over you is not the way to make that happen."

Katie slapped her napkin down on the table. "She's not walking all over me. I'm exercising patience. Which is something you might try for a change." Katie snatched the dishes off the table, her eyes snapping. "The girl is hurting. She's lost her parents—the only parents she's ever known. She's pregnant, she's in a strange town with no friends, and all of her life, she's thought of us as the bad guys. Don't you get it?"

"I get that you feel so damned guilty for something you shouldn't feel guilty about that you don't want to cross her."

"You don't know the first thing about how I feel." The plates clattered as she piled them on top of one another and strode into the kitchen.

Hell. She was probably right. He ran a hand down his face, blew out a sigh, then picked up the bowl of rice and the bowl of chicken and vegetables and followed her into the kitchen.

The plates clanged as she dumped them into the stainless-steel sink. Katie turned on the faucet. She picked up a plate and scraped its contents into the garbage disposal, then flipped the switch. The disposal roared.

"Would you like me to stick my head in there so you can grind it, too?" he asked over the noise.

"Great idea." She flipped off the switch. "Unfortunately, your head won't fit even in the sink, because it's so swollen with everything you think you know."

"I don't think I know everything. I just think the boy ought to be in on things, especially since Gracie's going to keep the baby."

"What if he doesn't want to be a part of things? What if you drag him into this and he's reluctant or angry or unreliable or just not there? Do you really think that's in the best interests of Gracie or the baby?"

He stared at her. "Is that what you're worried about?"

"Yes." She rinsed the next plate. "Believe me, there are worse things than not knowing your father," Katie said.

She'd never talked about her dad, other than to say he wasn't in the picture. Because of Katie's mother's barfly ways, he'd assumed she didn't know who he was. He crossed the kitchen toward her. "Are you talking from personal experience?"

"Yeah." She turned on the garbage disposal again.

The roar of the motor reverberated through him. "You knew your dad?"

She flipped off the disposal. "I wouldn't say that I actually knew him. He popped in a few times. Once he stayed a whole week. He made all kinds of promises about things we were going to do together and places we were going to go, and I believed him. And then he'd just disappear for another few years." She opened the dishwasher and pulled out the bottom rack with a clatter. "It would have been a lot better if he'd just stayed away."

His stomach felt like it was being squeezed in a juicer. "Kate—I didn't know."

"Why should you?"

"Because..." Because he'd thought they'd been close—closer than he'd let himself get to anybody else, at least as far as sharing stuff about himself. The poker games that summer hadn't started until eleven or later, so when he'd pick Katie up after work, they'd often just sat and talked. He remembered one night in particular.

They'd been sitting in his eight-year-old Ford Taurus in front of her run-down trailer, "Let's Get Rocked" by Def Leppard playing on his Radio Shack car-kit stereo. Katie had stared at her mother's dented blue Chevy Nova with the smashed-in fender and the mismatched black door, parked at a cockamamy angle. "I hate to go in there. I don't know if my mother is 'entertaining' or passed out, or if she'll be drunk and crying and I'll have to stay up half the night comforting her, as if I'm the grown-up." She looked at Zack. "It must be nice, having real parents."

. Zack let out a derisive laugh. "I don't have real parents. And it sure wasn't nice."

"What do you mean?"

"Real parents don't hit their kid just because he's standing there."

Katie's eyes grew round and concerned. "Your folks hit you?"

He'd never told anyone that before. He tried to downplay it with a shrug. "Nothing too bad. Just a slap or a backhand. And only if I interrupted one of their 'conversations.'" Meaning one of their long, drawn-out, pretty-much-continuous slurfests. "Most of the time they ignored me." Because he tiptoed around, trying to act invisible. "But when they got mad at each other, they'd yell at me, too. And then later they'd say, 'I love you.'" His voice twisted into a sarcastic falsetto. "'I love you, Zachary.' As if that made hitting me or screaming at me all right."

Kate had just sat there, her eyes urging him to keep on talking. So he had. "The worst part was, I had to say it back." His voice went into sarcasm mode again. "'Say it like you mean it, Zachary.' 'Zachary, tell your mother you love her so she'll quit crying and shut up.'"

He'd stared at the lightbulb on the front of Katie's trailer, illuminating the kicked-in dent on the mildew-covered, once-white door. "They acted like I was a big nuisance, like it was a real pain to take me anywhere or do anything for me, like they resented the fact I existed. When I was eleven, I found out why."

"Yeah?"

"I was in my room, and I heard my mom tell my dad

that he'd ruined her life. And he yelled back that she was the one who'd ruined it, getting knocked up with me."

"Oh, no," Katie breathed.

"Yeah. He said she'd gotten pregnant on purpose to trick him into marrying her. And she said it was the last thing she wanted, being stuck with a loser like him. And he said she should have gotten an abortion like he wanted her to. 'You know I couldn't,' she yelled back. 'I was too far along.'"

Katie's hand had reached for his. "Oh, Zack."

"I didn't know what an abortion was. I looked the word up in the dictionary at school the next day."

The jangle of silverware being jammed into the dishwasher pulled him back to the moment. God. He'd forgotten he'd told Katie all that. Knowing that about him must have made it really hard for Katie to call all those Fergusons in the Chicago phone directory when she'd learned she was pregnant herself.

He watched her angrily jab the plates into the dishwasher rack. "Why didn't you tell me you knew your dad?" he asked.

"I never talk about it."

Ever? Not even with her husband? It made him jealous to think that another man might have known something she'd held back from him.

Which was totally stupid. After all, they'd known each other for only six weeks that summer. It only made sense that she'd form a deeper bond with a man she'd been married to for four years.

The thing was, he'd never formed as deep a bond with another woman as he'd formed that summer with

Katie. Hell. Was he emotionally stunted or something? Apparently he'd peaked out on relationships in his teens.

But then, that had been his choice. He'd never wanted commitment and closeness and all that crap. He'd spent his childhood wanting his parents' love, and all he'd gotten were empty words shoved down his throat. Loving someone just gave them power over you, and he never intended to be in that position again.

He watched Katie storm across the kitchen and yank a couple of plastic storage containers out of a cabinet. Another thought occurred to him. "When you were pregnant with Gracie, were you worried that I'd be like your father?"

She lifted her shoulders. "Since I decided not to keep the baby, it didn't really matter."

It wasn't the outright "no" he'd hoped for. All that summer, he'd tried to be a stand-up kind of guy, to treat Katie the way guys in movies treated their girls. "Kate, I want you to know that I would have...I mean, I like to think that I would have..."

She cut him off. "None of us really know what we'd really do in a situation until we're in it, do we?" She dumped the chicken and vegetables into one of the containers, smashed on the lid, and slammed it into the refrigerator, then whirled toward him, her hands on her hips. "I don't even know why you're here now."

Zack didn't really know himself. He didn't know how to be a good father; he only knew how not to be the brand of bad father he'd had—disinterested, self-absorbed, and neglectful.

Zack had figured that being the opposite of his father meant being in Gracie's life, trying to form some sort of relationship with her and letting her know he gave a damn. He'd also figured that bringing Gracie and Katie together might, in some small measure, make things up to Katie. Hell. Was he succeeding at any of that?

Damn it all. He was accustomed to being sure of himself, to making decisions, taking action and not looking back. Ever since he'd set eyes on Katie, he'd been second-guessing just about every move he'd ever made.

He believed in playing by the rules, but he didn't know what the rules were in this situation. He was in uncharted territory. He knew how to be a good friend, a good sex partner, a good card player, a good business associate, a good drinking buddy. He had no clue how to be a good father, or a good... What? What the hell was he to Katie? An ex-lover? An ex-lovee? Even with an "ex" in front of them, the words made him sweat.

"I think it's time for you to go," Katie said.

It was his turn to have Gracie for the night, but under the circumstances, he wasn't going to force the issue. "Yeah. Talk to you tomorrow." He headed to the foyer and out the front door, locking it behind him. The sun was setting, but it was still so hot and humid that the air seemed to cling to his skin like plastic wrap.

He'd been so sure he knew what was right—so sure that finding the baby's father was the moral high ground. Now he wasn't so certain. The odds of being right were somewhere around sixty-forty, or even fifty-five–forty-five—too close to call, really. If he knew more about what kind of guy he was dealing with, he could make a better decision. He wanted to do right by Gracie and Katie and the baby, but damn it, he didn't know what the hell that was.

• • •

Gracie lay across the cream-colored duvet cover, iPod in her ears, looking at the ultrasound photo of the baby on her laptop, when the door opened thirty minutes later.

"Gracie?" Katie stood in the doorway, her face lined with worry.

Gracie yanked the buds from her ears. "Go away."

Katie stepped back into the hallway, but she didn't close the door. "Do you want something to eat?"

"No." She was hungry—starving, in fact—but she refused to do anything that Katie or Zack wanted. A hard wad of anger balled in her chest.

"You need to feed that baby."

Crap. Katie was right, but there was no way Gracie was going to admit it. She placed her hand on her stomach and sent a mind message to her baby. *I'll eat something later, after Katie goes to bed*, she silently promised.

"Are you feeling okay?" Katie took a step forward, looking like she was going to feel her forehead or do some other kind of mom thing.

"I'm fine. Just leave me alone."

Katie eyed her in silence, her eyes wounded. Oh, God. It was the same look her mother used to get whenever Gracie had treated her this way. Her throat tightened.

Katie moved to the door. "Well, there will be leftovers in the fridge if you change your mind. And I'm here if you need me."

"Don't hold your breath." Hot tears burned at her eyes as the door closed. She didn't want to need anyone, damn it. How dare they pry into her personal life!

She clicked on her phone. She had a text from Megan—no doubt in response to the photo she'd sent earlier.

Megan: OMG—Your baby pix are so cute!!!! Hard to
  believe that's growing inside U.

Gracie's fingers flew over the keys.

Gracie: No kidding.
Megan: Do U feel it moving?
Gracie: Yeah. I felt it while I saw it on the ultrasound.
Megan: When's it due?
Gracie: November 21st.
Megan: Wow! That's the day Thanksgiving break starts.
  Did I tell U my family's going skiing this year?

The thought of Thanksgiving made Gracie's chest
hot and tight. Oh, Jesus—how was she going to make it
through the holidays? Last year, she'd been xanaxed and
numb. And the year before...She squeezed her eyes shut
against the memory. Oh, God—her last year with her
parents, she'd been such a brat. She'd pitched a huge scene
because she hadn't gotten the Nintendo she'd wanted. She
couldn't believe she'd been such a bitch.

Megan: I'm looking at ski clothes online. Gotta look
  hot on the slopes!

Jeez, Megan's life wasn't just happening in another
town; it was happening in a whole other galaxy. Here she
was, getting fatter by the day, and Megan was looking at
ski clothes. Gracie drew a deep breath and typed.

Gracie: For sure.
Megan: So what R U doing now?

Gracie: Nothing. U?

Megan: Getting dressed 2 go 2 the mall with Christa
and Sarah.

Gracie: Wish I could go.

Megan: Me, 2. How are things with your BM and BD?

Gracie: Awful. Zack's prying into my life. He called my
old teachers.

Megan: He called my mom, 2.

Gracie stared at her phone for a moment, then texted
furiously.

Gracie: Why didn't U tell me?

Megan: Mom said not 2. Plus I didn't wnt 2 make U
mad @ your BD.

Gracie: U shld have told me!

Megan: Sorry.

Gracie: What did he ask?

Megan: Whoz the Dad. He wanted 2 know if it was
Justin.

Gracie: As if.

Megan: Yeah. Mom told him not likely. When they
hung up, Mom pumped me for like ten minutes.

Gracie: What did U say?

Megan: That I don't know. U wouldn't tell me because
I'm a lousy liar.

Gracie: Which is the truth!

Megan: Yeah. You're a brainiac 2 keep me in the dark.

Gracie: Yeah. I'm a real genius. Ha ha.

The only problem, Gracie thought, placing her hand
once more on her stomach, *is that I'm in the dark as well.*

CHAPTER FOURTEEN

"Hey."

Annette looked up over her reading glasses to see a black-and-blue-haired girl in her doorway. "Gracie!" Taking off her glasses, Annette put down the book she was reading and smiled. "Come in, come in. Katie told me you got a job here."

Gracie stepped inside. "Yeah. I'm the recreation assistant. We're going to be doing a picture-frame craft at two this afternoon, if you want to come."

"Thanks, sweetheart, but I have rehab then."

"Oh." Gracie looked at the book on her bed. "What are you reading?"

"*The Awakening*, by Kate Chopin. Dave brought it to me. He brought me a stack of stuff." She indicated a pile of books on the built-in chest by the bathroom.

Gracie looked through them. "Oh! The new Stephenie Meyer! I love her stuff."

"Feel free to borrow it."

"Okay. Thanks." She tucked the book under her arm and turned back to Annette. "How's your leg?"

"Getting better. Want to see?"

"Yeah."

Annette swung her leg out from under the covers and displayed the long scar.

Gracie peered at it intently. "Wow. That looks pretty good."

"Yeah. They took the staples out earlier in the week."

"Staples! Awesome. So if I become a surgeon, I won't have to learn how to sew."

Annette smiled. "I think you'd still need to know how. They use dissolving stitches for sewing up things on the inside."

"Oh, yeah. I guess that's right." Gracie looked at the book facedown on top of her bed. "So it must be cool, owning a bookstore."

"The store's not mine. It's Dave's. He opened it after he sold his insurance agency."

"But he's your husband, right?"

"Ex-husband. We're divorced."

The girl's eyebrows rose. "Really? You don't act like a divorced couple."

She supposed they didn't, Annette thought with surprise. Not lately, anyway. Dave came to see her every day—lately, twice a day.

"When did you two split up?"

"Four years ago."

Gracie sat in the chair by the bed. "How long were you married?"

"Thirty-two years."

"Wow." Gracie tipped the chair back into its recline position. "What happened? Another woman?"

Annette averted her gaze. "That's a rather personal question."

"So he did screw around." The girl eyed her somberly. "Wow. That sucks."

It did indeed.

"That happened to the mom of one of my friends, Gracie continued."

"Really?"

"Yeah. But she didn't know it."

"What do you mean?"

"Well, my mom was driving me home from art class and I saw my friend's dad with another woman in the parking lot of the Holiday Inn."

Annette believed in giving people the benefit of the doubt. "Maybe it was perfectly innocent. He could have been there for a business meeting. The woman could have been a colleague or his sister."

"I don't think he'd be playing squeeze-ass with a colleague or kissing his sister on the mouth."

"Oh. Good point." Annette couldn't help but wonder if any of her friends had ever seen Dave and Linda in a compromising position. How mortifying. "Maybe it wasn't really your friend's dad, but just someone who looked like him."

"Oh, it was him, all right. It was his car. I even memorized the license tag and checked it the next time I was at her house. They matched."

"Oh, dear." That was pretty damning evidence, all right. "How did your friend take it?"

"I didn't tell her." Gracie examined her nails. "I figured there wasn't really any point."

That took a surprising amount of restraint. "Did you tell her mom?"

Gracie lifted her shoulders. "I was going to, then I decided against it."

After she'd discovered Dave's affair, Annette learned that several of her friends had known for some time. "Why on earth," she'd demanded, "didn't you tell me?"

"I didn't want to hurt you," one had said. *As if my husband's continued infidelity would hurt less?*

"I figured you already knew," said another. *And you thought I wasn't doing anything about it?*

"I didn't want to embarrass you," her next-door neighbor had said. *As if being utterly humiliated behind my back was somehow better?*

Annette regarded Gracie now. "Why didn't you tell his wife?"

"Well, I figured if she knew, she'd confront him, and then there'd be a big fight. She might leave him and divorce him, and that would mess up my friend's whole life. Or she might not even believe me, and I'd never get to hang out with Sarah again." Gracie leaned her head back in the recliner. "I guess that last reason was kinda selfish."

"It was honest," Annette said. And showed a high degree of perceptiveness. When you don't want to hear something, it can be easy to discount the source. Would she have believed a teenager telling her something like that? She wasn't sure. "So you just kept the whole thing to yourself?"

"No. I talked to Mr. Malbury—I mean, my friend's father."

Annette raised her eyebrows. "No kidding! That took some courage."

"Yeah, well, I did it in kind of a cowardly way. I called him at work and pretended I worked at his bank, and that there was a problem with his checking account. I figured I could get past his secretary that way."

The girl was clever, she had to hand her that. Annette grinned. "So what did you say?"

"That I'd seen him kissing a blonde at the Holiday Inn and that if he didn't stop seeing her I was going to call his wife. He totally freaked and begged me not to."

"Wow. It must have been pretty awkward the next time you saw him."

"Nah. He never knew it was me." Gracie straightened the recliner. The footrest folded with a soft thud. "You know what I don't understand? He seemed like a really nice guy. He was a really good dad—he took my friend and her brother camping and canoeing, and he was always doing stuff with them." She shook her head. "I just don't get how he could be that two-faced."

"No one is all good or all bad, Gracie. Everyone does things they're ashamed of."

"Yeah, I guess." She placed a hand on her belly, looked down and sighed. "I mean, I'm not one to talk."

"Did you love your baby's father?" Annette asked gently.

Gracie let out a snort. "As if. Hooking up with him was the second worst mistake of my life."

"What was the first?"

Gracie rose from the chair. "I don't want to talk about it."

"I understand. I've made mistakes I don't like to talk about, either."

"They probably weren't very big ones."

Unwanted memories flooded Annette's mind. The night Dave had come home late after a night out with his buddies, reeking of beer and cigar smoke, and crawled into bed. His legs had pressed against hers, his chest warm against her back. His arm had reached around and his palm circled her breast. She'd slapped his hand away, angry that he'd spent yet another evening with his cronies instead of home with her. "Don't you dare touch me," she'd snapped, pulling away. "Go sleep in the guest room. In fact, I want you to move there permanently."

And so he had. It was just down the hall, but it might as well have been halfway around the world. The distance between them had just grown and grown. When she'd learned of the affair, they hadn't made love in more than a year.

By driving him from their bed, she'd destroyed more than their sex life. Too late, she'd realized that she'd destroyed another type of intimacy. Sleeping together had somehow calibrated their hearts.

She looked at Gracie. "Some of my mistakes have been doozies."

"At least you didn't get knocked up."

"Well, actually, my son wasn't a planned pregnancy. Dave and I thought we'd wait a few years before having a child."

"Really?"

Annette nodded. "He turned out to be the biggest blessing of our lives."

"I hope this turns out that way." Gracie put her hand on her stomach. "I hope I can be a good mom."

"You already are."

Gracie looked at her dubiously.

"You're feeding your baby. You're keeping him—or her—warm and safe. You're rocking him to sleep as you move. He thinks your voice is a lullaby. He's connected to you in a way he'll never be connected to anyone else, ever again."

"Wow. I never thought of it like that."

"The way you're feeling about your baby, Gracie… Well, that's the way Katie feels about you."

Gracie stiffened. "She gave me away."

"She gave you life, Gracie. She didn't have to do that. And she gave you the best circumstances to live that life that she could manage. If she had kept you, she would have been doing you a disservice."

"Do you think I'm doing that with my baby?" The defensive tone of Gracie's voice was offset by her wobbling lower lip. "Do you think I'm doing it a disservice by keeping it?"

A lump of sympathy formed in Annette's throat. "I can't answer that for you, honey."

"Well, when I turn eighteen, I'm going to get some insurance money, and I'll be able to support us."

"Money is important. But so is family. You're lucky to have Katie and…and…" Why was it so hard to say the man's name? A part of her, a dark, jealous part, hated that he existed. "…and Zack."

Gracie lifted her head. "They're not really family, and I'm not going to pretend they are."

"Shutting them out of your baby's life would be a mistake, Gracie. In fact, that might be one of the biggest mistakes of your life. You don't want to deprive your child of people who would love it."

"I'll love it enough to make up for it."

"You'll love it with everything you've got, I'm sure of that. But the love that surrounds a child in a family... well, that's something special. That makes a child feel connected. That makes a child feel like it belongs."

Gracie headed for the door. "I've got to go."

"All right, sweetie. Enjoy the book."

Annette leaned back against the pillow and stared at the blank screen of the turned-off TV mounted on the wall. She and Gracie had a lot in common. It was hard to put aside loyalties that you'd held for years. It was hard to look at things in a new way, hard to open your heart to the possibility that there was another side to the story. It could be really, really hard to admit that maybe you'd been wrong—or at least, not entirely right.

You teach what you need to learn. The old saying ran through Annette's mind like a burglar, unwelcome, startling, and intrusive. Not wanting to think about it anymore, Annette blew out a hard sigh and reached for the TV remote.

Zack pushed open the door of the tiny hair salon at the assisted-living center to see Katie standing behind the lone stylist chair, rolling a pink curler into the white hair of a little dumpling of an elderly lady, laughing at something the woman had said. Katie wore flat sandals, a sleeveless blue-and-white-striped shirt, and a short white denim skirt, and her hair was pulled up in a messy updo. His heart chugged hard at the sight of her.

He'd been out of town for the last three days—he'd had a presentation in New York that had been in the works for months—but Katie had been on his mind the whole time.

She was turning into an obsession. At first he'd told himself that it was because he hadn't been with a woman in a while—too long of a while, now that he thought of it. He'd told himself that while he was in New York, he should call one of the models he used to date and blow off some steam, but he hadn't been able to work up the interest.

He didn't just want to be with a woman; he wanted to be with one particular woman: Katie.

Which made no sense. Katie was a full-commitment kind of woman, and he was a live-for-the-moment kind of guy.

Still, she was driving him crazy. The memory of that kiss replayed in his mind over and over, popping to the forefront of his thoughts at the most inconvenient times. He couldn't recall ever being so haunted and intrigued and bewitched by a woman.

Oh, wait—he could. He'd been seventeen years old and crazy about a brown-eyed girl in the most colorful town in Louisiana.

Katie spotted him in the mirror. Her honey-colored eyes widened, and two pink spots formed on her cheeks. "Zack—hello!"

Good. It was only fair that his presence affected her, because God only knew hers affected him.

Her behavior didn't indicate she was glad to see him, though. Her gaze went right back to her client, and she continued putting rollers into the older woman's hair. "When did you get back in town?"

"Just now. I went by the salon and Bev said you were here."

Avoiding his gaze, she looked down at her client. "Dorothy, this is Zack Ferguson."

"Oh, you must be the warmie everyone is talking about!" the white-haired woman exclaimed.

"I think you mean hottie," Katie said softly to the lady.

"Yes, yes, yes. Hottie. And aren't you just! Why, you're a flat-out sheet-scorcher." The woman beamed at him. "I understand you made a fortune playing poke."

"Poke-er," Katie prompted. "You know—the card game."

"Yes, indeed."

Katie grinned. "Zack, this is Dorothy."

Zack dipped his head in a nod. "Nice to meet you."

"Likewise," Dorothy said. "So you're Gracie's father?"

"Yes."

"Oh, she's a darling girl! So sweet. We all just love her."

Zack's eyebrows rose. "Darling" and "sweet" were not descriptions he would have ascribed to the sullen teenager. Perhaps Dorothy had confused Gracie with another girl working at the retirement home.

"She's teaching us how to use Tubeface," Dorothy added.

Zack grinned at the malapropism. "No one does Tubeface better than Gracie."

"She showed us the funniest videos. And she's teaching us to swim the wet."

"I think you mean surf the Web," Katie prompted.

"Yes, that's it. And she turned shuffleboard into a drinking game."

Katie's brows pulled together.

"Oh, don't worry." Dorothy flapped her hand dismissively. "It was harmless fun, and she's not drinking herself. She's too young—and besides, she's got that baby to think about. The only person who had a problem was Iris Huckabee, and that was only because she was drinking prune juice."

Zack laughed.

"The stuff Gracie's teaching us about the computer is amazing. Why, I had no idea Oprah has a wetsite!"

Katie looked at Zack as she picked up a roller. "Gracie told me you've been calling and texting her."

Zack nodded. They'd communicated every day. It was actually easier to get information out of Gracie over her phone than it was in person. "I just saw her in the rec room, and she was calling bingo."

"Oh, she's great at that," Dorothy said. "And she's good at getting the folks on the rehab wing involved in activities, too."

That was surprising. Wonderful, but surprising all the same.

"She and my mother-in-law are bonding," Katie said, affixing the last roller at the bottom of the neat row down the center of the woman's head. "They like some of the same books." Katie pumped the metal bar on the chair, lowering it, and looked at Dorothy. "Ready to get under the dryer?"

"You bet." The woman took Katie's hand, rose from the chair, and bustled to the lone hair dryer. "I won't be able to hear a thing once I get under that contraption, so I might as well say good-bye now." She waggled her fingers at Zack. "Nice meeting you!"

Katie adjusted the helmet over the old lady's head, turned the blower on high, and handed her an Oprah magazine.

"So your trip went well?" she asked, moving toward the back of the small salon.

"Yes." The client had signed a huge contract, which would keep Zack's staff busy for the next few months. Usually he would have stayed longer to kick things off, but he'd left his vice president in charge. He'd been eager to get back to Chartreuse. "How are things between you and Gracie?"

"We're getting along better, as long as we stay away from sensitive topics."

He grinned. "Does that leave you anything to talk about?"

"Sure. Books and movies and music. Baby clothes and birthing classes." Katie opened a door in the back of the salon, stepped in, and came out with a broom. "And school. We visited the high school counselor and got Gracie enrolled. She'll attend most of the first semester and try to bring her grade point average up, then take her midterms online. After she has the baby, she can decide whether she wants to go back to school for her last semester, finish online, or test for the GED. She'll have some options."

"Options are good." Why didn't he seem to have any where Katie was concerned? Only one option came to mind—the same option that had led him to throw caution to the wind that night on the sailboat and to kiss her in the kitchen. He watched Katie set the dustpan at the styling station, beside a picture of Paul—Christ, she even had his picture here!—and start sweeping the perfectly clean floor. "What else is going on?"

"I made Gracie an appointment with a therapist yesterday, but she wouldn't go."

"Can't say that I'm surprised."

"I went instead." She swept up a few locks of white hair. "We talked about a lot of things."

"Such as?"

"The identity of the father." She stopped sweeping and looked at him. "The therapist said we shouldn't push Gracie. When she trusts us more, hopefully she'll tell us about him."

"I'm more concerned about Gracie telling the boy."

"We've been over this." Katie blew out a little sigh of exasperation and leaned on the broom. "Please don't start in on that again."

He didn't want to argue with her. He didn't know what the deal was with Gracie and the baby's father—it confounded him that despite all his snooping, he couldn't find out who he was—but there was nothing to be gained by alienating Gracie. And hell—for all he knew, it might be for the best if the guy just stayed out of the picture. Gracie wouldn't need child support; in addition to her inheritance from her parents' estate, Zack had more than enough money to care for her and her child.

"Okay," he said.

Katie eyed him suspiciously. "Okay, what?"

"Okay, I won't push Gracie about the baby's father."

"Oh." The capitulation seemed to leave her off balance. Her eyes softened. "Oh, good."

He stepped closer. "I'm glad you told me about your father. Now I understand why you feel the way you do about it." He didn't agree—he still thought Gracie should at least give the guy a chance to step up to the plate—but he understood, and he was willing to step back and let things unfold at Gracie's pace. "I'm glad you confided in me."

"Yeah." Her lips curved up in an embarrassed half smile. "Me, too."

"Why didn't you tell me that summer?"

She lifted her shoulders. "I was ashamed."

"Why?"

"I don't know. I guess I felt like there must have been something about me that was basically unlovable, and that's why my father always left."

His chest squeezed around his heart. He'd felt the same way about his parents—that it was his fault they fought, his fault they ignored him. He'd grown up thinking he was fundamentally flawed, and he'd spent his entire life trying to prove otherwise. Not to his parents—at some point, he'd quit caring what they thought—but to himself. He'd thought that success and money would do the trick.

He'd been wrong.

But he and Katie were different. They might have the same wound, but they'd recovered in different ways. He held himself away from others; she reached toward them.

"You know better now, right?"

She lifted her shoulders.

"Kate, you're the most lovable person I've ever known."

She looked at him, her brown eyes surprised, and time fell away. Suddenly they weren't just two people talking; they were two people connected to each other, deeply and intimately.

It had always been that way with Katie. From the

very beginning, there had been some intangible bond, something that drew him to her. It was as if her heart were transparent and he could see right into it and it was a safe place. She made him feel things he'd never felt with anyone else—understood and accepted and whole.

She looked like she was going to say something more, but instead she picked up the dustpan, bent and swept up whatever nearly invisible stuff she'd corralled with the broom, then dumped it into the trash can by her station. She briskly carried the dustpan and broom to the back room. She was running away from him, damn it. Without thinking, Zack followed her.

It was a tiny room, really little more than a walk-in closet with cabinets and a small counter, lit by a dim overhead bulb. Zack stood in the doorway, holding the door open as Katie busily hung the broom and dustpan on the wall at the back. She turned to the shelves on the right and reached for a fresh stack of towels, standing on her tiptoes.

"I'll get those for you," Zack said, stepping forward and reaching over her head. The door closed behind him. Katie stepped back, bumping into him. His hands went out to steady her, and landed on her waist.

A hot shock ricocheted through him; his groin was against her bottom, his nose in her hair. She smelled like herbal shampoo and Katie—a scent that reminded him of summer and desire and a nameless longing—a scent that made him so hard, so fast that he could have been seventeen again.

Neither one of them moved for long seconds. And then his fingers tightened around her waist as if they had a will of their own. His mouth moved against her hair.

She inhaled sharply, then gave a little moan. He dipped his head and kissed her neck, right where her pulse beat, right on the little brown birthmark. He felt her pulse flutter under his lips.

"Turn around, Kate," he whispered. "Turn around and kiss me."

He kept his hands on her waist, feeling her silky shirt slide under his fingers as she turned. Her eyes were dark, almost all pupil in the dim light.

"God, I've missed you," he told her. He felt like he'd missed her before he'd ever met her, like he'd missed her for a couple of lifetimes, like she was a missing part of his very soul.

He heard her quick intake of breath. He pulled her flush against him, then lowered his head and kissed her.

The kiss was slow and tender, but the effect on Katie was like a bolt of lightning—instantaneous, jolting, electric. It was as if someone had put a defibrillator on her heart, shocking it back to life, and all of a sudden her blood was pumping furiously through her veins and feelings, long lost, were flooding her body.

Something had happened in the other room. Zack had given her that look—the one that was tender and open and frank, the one that said, "I get you, I know you, and I think you're amazing," a look that said, "Your secret is safe with me," and "I'm on your side, no matter what." It was the look that had told her, "I'll defend you and watch out for you and make sure you get home safe"—the look that had made her fall for Zack all those years ago. God help her, he'd tripped the switch all over again.

His mouth moved over hers. Zack's hands slid from

her waist to her back. Her arms somehow wound around his broad shoulders.

She could feel the hard length of him, and it set her on fire. She moved against him, fitting her torso to his, her blood hot and fevered. She stood on her toes and wrapped her right leg around both of his, arching her spine, needing to get closer.

She couldn't get close enough. She wanted to touch his skin, to be naked underneath him, to feel him plunging into the part of her that ached to be filled. Desire, ravenous and mindless as wildfire, scorched through her. She needed... she wanted...

"Katie!"

Oh, dear lord. It was Iris Huckabee, her next appointment. Alarm shot through her.

"I—I've got to go."

"Okay." He didn't turn her loose.

"Katie?" Iris screeched again, her voice like metal rubbing against metal.

"Seriously," she whispered to Zack. "I've got to go. The longer it takes for us to come out of this closet, the worse this will look."

"Why do you care?"

"Because..." *She felt like she was cheating on Paul.* A sense of shame snaked through her.

"Dorothy, do you know where Katie is?" Iris shrilled.

Oh, God. Dorothy would know they were still in the closet together.

"Be right with you, Iris," Katie called, breaking away from Zack. "I'm getting some towels." She burst through the door, then realized she didn't have any towels in her hand.

Thankfully, Zack followed her, carrying a stack of towels.

Iris's painted-on eyebrows rose above her cat-eye glasses. "Who's this?"

"I'm Zack Ferguson." He smiled at the woman, then turned to Katie and held out the towels. "You really should put the towels on a lower shelf."

She followed his lead, grateful for the excuse. "Thanks for getting them down for me."

"No problem." As she reached for the towels, he whispered, "See you tonight."

"No." She couldn't. Her emotions felt like a scraped knee.

She was aware that Iris was watching them avidly. Dorothy had pushed the hair-dryer helmet up and was following the exchange as well.

She turned and carried the towels to her stylist station. "It's my book-club night," she said as casually as she could. And if it hadn't been, she would have found some other excuse. "Can Gracie stay with you tonight?"

"Sure."

"Good. Thanks for stopping by." As soon as he left, she'd explain to the two women that Zack had dropped in to discuss arrangements for Gracie.

"I'll see you tomorrow," Zack said pointedly.

Not if she could help it. She needed some time to gather her wits and work through her tangle of emotions.

He mercifully moved toward the door. She turned to Iris and motioned to her chair. "Have a seat."

She heard the door open, and although she didn't turn around, she knew the exact moment Zack left the salon. She felt the air change, felt it lose its charge and fizz, felt it flatten like a left-out soda, returning to the way it had been before he'd walked in.

CHAPTER FIFTEEN

"Good job, Mrs. Charmaine. Now turn around and go back the other direction."

Annette squinted against the late-afternoon sun shining through the window of the physical therapy room, then tightened her grip on the wooden bars on either side of her. It was hard to believe that the boy who'd been such a lackadaisical student as a teenager had turned into such a drill sergeant of a physical therapist. "I'm tired, Blake. I've been walking this cattle chute for half an hour."

"And you're doing great. Let's see you do it again. And this time, put more of your weight on that leg."

Annette scowled. "You're an unconscionable slave driver."

"Unconscionable." Blake shook his head and laughed. "Only an ex–English teacher would use a word like that."

"Humph." Annette rested her weight on her good leg and slowly turned around. "If you'd studied your vocabulary words half as much as you studied your football playbook, you might even know what it meant."

"Ow!" Blake clutched his chest. "You got me with that one."

She took a step forward on her new knee and winced. She was amazed at how much an artificial joint could hurt. "I think you're getting back at me for giving you a C on your book report on that Lindbergh biography."

Blake's eyes widened. "You remember that?"

"I most certainly do." It was funny that she could remember the topics of most of her students' biographical book reports. She'd always learned a lot more about the students than the subjects they'd reported on. "You spelled his name with a *u* instead of an *e*."

Blake laughed. "Spelling never was my strong suit."

"I'll say." She grimaced as she took a step.

He folded his arms across his chest and watched her. "As it turns out, it's a good thing I spent more time on football than English. If it weren't for football, I wouldn't be here with you today."

"And wouldn't that be a tragedy," Annette muttered, taking another painful step.

Blake laughed. "It would be, actually. You've got to work through the pain to get better, and you need someone to make you do it."

Annette was sure there was a lot of wisdom in the statement, but she hurt too much to contemplate it right now. "I fail to see the connection between torturing me and football."

"Well, if it weren't for football, I wouldn't have gone to college. And if I hadn't played, I wouldn't have gotten injured, and then I never would have gotten interested in physical therapy. And since I know what it feels like to be hurt, I can relate to my patients."

"Humph!" She took a pain-racked step and winced. "You relate about as well as you spell."

"Is she giving you a hard time again?"

Annette's head jerked toward the sound of Dave's voice. He was leaning in the doorway, his lanky frame filling it. The sight of him turned her heart into a pattering fool.

"Again? She never lets up," Blake complained.

"Don't I know it." Something in Dave's lazy grin made her stomach flip-flop. "How's she doing?"

"Well, she needs to put more weight on that leg, but overall, she's doing great."

"Glad to hear it."

"You two are talking about me as if I'm not even here," Annette complained.

"That's because I want actual information," Dave said. "If I ask you, all I'll hear is how Blake is trying to kill you."

Blake laughed. "You've got her number, all right."

"I should. I was married to her for thirty-two years."

Before he'd humiliated her in front of the whole town. Everyone knew he'd cheated on her, and they'd no doubt speculated on why. Her abilities or the lack thereof in bed probably had been dissected and discussed ad infinitum. It was one of the reasons she'd moved to New Orleans. She couldn't stand the embarrassment—plus the ever-present fear of running into Dave or that tart he'd taken up with.

It had been awful, trying to avoid them. She'd had to look for Dave's car in the parking lot before she dared go in the grocery store or drugstore or café. She'd begun to feel like a fugitive hiding from the law.

And then there was the whole issue of how everyone treated her. Her friends were sympathetic at first, but they didn't know what to say, and conversations grew stilted and awkward. After a while they started skirting around her, as if she were tainted with something contagious. She probably made them uncomfortably aware that their husbands could light out after fresh tail, too, if they took a notion to, she'd thought bitterly. After all, men remained attractive in their fifties, while women just seemed to grow invisible.

A nurse poked her head into the room, her forehead creased like an oriental fan. "Blake, I need some help!" Her tone was urgent. "Mrs. Anston fell. I don't think she's hurt, but I can't get her off the floor."

"I'll come help," Dave offered.

"Thanks, but only staff and relatives can physically assist residents," the nurse said. "You can stay with Mrs. Charmaine while Blake's gone, though."

Annette started to say that Dave was no longer a relative and therefore wasn't qualified to help her, either, then realized she would only be delaying getting help to poor Mrs. Anston.

Blake headed for the door. "I'll be right back," he called to Dave. "Just keep her walking the ramp."

"Will do."

A feeling of awkwardness settled over her as she found herself alone with Dave. He'd stopped by every day over the past two weeks—sometimes twice a day—and although she didn't want to admit it, she'd begun to look forward to his visits.

Although God only knew why. The man had broken her heart, ground it to bits, and stomped it into dust.

She hated the fact that she was starting to expect him to appear. Hadn't she learned the hard way not to expect anything from Dave? If she didn't expect anything, she wouldn't be disappointed when he let her down.

She hauled herself down the ramp as fast as she could. "You don't have to stay. I'm fine."

"I gave my word."

"Oh, and that means something?"

"It does these days."

She turned at the end of the ramp. She knew he'd gotten sober, and from everything she'd seen and heard, he had changed his ways, but she just couldn't—or was it *wouldn't?*—accept it.

Wouldn't, she reluctantly acknowledged. She didn't want to accept it. His personal transformation had come too late for her. She was being harsh and cold and judgmental and she knew it, but she couldn't seem to help herself. She forced her left leg forward. "What are you doing out here, anyway?"

He lifted his shoulders. "Seeing how my best girl is doing."

My best girl. It was a phrase he'd used when they'd first started dating. In light of his infidelity, it rankled. "I might have been the best, but I wasn't the last, was I, Dave?"

"No." He shook his head, his eyes filled with a forlorn angst. "And that's a mistake I'll regret till my dying day."

"You only regret it because your second marriage didn't last."

"Annette, what Linda and I had..." He ran a hand

across his balding pate. "It wasn't really a marriage. It never was. Not like with you and me."

"Oh, like it was so good between us?" She was glad to feel a surge of anger, glad to have the heat to hide behind. "The nights you didn't come home, the drunken arguments..."

He blew out a sigh. "You deserved a whole lot better."

"Damned right."

Dave smiled. "You never used to curse. It's a good sign. Maybe you're starting to get some of that anger off your chest."

A fresh spurt shot into her bloodstream. "It's not like a backpack I can just take off, David. It's not something concrete and finite. It's like a polluted well. Like systemic poison. Like a bad infection. It runs all through me. It's crippled me. It's wrecked my life."

"I know, sweetie. I know. And I'm so, so sorry." He spoke in a low, gentle tone, the same tone he'd used to soothe their colicky baby when they'd taken turns holding him and rocking him all through the night. The memory hurt worse than her knee.

"Infections can be cured," he continued. "Crippled parts can be rehabilitated. It takes time and work, but it can be done."

And he thought he could help her do that? "You can't fix me, Dave. You broke my heart. You're the breaker, not the fixer."

He lifted his shoulders. "Maybe I can be both."

"No. You can't."

"Well, I figure I'll keep coming around and let you take potshots at me until your poisoned well dries up. You'll feel a lot better if you let go of your anger."

"*You'll* feel a lot better if I do."

"Yeah. You're right." His head bobbed agreeably. "But this is about you."

She gave a derisive sniff. "It was never about me."

"Well, now, that's where you're wrong." His voice was maddeningly calm. "I wasn't perfect, but I always loved you."

I always loved you. The English teacher in her analyzed the comment. Was that past tense, or did the adverb *always* make it present and future tense, too?

To Annette's relief, Blake reappeared in the doorway. "Is Mrs. Anston all right?" she asked.

Blake nodded. "She's going to have a bad bruise, but nothing's broken and she's able to walk." He looked at Dave. "How did Mrs. Charmaine do?"

"She walked back and forth four times while you were gone."

"Wow. You must have really inspired her."

Annette huffed out an exasperated breath. Dave grinned. "Don't know about inspired, but I riled her up pretty good."

"I'll have to try that," Blake said.

"Don't bother. I'll come back tomorrow and do it for you." Dave gave that familiar little wink and ambled toward the door. "See you later, sweetheart."

Sweetheart? How dare he sweetheart her!

But before she could voice an objection, the door closed behind him. It popped open a second later. "By the way—you look really nice in that shade of blue."

Her skin prickled with pleasure, even though she longed to throw something at him. *Dad-blast that man,* she thought as the door swung shut behind him. Dave had a way of getting to her like no one she'd ever known.

"This book club is so much more fun than the one I used to belong to," Lulu said, settling on the red sofa in Anne's living room. "We never had margaritas and nachos at the library. Our book selection is spicier now, too."

"So are some of our members." Anne grinned as she handed Katie an enormous, salt-rimmed glass. A kindergarten teacher, Anne was a sparrow of a woman, tiny and trim, with a pixie haircut. "You've had a lot happen since our last meeting."

That was putting it mildly. Katie's face heated as she thought of the kiss in the closet that afternoon. She took a long sip of her margarita.

"I saw Zack at the Chartreuse Café the other day. My heavens, but he's gorgeous," said Sheila, a baby-faced blonde who worked at the post office.

"He was gorgeous as a teenager, too," said Nicole, a slender stay-at-home mom with sleek black hair sitting on the love seat.

Katie looked at her. "You knew him back then?"

"Not really, but I sure wanted to. I had a powerful crush on him. He was staying with Bruce Langdon's family."

"Oh, yeah," Lulu said. "Arnie Langdon was the mayor. He owned the marina and the boat repair shop. Apparently they didn't earn enough to keep up with his wife's spending habits, though. He got caught dipping into the city till and was run out of town a few years later."

"His son Bruce was a total jerk, but Zack was tall and mysterious and unbelievably cool." Nicole sighed dreamily. "I used to go to the marina all the time, just to watch him."

"I didn't know that," Katie said.

"Yeah, well, he didn't, either." She reached for a nacho on the pepper-themed platter and gave a wry grin. "He never paid me the time of day."

"Now we know why," Sheila said. "He had his eye on Katie."

"Oh, he wasn't interested in me like that," Katie said. "We were just friends."

"With benefits, apparently," Anne said.

The other women snickered.

"No!" Katie protested. "It was totally platonic, until the night it...wasn't."

The women all laughed. Anne lifted her glass. "And what a night that was!"

Katie took a sip of her margarita to hide her discomfort. They were just teasing, but it bothered her all the same. She and Zack had shared something special, and the ribald comments demeaned it.

Sheesh, she really needed to lighten up. There was no point in getting all defensive. She couldn't seem to help it, though. That kiss today had stirred up a lot of old, buried emotions. Or maybe not so buried, she thought guiltily. From the way her feelings had so quickly flared to life, maybe they'd been smoldering under the surface all this time.

Which was just unacceptable. She twisted her wedding ring. She couldn't have been harboring feelings for Zack while she was with Paul. She'd loved her husband with her heart and soul.

"Well, there's nothing platonic about the way he feels

about you now," Lulu added. "I've seen the way he looks at you. His eyes eat you up and lick the crumbs."

"Oh, yeah." Nicole fanned her face. "Just looking at the two of them gives me a hot flash."

Katie picked up her margarita glass and took another long swig. "Nothing is going on." Not if you discounted two kisses and enough sexual energy to run the local power plant. But that didn't matter; she couldn't change the past or who she happened to be attracted to. What mattered was what she did or didn't do, and from this point forward, she was *not* going to get involved with Zack.

She didn't like the way he interfered with her memories of Paul. It was bad enough that she could no longer smell Paul's scent on his clothes, but now she was having trouble picturing his face. When she lay in her bed at night, it was no longer Paul she fantasized about.

Zack had played too big a role in her life already. He was going to leave, and she didn't want him superimposing himself on her memories of her marriage.

Her head was starting to swim from the tequila. She leaned foward and lifted a cheese-and-jalapeño-covered chip from the nacho platter. "He's not going to stay in town, you know. When Gracie has the baby and turns eighteen, he'll head back to Vegas."

"No reason you couldn't go with him," Nicole said.

"Yes, there is. Nothing is going on!" Katie's tone was more strident than she intended.

Bev came to her rescue by changing the topic. "Who wants to open the discussion about the book?"

"Oh, let me make another pitcher of margaritas before we begin." Anne scurried to the kitchen.

"Is Gracie looking forward to school?" Lulu asked.

"It's hard to tell," Katie said. "I think she's nervous. It would be rough enough starting at a new school in your senior year, but when you're pregnant, too..."

The women all nodded. "Why doesn't she just earn a GED?" Nicole asked.

"She wants to take biology and chemistry, and those classes have labs."

"It takes a lot of nerve to go to high school pregnant," Sheila said.

Bev grinned. "Fortunately, that's one thing the girl is loaded with."

"Chip off the old block," Sheila teased her.

Not really, Katie thought. She'd left town when she'd discovered she was pregnant. "Gracie puts on a brave front, but at heart, she's just a scared kid—a kid who had her world shattered when the only parents she'd ever known were killed."

"The poor thing," Nicole said. The other women murmured sympathetically.

"Will she and the baby live with you after she gives birth?" Sheila asked.

Katie nodded. "For a while, anyway. Until she turns eighteen in February, at least."

"And then what?" Nicole asked through a mouthful of chips.

"I don't know." Katie shifted uneasily in the armchair. "I hope she decides to stay and finish school and maybe go to college nearby." Bringing up the future seemed to set Gracie on edge and set back the tenuous relationship they were beginning to develop. "I saw a therapist and she advised me not to push Gracie. She said I need to let her take things at her own pace."

"A baby and school—that's a lot to handle," Nicole said.

"A baby and anything is a lot to handle," Lulu added.

Katie's heart pressed against her ribs. She wished she'd had the chance to find out.

Anne returned with a fresh pitcher of margaritas. "What did I miss?"

"Nothing, Katie didn't tell us any more about the hunk," Sheila said.

"That's because there's nothing to tell," Katie retorted.

"Just wait," Lulu predicted. "There will be."

And that, Katie thought as she reached for her margarita, was exactly what she would not allow to happen.

CHAPTER SIXTEEN

"I'm not going to be able to make the meeting next week," Zack said into his cell as he paced outside the bookstore a week later under a gray and threatening sky. Through the window, he could see Gracie angrily stride toward the back of the store.

They'd had an argument as he'd driven her from her job to town to pick up a copy of *Fahrenheit 451*, which was the senior summer reading assignment. She'd badgered him about applying for her driver's license tomorrow. She still had a week to go before the agreed-upon month was up, and he'd told her she had to wait. She'd gotten angry and called him some names that by rights should move the whole process back another month.

Forming a relationship with Gracie was like climbing a mountain of ice. If things stopped moving forward, they started backsliding. He'd been out of town again last week, and it had caused a setback. Which was why he was canceling his plans to be gone for most of next week.

Overhead, lightning crackled in the sky. "I don't

like the idea that you're putting other clients ahead of me," said the man on the other end of the phone, who happened to be the president of Waterkey International Electronics in Seattle.

"I'm not postponing because of another client. I have a family situation." Family. The word felt weird in his mouth.

"I didn't know you had any family."

That makes two of us. "Look, I'll e-mail you the whole proposal, and my team will teleconference with you if you have any questions. I'll be at your board meeting a week from Tuesday."

He and his client discussed a few specifics, then ended their conversation. Zack sighed as he closed his phone and gazed up at the ominous-looking sky.

He could run the nuts and bolts of his consulting business from anywhere, but there were certain things that required his presence—things like proposal presentations, site inspections, board of director meetings, and zoning commission hearings. He could make Chartreuse his home base, but he still had to travel. He was going to have to leave Gracie and Katie more than he wanted to.

The thought of Katie made his pulse skip. There was something about the woman that just grabbed his heart and messed with his head. Not to mention the way she made him end up doing things he'd determined he wouldn't do again—namely, kissing her.

He couldn't even explain how it had happened. One minute they were talking about their daughter, and the next they were kissing like teenagers.

They'd both kept their distance since the last encounter at the retirement home, but the tension between them was almost palpable. His thoughts were taking a disturbing new twist. He'd always sworn he'd never settle down, but now the possibility was tugging at the corners of his mind.

He'd never thought people could change at such a fundamental level. Whatever you were, you were. Circumstances changed, but not human nature.

Or could it? Now he wasn't sure. One thing was for certain: He needed to stay the hell away from Katie until he figured it out. It wouldn't be fair to make any moves on her unless he was one hundred percent, absolutely sure he could give her what she needed, wanted, and deserved.

Fortunately, keeping his distance hadn't been hard, because she'd been avoiding him as if he had swine flu. They'd talked on the phone about arrangements for Gracie, but Katie had been emitting touch-me-not vibes since that close encounter.

Lightning zigzagged across the sky again. Zack pulled open the door to the bookstore, jangling the cowbell on the door. The air-conditioning was a welcome relief from the muggy August heat.

Dave sat on a stool behind the counter. He smiled and held out his hand as Zack walked in. "Good afternoon."

Zack shook it. "Afternoon. Looks like we're in for some weather."

Dave nodded. "We're supposed to get a heck of a storm."

Gracie ambled up with a paperback copy of the Ray Bradbury book and a handful of manga magazines. "Can I borrow these?"

"Sure," Dave said.

"I'll buy them for you," Zack said.

Gracie looked at him dismissively. "Dave said I could borrow anything I wanted."

"That's very nice of him, but you don't want to take advantage of his kindness. This is a bookstore, not a library, Gracie."

"It's okay. I want her to have them. My treat," Dave said.

Zack blew out an exasperated breath. Gracie plunked down the twenty Zack had given her for the book. Dave made change, and she tucked the book and magazines into that enormous ratty purse on her shoulder. "Thanks."

She pushed the door open, rattling the cowbells, without a glance at him.

"Hey—where are you going?" Zack called.

"To Katie's. I'm not going to stay with you."

"Don't you want a ride?"

"No. I'll walk."

"It's getting ready to storm."

"So? I like walking in the rain."

She'd told him during those first few days in Vegas that walking calmed her down. Given her current frame of mind, a walk would probably do her good. "Want me to take your books?"

Ignoring Zack, she turned toward Dave. "Have you got a plastic bag?"

Before he could answer, she reached over the counter and helped herself. She stuck the books in the bag and, without a backward glance, stalked out the door.

Zack shook his head as the door closed behind her. "Jeez. You'd think I was her sworn enemy."

Dave gave a sympathetic smile. "It's the age. My boy went through the stage, too. She'll outgrow it."

"I hope so. How long does it last?"

"'Til they're twenty-one or so." Sadness filled his eyes. "But then, my son and I went through it again after he was grown."

Zack looked at him, curious about the remark, but not wanting to pry.

Dave stuck his hands in his pockets. "I guess Katie told you about me, huh?"

Zack shook his head. "She hasn't told me anything."

"Ah. Well, you're bound to hear it somewhere or another, so it might as well be from me. One of the traits of a small town is that everyone knows everyone else's story."

Zack waited as Dave rubbed his jaw. "I wasn't much of a dad, and even less of a husband. Only thing I was really good at was drinking. One night I had too much to drink—that is, even more than usual—and I blacked out. I came to in my secretary's bed. That was the beginning of a full-blown affair. Annette caught me in the act and she divorced me." He looked down. "My son wouldn't have anything to do with me after that."

Out the window, lightning flashed across the sky. Thunder crashed a couple of seconds later. "He died before I could make things right."

"I'm sorry."

"Not as sorry as me. Katie was trying to get him to soften up when he..." He stopped, drew a breath, and swallowed. "When he was killed. It's funny how hard it still is to say that. Anyway, I've been sober a year and a half now."

"Good for you."

"Yeah. Well, it takes what it takes, I guess." He shifted

his stance. "At least you don't have a lot of baggage to wade through with your child."

"Not being around for her whole childhood seems like a pretty big piece of baggage to me."

"She'll come around. Just be patient and hang in there."

"Thanks." Zack reached for his wallet. "I'd like to pay for those magazines."

Dave waved his hand. "No. I see Katie as a daughter, so that makes Gracie family, too. I like being able to do things for family." He looked at Zack a moment. "You did a good thing, bringing Gracie back into Katie's life. She and my son...they wanted to have a child awfully bad." He cleared his throat, looked down, and straightened a stack of red-and-white bookmarks on the counter. "You know, Katie is a terrific woman."

"I know."

"She and my son—they were really happy together." He turned the bookmarks around. Zack read the title: *The Art of High-Wire Dancing.* Why did Zack get the feeling that's what Dave was doing?

"I'd like to see her happy again," Dave said.

"I would, too."

Dave bobbed his head as if they'd just settled something. Zack wasn't sure if he'd just been given a blessing to pursue her or warned off from doing so. Either thought made him uneasy.

A smattering of raindrops, fat and heavy, plopped noisily on the roof. Through the glass door, Zack watched one hit the pavement and explode. "I'd better get to my car before it starts pouring."

"Yeah. Try to stay dry."

"You, too."

Dave's lips curved into a wry smile. "Oh, don't worry about me. I'm not going to mess up a year and a half of sobriety."

Zack paused. "I didn't mean..."

"Oh, I know you didn't. That was just a little AA humor." He waved him out the door.

Zack ran through the rain and reached his car just as the heavens opened. Katie's house was only four blocks away, but he didn't know if Gracie had had time to get there. He didn't know if she was a fast walker or more of a stroller. The things he didn't know about that girl far outnumbered the things he did.

He started his engine and his windshield wipers, then carefully edged away from the curb. The wipers gave him only a second of visibility before the windshield returned to a gray, watery blur—a blur that echoed the shape of his life ever since Gracie had entered it and he'd learned that Katie had never really left it.

CHAPTER SEVENTEEN

Rain slashed horizontally against the windows. The branches of the massive oak in Katie's backyard scraped against the porch, screeching like a choir of owls.

Katie wrapped her arms around herself and stared out the living room window. Her last four appointments at the beauty shop had canceled because of the weather, so she'd closed the salon early. She'd sent Bev and Rachel home half an hour ago. Rachel lived all the way in Hammond, twenty miles away, and Bev lived out in the country off a dirt road that crossed Little Tchefuncte River and sometimes flooded.

Katie had texted Gracie and learned that Zack had already picked her up from work at three-thirty. They were probably at Zack's place, safe and sound and dry.

Katie wondered if Gracie shared her fear of bad weather. Probably not, she thought; Gracie had grown up in a nice house in the suburbs, not in a trailer park. Katie had spent too many nights huddled under the blanket of her bed, listening for the freight-train-like roar of a tornado, to ever be comfortable in bad weather. Everyone knew that trailers were unsafe in bad storms, but Katie's mother had never cared. After her nightly rounds with a bottle, her mother could sleep through anything—including the announcements broadcast from the loudspeaker atop the sheriff's car, ordering residents of the trailer park to seek safer shelter.

Lightning zapped the room in eery light and thunder shook the rafters, causing Katie to jump. That was close; the sound and the light had occurred almost simultaneously. Her heart pounding hard, Katie ran her hands up and down her arms. She was so nervous that she was actually shivering.

She'd go grab a sweater, she decided, then head to the kitchen and make some tea. Maybe that would calm her down—or at least distract her.

She'd just stepped into her bedroom closet and flipped on the light when another jolt of thunder, more deafening than before, rocked the house. Half a second later, she heard an even more earsplitting crash—a crash so close and acute and splintering that the walls seemed to shift and the floor seemed to move under her feet.

And then everything went black.

Zack found Gracie hovering under a live oak a block from Katie's house, clutching her purse and the plastic bag to her chest, her hair dripping in her pale face in dark spikes, looking like a drowned kitten. Relief surged through him, rapidly followed by irritation. Didn't she know that standing under a tree was just about the worst place to be in a thunderstorm? He braked, leaned across the passenger seat, and opened the door. "Get in," he said tersely, raising his voice to be heard over the rain.

She stubbornly hesitated. Another stab of lightning gashed the sky as an eardrum-jolting crash shook the ground. Gracie dove into the car.

"That hit something close," Zack said as Gracie closed the door. "You're lucky it wasn't you."

He turned back to the windshield. The wipers swept across the glass, giving him two seconds of vision. And in those two seconds, he saw a billow of smoke ahead on the right.

His heart jumped into his throat. He put the car into gear, pulled away from the curb, and drove through the slashing rain, telling himself that it couldn't be, it wasn't, there was no way that it was...

Katie's house.

"Oh my God!" Gracie stared out the side window as he pulled up to the curb.

Zack bent his head and gazed at the house, straining to see through the torrents of rain. His heart constricted to the size of a pea. The house was split in two, a giant water oak resting in the middle of it, right where half of the living room and the kitchen had been.

And Katie's car was in the driveway.

"Call 911 and stay put," he barked. He bounded out of the car like a jackrabbit on crack and raced toward the house, his eyes stinging, the water sluicing down his face.

"Kate!" he bellowed.

He dashed toward the house. The door was superfluous, because the wall next to it was flat as a pancake. He stepped onto the rubble. "Kate!" he yelled again as another roar of thunder crashed overhead.

Smoke rose from the side of the house. It was likely an

electrical fire; chances were that other live wires could be buried beneath the rubble.

But he didn't have time for caution. Katie might be hurt or trapped or...

"Kate!" he yelled again, taking another step into the wreckage. It was difficult—damn near impossible—to see through the deluge, but something red and moving caught his eye. He blinked against the rain and made out the form of a woman in a red blouse in a doorway. His heart vaulted with joy. *Katie.*

"Stay put!" he yelled. "I'm coming to get you."

He worked his way through the rubble toward the side of the house. Katie stepped out of the doorway of the closet into what was left of her bedroom and stared up, her face pale, her eyes blinking against the rain—no doubt shocked to discover her roof was gone.

She was likely to be in shock, period. She saw him and took a step forward.

He did the same, then heard a sizzle. Oh, God—a raw electrical wire whipped like a snake on the ground between them, shooting sparks, a mere two feet away from her. "Stop! Don't move! There's an electrical wire right in front of you."

She froze. He rapidly threaded his way through the wreckage, then grasped her arms and anxiously peered down at her. "Are you all right?"

She gazed up at him, her eyes large as knotholes, and nodded. Her whole body shivered.

"It's okay. I've got you," he said gently. Bending down, he hooked one arm under her knees and lifted her.

The acrid smell of burning plastic filled the air. Holding her tightly against his chest, he headed through the still-standing half of the living room, past the fireplace mantel.

"Wait," she whispered. "I can't leave..."

He knew what she wanted. Stepping closer to the mantel, he set her down and handed her the urn. As she cradled it, he lifted her again and headed out of the house, carrying her across the lawn. He reached the car to discover that the passenger seat was empty.

Oh, Jesus. Now Gracie was gone. His heart squeezed with alarm as he settled Katie in the front seat. "Just a moment," he told her, forcing himself to sound calmer than he felt. "I'll be right back."

He turned toward the house, ready to head back into it, when he saw a bedraggled black-and-white figure moving beside the house. He dashed toward her.

"Gracie—what are you doing? I told you to stay in the car!"

"I had to get my photo album."

Part of him wanted to explode at her that it wasn't worth risking her life for. Another part of him realized the pictures were her connection to her parents. Yet another part of him was so damned glad that she and Katie were all right that nothing else mattered.

Zack draped his arm around her as they headed to the vehicle and he opened the back door for her.

"Are y-you okay?" Katie asked through chattering teeth as Gracie climbed in.

"Yeah. You?"

Katie twisted around to look at her. "Y-yes."

Gracie looked at the urn in Katie's lap, then lifted her photo album. She leaned over the console between the front seats and gently touched the album to the urn in a solemn toast. She looked at Katie, her eyes warm. "Guess we got the important stuff out."

Katie gave a tremulous smile. "Yes."

Zack's heart squeezed tight. *We damned sure did, and it wasn't a bunch of ashes or pictures.* It was the two women who meant more to him than anything in the world—two women who seemed to be sharing a mother–daughter moment.

A siren sounded in the distance. He leaned his head back against the seat and drew a breath. It felt like the first one he'd drawn since he'd seen that tree on Katie's house. He'd never been so terrified in his life. If anything had happened to either Katie or Gracie...

He refused to let his mind go there. As the sirens drew nearer, he wiped his face with his hands, relieved that the rain could explain the moisture below his eyes.

CHAPTER EIGHTEEN

The events of the next hour were a manic jumble to Katie. Both of the town's two police cars arrived on the scene, followed by fire trucks and an ambulance. Against her protestations, Zack insisted that she let the medics check her for shock. When she passed muster, Zack drove Katie and Gracie to his house.

Katie carefully set the urn on a side table in the entry hall, then went upstairs to change into dry clothes. Only problem was, all of Katie's clothing and most of Gracie's were at Katie's house.

"I'll go back and get your things as soon as the fire marshal clears the site," Zack promised. In the meantime, Katie was forced to change into a pair of Gracie's sweatpants and a junior-sized Nickelback T-shirt.

Zack's gaze flicked over her appreciatively as she came down the stairs, self-consciously pulling the tight shirt away from her breasts. "You look seventeen again."

She tried to offset the way the compliment affected her with a show of casualness. "Thanks for the rescue," she said.

"My pleasure."

She grinned at him. "I was actually perfectly fine, but you looked like you needed a superhero moment."

He grinned back. Instead of easing the tension, her teasing seemed to accelerate it. "I appreciate your efforts to shore up my fragile ego."

There was nothing fragile about him. He'd changed into dry clothes as well, and looked so big and tough and strong in his worn jeans and navy T-shirt that she felt weak-kneed all over again.

The doorbell rang, providing a welcome interruption. Zack opened the door, and Katie saw the Gantors on the porch, holding a batch of warm brownies. The Chartreuse grapevine was apparently in full swing, relaying not only what had occurred to her home but also her current whereabouts. Over the course of the evening, half the town trooped through Zack's house—the police, who reassured Katie they'd keep watch on her house throughout the night to protect her possessions; the fire chief, who told her that the falling tree had caused an electrical fire in the hallway; and a parade of neighbors and friends, bearing cookies and casseroles and offers of help.

Katie's insurance agent, Gordon Stuart, stopped by to tell her he'd already seen the house and started the paperwork to file a claim. She was relieved to learn that she'd only be out the deductible; her policy would cover all her losses.

And it was a good thing, because those losses would be considerable. The tree had crushed through the main support beams, and the fire had ruined much of the rest of the house. Katie's home would need to be rebuilt practically from the ground up—and most of the contents were soaked.

"How long do you think it will take to rebuild the place?"

"It's hard to say," the insurance agent said. "I would guess about four to six months."

"Six months!" Katie exclaimed after she'd signed the claim forms and Zack had closed the door behind the gray-haired man. "Where am I going to live in the meantime?"

"That's simple," Zack replied. "You and Gracie will stay here with me."

"No," Katie said swiftly.

"Why not?" Zack demanded.

"No. It wouldn't work."

"Sure it would. This house has three bedrooms and three and a half baths, plus a garage apartment. There's plenty of room for all of us."

There wasn't enough room in the entire town for Katie to live with Zack, but she didn't want to tell him that. "It's not just Gracie and me; Annette is planning to stay with me when she's discharged from the inpatient rehabilitation next week."

"Well, she can stay here too."

Katie shook her head. "She won't be able to climb the stairs."

"So she can have the master bedroom and I'll move into the garage apartment. We'll make it work, Kate."

"Zack, that's really sweet, but I don't think she'd be comfortable here. She doesn't know you. And considering that you and I...that we..." Oh, God. What was she about to say? Have a history? Are attracted to each other?

Look at each other in ways that make other people in town assume something is going on?

"That we what, Kate?" he pressed.

She swallowed hard and went for the least inflammatory remark she could muster. "We have a child together."

"So?"

"So...she's my mother-in-law."

"You mean your ex-mother-in-law."

Every time someone applied that prefix to Paul or Annette, it rubbed her the wrong way. "No," she said curtly, shaking her head. "Ex implies a divorce, and that's not what happened."

"Former, then. Or late."

He was not going to negate or minimize her relationship with Annette. Anger flashed through her. "Annette will always be my mother-in-law. She's the mother I always wished I had. Nothing will ever change our relationship."

"Okay, okay!" He held up his hands. "Look—I didn't mean to upset you. I think it's great that you two have such a strong bond. I just don't see why her relationship to you means we can't all stay in the same place."

He did, too, damn it. He was trying to force her to admit that Paul was in the past. He thought Paul was no longer relevant, and he wanted her to think that, too. He refused to accept that Annette might be uncomfortable that her late son's wife had—correction; *had* had—a relationship with another man. And he was doing it in such a subtle, low-key, rational fashion that she looked like the unreasonable one.

Well, she would be the height of reason. She drew a deep breath. "Look—I really appreciate the offer, Zack. And I'd like to take you up on it for the next few nights, but as for the long term...Well, my insurance will pay for leasing a place while my home is rebuilt, and that's what I'd like to do."

"There's no decent rental property in this town. I looked into that before I moved here."

And that had been just a few weeks ago. Katie's spirits sank. The market was unlikely to have changed in that amount of time. Still, maybe Eula knew of something. "One of my clients is a real-estate agent. I'll give her a call." Katie rose to get her phone, only to realize that it was back at her house, along with her purse, her car keys, and everything else.

She had nothing. For the moment, she was completely dependent on Zack. "Can I use your phone?"

"Sure."

"And your phone directory, if you have one."

She sank onto Zack's couch and called Eula.

"Oh, I heard, dear, and I'm so sorry!" Eula exclaimed. "I already have several places in mind for you."

Katie's chest relaxed. "You do?"

"Yes. The Mercer place is for sale, and there's an adorable three-bedroom a couple of miles south of town..."

"Oh, I don't want to buy a house. I just need to lease a place for six months or so while I rebuild my home."

"You might want to rethink that, Katie," Eula said. "The nearest rental is in Hammond."

That wouldn't work. Gracie needed to live in Chartreuse in order to attend the local school.

Katie extracted a promise that Eula would do some checking, but when she hung up the phone, her mind was already whirling through other options. She knew Bev would take her in, but Bev and her husband lived in a tiny house with their son who'd moved back after college, and they didn't have room. Lulu and several of her other friends had a spare bedroom, but Gracie needed her own space, and then there was the matter of Annette.

"This is a no-brainer, Kate." Zack handed her a cup of hot tea and sank onto the far end of the sofa. "You and Gracie can stay here, and Annette is more than welcome to come, too. I'll be traveling a lot, so most of the time, you'll have the house to yourselves."

He was right. It seemed like a perfect solution. But still...

"There's no reason this can't work, Kate. Unless..."

"Unless what?"

His dimple flashed as he smiled. "Unless you're afraid you can't keep your hands off me."

Which was exactly what she feared. "In your dreams," she scoffed.

"Actually, that *is* my favorite fantasy." He grinned again, and then his eyes grew somber. "Seriously, Kate— let me help you out. I promise to behave. Nothing will happen between us that you don't want to happen."

Oh, God. That was not a promise that would be of much help—because when she was around Zack, she wanted things she had no business wanting.

"I'll move into the garage apartment," he said. "We won't even be sleeping under the same roof. I won't say or do anything that might make you uncomfortable."

She looked into his blue eyes, so clear and steady, and she believed him. Aside from the disappearing act—which she now knew was not his choice and not his fault—he'd never let her down. He was a man who played by the rules and kept his word. She could trust him.

She wasn't so sure about herself.

"Besides," Zack continued, "we're going to have a seventeen-year-old chaperone living with us."

That was true. There was no reason this couldn't work. It was a logical solution.

And really, she didn't have any other option. She slowly nodded. "Okay. We'll give it a try."

He gave her that smile, the one that made her melt. "Good. It's settled."

But Katie had never felt more unsettled in her life.

"Annette?"

"Sweetie!" Annette switched the phone to her other ear at the sound of Katie's voice. "I heard what happened. Are you okay?"

"Yes, yes, I'm fine. How did you find out?"

"Dorothy went by the drugstore, and Nellie told her that your house was practically cut in two by a tree. I've been trying to call you, but your cell phone went right to voice mail."

"My phone is in my purse, which is still in the house. I literally only have the clothes on my back." Katie gave a small laugh. "Well, truth be told, not even that. My clothes are in the dryer, so I'm wearing Gracie's clothes."

"Oh, no! So all of your belongings..." All of Paul's belongings!

"Yeah. But I did bring Paul's ashes."

Thank God. Annette hadn't wanted to ask. The topic was a sensitive one and she didn't want to make Katie feel bad, but it bothered her that Katie kept his remains in the house rather than putting him to rest.

"We'll have to go back and get the rest of the stuff

in the morning," Katie said. "The fire marshal won't let anyone back in tonight. The thing I'm most upset about is the photos."

All the photos from her wedding and marriage! Annette's chest ached at the thought.

"A lot of them are in the part of the house that's still standing, so I hope they'll be okay."

"They're only things," Annette said. "The important thing is that you and Gracie are all right."

"We're fine."

Annette hesitated, then charged ahead. "I heard you're staying at Zack's house."

"Yes. He has two extra bedrooms upstairs, and he's moving into the garage apartment. You can stay in the master bedroom downstairs when you're discharged."

"Oh, Katie—I don't want to put him out."

"It was his idea. He's going to be traveling a lot, so…"

The thought of staying with a man she'd never met— the father of Katie's child—made her stomach cramp. "Oh, Katie. I don't think…"

"Really. It'll be fine."

She didn't want to upset Katie any more than she already was. For heaven's sake, the poor girl had just lost her home.

The home she and Paul had built together. Annette pressed her hand to her stomach. Oh, dear Lord—Paul had put so much time and work into that place. Every weekend, it seemed, he and Katie had tackled one project or another.

"We'll worry about that later," Annette said. "Right now, you just need to focus on yourself and Gracie. Is she okay?"

"She's fine. She's been pretty much hiding out in her room, which is the same thing she did at my house, but she came out and ate dinner with us. You wouldn't believe the food people have brought over here."

That was one of the advantages of living in a small town, Annette thought; people cared for one another. In times of need, neighbors fortified each other with a timeless symbol of support and nurture: food. When Paul had died, she and Katie hadn't had to cook for a month.

Katie filled her in on the details of the house's damage.

"I'm so glad you're okay, dear," Annette said. "I was terribly worried."

"How about you? How are you feeling today?"

"Oh, I'm fine. I walked the full length of the corridor three times today using a walker. Blake is a slave driver, but he says I'm making progress."

"That's wonderful!"

"I'm about to go downstairs and have dinner with Dorothy and Harold in the dining room. I'm taking the elevator, of course, but it's a much-needed change of pace."

"Have a great time. I'll see you tomorrow."

"Katie, I'll understand if you miss a day. You're going to be awfully busy."

"I'm never too busy for you."

Annette hung up the phone and sighed. She loved that girl, and she knew Katie returned the affection. So why did she feel as if she was losing her?

No, that wasn't what she was feeling at all. She felt like *Paul* was losing her. Which made no sense, but it grieved her heart all the same.

• • •

"We're so glad you could join us for dinner," Dorothy said as Annette shuffled into the dining room using her walker. The hostess led them to a table by the window, and Harold pulled out Annette's chair. Dorothy folded the walker and set it to the side, then smiled as Harold pulled out her chair in a courtly fashion.

Annette never failed to be impressed by Harold's impeccable manners. He had early stage Alzheimer's and often forgot things, but manners were never one of them.

Annette smiled at the couple as she unfolded the black cloth napkin on her lap. "Thank you for inviting me. It's so nice to get out of my room for a change."

"Have you talked to Katie?" Harold asked.

"Yes." Annette was filling them in on the details of her phone conversation when the waitress stopped by their table. "Will there just be the three of you this evening?"

"No, dear," Dorothy said. "We're expecting someone else to join us."

Annette's eyebrows rose in surprise.

Dorothy looked up and grinned. "And here he is now."

Annette turned to see Dave standing behind her, tall and handsome in a navy sports jacket and open-collared shirt. "What on earth are you doing here?"

"Actually, dear, Dave arranged this dinner." Dorothy's eyes gleamed with mischievous excitement. "He thought you wouldn't come if he just invited you to dinner himself."

"He was right about that," Annette muttered. Despite all logic, her pulse thrummed at the sight of him.

Dave pulled out a chair and sat down next to Annette. The spicy scent of his aftershave kicked her heart into a faster gear. "I thought it was time to get you out and about."

"That's right," Dorothy said, nodding vigorously. "It won't be long before you're a goner."

"What?"

Dave smiled. "I think she means before you leave here."

"Oh! Right." Annette smiled at Dorothy.

Dave picked up the cloth napkin and unfolded it. "Sorry I'm late. I stopped by to see Katie."

"How was she?" Annette asked.

"Fine. Shaken up by the whole thing, but fine." Annette watched him drape the napkin across his thigh. She'd always loved Dave's thighs, always loved the way they felt so firm and solid and masculine. It was probably her favorite body part on a man. When Dave used to kneel over her when they were making love, his thighs used to...

"Katie said you're going to stay at Zack's when you're discharged."

Dave's words pulled her back into the moment. She brushed back a strand of hair, hoping her face didn't look as flushed as it felt. "That isn't decided yet. I don't even know the man."

"Living with him is a pretty good way to get to know him," Harold commented.

"That might be the way young people do it today, but it's not exactly my preferred arrangement," Annette said.

Dave and Harold laughed.

"Besides, I'm afraid I'd just be in the way." Annette took a sip of water.

"Well, I have a solution." Dave folded his hands on the table. "You can stay with me."

Was he crazy? "No." She adamantly shook her head. "No way."

"Why not? I have a one-story house, and all the rooms are handicap-accessible. It even has grips in the bathroom."

"Oh, that's right. You bought your house from Mamie Duncan," Dorothy said. "She was wheelchair-bound after her stroke, and her kids fixed the house so she could get around."

Dave nodded. "It's the perfect arrangement for you."

Perfect, except for the fact that Dave would be there. Annette shook her head. "It's kind of you to offer, but I can't stay with you."

"Why not?"

"We're not married anymore."

"So? Katie's not married to Zack."

"I know," Annette said. "And that bothers me."

"You want her married to Zack?" Harold asked.

"No!" The word came out more vehemently than she'd intended. Iris Huckabee and Myrtle Mann at the next table looked over at her. Annette lowered her voice. "I don't want her seeing Zack at all, to tell you the truth, and it bothers me that she's staying with him."

"Why?"

"He's a—a poker dude."

Dave's lip curved in amusement. So did Harold's.

"That's what Gracie called him," Annette said defensively.

Dorothy's eyebrows knit together. "Gracie thinks he pokes her?"

The ladies at the next table leaned forward, dropping all pretense of not listening.

"No!" Annette whispered. "He's a professional gambler."

"Not anymore," Dave said. "He owns a risk-management firm that counsels some of the largest companies in the world. He's entirely respectable."

It figured that Dave would stick up for him. "There's no such thing as a respectable gambler. Besides, I don't think Paul would have liked the idea of Katie staying with him."

Dave leaned back in his chair. "Under the circumstances, I'm not so sure."

Annette stared at him. "You can't be serious! You know how people gossip in this town."

"Well, they're gossiping anyway." Dave took a sip of his water. "They do have a child together."

Annette's chest tightened. "That was years before she met Paul."

"Yeah, but it's still grist for the gossip mill."

"Well, living with him will just make it worse. Everyone will think that something is going on between them."

"What if something is?"

Annette's heart squeezed. She rubbed her temples. "Do you think it is?"

"Well, I wouldn't blame her. He's a toastie, that's for sure," Dorothy said.

Annette looked at her blankly.

"I think she means hottie," Harold said.

Great. A hottie. Just the kind of man she wanted her daughter-in-law living with.

"Katie and Zack's relationship really isn't any of our business," Dave said gently.

Annette's brow knit. "Do you think they're having one?"

"I think we should stay out of it, and I think you'd be a lot more comfortable staying with me."

Comfortable? How did he figure that? Annette opened her mouth to protest.

Dave held up his hand. "Don't give me an answer right now. Take your time and think it over. You'd have a private bedroom and bathroom, and I'd be happy to drive you to and from physical therapy. Katie's likely to need help with that, anyway. She's going to be busy rebuilding her house and seeing to Gracie."

It was true. Neither Gracie nor the storm damage to her house had been in the scheme of things when she'd made plans to stay with Katie during rehab.

She didn't have a lot of options. She couldn't go back to her own home in New Orleans; it had been raised twelve feet off the ground after Hurricane Katrina and now had a twenty-four-step porch, and she wasn't supposed to climb stairs on her own. Her insurance wouldn't pay for her to stay at Sunnyside after the end of the week, and the rates in the rehabilitation wing were too expensive for her to cover on her own.

"I'd welcome the opportunity to help you, Annette." Dave's eyes were warm, his voice earnest. "God knows I owe you. It would be a small way of making amends." He put his hand over hers. The warmth of his palm sent a shock wave through her, right through her skin, straight into her bloodstream. "Promise me you'll think about it."

"Okay." She nodded. "I'll think about it."

In fact, until she made a decision, she was unlikely to think about anything else.

"So here's your room." Zack opened the door to a bedroom at the end of the hall with two dormer windows overlooking the backyard.

Katie followed him inside, carrying the urn. "Oh, this is lovely!" The room was decorated in white and spring green with splashes of coral, in a mix of gingham and floral fabrics.

"The interior designer intended for this to be Gracie's room, but Gracie said it looked too girly." He leaned against the doorframe and watched her as she set the urn on the dresser.

She fingered a green gingham pillow. "Well, her loss is my gain. I love it." She ran her hand over the top of a white vanity with a a tufted floral stool. "This is the sort of room I dreamed about having when I was a girl."

He nodded. "I remember you showing me a room with green checks and flowers in a magazine."

She stared at him. She'd found the photo in an issue of *Redbook* that a bait shop customer had left behind. She used to lie on the saggy mattress on the built-in bunk of her mother's trailer, put a transistor radio under her pillow to drown out the sound of her mother with men in the next bedroom, and pretend that she was in the room in the photo. "You remembered that?"

He nodded. "I remember a lot about you."

She gave him a dry smile. "I'm sure I was at the top of your mind when you were dating Cameron Diaz."

"Actually, I googled you when I was dating her."

She hated the way the news pleased her. She gazed out the window as a distant bolt of lightning streaked across the sky. A string of thunderstorms was rolling through southern Louisiana, and it looked like another one was on its way. "Really? Why?"

He lifted his shoulders. "She reminded me of you."

Cameron Diaz had reminded him of *her*? Pleasure curled through her like a warm toddy.

"So what did your Google search turn up?"

"You and your husband had bought a house." He picked up a vase on the dresser and looked at it. "It made me kinda sad."

"I should have thought you'd be happy for me."

"I thought that, too. That I should be glad you'd gotten what you wanted." He looked at her, and his voice dropped. "I wasn't."

Her chest suddenly hurt, as if her heart was having to work too hard. "Why not? You had what you wanted, too."

"Yeah, but it wasn't what I thought it would be."

The ache in her chest grew stronger. Zack turned the vase upside down and looked at the bottom. "Was your marriage?"

She tried to remember what, exactly, she'd thought marriage would be like when she was a girl. "Yeah. In a lot of ways, it was even better. Maybe not in the candlelight-every-night way, but in a real, we-can-have-fun-even-though-we're-just-doing-laundry way. We—"

The door down the hall banged open, startling Katie.

She heard footsteps in the hallway, then Gracie appeared in the doorway.

"Hey." She looked from Katie to Zack. "What's going on?"

"Nothing," Katie said, feeling oddly guilty.

"Just showing Katie her room," Zack said.

Gracie made a face. "I told you it was lame."

"I think it's beautiful." Katie smiled at Zack. She couldn't believe he'd remembered that magazine picture. If she wasn't careful, she might just begin to think that he'd really cared about her, that their time together had meant something, that he'd felt that gut-deep connection, that he felt it still. And if she allowed herself to think that, she might begin to hope for something more.

And she didn't want more. She twisted her wedding ring. She didn't want to open her heart again. She'd already had more than most people ever got. She wanted to just be content with what she'd had.

So why wasn't she?

"What was it like when that tree fell on the house?" Gracie sauntered into the room and sat down on the bed beside Katie.

A bolt of joy struck Katie's heart. It was the first time Gracie had made any kind of move to seek out her company. Maybe Gracie was starting to thaw.

"It happened so fast, I didn't have time to think. I heard this deafening crash and felt the floor shake, and then the electricity went out, and since I was in the closet, it was dark. I opened the door, and half the bedroom wasn't there, and I smelled smoke. I think I kinda went into shock, because the next thing I knew, you all were there."

"Good thing, huh?"

"Absolutely." She smiled at the girl. "Did your photos get wet?"

"No. Just the outside of the album."

"Good."

Gracie gestured to the urn on the dresser. "Looks like your husband made it out okay."

"Yeah," Katie said. Funny how she and Gracie were bonding over the things they'd saved from the house. Paul and Gracie's parents were bringing them together.

Across the room, Zack's jaw tightened and his lips pressed hard together.

"Do we have any chocolate?" Gracie asked. "I've got a really strong craving."

"Lulu brought over a chocolate cream pie. Let's go see if it's as good as it looks."

Gracie popped up from the bed, and Katie followed her down the stairs. Zack took his time following behind.

"Want some pie?" Gracie asked him when he finally arrived in the kitchen.

"No, thanks. I think I'll turn in." He headed for the kitchen door.

"Where are you going?" Gracie asked.

"I'm going to sleep in the garage apartment."

"Why?"

Zack cut a quick glance at Katie, then rubbed his jaw. "Well, Annette will be moving into the downstairs bedroom."

"Not tonight."

Zack shrugged. "Might as well go ahead and get used to it." Without looking at Katie, he walked out the door.

CHAPTER NINETEEN

The morning after the storm, the world seemed wiped with Windex. The air smelled fresh, the grass was a perkier shade of green, and the sky was a dazzling azure. The beauty of the day was a stark contrast to the wreckage of Katie's house.

Katie surveyed the damage, her chest tight, as she climbed out of the U-Haul Zack had rented in Hammond earlier in the morning. "Good heavens," she breathed. The trunk of a pine tree stood like a giant scorched matchstick, the victim of a lightning strike. The top half of the seventy-five-foot-tall pine had fallen on the enormous water oak in her backyard, knocking it over. The oak lay through the center of the house, its branches an incongruous fresh green, its root-ball twice as tall as Katie.

"It's even worse than I thought," Katie said.

"Well, let's see what we can salvage," Zack said.

Instead of wading through the debris, they went to the kitchen door, which was, ironically, locked. Katie's hand shook as she inserted the key. "My insurance agent said the kitchen was a total loss."

She pushed the door open and gasped. It was beyond a loss; it was gone. Sunshine streamed onto the floor, which was covered with splintered beams, crumbled drywall, and broken furniture. The back and side walls lay flattened beneath the trunk of the enormous tree.

Katie tried to draw a deep breath, but her rib cage seemed to have shrunk. She bent and picked up part of a photo from under the tree. It was one of her favorites—a picture of her and Paul on their wedding day, the one where he was feeding her a piece of cake. The picture had been cut by the broken glass of the frame, and what was left was wet and warped.

Tears formed in her eyes. "All the pictures on this wall..." Her voice choked. The pictures were now under the trunk of the tree. All the mementos of her life with Paul—their vacations, their holidays, their wedding— were gone.

Zack put his arm around her and pulled her close. "Hey—I'm sorry." She smelled his shaving cream on his neck. His chest was hard and firm, and she could feel the bulge of his biceps as his arm curled around her. She knew he meant to comfort her, but being consoled by Zack right now made her feel disloyal to Paul.

She pulled away. "Let's see what the bedrooms are like."

She led the way through the hallway to Gracie's room, which looked just the same as before the storm, except for the view out the window of the overturned tree's roots. "Thank God," she breathed. Gracie's things, at least, were intact.

She made her way down the hall to her room. Half of it was gone. The wall on her side of the bed was missing, smashed by the tree. The other half of the room looked weirdly normal.

Zack stepped in behind her. "Jesus." He wasn't looking at the leveled wall. He was looking at the things on Paul's nightstand—a baseball cap, a key chain, a book about the NFL. A trouser press holding a man's jacket rested beside it.

Her face heated. She suddenly saw the room from a fresh perspective, the way Zack must see it. She could only imagine what he thought—that she was pitiful, that she was weird, that she was stuck, that she couldn't move on. All of which might be a little true, but mostly—at least, lately—she simply didn't notice the stuff on Paul's nightstand, because she was so used to it being there. At first she'd agonized about what to do with it. When she cleaned house, she'd just dusted around it. And then, after a while, it was a habit, and she didn't even really see it.

One thing she knew for sure: She didn't want Zack standing there, looking at it.

Apparently he didn't want to be there, either. "I'll go bring in some more boxes."

He turned on his heel and left the room.

His stomach wadded into a giant spitball as he headed out to the truck. He'd known Katie kept pictures of her husband all over the house, but keeping his things on the nightstand, as if he still slept with her...

Well, it was pathetic. Downright pathetic. He knew she'd loved the guy—he could see it in the way her eyes went all soft when she talked about him, and the way she still wore her wedding ring—but something about seeing Paul's stuff on the nightstand had hit him right in the gut.

Did she look over at that stuff before she turned out the light and pretend he was in the other room, about to come to bed? Did she lie there and fantasize about how they would make love when he joined her in the queen-sized four-poster? Did she touch herself and pretend it was her husband doing the touching—the way Zack thought about Katie?

Yearning, sharp and intense, hit like a hunger pang. What would it be like to be loved like that? To know that a woman like Katie cared about you so thoroughly and completely, to know that she carried you in her heart and soul? The thought bounced around an empty place inside him like an echo in the Grand Canyon.

He muttered a curse, grabbed a box, and stalked into Gracie's room, where he packed up her things in record time, then carried them to the U-Haul.

A few minutes later, he stepped back into Katie's room to see how she was progressing.

She'd cleared off that shrine of a nightstand, thank God—along with the top of the dresser across the room. But he found her in the walk-in closet, holding a man's shirt as if it were a religious artifact. One entire side of the closet was filled with men's clothing. Apparently she hadn't gotten rid of any of her husband's belongings.

His muscles tensed. He cleared his throat to alert her to his presence.

She whipped toward him, her face alarmed. He felt like he'd interrupted her in the middle of a prayer or meditation or something.

He put a hand on the closet doorjamb, trying to look casual, and forced his voice into what he hoped was a normal tone. "Want some help?"

"No." She folded the shirt as if that was what she'd been doing all along, instead of gazing at it like it was the Shroud of Turin. "I've got this covered."

"Okay. Let me know if you need more boxes."

He stalked toward the living room, trying not to think about her in that closet, trying not to think about the look on her face or the way she'd held that shirt. That empty spot inside him stretched wider and deeper. He tried to reason it away. Why did he care, anyway? It wasn't any of his business.

But it felt like his business, and he couldn't get it off his mind.

He waited half an hour, then went back in to check on her. A stack of boxes stood outside the closet. He gestured toward them. "Want me to take these to Goodwill or something?"

"No."

"Okay. I'll take them to the storage unit, then." He'd rented one for her furniture when he'd picked up the U-Haul.

"No. I want to keep them with me."

"All of them? Everything that was in this closet?"

She tilted her chin up, as if daring him to argue. "Yes."

She wasn't ready to let go. A lump the size of the moon lodged in his throat. Okay, it was no skin off his nose. Why should he care? And yet, part of him wanted to punch his fist through the wall.

Which made no sense. He was crazy about Katie, but he wasn't planning on doing anything drastic or permanent. It wasn't like he seriously wanted to take her husband's place.

He needed to get a grip. If she wanted Paul's stuff at his house—why the *hell* did she want to bring her dead husband's stuff to his house?—then that was where he'd put it.

He ran a hand down his face. "Okay. I'll load these boxes with Gracie's stuff."

Zack picked up one of the four boxes carefully labeled "Paul"—not "Paul's Pants" or "Paul's crappy suits." Just "Paul," as if the man himself were in there—and carried it out to the curb.

Thirty minutes later, a blue Toyota parked in front of the house as Zack started to load the pile of boxes into the bed of the truck. A familiar lanky man climbed out. "Thought maybe you and Katie could use some help."

"Dave—hello!" Zack climbed down from the back of the truck and shook his hand. Dave had come by yesterday afternoon to check on Katie and Gracie, and he'd offered to come back today to help clean things up.

The older man surveyed the house, then shook his head and let out a low whistle. "Looks even worse in the light of day."

"Yeah." Zack nodded. "It's a mess."

"Let me give you a hand with those boxes," Dave said.

Zack hesitated. "Are you supposed to be lifting things with your heart condition?"

"As long as they're not too heavy, I should be fine. My doctor wants me to exercise."

Dave bent to pick up a box, then froze when he saw the name "Paul" scrawled on the side in neat magic marker. "Is this the urn?"

"Oh, no. Katie wouldn't leave the house without it last night. It's at my place."

His frown relaxed into relief, then his brow furrowed again. "So what's in here?"

Zack waved a hand at the other boxes. "Paul's clothes and stuff."

"Wow. She's still got all his things?"

"Looks like it."

Dave blew out a sigh and shook his head. "She needs to let go and move on." He ran a hand over his head. "Maybe this disaster is just what she needed."

"What do you mean?"

"Sometimes we have to lose the things we're attached to before we can see the stuff that really matters."

"She already lost the only thing that ever mattered." The words came out harsher than he'd intended. Hell, he hadn't really intended for them to come out at all. He was talking to Paul's father, for Christ's sake. At least Dave didn't seem to take offense.

"Katie's stuck in the past," Dave said. "She's hiding behind it."

"Hiding, how?"

"Well, when people are afraid of something, they divert their attention so they don't have to face it. Some people hide behind booze or work or computer games. Others use hobbies or shopping or parties or a defeatist attitude, or staying busy all the time—or traveling and dating lots of beautiful women."

Zack chose to ignore the obvious jab at his lifestyle. "What do you think Katie's afraid of?"

"Of moving on. Of getting her heart broken again."

Zack picked up a box and shoved it into the truck.

"Do you think she'll ever be able to feel about someone else the same way she felt about Paul?" He hadn't meant to ask the question; it just kind of burst out. What was with him today? He climbed into the bed of the truck and pushed the box to the back.

"Oh, I think she'll fall in love again. But I suspect every love is different."

Meaning what? Any other love would be second-best?

"But I'm not really qualified to answer that," Dave continued. His mouth pulled into a rueful smile. "I've only loved one woman my whole life. I just did a really bad job of letting her know it." He lifted a box and shoved it into the truck, breathing hard.

Zack looked at him, worried about the older man's heart. "You okay?"

"Yeah. Just not in as great a shape as I used to be."

"Tell you what—why don't you go inside and give Katie a hand packing things up? I'll handle these boxes."

"Okay. Guess I'll do that." Dave clapped him on the shoulder. "Thanks for being here for Katie."

"Where else would I be?"

Wherever the hell you were between 1992 and now, Zack's brain chided him. He watched the older man amble toward the house, his words replaying in Zack's mind.

Apparently Dave thought Zack was afraid of something, too—probably commitment. He'd had plenty of women tell him he was a commitment-phobe.

And hell, he was, but that didn't mean he was hiding from anything. Just because he chose not to get all tied up and emotionally entangled didn't mean something was wrong with him; it just meant he was smart. He'd spent the first seventeen years of his life trying to get his parents' affection, and all it had gotten him was pain.

He'd seen too many people carry neediness from a bad childhood over into adulthood, only to get hurt again and again. He refused to stay stuck on that hamster wheel.

But nearly losing Katie yesterday—well, it had scared him to death. When it came to her and Gracie, he damn sure hadn't felt detached and uninvolved. He felt involved up to his eyeballs.

His thoughts were interrupted by the arrival of Lulu and a gangly man in cowboy garb. "Hey there, Zack!" Lulu waved as she stepped out of a red pickup truck, wearing pink jeans, pink sneakers, and an orange-and-pink shirt. "My husband and I came to help out."

Rachel and Bev and their husbands drove up right behind them, and were promptly joined by eight of Katie's neighbors and the youth group from the Methodist church.

By twelve-thirty, the tree had been sawed and removed, and all of the retrievable possessions had been boxed up, carted away, and stored. The volunteer effort had apparently been well coordinated, because someone had brought a tray of sandwiches, someone else provided a cooler of cold drinks, and yet another person had baked several dozen brownies. Lulu set the feast out on the tailgate of her red pickup and everyone ate their fill.

"Thank you so much," Katie called as everyone trooped back to their homes or cars.

"Glad to help. Just a little payback for how you helped

me out during Hurricane Katrina," one of her neighbors said.

"And you've saved my sorry ass from more messes than you can shake a stick at," Lulu said.

"You were a rock for me when Sydney got sick," said another.

Katie's eyes grew misty. "Aw. You guys are the best."

"You have some great friends," Zack said when they'd left.

"Yeah," Katie said. "I'm really lucky."

"There's no such thing as luck. You've got good friends because you're a really good friend yourself."

She lifted her shoulders. "That's what life's all about, isn't it? Caring for others."

"It's that simple, huh?"

"Pretty much." The corners of her eyes crinkled as she smiled. "Just that simple, and just that complicated."

She really believed that. To Katie, life wasn't about achievement or challenge or winning or money or any of the things that drove most people—the things that had always driven him. To Katie, life was about caring for others.

The very thing he'd spent his whole life avoiding.

A bead of sweat trickled down his spine. Was it possible she was right? Was it possible that keeping his distance was the bigger risk? He'd always been a loner, figuring that you couldn't get burned if you didn't get near the fire. Maybe always feeling cold was an even worse fate.

Maybe Dave had been onto something, after all.

CHAPTER TWENTY

"Annette—are you sure about this?" Katie asked for the umpteenth time four days later.

"Yes, dear. It only makes sense." Annette zipped her makeup bag and set it in her purse, then placed her purse beside the packed suitcase on the floor of her room in the rehabilitation wing. "Besides, I'm making such good progress that Blake says I'm likely to only need two more weeks of therapy instead of three."

Katie regarded her with worried eyes. "If you change your mind at any time..."

Katie was such a mother hen. Annette smiled at her reassuringly. "I know, dear. I can call you. And if I need to, I will."

"Don't wait until you need to. Call me if you feel the least bit uncomfortable."

"I will. But I'll be fine. I lived with the man for thirty-two years. I'm sure I can stay with him for two or three weeks."

A knock sounded on the door. Dave walked in, wearing a blue polo shirt and a pair of khakis, his face freshly shaved, his hair combed. He looked fit and dapper, and he smelled like Aramis. As always Annette's foolish heart jumped at the sight of him.

"All set?"

"No," Annette said. Now, why had she said that? It had popped out automatically, the way the word *fine* popped out when people asked how she was doing. She guessed that was her knee-jerk reaction to Dave. She'd had an automatic no answer to his every suggestion even before they'd split.

"Well, you better get that way." He pulled a wheelchair from the hall and wheeled it into the room. "Your chariot awaits."

Annette made a face. "I hate those things."

"This is just to get you from your room to the car. After that, you'll be on your own."

"I'll wheel your suitcase," Katie volunteered.

Now that the moment had come, Annette felt a little nervous. Her palms grew damp as Dave helped her into the chair.

A few minutes later, he opened the passenger door of his Camry just outside the entrance. Dave got her safely inside, then Katie bent and kissed Annette's cheek. She turned and hugged Dave. "Take good care of her."

"I will."

Dave was merely giving her a place to stay; she was perfectly capable of taking care of herself. Annette opened her mouth to say as much, then promptly shut it. Good heavens, what kind of crass ingrate would say such a thing? Her mother would roll over in her grave. For the second time since Dave arrived, she realized she wasn't accustomed to treating him with the same courtesy she afforded other people. The thought stung her conscience.

Katie looked at Annette, then Dave. "Call me if you need anything."

Annette nodded.

So did Dave. "Will do." With a wave to Katie, Dave closed Annette's door, rounded the car, and climbed in.

As he started the engine, Annette felt a moment of panic. She would not—repeat, *would not*—let him back into the driver's seat of her heart.

Dave pulled the car into the driveway of a low-slung ranch house on the east side of town and killed the engine. His gut knotted with teenager-ish anxiety. He hoped Annette would approve of the place. "Sit tight. I'll come around and help you out." He grinned. "Just like when we were dating."

"Not exactly," she said dryly. "Back then, you weren't helping me with a walker."

His smile widened. "Back then, it was just an excuse to take your hand."

She rolled her eyes. "Like you needed an excuse."

"I thought I did." She'd sat next to him in sophomore English at LSU, and he'd been smitten from day one. It had taken him two weeks to work up the nerve to talk to her. "I have a confession to make. I didn't really forget my pen the day I asked if I could borrow one. I deliberately left it in the dorm."

"What if I hadn't had an extra?"

"I would have asked to borrow your notes. Which

would have been even better, because then I'd have had to find out where you lived to return them."

Something flickered in her eyes. She looked away before he could name it.

"You were so beautiful I could barely breathe in that class," he said.

"Well, that's certainly changed."

"No. You're just as beautiful as ever."

She rolled her eyes. "And you're just as full of it."

Grinning, he circled the car, opened the back door and pulled out her walker, then opened her door. He held out his hand to help her up, and a rush of heat shot up his arm as she gripped his fingers. She quickly released his hand and took hold of the walker. He pulled her suitcase out of the backseat and wheeled it behind him as he walked to the porch. "You move pretty well with that walker."

"I can't wait to get rid of it. I can move to a cane as soon as the cast comes off."

"You're doing great." He unlocked the door and pushed it open, wondering what she would think. He'd purchased this little place after he'd divorced Linda. The house that he and Annette had lived in had been bought years ago by a young family raising three children. He'd driven by it the other day, and noticed that they'd painted the shutters black and relandscaped the front yard— all things he probably should have done when he and Annette had been together.

"The place needs a little fixing up," he said apologetically as Annette stepped through the front door. She paused and looked around. The room had a sofa and a TV, and that was it. "I'm going for the minimalist look," Dave joked.

"You've achieved it." She moved farther into the room. "Looks like Linda cleaned you out."

"Actually, she didn't. Marty talked me into getting a prenup."

"Marty's been a good friend to you."

Dave nodded. "The best. He's my AA sponsor."

Her eyes widened. "Marty? I never knew him to take a drink."

"That's the whole point of AA. He's been sober twenty-seven years."

"Wow. And he still attends meetings?"

"Yeah. To help newbies like me."

"I have to admit, I'm surprised. I always pictured the meetings full of people just holding on by their fingernails."

"There are some of those," Dave said. "But most members have been sober a while."

"I had no idea."

"Yeah, well, helping others achieve and maintain sobriety is part of the program."

She looked at him, really looked at him, as if she were seeing him for the first time in a long while. "And you're working it."

"Trying to." He gestured down the hall. "Your room's back here."

She followed him to a room with a bed, two nightstands, and a matching dresser. He'd bought a blue floral comforter for the bed and a reading lamp. He'd put the lamp on the nightstand on the side of the bed she used to sleep on.

She smiled. "This is nice. It all looks brand-new."

He shrugged. "I didn't want to keep any of the

furniture Linda had picked out, so I let her take it. You were my incentive to start furnishing this place."

"Oh, Dave—you shouldn't have done that."

"Sure I should have." He swung her suitcase onto the bed. "Need some help unpacking?"

"No, I can get it."

"Do you need anything washed? I have a washer and a dryer."

"No. Katie took care of my laundry."

He watched her pull three sets of jogging suits out of her bag and stepped forward to take them. "I'll put these in the bureau for you." He put the pants and T-shirts in a drawer, then returned to her suitcase. Sitting on top were three pairs of lacy black panties and three lacy black bras. His mouth went dry. The thought of Annette in nothing but her undies stirred up a hornet's nest of memories. The night they'd made love at the river. The first time they'd made love after their wedding. That time at the cabin in the woods.

He realized he'd been standing there, staring at her underwear.

The fact didn't escape Annette's notice. "Developed an underwear fetish?"

"I've always had one where you're concerned."

"What about Linda? Did you like her underwear, too?"

Dave sank down on the bed. "It wasn't the same with her. It was never the same."

"Is that so." Her tone was dry and disbelieving.

"Yeah." He looked up and met her gaze. "I never intended to get involved with her. I don't even remember the first time. I was in a blackout. When I came to, I was in her bed." He looked down at his fingers. A hangnail hung in a red gash off his thumb. "I was horrified."

"Yeah, I bet."

"I was." He needed her to believe him. "My first thought was 'Oh, God—what have I done? I've got to get out of here and make sure Annette never finds out and it never happens again.'"

"Failed on both accounts." Her head tilted to the side as she regarded him. "Is that really the truth? Is that really how it started?"

He raised his hand. "Swear to God."

"I hate to think how many times you swore to God you'd stop drinking."

"This is different. Now I believe in him."

The skepticism in her eyes softened for a moment. And then she lifted her chin, and it was back. "For a guy who didn't want to get involved with Linda, you sure got in awfully deep awfully fast."

"When you kicked me out, I had nowhere to go. I couldn't stay in the motel forever. She offered to let me stay there, and, well…"

"I'm sure it was a terrible hardship."

"Hey—I was a total ass. A drunken, stupid, take-the-easy-path ass. I'm not trying to excuse my behavior. But I want you to know that Linda and I—well, it was never what you and I had."

The hard glint in her eye softened again. "How was it different?"

"We never really talked to each other. There were a lot of awkward silences, and we didn't make each other laugh. We just didn't have any fun together."

"Not even in bed?" The skepticism was back.

"Well, that part was exciting at first, because it was new, and she..." He hesitated. He wasn't supposed to say anything that might hurt her or put blame on the person he was making amends to.

"She what?"

"Never mind."

"No. I want to know what she had that I didn't have."

"She didn't have a thing."

"You started to say something, Dave. If it wasn't something she had, it was something she did. What was it?"

"She...wanted me." He looked down at his hands again, embarrassed. "It's no excuse, I know that. But... I felt like such a failure with you. Hell, I *was* a failure. Every time I looked at you I saw how unhappy I made you, and I just felt like the world's biggest loser. Linda acted like I was wonderful and clever and exciting and..." He stopped and swallowed. "Hell. She made me feel good about myself."

Annette stared at him. He couldn't read her expression, couldn't tell if it was disbelief or derision or surprise. He looked back down at his thumb. His guilt felt like that—a hangnail of the heart, raw and ugly and painful. "Of course, that didn't last. She figured out I wasn't much of a prize pretty quickly. And as for her—well, she never could hold a candle to you."

The phone rang. It felt like a reprieve. He jumped to his feet. "I'd better go get that."

She nodded.

He hurried from the room, glad of an excuse to escape, aware of Annette's eyes following him with that inscrutable expression.

• • •

"So you've been living with Zack for two weeks now. How's it going?"

"Okay." Katie cradled the phone against her shoulder as she straightened her salon before it opened for the day. Her friend Emma had called from Italy, and they'd already talked for ten minutes. Emma had told her all about her family, the things they'd done on their travels, about her upcoming TV special in late October and how Harold and Dorothy planned to join them. Katie had told her about the storm, how she'd hired a contractor and begun rebuilding her home, and how she and Gracie seemed to have reached at least a détente.

But she'd been uncharacteristically hesitant to talk about Zack. Probably because she didn't quite know where things stood between them herself.

"Well, aren't you a fount of information."

Katie swiped the feather duster over nail polishes at the manicure station. "He's gone a lot."

"How much is a lot?"

"About five days a week."

"So what happens on the days he's there?"

"Nothing, really. Just normal stuff. We eat together."

"Who cooks?"

"We all take turns."

"He cooks? And Gracie cooks?"

"Yeah. Gracie does a lot of Hamburger Helper, but still, she cooks. And Zack is amazing. He never does anything halfway. He's bought books and videos on cooking, and he takes it very seriously. He's really good. Even Gracie thinks so."

"Wow. There's nothing sexier than a man who cooks. Except maybe for one who cleans up after himself."

"Actually, Zack does that, too."

"Honey, you've got a keeper there."

"I'm not looking for a keeper." Katie decided to change the topic. "Gracie is feeling the baby move pretty regularly now. She's starting to a childbirth class at the hospital this week."

"Are you going with her?"

"No. She says she wants to do it alone."

"Maybe she'll change her mind."

"I hope so." Ever since they'd moved into Zack's house, Gracie had been less hostile, but she still kept Katie at a distance. "She's still pretty withdrawn. She spends a lot of time alone in her room."

"Sounds like that leaves you and Zack with lots of time alone."

Too much time alone, Katie thought, running the duster over the product display counter.

"So what do you two do when you're not cooking and eating?"

"Watch TV, listen to music, check out progress on my house, talk."

"What do you talk about?"

"Anything and everything." Literally. From the origins of life to politics, from their childhoods to the possibility of life on other planets. It was the darnedest thing, the way they could talk so easily to each other.

"So is a romance blooming?"

"No." The word came out fast and hard.

"Why not?"

"I don't want to get involved."

"That isn't much of a answer," Emma said.

"Well, it's the best I can do."

"Do you have feelings for him? Is there any chemistry?"

Oh, there was chemistry, all right so intense it was a wonder they didn't both burst into flames. She couldn't spend any time alone with him without remembering the kisses they'd shared and fearing she was about to kiss him again. "Chemistry's not enough."

"Ooh, sounds like a yes to me."

"Emma, I just don't want to get anything started."

"Why on earth not? You know him well, you like him, and you have a good time together."

"There's more to life than that."

"Yeah. There's sex."

Katie shifted the phone to her other ear.

"I don't want to end up heartbroken again."

"What makes you think you will?"

"For starters, Zack isn't planning on staying in Chartreuse. Then there's the fact he's a commitment-phobe who's never had a long-term relationship."

"Lots of men change their minds about commitment when they meet the right woman. And you could move, or he could decide to stay in Chartreuse."

"Yeah, well, if we get something started and it doesn't last, it'll be tough on Gracie."

"Gracie's nearly grown. She'll be starting her own life."

"Emma, I don't want to get my heart broken again."

"That's the second time you've said that."

Katie sigh, I guess that's the bottom line. It hurts to lose someone you love. I don't want to risk it."

"Honey, you're letting fear steer your boat. Do you want to live alone the rest of your life?"

"No."

"Well, then, you're going to have to take a chance at some point in time. And chances at love don't come around every day."

That was true. After Zack, she'd waited twelve years to find Paul.

"I want you to ask yourself, 'When all is said and done, which will I regret more: not taking a chance on love, or giving love a chance?'"

"That's not the question." Katie frowned. "The question is, 'What if I take a chance and lose?'"

Emma sighed. "The Katie I used to know wouldn't look at things in those terms."

"That Katie hadn't been widowed."

"Well, this Katie is going to end up growing old by herself if she doesn't change her attitude." Emma's voice softened. "Just open your heart to the possibility." A baby's cry sounded through the phone. "Oops—I've got to go. Just think about it, Katie. And think about coming to Italy to do my hair for the special."

Katie hung up the phone, more confused than ever.

CHAPTER TWENTY-ONE

Gracie stood uncertainly in the hospital hallway, looking into a meeting room, where a woman with short, dark hair leaned against a lectern.

"Is this the birth class?" Gracie asked her.

"Yes. Come in, come in." The woman smiled and motioned her in. Gracie took a couple of steps forward, then stopped. Oh, jeez. The participants were all couples, and they all looked twice her age.

"Come on in." The woman waved her arm again. Eight pairs of eyes stared at her. Gracie swallowed, squelched down the urge to flee, and slunk into the room. She sank into the first available chair at the back.

"We were just sharing our names with each other," the woman said. "I'm Marianne Caville. Let's go around the room and bring our new arrival up to speed."

"I'm Misty," said a pretty blonde in the front row. She turned to the handsome man beside her. "And this is my husband, Steve."

"I'm Carla, and this is Jack," said the long-haired brunette sitting next to her.

"I'm Sara, and this is my husband, Pete." A fireplug of a woman who had to be close to forty put her hand on the leg of a balding, beefy man in the second row.

"I'm Tamika," said the woman in the red sundress two chairs down. "And this is Richard." The man in the Hawaiian shirt beside her lifted his hand.

Everyone turned and looked expectantly at her. "I'm Gracie." She put her hand on her stomach. "And this is my baby, as yet unnamed."

"Hi, Gracie," everyone called in unison, as if it were some sort of cult.

Marianne smiled out at them. "We have a lot to cover, so let's get started. As you know, the purpose of this class is to assist you in labor. We'll teach you pain-management techniques like breathing sequences, massage, and hydrotherapy.

"Now, each of you will need a birth partner. The baby's father is the ideal partner, because the birthing process will help him bond with his child." She paused and looked at Gracie.

Gracie's stomach went tight. Oh, God. She wished she could just crawl under the tile.

"If the father is unavailable, your mother or grandmother or a friend can serve as your partner."

Gracie was relieved when the blonde at the front of the room raised her hand. "My husband travels a lot. He's probably not going to be here for every session."

"That's fine." Marianne smiled at the blonde's husband. Jeez, couldn't the guy talk for himself? "Just try to attend as much as possible." The man nodded.

Marianne turned her gaze to Gracie. "Gracie, do you have a partner in mind?"

"I, uh—" She ought to say she didn't need a partner, that she was going to raise the child alone, so she might as well get started doing things alone from the outset. Instead, she found herself saying, "Sure."

"Good. Try to bring him next time."

Him. Oh, God. Was the rest of her life going to be one long, massively uncomfortable moment? Gracie's stomach clenched again.

"All right, then," Marianne said. "I thought we'd start with a movie of an actual birth."

The lights dimmed.

By the time they came back on, Gracie's belly was a hard knot of nausea. She sat perfectly still, gripping her hands together, trying to process what she'd just seen.

No way. No way! There was no way in hell she was going to go through that. And yet— Gracie's stomach heaved. She rose to her feet.

"Gracie—are you all right?"

"Yeah," she managed to choke out. "I just need to go to the restroom."

She fled the room and stumbled to the ladies' room, where she turned on the faucet and splashed water on her face. The thought of going through all that gross stuff made her feel as if one of those medieval spiked balls was rolling around her insides.

She shouldn't have come here tonight. She could have watched a birth on YouTube at any time, but she'd deliberately avoided doing so, figuring, why freak out before she had to?

She splashed water on her eyes, wishing she could erase the images burned on her corneas. No way.

Absolutely no way! And yet, the baby was inside her—she'd seen it on the ultrasound. It was definitely in there, and it had to come out somehow.

The restroom door squeaked open. In the mirror over the sink, her water- and tear-soaked eyes made out the blurred image of a slender woman in black capris and a blue-and-black print top. "Gracie—are you okay?"

Oh, great. It was Katie. She'd driven Gracie to the hospital and said she was going to visit a friend recovering from surgery while Gracie took her class. "Yeah. I'm just dandy."

Katie stepped closer, her eyebrows pulled together in concern. "What's wrong, honey?"

"Nothing." *Everything.* "I, uh, had something in my eye."

The door opened again. The short, stubby woman from her class stepped into the restroom, and grinned when she spotted Katie. "Katie!" She gave her a hug. "What are you doing here?"

"I dropped my daughter off for a birthing class, then went to see a friend who just had an appendectomy."

"Gracie's your daughter?"

"Yes."

Gracie thought about mounting her not-my-mother protest, but decided to let it go.

"I came in to check on her." The woman smiled at Gracie. "Honey, are you all right?"

"I'm fine." Gracie wiped her face with a paper towel. It felt like sandpaper on her skin.

"What happened?" Katie asked the woman.

"They showed a movie of a birth."

"Oh, sweetie—no wonder you're upset." Stepping

closer, Katie opened her purse, pulled out a Kleenex, and held it out. Gracie took it and inelegantly blew her nose.

"I watched a movie like that when I was pregnant with you," Katie said, "and it totally freaked me out."

"This one was really bad. It freaked *me* out," the woman said, "and I've already had two children."

"If you've had two kids, why did you sign up for the classes?" Gracie asked.

"Because the breathing techniques really help. It's been years since I had my last child, and I've forgotten everything I learned." She touched Gracie's arm. "I'm going back to class, since your mom is here. Just remember—it's all going to be all right. I've been through it twice, and here I am, about to do it again."

"I don't know why."

"Once you hold that baby in your arms, you'll forget all about the delivery. Right, Katie?"

Tears formed in Katie's eyes. "Right."

Gracie swallowed. Katie had said that giving her up was the hardest thing she'd ever had to do. Seemed like the giving-birth part would have been the hardest.

The door swung closed behind the woman, leaving Katie and Gracie in awkward silence. Katie pulled another tissue out of her purse and dabbed at her own eyes.

"That movie was so gross," Gracie said, hoping to defuse the emotional tension. "I can't imagine having my va-jay-jay hanging out there for everyone to see."

"When you're giving birth, you don't think about that." Katie gave her a wobbly smile.

"Did you have a birth coach?"

Katie nodded "A lady with the adoption program served as my coach. She was awesome."

"Did you stay in touch with her?"

"I wanted to, but she refused. She said I needed to put the experience behind me." Katie gave arwful smile. As if you could ever put a life-changing event like that behind you."

Gracie twisted her Kleenex.

"I could be your coach, if you like," Katie offered.

Part of her wanted to say yes. Another part—the stubborn part, the part that needed to cling to the way she'd always been, because who would she be if she wasn't that person?—wanted to keep Katie at arm's length. She couldn't betray her real mom by getting too tight with Katie.

She shook her head. "I don't need a birthing partner."

"Everyone needs someone, Gracie."

Gracie hugged her macraméd purse, the one her mother had made her, to her chest. "Let's just get out of here."

"What about the class?"

"Forget it."

She thought Katie was going to argue with her. She was relieved when she nodded. "Okay."

The parking lot was hot, and so was Katie's car when they climbed into it. Emotion simmered in Gracie's chest.

"Every one of those women was married," she found herself saying. "I felt like a freak."

Katie didn't say anything. She shot her a sympathetic glance and pulled out of the parking place.

"The teacher wanted me to bring the baby's father to the class. She said it would help him bond with the baby." Gracie stared at the blur of trees out the window.

"She didn't know that he lives in Pittsburgh," Katie said.

The truth built up in her chest like steam in a pressure cooker. "He doesn't. I don't even know where he lives."

Katie glanced at her.

"I don't even know his name!" Gracie blurted. There. She'd said it. She closed her eyes, hot tears coursing down her face. "But it's not like Zack thinks. There weren't a lot of guys. There was just one, and..." Her chin shook, making the word wobble.

"Oh, sweetie." Katie pulled the car to the side of the parking lot and stopped. Gracie ventured a look at her face. Instead of the horror she feared seeing in her eyes, she saw concern and sympathy. "It's okay, sweetie," Katie said softly. "Whatever happened, it's okay."

A fire hose of words gushed out. "I—I was mad at my aunt. I wanted to go to a concert and she wouldn't let me. She wouldn't let me do anything! She was a complete hard-ass. She wanted me to be just like her perfect grown daughter had been, and that's not me. I couldn't let her define me, you know? I wasn't like her. I would never be like her. I hated her. I was just so...so alone."

"You were grieving your parents," Katie said.

"Yeah. And she wasn't anything like them. And I hadn't made many friends at the school..."

The words tumbled out, fast and furious, falling all over each other, like water over a waterfall.

"Anyway—it was an outdoor thing, not even really a concert, just a thing happening in the park near their house. I met these older kids. They all introduced themselves at once, and it was hard to hear over the music, and..." And she hadn't wanted to seem uncool, having to ask again, so she pretended she'd heard them. "I think his name was Kurt or Kirk or Dirk or Burt, but I'm not even sure about that." She drew a ragged breath. She'd thought about it over and over and tried and tried to figure it out, and the more she thought about it, the more she thought maybe she was just making it all up. "He said he was from California. He was on spring break and either headed to or from New York."

"Did he say what part of California?"

Gracie shook her head. "They were passing around a bottle of vodka," she continued, "and I drank some. Then they passed around a joint, and I smoked a little." A lot, actual "One of the guys was really cute, and... well, he put his arm around me." She wiped a tear off her chin. "I don't think anyone had put their arm around me since I moved to my aunt's house. My aunt was kind of cold, you know? Not that I wanted her to touch me, but my mother—well, she used to hug me all the time, and I think... I think I missed being held. And so when he put his arm around me..."

"Oh, sweetie." Katie drew her into her arms.

Gracie let her. She leaned against her shoulder and sobbed while Katie murmured words of reassurance and stroked her head. At length, Gracie pulled back and wiped her nose with the tissue. "He—he asked if I wanted to go make out, and... and I said, sure. I never had, and he was really, really cute, so we moved away from the crowd and went to his pickup and..." Words wouldn't follow.

Katie softly stroked her hair. "Did he rape you?"

Had he? Memories of that night swirled through Gracie's head. "No. I mean, I don't think so."

"Did you tell him no?"

"I—I tried. But I was drunk and stoned, and I don't think I ever got the words out."

Making out had been fun, at first. Romantic. Exciting. He'd had a sleeping bag in the back of his pickup, and they'd stretched out on it and kissed and touched. She'd felt all kinds of thrilling sensations she'd never experienced. And then she'd realized that this guy had moved from stroking her thighs to pulling down her underpants, and he'd already unfastened his jeans.

"Wait...," she'd said—or maybe she'd just meant to say it. The vodka and pot had made everything seem fuzzy, like she was seeing things through a pane of painted glass. She remembered that a sign had flashed out the back window—HOTCAKES. She'd felt like she was in a thick gray fog, or having a dream, but just starting to wake up. "Slow down," she'd told him.

"I can't, babe. You feel too good." Her panties were moving down her thighs. He pulled off her shoe and edged one leg out.

Through her fog-enshrouded brain, she felt a skitter of alarm. "Wait. I don't want..."

His fingers had been back at her crotch.

"Please. I'm not...I've never..."

"Okay." He moved his hand. She thought he was completely backing off. He'd cradled her face and kissed her. "It's okay. Put your arms around my neck."

She thought they were going back to just kissing. Relieved, she wound her arms around his neck.

And then he'd rammed into her, hard and fast. It felt like a red-hot butcher knife, splitting her in two.

"I—I screamed," she told Katie.

"Did he stop?"

"Yeah, but not right away."

He'd thrust into her again, then again. His eyes had been closed, his mouth all twisted. She'd screamed again, and he'd driven into her even harder. His face had been right above hers, contorted in a scary kind of way.

"Get off!"

She'd wanted to push him away, but her arms were locked by his body weight, and all she could do was flap her wrists. His breath blew hard into her face. He'd grunted and thrust, and then it was all over.

"It happened so fast," Gracie told Katie. "I didn't know he was even going to, and then he did, and then... he was done."

"Wow. That was awesome," he'd said when he rolled off her, as if everything was just fine.

Shaking, Gracie had climbed out of the pickup bed, then promptly vomited on the parking lot.

"I—I just wanted to get away. My aunt's place wasn't far, so I—I ran."

She'd only had one shoe, and her panties had been clumped around one ankle. She'd nearly tripped over them. She'd stopped, pulled off the shoe and her underwear, then run as fast as she could.

"Do you know what kind of truck it was?" Katie asked.

Gracie shook her head. "Just a pickup. It was black. Or maybe dark blue."

"Did you see the license plate?"

She shook her head.

"Do you know anything about the other kids with him? Their names, or where they were from?"

She shook her head. A fresh sob rose in her throat. "What am I going to tell my baby when he's old enough to ask?"

"It'll be okay, honey." Katie rocked her. "It'll be okay."

CHAPTER TWENTY-TWO

Zack's fingers knotted in his palm. He wanted to smack something—specifically, the face of the prick who'd done this to his daughter. "That's all she knows?"

"Yeah." Katie nodded. "I'm pretty sure she told me everything."

"That's not much to go on."

"I know."

Katie had waited to tell him until she'd taken Gracie to work at the retirement home the next morning. Zack had been sitting at his office desk as she delivered the news, but now he needed to move, needed to dispell the energy blazing inside him like an oil field fire.

He paced the room. "Damn it. The odds of finding this guy are worse than nil. We don't even know where to begin looking." He stopped as a new concern hit him. "Was she tested for STDs?"

Katie nodded. "I called her ob-gyn. It was an automatic part of her pregnancy workup. She's okay."

"Well, thank God for that." Zack strode back across the room. "The asshole didn't even wear a condom!" He froze and looked at Katie. Guilt oozed to the top of the toxic sludge in his chest. He ran a hand down his face. "Hell. That's the pot calling the kettle black, isn't it?"

"It's not the same."

"It was no more okay for me not to wear one than it was for this guy."

"We were different, you and I. Entirely different. We knew each other. We were friends. I was... willing." She looked down at the desk, then back up, her mouth curved in a wry smile. "More than willing."

She abruptly rose from her chair and carried her coffee cup to the kitchen. He followed her.

"She should file a police report," Zack said.

"I asked her if she wanted to." The cup clattered as Katie set it in the stainless-steel sink. "She said she doesn't want the baby to be burdened with that kind of baggage. Besides, she isn't sure she really told the boy no."

"Damn it, any hesitation on the woman's part is a no."

Katie looked at him, her eyes soft. "Too bad all men aren't like you, Zack."

Something jumped between them, something beyond chemistry, something deeper and more tender. She turned away from him again. "Gracie's agreed to talk to a counselor. I'm taking her for her first session tomorrow afternoon."

"That's good." Zack rubbed his jaw, rage and outrage and a raw, nameless pain bubbling through his veins. Everything Katie was saying made sense, but damn, it was all passive. He needed to take some action. He strode the length of the kitchen, biting the inside of his mouth.

"Are you okay?" Katie asked.

Okay? He had homicide brewing in his heart. "I'm so damn mad I can't stand it." For the first time in his life, he could understand how someone could be angry enough to kill. He paced back into the kitchen, balling his hands into fists. "I've got to do something."

"You said it yourself, Zack. It's impossible to find this guy. And any attempt to do so is just going to upset Gracie further. The best thing you can do is nothing."

"I've never done well with nothing as a goal."

"Well, then, here's a positive goal. Go take a long, hard run, and get your feelings under control. Gracie knows I'm telling you this, and she's really worried about what you'll think of her."

His chest hurt. "She is?"

"Yeah. She needs to know that you care for her and accept her and aren't judging her."

"Why the hell would I judge her?"

"She's ashamed, Zack. She feels like she brought this on herself. And regardless of how she acts, your opinion means a lot to her." Her gaze rested on him. "If you're angry, she'll think you're angry at her."

"God." Zack looked at Katie, drawing strength from the softness in her eyes. "So what do I do?"

"Let her know you care about her and this doesn't change that. Reassure her that you're going to let her make the decisions."

"But this guy should be locked up!"

"We don't know who he is or where he's from. You yourself said he'd be impossible to find." Katie's eyes were soft, almost pleading. "Zack, Gracie can't handle a big legal deal right now."

"You're right, but damn it..." Zack blew out a sigh.

Katie picked up her purse and headed for the foyer. "I've got to meet with my contractor, then get to the salon." She pulled out her car keys. "Think you can handle picking up Gracie this afternoon?"

Oh, God. What was he supposed to say to her?

Katie must have read his expression. "I have appointments all afternoon, but if you need me, Bev can cover for me."

I need you. He almost said the words, but years of habit kept him silent. "Nah. I'll be fine."

She gave him a long look, and he got the feeling she could see right through him, right through the boiling cauldron of anger, to the fear at the white-hot center. "I'll call you this afternoon and see how things are going," she said as she went out the door.

Zack paced the house some more. The more he thought about this A-hole and Gracie, the madder he got. He wasn't good at dealing with anger. He usually just stuffed it down, but this was too big to stuff. This thing blew off the lid.

For lack of a better plan, he opted to take Katie's advice. Despite the heat, he ran five miles, then took a cold shower. That barely took the edge off. His chest still felt like a pressure engine about to blow.

He needed to hit something. He stormed to his computer and looked up boxing clubs, then drove to a ratty old gym in Hammond and reserved an hour with a punching bag.

He tied on the rented gloves, pulled back his right arm, and rammed his fist at the bag, right at face level—right where he wanted to hit Kirk or Dirk or whatever the bastard's name was. Dirt. He'd call him Dirt. He threw a punch with his left, hitting the other side of the A-hole's imaginary face, and muttered a foul oath. He threw another right, then a left, battering the punching bag with one-two punches, combining every blue word he'd ever heard in new and inventive ways. Wth every blow, he cursed Dirt and Dirt's mother. He called down various plagues on all of Dirt's personal body parts. He wished him catastrophe upon catastrophe, all of which would result in his slow and torturous death. He wanted the scumbag to suffer. He smashed his fists into the bag again and again, until his knuckles were bruised, his muscles burned, and his hour was up.

Breathing hard and aching all over, he limped to the shower. He stood under a stream of hot water, then washed up and headed back to Chartreuse.

He was waiting in the parking lot when Gracie got off work.

She stepped out the door, looking small and vulnerable. Everything about her looked sad and lost and a little off-kilter—her choppy black-and-blue hair, her bulging belly, her big saggy purse. A tenderness so intense he could barely breathe swelled in his chest as he watched her.

She scanned the parking lot, spotted his car, then dropped her gaze to the pavement. The tenderness moved to his throat and formed a lump so large and unwieldy he couldn't swallow. Oh, God—she was ashamed, maybe even scared. She didn't want to face him.

He watched her skulk to the car, her eyes downcast, one hand on her belly. A wave of emotion crashed over him, immersing him in a truth so profound that for a moment, he couldn't move. *He was no longer unattached. He was attached at the heart, double-bound to this girl and her mother. Gracie and Katie were his girls, and he'd do anything in his power to protect them, to take care of them, to make them smile.*

He climbed out of the car and circled it just as Gracie reached the passenger door. She froze, unsure what to do. She wouldn't look him in the eye.

"Gracie." His voice cracked as he said her name. "Gracie, honey—it's okay."

He opened his arms, and she fell into them. He could feel her baby bump pressing against his side, could smell the scent of Juicy Fruit gum and Clearasil. His heart felt like it was breaking and growing at the same time—as if it had a shell around it that was cracking open, and some new, awkward life-form was floundering out, as clumsy as a just-hatched chicken.

He patted her back as she clung to him and sobbed. They stood there for a long time, long enough that a couple of senior citizens waddled out of the building to stare at them. "Are you okay?" he finally asked Gracie.

"Yeah." Gracie pulled back and sniffed, wiping at her eyes with the backs of her hands.

Hell. He didn't know what to say. He wasn't any good at this touchy-feely stuff. He shifted his stance and blurted out the most comforting thing he could think of. "Want to go test-drive some cars?"

Her eyes lit up. "Really?"

"Yeah. Let's drive over to Hammond and check out some wheels. Maybe Kate can meet us there when she gets off work, then we'll go for Chinese or Mexican or something."

"Okay. Cool!"

Just like that, things were back to normal. Zack gave a sigh of relief as he climbed into his car. Sometimes you didn't need to get all wordy. Sometimes the things people needed to hear weren't things that were said out loud. Sometimes they just needed to know that everything was okay, and the best way of showing that was to act as if nothing had happened.

He hoped the same approach would work with Katie. Yakking about his feelings had never been his style.

CHAPTER TWENTY-THREE

"Not every kid gets to take her driver's test in a brand-new Toyota Prius," Katie said later that night, after they'd arrived home and Gracie had gone up to bed. She and Zack were in the kitchen, and he was opening a bottle of wine.

"Hey, they're great cars. They're environmentally friendly and they have great crash ratings." He popped the cork, then opened the cabinet and pulled out two wine glasses. The fragrance of chardonnay filled the air. He poured her a glass and handed it to her. "You're okay with it, right?"

She took a sip and nodded. "Yeah." He'd called and talked to her about it on the phone. She'd joined them at the dealership, and Zack had made sure she was part of the decision.

And then they'd ordered the car, and he'd pulled out his debit card and paid for the whole thing. That part had made her a little uneasy, but she'd come to terms with it. The fact was, he had resources she didn't. If he wanted to share them with Gracie, well, that was his prerogative.

"This whole parenting thing is a lot harder than I real-ized," Zack said.

"Yeah."

"I never thought I'd get so..."

"So what?"

He shook his head, as if he'd changed his mind about whatever he was going to say.

"Nothing." He splashed some more wine in her glass. "Anyway, thanks for your advice. Left to my own devices, I would have gone off the deep end, and that wouldn't have been good for Gracie." He took a sip of wine, then set down his glass. "So—when did you get so wise?"

She grinned. "I've always been wise. You've just been too much of a wiseass to notice."

"Actually, I noticed." His dimple flashed. "Your wisdom first revealed itself when you prevaricated that summer."

Katie's eyes widened. "I can't believe you remember that!"

They sat on the hood of his car in the bait shop park-ing lot, and he asked her how old she was. She lied, and he called her on it.

"How could you tell I was lying?" she asked.

"Because you hesitated, then you looked away."

"I'll have to remember not to do that."

He grinned. "The next time you tell a lie?"

She tossed her hair over her shoulder. "The next time I deal with a rude Yankee."

"What did I do that was rude?"

"You asked me my age, and then you directly called me on an indiscretion."

"An indiscretion?" His lips twitched up in amusement. *"Is that what a lie is called around here?"*

"Well, it's a much nicer term than 'liar.' And a Southern lady is allowed to prevaricate about her age."

"Prevaricate *about* indiscretions? *Have I fallen into some kind of* Gone with the Wind *time warp or something?"* he quipped.

He grinned at her now. "As I recall, every time you learned a new word, you tried to use it in conversation."

She nodded. "My English teacher said if you use a word three times, it's yours."

"And you'd learned that word because you were working your way through a list of books that were required reading for 'persons of refinement and good breeding.'"

Her face heated at the memory. "I didn't want to be ashamed of who I was and where I was from and what I didn't know. I didn't want to spend my life feeling less than other people."

"You said you wanted to be somebody you could be proud of."

"Yes." She took a long drink of wine, moved and a little embarrassed that he recalled all that.

"Remember what I said?" he asked softly.

Oh, she remembered, all right. They were some of the favorite words anyone had ever spoken to her. She'd held them close and etched them on her heart, hoping they were true.

"I told you that you already were," Zack said.

She glanced at him, then glanced away. His eyes were warm and intent, and she felt exposed to the soul. She nervously took a long draught of wine. "You have an amazing memory."

"Well, everything about you was pretty unforgettable."

Her heart thudded hard. "You were, too." Oh, dear—why had she said that? Maybe it was the wine. Maybe it was the emotion of the day.

Maybe it was just true.

The clock ticked loudly. Seconds passed, then more seconds. She lifted her eyes and looked into his, and what she saw there made time seem to stop.

Her gaze must have mirrored his, because he said, "Don't look at me like that, or I'm going to do something I'll regret."

"Why would you regret it?" Was that really her voice? It was barely a whisper.

"Because I promised I wouldn't."

Her nerves stretched like a tautly pulled rubber band. "Maybe you were prevaricating when you made that promise."

His dimple winked in his cheek. Her nerves stretched tighter.

And then his smile was gone. He set down his glass and turned fully toward her, his eyes somber and direct. "Kate—I don't want to do anything you would regret."

Emma's words rang through her mind. *When all is said and done, which will you regret more: not taking a chance on love, or giving love a chance?* Her empty glass made a little tinkling sound as she set it on the granite countertop. "What I will regret," she said, taking a slow, deliberate step toward him, "is waiting one more minute to kiss you."

She stepped right up to him, toe to toe, and tilted up her face. Zack's heart felt too full to beat right. "Kate,

don't start something you don't want to finish. I have
a pretty bad track record of self-control around you."
Which was why he'd decided to continue sleeping in the
garage apartment even though Annette was at Dave's.

She put her hand on his chest. "I don't want you to
have any self-control."

He swallowed. "None whatsoever?"

"Well, you'll need to have a little." She edged closer
and kissed his neck.

His arms ached to wrap around her. He resolutely kept
them at his sides, his hands clenched in tight fists. "How
much?"

"Enough to let me take your clothes off." Her palm
moved from his chest to his face, then slid across his
cheek, cool and soft. "And then you'll need to take off
mine. Then I intend to kiss you from head to foot and
back again, making sure to hit every spot in between.
And then I want you to do the same to me."

Dear God. His hands flexed. His fingernails dug into
his palms. "I don't think I have that much self-control. At
least not the first time."

"Well, then…" Her breath tickled his skin. "We'd better get the first time out of the way so we can get to the
second time."

She stood on her tiptoes, pulled down his head, and
kissed him. It was more than lips on lips; it was heart on
heart, soul on soul. She was in his arms, his mouth was
on hers, his body pressed against hers. All the rage he'd
felt today had been a crucible, burning away everything
but one immutable truth: Katie was a part of him. Just
like the child they'd created together, Katie was a part
of his soul.

He'd been lying to himself all these years, pretend-ing he was detached, disengaged, and uncommitted. The whole time his heart had belonged to Katie, and he'd been in denial. He'd told himself that women came and went, that sex was just sex, that relationships were interchange-able, and he'd believed his own lies. But the truth was in his arms. There was no one like Katie.

She made him feel things beyond the physical, things beyond words or even music.

He couldn't get close enough. He needed to be over her and in her and joined with her. He lifted her off her feet. She wrapped her legs around his hips. One hand on her back, another under her bottom, he carried her out the kitchen door, across the dog run, and through the side door of the garage.

He staggered up the stairs to the apartment, kissing her as he carried her, her fanny bumping against his thigh with every step. He pushed the bedroom door open with his foot. The hinges squeaked and the door flew wide. So did Katie's heart.

Katie felt the bed give beneath her as he gently set her on it, then leaned in to kiss her again. She inhaled his breath, wishing she could inhale all of him, want-ing to just take him in. She tugged up the bottom of his polo shirt, anxious to feel his skin, needing tactile proof that he was here and she was with him and this wasn't a fantasy.

He yanked the shirt over his head, then set to work on the buttons of her black linen top, starting at the top and working his way down. He pulled the fabric apart and unfastened her black front-open bra, exposing her breasts. "Kate," he murmured. "My beautiful, beautiful Kate." Carressing her softly, he leaned in and closed his lips around her nipple.

A hot wire of pleasure burned straight to her core. He unfastened the button on the front of her khaki skirt and pulled down the zipper. It was the same skirt she'd been wearing the day he'd come back into her life. She realized she'd been waiting for this moment ever since he'd walked into her salon.

Why had she fought the inevitable? Zack was like gravity. As surely as a dropped spoon would fall to the ground, she would fall for Zack. He was like oxygen—essential and elemental. The lack of him left her gasping.

No, wait—the nearness of him left her gasping. A moan of pleasure escaped her throat as his mouth moved to her other breast.

Her head lolled back. If a person could die of pleasure, she was in imminent danger. And she didn't even care. Her heart was singing as Zack played her body, kissing her breasts, working down her skirt. She felt as if she were both dreaming and waking up, both going away and coming home. Zack was familiar and new, exciting and reassuring, all at once.

His mouth moved up to her neck, then on to her ear. Her skin pebbled in goose bumps of pleasure. "Kate," he murmured, as if her name were a prayer.

His hands touched her face, and she thought she would die from the tenderness of it. His forefinger traced the outline of her lower lip. His gaze had weight and warmth, a caress in and of itself, as he looked at her. He kissed her again, and then his mouth moved lower, back to her breasts, down to her rib cage.

He eased down her skirt, his lips following.

"Wait," she murmured.

He immediately froze and looked up at her.

She smiled. "You're wearing too many clothes."

His teeth flashed in a grin. "Well, 1 can fix that." The muscles on his flat stomach rippled as he stood and kicked off his loafers. He reached into the pocket of his jeans and pulled out his wallet, then extracted a foil packet and tossed it on the bed. He peeled off his jeans and boxer briefs, revealing his enormous arousal. Her mouth went dry at the sight of him.

And then he was back at the bed. He pulled off her skirt, then gently lifted her left foot and removed her sandal. He did the same with the right one, kissing the top of her foot as the shoe dropped to the floor. His mouth moved to her ankle, then up her calf, to her knee, along her inner thigh, all the way up to the edge of her scanty black panties.

The ache inside her became a throb, and then a hungry, pulsing need. "Please." The word came out half whisper, half moan as he peeled her panties down her legs.

He parted her with his thumbs and kissed her there, where she was dying to be touched. He stroked her with his tongue and fingers until she was panting and quaking, shuddering on the edge, but not wanting to fall alone. "Zack," she whispered. "I want...I need..."

You. All of you. Filling me, completing me.

He reached for the packet of foil, and then he was over her. He took his time, moving slowly, filling her inch by exquisite inch, inciting her with his deliberate slowness until she was gripping his hips and urging him on.

And then they were moving together—rising and

falling, taking and giving, leading and following each other to the edge of the world, to a cliff so exquisite, so beautiful, so intimate, so deep that all she could do was close her eyes, hold on, and fall.

He followed her there. They lay together, spent and sated and weak-limbed. He rolled over onto his side, one arm behind her head, the other on her belly.

"Wow," he said.

"Yeah. Wow."

"Are you okay?" He searched her face, his eyes dark as deep water. She could read his mind—she felt that connected, that close. He was worried that she was regretting it.

"I'm fine." She put her hand over his on her belly. "Better than fine."

"Good." His dimple winked at her. "Because in a few minutes, I'm afraid we're going to have to do that all over again."

"Really?"

"Yeah." He lifted his hand and twirled a lock of her hair around his finger. "We've got a lot of time to make up for."

They made up for lost time twice more that night. The second time was a slow, leisurely, full-bodied adoring and exploring of each other, emotional and soulful, that unexpectedly burst into something hot and wild that ended with Katie straddling his lap, then pushing him down and having her way with him. The third time was a hilarious romp full of laughter and inventive positions, which took an unexpected turn to tender at the end.

Zack fell into a deep sleep, fulfilled and happy and

warm, his arm tight around Katie. He awoke at dawn to find her moving out of his arms, then out of the bed. He opened his eyes and saw her gathering her clothes. He sat up in bed, alarmed. "Where are you going?"

"Back to my room. I don't want Gracie to know about this."

"Gracie's no dummy," Zack said, propped up against the pillows, his hands behind his head. "She's going to figure things out."

"*I* need to figure things out first."

"What's to figure out?"

"Everything." She knelt and pulled a sandal out from under the bed. "What are we doing?"

He adjusted a pillow behind his head. "We're having a great time."

"Yes, but what does it mean?"

"That we're crazy about each other."

"Besides that."

"That's not enough?"

"No." She found the other sandal and straightened. "I need to know where things are going."

Zack's stomach clenched. Man, he hated these let's-talk-about-our-relationship conversations. He wasn't even awake yet. "Kate, it's a little early to be having this discussion."

"Until we have it, it's too early for Gracie to know about us."

The stubborn tilt of her chin sent him into risk-management mode. The first rule of risk management: Identify and avoid the worst-case scenario. In this case, the worst scenario would be Katie calling the whole thing off. "Okay. How do you want to handle this?"

"Well, for starters, we can't see each other until Gracie's asleep."

He grinned. "By see each other, you mean see each other naked."

She gave him a look that was supposed to be stern but only made him laugh.

"This isn't a joke. I'm very serious."

"I can see that." Second rule of risk management: Don't do anything that would jeopardize efforts to enact rule one. "What do you suggest we do?"

"Well, whenever Gracie's around, we'll need to act perfectly normal."

"By normal, you mean..."

"Nonromantic. Nonflirtatious. Noninvolved."

He didn't think they were going to fool anybody, least of all Gracie, but he'd do anything Katie wanted. Anything at all. "Okay."

She smiled. Wow, it was amazing how her smile could just light up a room. And not just the room; she made him feel all lit up, as well.

He patted the bed beside him. "Before you leave, I think you need to come over here and show me exactly what it is we're going to pretend we're not doing."

She hesitated. For one thrilling moment, he thought she was going to comply.

Then she raised a finger, the strap of her sandal dangling from it, and gave him a mischievous grin. "Hold that thought until tonight," she said before disappearing out the door.

He leaned back against the pillow and sighed. He wouldn't be able to hold any other thought in his head all day.

CHAPTER TWENTY-FOUR

"So are you going to talk about it?" Bev shot Katie a sidelong glance a week later as the two women readied the salon for the day.

"Talk about what? Gracie starting school? She hasn't had a lot to say, except that the kids are stupid but classes are good."

Bev grinned. "That sounds about right. But that's not what I meant."

"Oh, you mean Gracie's doctor's appointment yesterday afternoon." Katie opened the cabinet in the storage room. "Dr. Greene said the baby is growing beautifully. The placenta is still too low, and that's worrisome, but the doctor still thinks it will grow upward from here on out. She asked Gracie if she wanted to know the baby's gender. Gracie's not sure."

"That's all very interesting, but that's not what I was referring to." Bev reached into the dryer. "I was wondering if you want to talk about the reason you're humming and smiling and floating around like you're in a Heavenly Hash commercial." Bev pulled out a towel and folded it in thirds. "I kept my mouth shut all last week, figuring you'd say something when you were ready, but Rachel is starting to take bets."

"Bets?"

Bev nodded. "On how long you'll keep pretending nothing's going on between you and the hunk."

Katie felt her face heat. "Is it that obvious?"

"Yeah." Bev's face broke into a big old smile. "And I think it's wonderful."

It *was* pretty wonderful. Beyond wonderful, actually. Katie smiled back, her heart feeling like a kite on a string. "Zack and I have a really good connection."

Bev raised an eyebrow. "Is that what they're calling it these days?"

Katie laughed as she pulled a gallon jug of shampoo off the shelf in the storage room. "Everything is so good that it scares me. I'm afraid it's not going to last." She took the jug to the shampoo sink. "I don't want to get in over my head."

"Too late, I'd say."

Katie grinned. Her friend never pulled any punches.

"Honey, none of us ever know how long anything is going to last or where it's going to lead. There are no sure bets in this world." Bev placed the folded towel on the washer and pulled another one out of the dryer. "What made you decide to stop sitting on the sidelines and get into the game?"

"Something Emma said. She made me realize that I *was* taking a chance by *not* taking a chance."

Bev nodded. "No decision is a decision. Inaction is an action."

"Sounds like you two read the same book." Katie

unscrewed the lid of the large shampoo container, then removed the lid of the smaller sink-side bottle. "I just didn't realize how fast I'd get in so deep."

"You were already in deep, Katie. And it's only natural; you two have a shared history. Heck, you have a child together!" Bev stacked the second towel on top of the first. "He's got deep feelings, too. He wouldn't be in Chartreuse if he didn't."

She hoped that was true. Zack had been completely closemouthed about his emotions. "I asked him where this was going, and he said it was too early to talk about it."

"Typical male response."

"Typical Zack response."

"Well, it *is* too early. Easy does it, honey. Just take it one day at a time."

"You sound like Dave, using all those AA sayings."

"How is he? And how are he and Annette getting along?"

"They're doing really well." The herbal scent of shampoo filled the air as Katie filled the small bottle. "Better than I ever would have predicted."

"Any chance they'll get back together?"

"I don't know if Annette can get over what he did."

"What does she think of Zack?"

Katie's conscience gave a twinge. "She gets a funny look whenever his name comes up. She hasn't met him yet."

Bev gave her a pointed look. "She's going to need to."

"Yeah. I'm thinking about inviting her and Dave over to dinner."

"Great idea. But maybe you should wait another week or so."

"Why?"

"To let some of that new-love sparkle that's all over you burn off a little." Bev grinned. "You don't want to blind her."

Two weeks later, Annette sat between Gracie and Dave at Zack's dining table. Katie hovered nearby, coffeepot in hand. "Would you like more coffee?"

"No, thank you." Annette put her yellow cloth napkin next to her place mat and glanced at Dave. "We really need to be going."

"That was a wonderful meal," Dave said, scooting back his chair. "Thank you for inviting us."

"It was our pleasure," Zack said.

"Your gumbo is always delicious, Katie, but this time you outdid yourself." Annette looked at Zack. "And that was probably the best Caesar salad I've ever had. I'm impressed that you made it from scratch."

Zack grinned, a dimple indenting his right cheek. "I got the recipe off a YouTube video." Good heavens, but Zack was an attractive man—and just as charming as he was good-looking. Annette could see why Katie was crazy about him.

And she was clearly crazy about him. Throughout the meal, Katie had avoided eye contact with him and kept a careful distance at all times, but it was impossible to miss the spark between them.

"How about the cookies?" Gracie prompted.

"Oh, my heavens, Gracie—those were to die for!" Annette placed both hands on her stomach. "I must have eaten a half dozen of them. You'll have to give me the recipe."

The girl beamed. "It's easy. Just peanut butter, eggs, and sugar."

"No flour?"

"Nope. Just three ingredients."

"She's been baking them a lot lately," Zack said. "Peanut butter is her latest craving."

Dave grinned at Annette. "You went through a stage like that. I remember going out at midnight to buy you a jar of Skippy."

The memory caused a little stitch of pain. She wondered if she'd ever be able to think of Paul without feeling loss. She glanced over at Katie and felt it again. It was so odd, seeing Katie here, looking like a member of another family.

Dave came around the table, took Annette's arm and helped her up, then handed her her cane. She put it in her right hand, then rested her left one on Dave's arm.

"I can't believe how well you're getting around," Katie said.

Annette nodded. "I kicked that walker to the curb. I see the doctor next week, and if things go well, he's going to release me from therapy and let me get around unassisted."

Gracie's brow furrowed. "So you'll be moving back to New Orleans?"

"I don't think she should go for another few weeks," Dave said. "She's not ready to deal with twenty-four stairs every time she leaves her house."

If Dave had his way, she'd never be ready. But then, she wasn't really ready herself. She never would have believed it was possible, but she was having a wonderful time living with Dave. He was considerate and kind, and he'd been careful to give her privacy. She'd forgotten how funny and thoughtful and insightful he was. She'd forgotten how much fun it was to just spend time with him.

But then, during the last years of their marriage, he hadn't been around to spend much time with.

"I think you should stay in Chartreuse for good," Gracie said.

Annette smiled. She'd grown very fond of the girl. Since she'd moved to Dave's, she was just three blocks away from Zack's home, and Grace often dropped by. She never stayed very long—just five minutes or so—but Annette was glad she was continuing to visit as she had at Sunnyside.

"I second that," Katie said.

"And I third it," Dave agreed.

"Hey, I have an idea!" Gracie said. "You could remarry Dave, and you wouldn't even have to move out of his house."

Trust a teenager to say the most awkward thing possible. Annette felt her face heat.

"Now there's a grand idea," Dave said, grinning down at her.

Taking a page from Gracie's book, Annette rolled her eyes. Everyone laughed.

"You could teach at the high school again," Gracie added, "and I'd get to see you every day."

"They'd have to fire someone to hire me back."

"I bet they'd do it."

"I bet they wouldn't. And if they did, it wouldn't make me very popular with the other teachers."

Annette squeezed Dave's arm. He took the hint and stepped with her toward the door. Even after all they'd been through, they still had a way of communicating without words. The thought sent a pang of longing through Annette's chest. She'd never felt this deeply connected to anyone else, and she doubted she ever would. Her cane softly thudded on the hardwood floor. "Zack, thank you for having us to your gorgeous home. It's wonderful to finally meet you. And Katie, honey, thanks for everything."

Katie kissed her on the cheek. "You're more than welcome. I'll see you tomorrow or the day after."

Annette nodded and kissed Gracie. "Don't forget to send me that cookie recipe."

"Or better yet, just make us a batch and bring it by," Dave said.

As everyone laughed, they walked out onto the porch. Dave helped Annette down the stairs and sidewalk, then into the car.

"So that was Zack," she said as Dave closed the door and settled into the driver's seat.

"Yep." He turned the key and put the car in reverse.

"He's a nice guy."

Nodding, Dave put his arm over the back of the seat and turned his head as he backed out of the drive. "I like him a lot."

"So does Katie, apparently." She gazed out at the street as Dave shifted gears. "She positively glows around him. I think she's in love."

"Really?"

Men. Didn't they notice anything? "Yes."

"Now that you mention it, she does seem happier than

I've seen her in a long time." Dave cast her a sideways glance. "I'm glad to see it. It's time she moved on."

Moving on meant moving away from Paul. Annette still had mixed feelings about it, but the tight band of resistance that had bound her into knots at first was loosening and softening.

"It's time she found a little happiness," Dave said. "It's time we all did."

Oh, dear—she had a feeling he was going to turn the topic to something uncomfortably personal, and she didn't want to go there. "Gracie told me that Katie's been sneaking into Zack's room at night."

Dave laughed.

"You think it's funny?"

"It *is* funny." He pressed his foot to the accelerator, his mouth curved in amusement. "Does Gracie have solid evidence, or is she just suspicious?"

"She said Katie's bedroom door opens about thirty minutes after Gracie goes to her room."

"Purely circumstantial. Maybe Katie's just going to the bathroom."

"I mentioned that. But Gracie said the toilet doesn't flush. One night she got up and checked, and both Katie's room and the bathroom were empty."

"Maybe Katie went down to the kitchen."

"Gracie said she checked the whole house. Katie's car was still in the drive, but she was nowhere to be found. So she must have been in the garage apartment with Zack."

Dave's smile widened. "I wonder if Grace put on a Sherlock Holmes cap to conduct this investigation."

"Gracie also said she's heard Katie sneaking back into her room around five or six in the morning."

"Case closed, I'd say." Dave chortled.

"You seem awfully amused."

"Come on, Nettie." The use of his old pet nickname disconcerted her. "Two grown-ups sneaking around their teenager, instead of vice versa." Dave shook his head. "Remember how we caught Paul sneaking in at three in the morning when he was sixteen?"

As if she could ever forget. They'd been waiting for him in the dark. When he'd stepped inside the house, they'd flipped on the lights and given him the scare—and the lecture—of his life. She smiled.

"That Gracie—she's a pistol."

Annette nodded. "That she is."

Dave looked over at her as he pulled into his driveway. "I have to say, I liked her suggestion that you remarry me."

Annette's heart pounded. "She's the queen of the outrageous statement."

"Do you really think it would be so terrible?" He glanced at her as he shifted the car into park. His hand moved from the wheel to the back of the seat, close to her neck.

"Yes."

"I think you feel duty-bound to treat me badly."

There was probably some truth to that. "Well, you deserve it."

"You'll get no argument from me." His hand lifted off the seat, and his finger touched her hair. The follicles suddenly seemed electrified, sending little crackles of energy down her spine. "Did I tell you how beautiful you look tonight?"

Annette's pulse fluttered in her throat, fast as hummingbird wings. "No. And I don't want you to now."

"Why not?"

"Because it makes me uncomfortable. It's too personal."

"It's just an observation."

"It's the sort of thing a man says to a woman when he's trying to get on her good side."

"It's also a thing a man says when he looks at a woman and thinks, 'Wow, she's really beautiful.'" He turned off the ignition, throwing them into acute silence. Outside, tree frogs and cicadas trilled their evening serenades. "You *are* beautiful, Nettie. I didn't tell you often enough when we were married."

Her heart was pounding, and she didn't like it. She felt breathless and confused and out of her depth. "Well, it's too late now."

"It doesn't have to be." His finger moved to her ear.

Her breath caught. He knew that her ear was sensitive, knew that the slightest touch to it gave her goose bumps. He was doing that on purpose. She should move her head or swat his hand away—and yet for some reason, she couldn't bring herself to do it.

"Nettie—I'd like to start over."

"No." The word was a reflex.

"Why not? We could date, like two people who'd just met each other. We could go to dinner and talk—all the stuff we're doing now. And who knows? Sooner or later, we might even kiss."

"I don't want to kiss you."

"Are you sure?" His fingers moved against her ear again. He leaned in closer, close enough that she could

smell his Aramis, close enough that her brain grew
muddled and her thoughts got loopy. "I sure want to
kiss you."

All of a sudden, it was flooding her—all the old attraction, all the old tenderness, all the old, sweet memories.
He was circumventing her brain. He was getting to her
on a primal level.

"Just relax and let it happen," he murmured, moving
closer.

The words were oddly un-Dave-like. He wasn't a
relax-and-let-it-happen kind of guy. Those sounded like
the words of someone else.

And she knew just who. Her body went rigid. "Is that
what she used to say?"

"What?"

" 'Relax and let it happen.' Is that something Linda
said to you?"

He dropped his eyes.

Oh, God—she was right! Annette struggled to open
the car door. She was so stiff with anger that her fingers
wouldn't fold around the handle.

"Wait," Dave said. "Sit tight. Let me come help you."

"I don't need any more of your help."

"Yes, you do. I'll get your cane, then I'll help you into
the house."

Damn it. She was still a week away from being able
to walk and climb the porch stairs herself. She closed her
eyes and pressed her lips tightly together, furious at him,
at herself, at the whole damned situation.

She hated that she needed him. Being physically
dependent on him was bad enough, but God help her, she
was getting emotionally dependent on him, too.

Let it happen, indeed! He was the one who'd let it happen, who'd let the stranger into their marriage, who'd broken their wedding vows. He was the one who'd ruined things.

He held out his hand. It stung her pride to take it, to have him help her out of the car. It burned her ego to feel his arm under her hand as she walked stiffly to the house.

So help her, as soon as she could go up and down stairs safely on her own, she was out of here.

Dave's pace slowed as they neared the house.

"Damn it, Dave, hurry up. Don't make me hang on to you any longer than I have to."

To her annoyance, his speed slackened still further. "Annette, as soon as we get to the porch—grab the railing."

"What?"

His steps were now mere shuffles. "Grab the railing." He put his free hand on his chest.

That's when she realized something was wrong. "Dave?"

He inched forward, up to the edge of the steps, then doubled over.

She reached for the railing—just as he tumbled over and fell into the flower bed.

"Dave!" Panic surged through her chest. Casting aside the cane, she used the railing to lower herself to the ground beside him.

He lay on his side, crumpled in the cypress mulch, his hand over his chest.

"Dave! Dave!" She knelt over him on her good leg, grabbed both of his shoulders, and turned him on his back.

In the porch light, his face was a mottled, bluish purple. "Can't... breathe," he gasped. "Nitro. Pocket. Pants."

She reached into his left pocket and pulled out a cell phone. Dropping it on the ground, she stuck her hand into his right pocket and found a bottle of pills. Her hand shook as she struggled to open it. The lid finally flew off, spraying pills into the mulch, where they landed like flower seeds. Three pills remained in the bottle. She put one under his tongue, then grabbed his phone and dialed 911.

"What's the nature of your emergency?" asked a maddeningly calm male voice.

"My husband." The word was out before she had time to think about it. "I think he's having a heart attack. We're at..." She looked up at the house numbers on the porch. "Forty-two-oh-nine Cypress Way."

The man repeated the address in a robotic fashion. "He has a heart condition," Annette said. "I gave him nitroglycerin."

"Is he conscious?"

"Just barely. He's having trouble breathing."

"Annette." Dave called her name. It came out as a low, inhaled rasp. "You were the best part of my life."

"Stop talking like that!"

"Tell him not to talk. He needs to lie still and take deep breaths," said the insanely calm operator.

"Dave, you're supposed to lie still and take deep breaths," Annette relayed.

"Got to say this," Dave gasped. "May never get another chance."

He thought he was dying. Terror filled her.

"Dave, just lie still."

"No. You need to know. Annette—love you. Always loved you." His breathing was labored. His face looked like unbaked bread dough. "That's why Linda left. Because I'd never love her like I love you."

He was dying. Oh, God—if he died, she'd die, too.

"Don't you dare die on me, Dave Charmaine." She shook him. On some back burner of her mind, it occurred to her that it was probably a bad idea to shake a man having a heart attack, but she couldn't help herself. "Do you hear me? Don't you dare check out after making me fall for you again."

"Ma'am?" The operator's voice sounded through the phone on the ground beside Dave.

Tree frogs and cicadas burst into a loud chorus. Dave went limp in her arms.

Annette picked up the phone, frantic. "He's unconscious! I need help!"

"Is he breathing?"

She bent down and put her ear to his mouth. Nothing.

"Ma'am? Are you there?"

Ignoring the operator, she fit her mouth over Dave's. He tasted like home. Oh, God, she loved this man. She'd never stopped loving him. He was the best and the worst of her. Together they'd made and lost a son—unspeakable joy, unfathomable grief. She loved him. Why hadn't she fought for him when Linda had tried to lay claim to him?

Damn it, she'd fight for him now. Despair morphed into desperation, desperation into determination. She blew into his mouth, willing him to breathe. She pulled back, stacked her hands on his chest, and pumped on his stubborn heart, willing it to beat. "Damn it, Dave, I'll kill you if you die on me!" She dipped her head and filled his lungs again, then pumped his chest again.

She repeated the cycle for what seemed like forever, until the wail of a siren cut through the night. She continued alternating the chest compressions with hard huffs of air into his mouth, until a medic took her by the shoulders.

"We've got it, ma'am."

Another medic rushed up with a stretcher. She stood back and watched them set to work, her hand over her mouth, her heart splitting apart along seams she hadn't even known had mended.

CHAPTER TWENTY-FIVE

"Mrs. Charmaine?"

Annette felt Katie grip her fingers as the surgeon called her name in the surgery waiting room at Our Lady of the Lake Hospital in Baton Rouge. Actually, it was both of their names. What a weird thing to notice—but then, a person tended to notice weird things when she'd been up all night, worrying and praying and bargaining with God.

Annette had phoned Katie seven or eight hours ago and told her that Dave had been helicoptered here for emergency open-heart surgery. Katie had immediately driven to Baton Rouge to join her. She'd said that Zack had wanted to come, too, but Katie had insisted he stay home with Gracie.

Annette looked up at the scrubs-clad surgeon, trying to read his face, her heart quaking. "Yes?"

The lines in the doctor's face shifted into a smile. "Your husband came through just fine."

It was a good thing she was seated, because otherwise her legs would have buckled. "Oh, thank God."

"We ended up doing a triple bypass," the doctor said. "He should have had the surgery when we first recommended it."

Annette frowned. "When was that?"

"About eleven months ago."

Dave had known he'd needed surgery for eleven months, and he hadn't done it? He hadn't even told her. It took an effort to pull her focus back to the doctor.

"There was very little damage to his heart. He was fortunate."

"Fortunate," she echoed.

"He's going to be in intensive care for the next forty-eight hours. You should go home and get some rest."

"No. I'll stay here."

"Are you sure? You can only go in to see him once every two hours, and then only for ten minutes at a time."

"That's okay. I don't want to leave him." Ever. Ever again.

The doctor nodded. "He's in recovery right now. We'll let you know when we transfer him to ICU."

"Thank you."

The minutes ticked by like hours. At length, a nurse came and got her. "Mrs. Charmaine? You can see him now."

She hobbled in, leaning on the cane and Katie's arm.

Oh, God—he looked like death. A tube protruded from his throat, connecting him to a machine forcing air into his lungs. "Dave—I'm here." He didn't move. Annette lifted his hand. It was cold and limp.

"I'm here, and I'm not going anywhere." She leaned down and spoke into his ear. "And damn it all, you'd better not go anywhere, either. We've still got a lot of living to do." His fingers moved in her hand. He opened his eyes for a second—just long enough to look at her. The ventilator was taped over his lips, so he couldn't have moved his mouth, yet she could have sworn he smiled. He closed one eye, and then the other.

The nurse gasped. "It looked like he winked at you!"

"He did," Annette said. She squeezed his hand, her heart light—light and buoyant and floaty, free of the anger and resentment that had weighed it down for so long.

Gracie: Remember the guy who runs the book store who's kinda like my granddad? He had a heart attack 3 days ago.

Megan: OMG Is he ok?

Gracie: Yeah. He's in the Baton Rouge hospital for a week or so. Katie and Annette r staying at a hotel there 2 be with him.

Megan: So ur living alone?

Gracie: Nah. Zack is here.

Megan: How is that?

Gracie: OK. He lets me drive his car. Mine won't be delivered for another 2 weeks.

Megan: Bet U can't wait! How's school?

Gracie: Totally sucks, except for biology and chemistry. How's yours?

Megan: Awesome. John Rogers invited me 2 the homecoming dance.

Gracie: OMG!

Megan: I know. I'm going 2 the mall with Jana 2 shop for a dress.

Gracie: I'm jealous. I can't fit into anything but yoga
    pants. My belly is gi-normous.
Megan: How's the baby?
Gracie: OK. The placenta's still low, though.
Megan: Bummer. Gotta go. Jana's here.
Gracie: Have fun!

Gracie closed her phone and rolled over on the bed,
fat tears plopping down her cheeks. She wished she could
wear cute clothes and look forward to things like the
homecoming dance. She wished she could go to the mall
and hang out with other kids and just have a normal life.

It wasn't fair, how completely one bad decision had
changed everything. She wished she could get a do-over.
She wished she'd never gone to that guy's truck or never
gone to that stupid concert at all. She wished like crazy
she wasn't pregnant.

Guilt soaked through her. What kind of expectant
mother had thoughts like that? She was going to be a
lousy mother. What if she couldn't love the baby? What
if she hated it? What if all she felt for it was shame and
loathing, like she felt about herself when she thought
about the night she conceived? She grabbed her pillow,
hugged it tight, and cried.

"Thank you so much for letting me stay here," Annette
said as she limped into Zack's house a week later. Zack
followed behind her, carrying her and Katie's suitcases.
Annette was still using the cane, but she was walking
without holding on to anyone. "I hate to be in your way."

"You won't be in the way," Zack said. Well, that wasn't
exactly true. As long as Annette was in the house, he was

pretty sure Katie wasn't going to visit the garage apartment. But that was a sacrifice he'd willingly make; he was glad just to have Katie back in the house. During the past week while she'd been in Baton Rouge, he'd missed her more than he'd known he could miss anyone.

"I tried to tell Katie that I'm perfectly capable of staying on my own at Dave's place, but she wouldn't hear of it."

"We've already settled this," Katie said firmly. "You were just released from therapy this week. It's not a good idea for you to be staying alone yet."

"When Kate makes up her mind about something, there's no point in trying to change it," Zack said.

"Isn't that the truth. My son used to say that she could out-stubborn a rock."

The mention of Katie's husband made Zack's chest tighten. He placed Annnette's suitcase on a chair by the window. "We'd like Dave to come stay here, too, when he gets out of Sunnyside," he said. Dave had been discharged from the Baton Rouge hospital on the condition that he stay in the facility's rehabilitation wing for another two weeks.

Annette smiled. "That's very sweet. But by then, I'll be more than strong enough to care for him."

"So you're going to stay in Chartreuse for good?" Gracie asked. Her mouth was purple from licking a grape Dum-Dum. The girl was trying to act indifferent, but she wasn't fooling anyone. She was clearly thrilled to have Katie and Annette back. She'd been bouncing around all afternoon, helping get the place ready for their arrival, and now she was glued to the two women's sides.

Zack was glad to see it. Gracie had been glum and

morose and unnaturally silent lately. He had a feeling she was having a hard time at school, but she refused to talk about it.

"Dave and I haven't had a chance to really discuss our plans yet," Annette said.

"But you might stay," Gracie persisted.

"It's possible."

"Awesome!" Gracie gave a big purple grin.

"Totally awesome," Katie said, smiling just as wide.

Zack had talked to Katie daily, and she'd told him that Annette had had a complete change of heart where Dave was concerned. "Those two belong together," Katie had said. "Neither one has really been happy since they've been apart."

After a week without Katie, Zack was beginning to know how they felt.

Katie was curled under the green-checked comforter reading a romance novel when she heard a knock on the door. "Come in," she called.

Gracie opened the door.

Katie put down the book, delighted at the unexpected visit. She had texted and called Gracie while she was in Baton Rouge, but she'd really missed the girl. "Come in!" She patted the bed beside her. "Sit down. How are you doing?"

She shrugged. "Okay, I guess."

"What's on your mind?"

Gracie sat on the bed. "Well, I've been thinking."

"Yes?"

"Next time I go to the doctor, I think I want to know the sex of the baby after all."

Katie smiled. "So you can pick a name and clothes and stuff?"

"Sorta. But more because I don't like the idea of the doctor knowing something about my baby that I don't know. It seems dumb to be deliberately ignorant." She looked at Katie. "What do you think?"

It was the first time she recalled Gracie actually asking her opinion about anything. Katie considered the question thoughtfully. "I think it's a personal choice, and it's entirely up to you."

"Did you know my sex when you were pregnant with me?"

Katie's throat grew thick. "No. The doctor said I was better off not knowing. He said it would only make me more attached, and that would make it harder for me to do what was best for you."

Silence loomed between them for a long moment.

"Do you think giving my baby away would be best for him or her?"

It was the second time Gracie had asked her that question, so it must really be weighing on her. Katie answered straight from the heart. "No."

"Why not? I'm the same age you were."

"But you have resources I didn't have. You have Zack and me. You'll be able to get an education and afford child care." Katie hesitated, then decided to just go ahead and say what had been on her heart for months. "Gracie, sweetheart, if you don't feel ready for motherhood, I would be honored to raise your baby."

"No." She shook her head, her mouth tight. "No way. It's *my* baby."

"I understand." Katie lifted her hands. "Totally. I just wanted to lay that out as an option. I also want you to know that I'll be here to help in any capacity you want or need."

"I don't intend to lean on you."

"I admire your independent spirit. But I'm here, and I'll be happy to babysit if you want a night out or anything."

"Okay."

Gracie looked down at the comforter and traced one of the green squares with her finger. "My mom said you picked out my name."

"Yes."

"Why did you name me Grace?"

Katie grinned. "Because you were amazing. Why else?"

"Seriously."

"Because it's such a beautiful word. It means God's unmerited favor. In other words, love without any strings. It's affection and forgiveness and protection and beauty, all wrapped up together—and we don't have to do anything to earn it. He gives it to us regardless of how badly we behave." She grinned. "That concept seemed like the most beautiful thing I'd ever heard."

Gracie sat very still for a moment. "What were you going to name me if I was a boy?"

"Joseph. I thought that he must have been the best man who had ever been born, if God trusted him to be Jesus' earth dad. Plus he listened to his dreams. He was thinking he shouldn't marry Mary when he found out she was pregnant, but he had a dream where an angel told him to go ahead and take her as his wife, so he did." Katie smiled at Gracie. "I think that's a good example of listening to your heart."

"Yeah." Gracie looked at her thoughtfully for moment. "If I have a boy, maybe I'll name him Joseph, too."

A moment of harmony pulsed between them. "Is school going okay?" Katie ventured.

Gracie's face shut down. "It sucks."

"High school is hard enough when you're not new or pregnant. I think you were really brave to decide to attend for a semester."

"I have to, in order to do the chemistry and biology labs."

"Still, I think it's brave. And if you ever want to talk about any problems you're having with the other kids or anything..."

"No." Gracie stood up. "When I'm not there, I don't like to think about it."

"Okay, sweetie."

Gracie went to the door. "Good night."

"Good night." Katie watched the door close, then dipped her head and closed her eyes. *Please, God—be with Gracie and her baby. And help me to be the mother you want her to have.*

Four nights later, Zack headed up to the garage apartment to watch a Saints game on TV. At halftime he decided to go to the house for some ice cream. He'd just walked in and was reaching for the kitchen light switch when he heard Katie and Annette talking through the open master bedroom door.

"You've never told me anything about Zack's family," Annette was saying.

"He's an only child," Katie said. "His mother's dead, and his father...well, they don't stay in touch."

"What's the situation?"

"Well, Zack didn't come from a very nurturing environment."

That was putting it mildly. Zack stood in the dark and shamelessly listened.

"His parents had a horrible marriage, with lots of quarrels and jealousy and anger and accusations," Katie continued. "That anger spilled onto Zack. They'd yell at him and sometimes hit him for not much more than being there. Afterward, they'd try to make nice by telling him they loved him, and they'd coerce him into saying it back to them."

"Oh, dear."

"He always felt unwanted, and as it turns out, he was." She paused. "One time he overheard his father accuse his mother of trapping him into marriage by getting pregnant."

Annette made a tsking sound. "That kind of home life leaves scars on children. I saw it when I used to teach. " Annette paused. "When a kid feels unwanted, it makes it hard for them to ever form close relationships."

Katie murmured something he couldn't make out.

"Be careful, Katie," Annette said. "You and Paul had such a special love. I'd hate to see you settle for anything less."

Katie's response was too soft for him to hear. Zack's throat tightened. Was Annette right? Was he damaged goods?

Too damaged to be good for Katie?

"I'd better let you get some sleep," he heard Katie say. He heard the master bedroom door squeak all the way open.

Deciding he didn't really want any ice cream after all, Zack turned and headed back to the garage, pulling the kitchen door quietly shut behind him.

The second week in October, the heat temporarily broke. The day Dave came home from Sunnyside wasn't cool, exactly, but it lacked the oppressive humidity that had lasted all summer. Katie and Zack picked him up and drove him to his little ranch house, where Annette was already waiting.

"Are you sure you two are going to be all right?" Katie asked. She looked at Dave, leaning back in the new leather recliner she'd helped Annette pick out four days ago, then at Annette, sitting beside him in a matching chair.

"We're great," Annette said.

They looked so cute in their matching recliners that Katie's eyes misted.

"Anything we can get you?" Zack asked. "Need us to run any errands or bring you dinner?"

"I think everyone in town has brought us a casserole," Annette said. "We've got meals for a month or more."

"I'll be checking in every day, " Katie said. "And you know we're just a phone call away."

"I know," Dave piped up. "And if she doesn't treat me right, believe me, I'll be calling." Dave shot Annette a wink.

Annette rolled her eyes.

Katie exchanged a grin with Zack, then smiled at Annette. "Looks like you're going to have your hands full. I feel for you."

"What about me?" Dave asked. "Don't I get any sympathy?"

The man was making an amazing recovery. His color was good, his appetite was returning, and he was walking more and more each day. "You get no sympathy at all, buster," Annette said, shaking her head. "Waiting eleven months to have surgery and not telling a soul you even needed it!"

There was a lot of love behind Annette's scolding, and judging from the grin on his face, Dave knew it. More than Dave's arteries and Annette's leg had done a lot of healing over the last couple of months. "I think you're both in wonderful hands," Katie said softly.

Dave and Annette smiled at each other. It was pretty obvious they thought so, too.

As soon as Katie and Zack climbed into Zack's car in the driveway, he leaned over and kissed her. "I've missed you."

"Likewise." While Annette had been staying with them, Katie had kept her distance from Zack, not wanting to make her mother-in-law uncomfortable.

He lifted a strand of her hair and looked at her in a way that made little tendrils of emotion unfurl inside her. "How about coming up to the garage tonight?"

She gazed into his blue eyes and responded to his irresistible smile with one of her own. "I thought you'd never ask."

Gracie: It's a girl! I found out the baby's a girl!

Megan: Cool. Got a name?

Gracie: Not yet. But I've got lots of name books, and I'm picking out clothes and furniture and junk.

Megan: Where will U live after U have the baby?
Gracie: Not sure. With Katie for a while, I guess.
 She's rebuilding her house with 2 bedrooms right
 together and one will be a nursery. Whatzup
 with U?
Megan: Callie's throwing a big Halloween party. I'm
 going as a sexy witch.

Longing punched Gracie's gut, harder than the baby's kicks. Halloween had always been her favorite holiday.

Gracie: I could go as the Great Pumpkin, and I
 wouldn't even need a costume.
Megan: LOL. My mom thinks my costume's 2
 skimpy, but I think it's hot.

Tears beaded in Gracie's eyes. Her stomach was so enormous that her belly button had turned into an outie. She wondered if she'd ever look hot again. Megan didn't realize how lucky she was.

Gracie: Guess you're getting pumped about your ski
 trip.
Megan: Yeah. Gonna look at colleges on the way.

Another fist of longing hit Gracie's gut. If it weren't for Kirt or Dirk or Dork or whoever, she'd be doing stuff like that, too.

Megan: How are things with Katie and Zack?
Gracie: OK, I guess.

Actually, Katie and Zack had turned out to be pretty cool. She liked them, and that made her feel kinda guilty. Sheesh—why did everything have to be so complicated? Even good stuff made her feel bad.

Megan: Are they still hooking up?
Gracie: Yeah. Every night, except when he's gone on business. They think I don't know.
Megan: Pretty funny.
Gracie: Yeah. Grown-ups are so weird.

Dawn light filtered through the window of the garage apartment a week later. Katie moaned as Zack moved deep within her. He showered her face with kisses, then buried his face against her neck, his breathing hot and labored.

Katie clutched his back, her legs wrapped around his. All of her senses converged like sunlight through a magnifying glass, tapering and focusing to the feel of him inside her, filling her, thrilling her, pushing her higher. He thrust, then thrust again, over and over, driving her onward, up and up and up until everything shattered in a brilliant, beautiful explosion of emotion.

"I love you so much!"

The words burst out of her throat before she even knew she was thinking them. No, that wasn't quite right; she'd been thinking them for a few weeks now and feeling them for some time before that, but she hadn't intended to say them.

Over the past month, she and Zack had grown increasingly close. He'd drastically cut back on his travel and was gone only one or two nights a week instead of five or six. Katie's feelings for him had reached the point that they'd just spilled out.

But that wasn't a good thing, judging from the way Zack had gone perfectly still above her. Oh, dear heavens—she hoped she hadn't freaked him out.

They didn't have a great track record where the L-word was concerned. She'd told him she loved him that summer, and he'd tried to convince her that she didn't.

He had a real aversion to those three little words. On more than one occasion and to more than one source, he'd said that he didn't believe in love. Katie didn't believe he really didn't believe, but she believed he believed that he didn't believe. One thing was for certain; she hadn't intended to be the one to utter the loaded phrase first again.

"I love so much how you make me feel," she said, hoping he'd think that's what she'd meant a moment earlier. "I love your body."

He began to move again, and moments later, he found his own completion. She waited until his breathing slowed.

"I love being with you," she said, still hoping to fix things. "I love making love to you. I love the feel of your skin on mine."

He pulled back and looked at her, his gaze inscrutable. She almost said the dreaded words again, but stopped herself in time.

"Kate." He stroked her hair back from her face. "You talk way too much."

"I thought you liked it when I talked during sex."

"Only if you're giving me instructions or saying something dirty."

"Oh. I didn't know there were parameters."

"Yeah, well, now you do." He planted a kiss on her lips and rolled off.

His tone was joking, but there was tension in the way he moved away from her, and he was wearing his poker face—the one where she couldn't tell what he was thinking or feeling.

Katie frowned, wondering if she should say something, then her gaze lit on the bedside clock. Six-twenty. Oh, no—Gracie's alarm went off at six-thirty!

She scooted out of bed and started scrambling for her clothes. "I've got to hurry, or Gracie will be up before I get back to the main house."

Normally Zack would grin and say something teasing, such as, "And she would keel over in shock, because you're totally fooling her," or "Better hurry or she'll ground you." But today, he just said, "Okay," then climbed out of bed and headed for the bathroom.

Katie pulled on her pajamas and bathrobe. Ever since Gracie had started school, Katie had skipped the sneaking-back-to-her-room part and gone directly to the kitchen to make Gracie breakfast. Hopefully Gracie thought she'd slept in her own bed and just set her alarm early.

Katie grabbed the sash of her bathrobe and headed for the door. Saying "I love you" had freaked Zack out, all right.

Well, it was true. He might not want to hear it and she might not want to admit it, but she was in love with him. She was beyond the following-her-heart-and-seeing-where-this-might-lead stage; she was completely, thoroughly, head-over-heels, wildly, madly in love with him.

And when she was in love, she was accustomed to saying it out loud.

But Zack wasn't like Paul. Zack wasn't comfortable with emotions.

A lump formed in Katie's throat. Paul had wanted to fall in love, to get married, to settle down, to have a family.

Zack...didn't. He had trouble with commitment. He had trouble articulating his feelings. Heck, he had trouble feeling his feelings. But Katie thought—at least, she hoped—that he *did* have feelings for her.

She desperately hoped he did, because her feelings for him were deep-rooted, far-reaching, and long-ranging. She wanted a future with him.

Before she was ready to address the future though, she needed to deal with the past. She glanced down at the diamond solitaire and the gold band beneath it on her left hand and made a sudden decision.

It was time—way past time—to put Paul to rest.

Thirty minutes later, Katie sat at Dave's kitchen table, her hand curled around a cup of coffee, her heart pounding at an erratic pace.

"So what's on your mind, dear?" Annette asked.

Katie drew a deep breath. "I think it's time to put Paul to rest."

They looked at each other. Dave cleared his throat. "We do, too, Katie. We have a cemetery plot, if you want a place to bury him."

So Annette and Dave had talked about this. They'd no doubt wondered what had taken her so long. A stab of pain shot through her. "Paul didn't want to be buried.

He wanted his ashes scattered over the lake, off the old fishing pier."

Annette looked at her in surprise. "He told you that?"

Katie nodded. "A week before he left for his first tour of duty."

They'd gone for a moonlit walk along the lakefront and ended up at the end of the old pier where he'd proposed to her. "Did you bring me here to give me another ring?" she'd teased.

"Sorry." He gave her that lopsided grin she knew so well and loved so much. "Fresh out."

"I can think of something else you can give me." She took a step toward him. "A baby."

He cradled her face in his hands and kissed her. "We'll go home and work on that. But first, we need to discuss something serious." The somberness in his eyes made her blood run cold. He moved his hands to her upper arms. "Katie—if something happens to me over there..."

She shook her head, wanting to shake off the topic. "I don't want to talk about it."

"I don't, either. But we've got to." He smoothed a strand of hair behind her ear. "If something happens, I want you to scatter my ashes here."

"Nothing's going to happen." She forced a smile. "Not until we get home, anyway. And then I intend to jump your bones."

"Katie, you've got to hear me out."

The icy lump in her throat made it hard to swallow, much less speak. Paul's hands slid down her arms. "I hate the idea of being buried. But the thought of being here, a part of the lake and the swamp and the sky, at my favorite fishing spot, the spot where you agreed to marry me...well, that idea is kind of peaceful." Maybe it was the three-quarter moon behind him, maybe it was the sheen of tears clouding her vision, but for a moment, he'd looked like he had a halo glowing around him, as if he were shimmering and disappearing, as if she were already losing him.

She was desperate to break the mood, to de-ice the fear freezing her soul. She gave him a wobbly smile, then raised her hand in a snappy salute. "Message received, Captain. Your wishes have been duly noted and filed."

"If it happens, don't send me off with a lot of angst, Katie." He looked into her eyes. "You know what I believe—life doesn't end with death. So promise me you'll send me off with a peaceful heart."

It took her a moment to find her voice. "How can I do that?"

"You'll find a way. I just need to know, going over there, that if something happens, your life won't end, too." A cloud passed in front of the moon. He pressed her fingers. "Promise me."

The only way to end this horrid conversation was to tell him what he needed to hear. She swallowed, looked away from his shadowed face, and said a word she didn't mean. "Okay."

"Okay." His hands moved back up her arms. "I hereby declare this difficult conversation officially over."

"Thank God."

He smiled, kissed the top of her head, then looped his arm around her waist. "Now, about this bone-jumping you mentioned..." They walked off the pier together.

Katie hadn't been back to the pier since.

She looked at Annette and Dave now. "I promised I'd send him off without a lot of angst. I haven't felt able to do that until now."

Annette rested her hand over Katie's. "Well, then, honey, I think it's time you kept your word."

Katie's eyes grew moist. "Would you two like to come with me?"

Dave looked at Annette. Annette nodded.

"Sure," he said. "When?"

"Are you up to it now?" Katie wanted to do this before she lost her courage. "I can drive us right up to the pier, so you won't have any distance to walk."

Dave nodded. "I'm up for it."

Katie swallowed. "I have the urn in my car."

Again, Dave looked to Annette.

The older woman nodded. "Let me get my purse."

Zack entered the house around twelve-thirty. "Kate?"

He'd called her salon and learned she'd taken the afternoon off. Her car was in the drive, so he knew she was home. He searched the downstairs, then headed up the staircase.

He hadn't handled things well this morning. He couldn't bring himself to say a lot of empty words—his parents used to ram "I love yous" down his throat, then force him to parrot the phrase back—but he needed to let Katie know he cared.

Action was more his style, and everyone knew actions spoke louder than words. Working out of a coffee shop in Hammond, he'd spent the morning on the phone and the computer, developing an action plan that would show Katie how much he cared. He'd combed over his schedule, along with the schedules of his top three staff members, all with the intent of shifting a lot of his travel responsibilities onto them.

His staff frequently accused him of micromanaging things—and hell, he did. Not because he didn't trust them, but because novel settings and situations, combined with an overload of work, kept him busy, and when he was busy, he didn't notice the ever-expanding emptiness inside him. He'd traded in poker for corporate risk management because he'd thought a new challenge would keep the dark feelings and doubts at bay, the thoughts that surfaced in the middle of the night and circled like hungry sharks—thoughts like *Nothing matters. Nothing lasts. Nothing has meaning.*

Being around Katie and Gracie had started him thinking. Maybe he was going at things all wrong. Maybe there was another side to life, a side he'd deliberately avoided. Maybe Katie was right about relationships and connections. Maybe he could even move his headquarters lock, stock, and barrel to Chartreuse.

He might not be able to tell Katie the three little words she wanted to hear, but he could give her some concrete evidence that he wanted to be with her and that he intended to stick around for the long term.

He got to the top of the stairs. "Kate?" he called again.

The door to her bedroom was open. He pushed through it and then jerked to a stop.

She was sitting on the floor of the closet, her back to the door. She wore a large man's white dress shirt, the cuffs flopping over her wrists, and she was clutching a gray T-shirt to her face. Earbuds in her ears were attached to an iPod. Several boxes marked "Paul" were open around her.

He abruptly stepped back, feeling as if he'd been slapped. As if a big pitcher of cold water had been dumped on his head. As if someone had punched him in the chest while kicking him in the kidneys, knocking all the wind out of his lungs.

Turning on his heel, Zack hurried down the stairs. His heart took the express elevator.

Damn it. Katie might be sharing his bed, but apparently her heart was still pining for Paul. Had she been fantasizing about her husband while she was making love with him? Was that "I love you" meant for Paul?

His throat felt like he was wearing an overly tight tie. At the very least, Katie was conflicted. Maybe that explained why she had tried so hard to cover up by saying she loved him. His fingers dug into his palm. He headed down the stairs and to the kitchen, where he snatched his car keys off the counter, his stomach curling into a hard fist.

To hell with this. This was why he didn't do emotion. This was exactly why he never let women get close. All that muck his parents had rolled around in—anger and hurt and jealousy and blame—well, that was not for him. He didn't do deep attachments, not with Katie or anyone else. He was out of here as soon as Gracie had her baby and got her life settled.

That was the plan, and he seldom deviated from a plan, once he'd formed one.

Except, in this case, he'd been ready to change the plan.

He scrubbed his hand down his jaw as he stormed out

to his car. Jesus, what a sap. He'd never thought he'd turn into one of those touchy-feely guys. And yet, he never thought he could feel anything as deeply as what he felt for Katie.

Apparently, though, she wasn't over her husband. He didn't want to be all gaga over her if she was hung up on someone else. He didn't want to just be a substitute. He didn't want to be second-best.

He wanted Katie to feel about him the way she'd felt about her husband, damn it. He wanted to have what they'd had—a real-deal, heart-and-soul, in-with-both-feet, whole-enchilada, forever-and-always, equally matched, lover-lovee relationship.

He wanted it all. He wanted everything and more.

And if she couldn't give him that, he wanted nothing at all.

Katie pulled the buds out of her ears and shrugged out of Paul's shirt. Their favorite song no longer made her feel like she could hear him singing along, and his clothes had lost their mojo. She could no longer smell Paul's scent, could no longer feel his presence. This time she didn't bother to put Paul's T-shirt back in the plastic baggie; she just placed it on top of the other clothes and folded over the flaps on the top of the last box.

She'd donned the shirt and pulled out the T-shirt as a kind of Auld Lang Syne while sorting through Paul's things. She'd asked Dave and Annette if they wanted any more of their son's belongings—she'd let them help themselves to his things after his death—and they'd declined. They'd suggested that she give Paul's clothes to two different charities in New Orleans: the Salvation Army and

Bridge House, an alcohol treatment facility that ran a used-clothing store. She'd equally divided the belongings, and Bev's husband had offered to pick up the boxes and deliver them to the charities.

Dispersing Paul's ashes at the lake had been an emotional experience for Katie, Annette, and Dave. Katie had cried, and so had Annette. The three of them had hugged, and then Dave had wrapped his arms tightly around Annette, and Annette had squeezed him back.

They'd needed the closure, Katie thought. Annette and Dave had been estranged at the time of Paul's funeral. They'd needed to comfort each other and grieve their son together.

And as for herself...well, it had been difficult and emotional, but she was glad she'd finally done it. There was only one thing left to do.

Drawing a deep breath, she eased the wedding rings off her finger and crossed the room to her wooden jewelry box on the dresser. With shaking hands, she opened the bottom drawer and set the rings inside. The diamond twinkled against the black velvet.

"Good-bye," she whispered.

Her throat felt swollen as she closed the box. She inhaled deeply, then headed for the door.

It was time to move on. Paul was gone, and she needed to make space in her life for a new beginning.

Around four that afternoon, Lulu eyed Katie in the salon mirror. "Why do you keep checking your crackberry every two minutes?"

Trust Lulu to catch her doing something she'd hoped no one would notice. It was a good thing she was wearing gloves so Lulu wouldn't notice she wasn't wearing her rings.

Katie placed her BlackBerry on the counter of her workstation and picked up the bowl of strawberry-blonde highlights she was applying to Lulu's red curls. "No reason."

"Yes, there is. There's only one reason a woman keeps checking for messages like that," Lulu said. "You're hoping to hear from a man."

Across the room, Rachel nodded.

"That's right," said Josie, who was soaking her fingers in the manicure bowl.

Everyone stared at her. "What happened, honey?" Lulu pressed. "Did you and Zack have a fight?"

"Why would they fight? Nothing's going on between them." Rachel looked up from the manicure station and gave a broad wink.

Lulu, Rachel, and Annie all giggled. Katie focused on stirring the highlighter, her fingers tight around the wooden-handled brush. Aside from Bev, whom she'd sworn to secrecy, Katie hadn't admitted to anyone that she and Zack were romantically involved. Katie didn't want it public knowledge before Gracie knew, and she didn't want Gracie to know until Katie had at least an idea where the relationship was headed. After Zack's reaction to this morning's pronouncement of love, it appeared to be going directly south.

"How long are you going to keep pretending you and the hunk are just friends?" Lulu asked.

Katie picked up a piece of Lulu's hair and slathered it with highlighter. "I bet your husband wishes you'd concentrate on your own love life the way you're fixated on mine."

Everyone laughed.

"Was that an admission that you've got a love life?" Lulu asked.

"It wasn't an admission of anything."

Besides, she might not have a love life anymore. She'd been trying to call Zack since early afternoon, but he hadn't picked up. She'd texted him and e-mailed him, and she'd still gotten no response. Which was highly unusual. They'd fallen into the habit of touching base several times a day. Apparently the L-word had been a bigger gaffe than she'd realized.

After getting Lulu highlighted, blow-dried, and out the door, Katie picked up her phone, strode into the store-room, and called Gracie.

"Hey, sweetie. How was school?"

"Okay." The teen's voice didn't sound okay. She grew sullen whenever the topic of school came up, and she was getting more withdrawn with every passing day. Gracie would talk freely about her classes—especially biology and chemistry, which she loved—but she refused to offer any information about her social life or the lack thereof. Katie had tried to talk to her. She'd told her how she'd been ostracized at school because of her mother's reputation. Gracie had remained close-lipped and hadn't offered to share any of her own experiences.

"Do you have a lot of homework?" Katie asked.

"Yeah. Tons. What's for dinner?"

"I don't know. It's Zack's turn to cook."

"Gonna be kinda hard, considering he's in Vegas."

"What?"

"He texted me and said he's in Vegas. You didn't know?"

She didn't. He hadn't said a word. In fact, just yesterday he'd said he planned to be in town all week. Katie's stomach plunged to her toes. "I, uh, forgot," Katie said, not wanting Gracie to know anything was wrong. "Did he say how long he'll be gone?"

"Maybe three weeks." She heard Gracie chew something that sounded like a carrot.

"Three whole weeks?"

"That's what he said." Another crunch sounded through the phone. "I thought you knew."

"I, uh, didn't realize he'd be gone that long."

Katie hung up, feeling as if she'd eaten a bag of green apples. Her hand shaking, she dialed Zack again. To her surprise, this time he picked up.

"Hi, Kate." It was his poker voice, the one that went with his poker face. It was completely inflection-free. "What's up?"

Anger joined the fear churning in her belly. "You tell me."

"What do you mean?"

How dare he act like nothing was amiss! "Gracie says you're in Vegas."

"Yeah. Something unexpected came up."

"Something that's going to last three weeks?"

"Maybe."

Katie blew out an exasperated breath. She didn't want to play any games. "Zack—what's really going on? Is this about what I said this morning?"

"What did you say?"

"You know exactly what I said. All the talking . . . while

we were..." Was he trying to get her to say it again? She'd be damned if she would. It was hard to keep her voice from shaking. "Just tell me straight out what's going on."

A long sigh blew through the phone. "Look, Kate... this whole thing with you and me...I think we need to take a breather."

"A breather." Funny how the word *breather* stole all the air from her lungs.

"Yeah. I'm just not...I just don't..." He blew out another harsh breath. "I think we need some space."

"I see." He was doing it again—the same damned thing he'd done that summer. As soon as she told him how she felt, he shut down and backed away. She whipped around, paced six steps across the tiny room, then turned around and crossed the room again. Anger vied with hurt for top billing, duking it out inside her like rival prize-fighters. Anger won. "Well, there's probably about two thousand miles of space between Vegas and Chartreuse. I hope that's enough for you. Because as far as I'm concerned, you can just stay there. Permanently."

"Come on now, Kate."

"You obviously can't handle closeness, so I want to give you all the space you need." She clicked off the phone and burst into tears.

Bev came into the storeroom five minutes later to find Katie sitting on the washer, crying.

"Katie, honey—what's wrong?"

Amid a fresh spate of tears, Katie told her.

"Oh, sweetie." The older woman pulled Katie to her bony chest and patted her back. "He's running scared," Bev said. "He just needs some time."

"I don't know, Bev. He sounded awfully distant."

"He'll be back."

"I don't know that I want him back. This is what he always does. I don't want a man who runs away every time we get close." She burst into new tears. "I want a man who loves me back. A man like Paul."

"Oh, sweetie." Her hands on Katie's shoulders, she drew back and looked at her. "Putting Paul to rest this morning had to be so rough on you."

It had been. But not nearly as rough as she'd feared, because at the time, she'd thought she had a future with Zack.

Bev pulled a tissue out of her pocket and handed it to Katie. "You know, this is all new territory for Zack. It's hard to break lifelong patterns, sweetie."

"What's so hard about letting someone love you and loving them back?"

"My guess is he thinks you're going to jerk the rug out from under him once he puts his heart out there. It's what he saw growing up."

Bev was right, but that didn't make it okay. Katie dabbed at her eyes.

"When you think about it, he's made a lot of concessions already. He's moved to Chartreuse, he's taken in Gracie, he has the two of you living with him. He even took in Annette for a while. My guess is he needs some time to process it all before he moves to the next step."

"He could just tell me that."

"Oh, honey, men are strange animals. They hate to admit to the slightest weakness."

"Caring isn't weakness."

"Yeah, well, from everything you've told me, Zack thinks it is. He thinks it gives you power over him."

"I don't want power. I just want love."

And the really frustrating thing was, she was pretty sure Zack loved her. After all, how could he act so considerate and attentive and kind if he didn't love her, at least a little?

What was so awful about what she'd said, anyway?

A fresh spurt of anger shot through her. "Why does he get to set the limits on what is and isn't allowable in our relationship?"

"He doesn't. And I suspect that's a lesson he's learning right now. My guess is he's even more miserable than you are."

"I hope so."

Bev gave her an encouraging smile. "This will all work out, honey."

"I don't know." Katie's heart felt as if it were tied to a concrete block. "Love isn't just a feeling; it's a choice. You have to want to be in a relationship. I don't want to love someone who doesn't want to love me."

Bev patted her back. "You've had a rough day. Why don't you go home and spend some time with that daughter of yours? I'll close up here."

Katie gave her a grateful smile. "Thanks, Bev."

"Don't mention it." Bev gave her a hug. "And Katie—things will work out."

But Katie wasn't so sure. She knew what it was like to be wholly loved by a man, and she wasn't willing to settle for anything else.

CHAPTER TWENTY-SIX

"Don't forget your lunch," Katie said, holding out a brown paper sack a week later.

"Thanks." Gracie took the sack and stuffed it into her book bag. It made her uneasy, having Katie do things for her that her mother used to do. She didn't even think about her mother very much anymore, and that made her feel guilty and confused.

A lot of things confused her. For one thing, she didn't know what was going on between Katie and Zack. They must have had a big fight, but neither of them admitted it. At least they weren't mad at her. Zack texted and called her all the time, and Katie was kind and caring and, well, Katie-like. Katie seemed awfully sad, and Gracie found herself trying to cheer her up.

Gracie's feelings about the baby were all jumbled up, too. She fluctuated between feeling excited and tender to feeling resentful and scared to death. She was more than a little horrified at the way the baby was changing her body. Her breasts kept getting bigger and heavier, and her stomach was getting these weird red lines that made it look like a road map. Was she going to be deformed for the rest of her life?

And then there was the whole giving-birth thing— God, that was beyond terrifying. And what about being a mother? Would she be able to calm the baby when it cried? Would she be able to change the diapers without puking?

And what about her own life? She'd hoped to someday find a cool guy and fall in love. Would anybody ever want to date her if she already had a baby? And what about college and a career? She'd been thinking she might want to be a doctor, but that took a lot of school and studying and work, and she didn't know how she'd do that and raise a child.

She was confused about other things, too. She had these dark thoughts she was ashamed to admit, even to herself. She was angry, and she didn't even know at whom. She sometimes felt like the baby was a big parasite just leeching the life out of her. Sometimes she even wished the baby would die and she could just be a normal seventeen-year-old, and then she'd hate herself for having such an awful thought.

Katie handed her a fruit cup and a spoon. "I forgot to put these in your lunch."

"Thanks," Gracie muttered, sticking them in her bag.

"It's too bad the school food is so rotten."

The school food wasn't the problem. The problem was the kids in the cafeteria. She'd steered clear of the place ever since the first day.

Just the thought of that day made her kinda sick. Gracie had carried her tray of spaghetti through the cafeteria only to find all the tables at least partially occupied.

Everyone had gawked at her as if she were some kind of freakzoid.

She'd finally just sucked up her fear and plopped down in a spot. Ignoring the girls already seated at the table, she'd picked up her milk carton and started to open it.

"Hey, you're in my seat."

Gracie looked up to see a brunette with deep-set eyes standing beside her, her hand on her hip, a lunch box dangling from her wrist.

"I didn't see a reserved sign," Gracie commented.

"But I always sit there!"

"Not today." The milk carton opened too hard, and chocolate milk splashed all over Gracie's baggy white shirt.

"What a slob." The girl huffed out a disgusted breath and looked at the plate of spaghetti on Gracie's tray. "You know, you really shouldn't eat those carbs. They'll make you even fatter."

Gracie's face burned as the girl stalked off. "I'm not fat," she called after her, loud enough to stop conversations across half the room. "I'm pregnant."

"Told you," whispered a freckled, sandy-haired girl at the end of the table. The room buzzed loudly as all the kids turned and stared at her.

Gracie focused on getting her straw out of the wrapper and into the milk carton.

"So how did it happen?" a cherub-cheeked blonde at the table inquired.

Gracie frowned at her. "You're kidding, right?"

The other girls at the table snickered. The one on the far left, a brunette wearing a tight red shirt over a cami, leaned forward. "She means, did a condom break or something?"

Or something covered a lot of territory. "Yeah." Gracie stuck her fork into her spaghetti, hoping to signal that she wanted to eat, not talk.

"You're from Pittsburgh, right?"

"Actually, I'm from Kansas City." She refused to be defined by the year she'd spent at her aunt's.

"You're Gracie, right? I'm Kayla, and this is Lauren, and Gabby, and Alex and Jennifer."

"So . . . tell us about the baby's daddy." The ponytailed girl in the middle of the opposite side—Gabby or Alex, Gracie wasn't sure which—leaned forward. "Are you in love with him?"

"Yeah. What's he like?" the brunette asked.

Gracie forked a bite of spaghetti into her mouth. Maybe by the time she finished chewing, they'd have moved on to another topic.

"Is he going to help raise the baby?"

"Is he going to move here, too?"

The spaghetti tasted like shredded latex. It took a monumental effort to swallow. "He's not in the picture," Gracie finally managed to say.

"Why not?" asked the brunette.

Jeez, what was with all these questions? It wasn't like they actually cared. They just wanted information so they could gossip about her. "Because he's a freakin' rat."

"If he's a rat, why did you sleep with him?"

Her palms were perspiring so much it was hard to hold the fork. She jabbed it back into the spaghetti. "I didn't know he was a rat until it was too late, okay?"

"He freaked out when he learned you were pregnant, huh?" the ponytailed girl said knowingly.

Gracie's stomach felt tighter and tighter. She hunkered down over her tray. "I really don't want to talk about it."

"Is he somebody famous?" The brunette turned to the other girls. "Her dad hangs out with all kinds of famous people. And her mother is Emma Jamison's best friend. I bet her boyfriend is somebody famous, too."

Gracie felt like crawling under the chair, but she didn't want to let them know they were bothering her. "Wow. And here I thought my secret was safe."

The ponytailed girl slapped her palm on the table. "I knew it!"

Jeez, didn't these girls understand the concept of sarcasm?

"Is she kidding? I think she's kidding," said the cherub-cheeked blonde.

"Why would she kid about a thing like that?" the brunette asked.

"I dunno." The ponytailed girl looked at Gracie. "Are you kidding?"

If they couldn't figure it out, Gracie felt no inclination to enlighten them. She lifted her shoulders.

"Oh my God! She's *not* kidding!" Freckle Face leaned forward, her eyes wide.

"I knew there was a reason you and your dad had moved here," the brunette said excitedly. Her eyes were big as saucers. "It's to lay low while you're pregnant, isn't it?"

"It can't be anyone famous," said Cherub Cheeks. "She said the dad was a rat."

"So? Famous people can be jerks."

Ponytail Girl lowered her voice. "Who is it? We promise we won't tell."

Gracie should have just said, "I'm joking," or "Get real," or even "Just how stupid are you?" But Gracie had never been able to resist pushing the envelope. "Well, if you promise not to tell..."

"Promise." The brunette raised her hand like she was taking an oath.

"Scout's honor," said the girl next to her, raising two fingers.

"Yeah. Who is it?" Freckles asked.

"Well"—Gracie leaned over her tray and spoke in a loud whisper—"it's one of the Jonas Brothers."

"Oh my God!" Ponytail Girl clasped her hands to her chest. "Which one?"

"I can't say." Mainly because she hated their music and didn't even know their names.

"Oh, come on," the brunette wheedled. "You've told us this much. You've got to tell us!"

"Yeah. We promise to keep it secret."

"I can't tell you, because I don't know." Gracie paused dramatically and looked at their puzzled faces. She shot them a wicked smile. "I did all three of them."

The girls collectively gasped. Gracie picked up her tray, marched to the return window across the room, and slid it through the opening.

The lunch lady on the other side looked at her practically untouched meal. "Didn't you like the food, honey?"

"I lost my appetite," Gracie said.

As it turned out, the lunch lady knew Katie, and

reported that Gracie had barely touched her meal. The next day, Katie had started making Gracie's lunch.

"Are you making any friends?" Katie asked now as Gracie shoved her arm through the strap of her backpack.

"Not really."

"Amber Drindle is nice," Katie said. "I cut her hair. I can talk to her mother and see about getting you girls together."

What Katie didn't know, and Gracie was too proud to tell her, was that being seen with Gracie would be social suicide.

"No, thanks."

"Who do you sit with at lunch?"

"No one in particular." The truth was, she'd started spending her lunch hour hiding out in the girls' rest-room.

Word had quickly spread about her Jonas Brothers' comment. "As if the Jonas Brothers would touch that," a Barbie look-alike had said to her friend as they'd passed in the hall.

"It was a joke," Gracie had snarled. But no one seemed to think it was funny. For more than a month afterward, she couldn't walk down the hall without overhearing comments like, "pathetic," "liar," and "slut." A particularly obnoxious jock thought it was funny to holler, "Will you have my baby if I sing 'Please Be Mine'?"

Eventually, things had kinda died down. Now everyone just mainly cut her a wide berth, as if she were contagious.

Gracie slung the book bag over her shoulder and headed out the door.

"Have a great day, sweetie," Katie called.

Gracie snorted. "As if anything could be great about school."

Although the truth was, she didn't really mind the classes. She liked them, in fact. Once she was safely behind a desk, she felt like she could actually breathe. She was a fast learner, she liked her teachers, and she was getting good grades again. Plus today was dissection day in biology. They were going to cut up rats, which sounded gross to most kids, but Gracie was looking forward to it. She was interested in the way living things were put together.

The school was a regional high school, which meant kids from the entire parish attended it, so it was a lot bigger than she'd thought it would be when she first moved to this tiny town. It was only three blocks from the house, so she walked.

She climbed the concrete stairs of the old brick building, past the groups of kids clustered at the door, and strode down the hall to her locker. She turned the lock—three left, five right, four left—and tugged the door open.

A dead rat fell out, a pacifier and a large note tied around its neck. The note read, "Gracie's baby."

She jumped back and screamed.

Loud laughter sounded behind her. She turned around and realized that a crowd of kids were standing behind her, just cracking up. Apparently the practical joke had been a group effort.

Tears flooded her eyes. Dropping her books on the floor, Gracie turned and fled down the hall, out the school door, and down the street.

The contractor rebuilding Katie's house pushed his mirrored sunglasses up his balding head, under the rim of his cap that read Flautere Home Construction and Remodeling. "We're way ahead of schedule," he said in a lilting Cajun accent. "If ever't'ing goes well, we'll have you fix't up and moved back in less'n a month."

Katie squinted at the new roof of her house. "I thought it was going to take at least two or three more months."

"We been lucky, cher. The weather's been dry, and the slow econ'my has work't in our favor. The stores had all the supplies we needed in stock, and all the subcontractors have been 'vailable when we needed them. We're sailin' along."

"Well, great."

So why didn't it feel great? Her stomach clenched as she acknowledged the answer: as long as she lived at Zack's house, she could delude herself into believing that she and Zack had a chance of working things out.

Yeah, right. It was going on two weeks, and she hadn't heard a word from him. He stayed in regular touch with Gracie, but as far as Katie was concerned, he'd been entirely incommunicado.

Not that she'd tried to contact him, either. As far as she was concerned, she'd handed him her heart, and he'd rejected it.

With each passing day, the facts were becoming more obvious: Zack was not now, and never would be, commitment material. She couldn't build a life with someone who bolted the minute things got emotional.

Her cell phone rang. In spite of herself, her pulse rate spiked at the thought it might be Zack. She reached into her purse, pulled it out, and looked at the number. Not Zack. It was a local number she didn't recognize.

A female voice spoke through the earpiece. "Katie,

this is Jeanne at the high school. I was calling to see if Gracie's okay."

"Why wouldn't she be?"

"Well, she isn't at school. She was here before the bell rang for first hour, but she never went to class."

Alarm jangled down Katie's spine.

"I hoped she was there with you."

"No."

"Oh. Oh, dear."

The alarm ratcheted up to panic. "Oh, dear, what?"

"Well, there was an incident at her locker. She was upset."

"What kind of incident?"

"Somebody put a rat in her locker."

"A *rat*?"

"It was one of the ones the kids dissect in advanced biology. It was a prank."

"Oh, no." Katie tightened her grip on the phone.

"We don't know who did it," Jeanne continued, "but when we find out who it was, Principal Burton intends to suspend them."

They ought to be strung up by their toes, but that wouldn't help Gracie, and helping Gracie was all that Katie cared about. "This was what—two hours ago? Why did you wait to call me?"

"We hoped she'd come back."

Katie speed-dialed Gracie's phone. Voice mail immediately kicked in, meaning her phone was turned off. She called Annette and Dave. They hadn't heard from Gracie, either. Dave suggested she call the bookstore, which was being run by the assistant manager during Dave's convalescence. No luck there, either.

Maybe she'd gone home. Katie rushed down the block, only to find Zack's house empty. Gracie's Prius was in the driveway. She hadn't driven anywhere.

There was only one other person whom Gracie might call. Drawing a deep breath, Katie dialed the number.

Zack picked up on the first ring.

"Have you heard from Gracie today?" she asked.

"No. What's going on?"

Katie rapidly filled him in.

Zack muttered a low oath.

"I don't know where else she'd go," Katie told him.

"She likes to walk when she's upset," Zack said. "That's what she was doing when your house was struck by lightning. Are there any walking paths around the school?"

"The park at the lakefront is about half a mile away."

"Look there. And keep your phone with you. I think she'll call."

A blackberry bramble grabbed Gracie's hair as she hurried around a bend on the lakeside trail. She stopped, breathing heavily, and swatted at the branch to free her hair. A thorn ripped the tender white skin on the inside of her wrist. "Damn it," she muttered as blood beaded up along the inch-long red line. Panting, Gracie raised her hand to her mouth and sucked on the wound, then looked at it. It was just a superficial cut. Too bad; if it were deeper, she might bleed to death, and then the world would be a better place.

She swiped at the tears coursing down her face. She'd thought she was out of tears, after crying for the past couple of hours, but apparently not. How much misery was one person supposed to handle?

Probably as much as they brought on themselves. After all, everything bad that had happened to her was her own fault.

Her parents' death. Her pregnancy. Even the way the kids at school treated her.

The thought of that rat falling out of her locker made her shudder. Not because it was a dead rat, which was pretty gross, and not even because it was dyed yellow with blue veins—that was so you could see the venous system when you dissected it. The thing about the formaldehyde-soaked rodent that had totally creeped her out had been the tag on its foot: "Gracie's baby."

As if she had a dead, limp, yellow-and-blue rat inside her. It was like coming face-to-face with her worst fear. The guy who'd knocked her up had been a rat of the first order. Maybe her baby was going to be a rat, too.

The thought made her sick. She didn't want anything to do with that creep, and yet here she was, having his baby. Last night she'd had another nightmare about him. She'd dreamed she was wearing a puffy pink dress, kinda like the princess costume she used to dress up in when she was little, and she was in a car going to a prom or something. She couldn't see the face of her date, but she was all happy and excited. And then he turned toward her and it was him, only his face was really a mask. And she'd gotten really scared and closed her eyes, because she just knew he was so horrible she would die if she really saw him, and then all of a sudden they were out of the car and he was pinning her down and she couldn't breathe, and she woke up feeling like her heart was going to pound out of her chest.

For the trillionth time, she wondered what her mom would say if she knew she was pregnant. Her mother would have been so disappointed that it would have killed her if she weren't already dead.

Another tear flashed down her face. Why was she such a jerk? Her dad had once told her that she charged at life as if it were an enemy. Why did she do that? She didn't know. Something was wrong with her. Something about her just didn't fit in with the rest of the world.

She tried to pretend she didn't care, but she did. She cared so much it hurt. The truth was, she cared so much that she preemptively treated people with disdain, so it wouldn't hurt when they rejected her.

Could she really love this baby, when she couldn't even love herself? Was she going to think about Kirk or Kirt or whoever he was every time she looked at it? The bigger her belly grew, the more scared she got.

She was a total fake. She pretended she had it all together, but she didn't know what the hell she was doing most of the time. If she couldn't manage her own life, how the hell could she manage someone else's? Her baby was going to be even more screwed up than she was. She had no business procreating her own wretched existence. She wished the baby would just go away.

She resumed her march along the deserted lake trail. The trees and bushes had thinned out as she neared the lake, then gave way to a mowed stretch that ran beside the road. The sun crept out from behind the clouds, and although it was October, the sun beat down like a blowtorch. Jeez, did it ever cool off in Louisiana, or was it always hot? She sat down on the grass and pulled up her leg, then noticed some blood on the thigh of her jeans. That stupid thorn had really made her bleed. She glanced at her wrist, and saw that the cut was just a thin red line.

The blood wasn't coming from her wrist. It was coming from...

Holy crap! She was bleeding. Bad. Was she losing the baby? She didn't feel any cramps or anything. Still, this was a lot of blood.

The breath froze in her throat, as if it couldn't go in or out, and her chest ached. Oh, God—it was all those bad thoughts. That book *The Secret* that Annette had loaned her said that people made things materialize by thinking about them. Had she killed the baby by wishing she wasn't pregnant?

"I didn't mean it," she whispered. Her heart pounded like a tom-tom. She stood up, then felt a sticky warmth between her legs. She sat back down, panic making her breath come in fast spurts. *Oh God. Oh God. Oh God.* She reached in her purse, pulled out her phone, and hit Katie's speed-dial button.

"Help," she said as soon as Katie answered. "I think I'm losing the baby."

CHAPTER TWENTY-SEVEN

Katie stroked Gracie's hair as Dr. Greene ran an ultrasound over the girl's stomach thirty minutes later at the hospital. Katie was quaking inside, but she tried hard to project a sense of calm for her daughter's sake.

"It's what we hoped wouldn't happen," Dr. Greene told Gracie. "Your placenta has grown over your cervix."

Worry coiled through Katie's body.

Gracie raised her head. Her eyes were swollen from crying. "Is the baby okay?"

"Looks fine." The doctor pointed to the screen. "There she is. And her heartbeat sounds good and strong."

"Oh, thank God." Gracie lay back and stared at the screen.

The tightness in Katie's chest loosened a bit.

"That's the good news. The bad news is, you are now on complete bedrest."

"For how long?" Gracie asked.

"The rest of your pregnancy."

"No way. That's more than a month!"

"There's no other option."

"So this is serious?" Katie's brow pulled together.

"I'm afraid it is. Gravity is the enemy—especially as we get closer to her due date, and the cervix softens and thins. And she's definitely going to need to be delivered by C-section."

The doctor turned off the ultrasound machine. "I want to keep you at the hospital until the bleeding stops. If it doesn't stop or you have any further bleeding once you get home, you'll have to stay here until you deliver."

Gracie grabbed the doctor's sleeve as Dr. Greene rose from her seat by the side of the exam table. She stopped and turned. Gracie peered up at her with anxious eyes. "Did I do something to cause this?"

"No, Gracie. It's just something that happened."

"Are you sure? It's not because I got upset or walked too fast or too far or got too hot or…or…" Her voice shook, and her eyes filled with tears. "Or thought bad thoughts?"

The doctor patted her hand. "No. Placenta previa is just one of those things. There's absolutely nothing you could have done to cause it or prevent it."

Gracie swallowed and nodded. Katie didn't think she looked entirely convinced.

"There is one more thing," Dr. Greene said. "There's a very strong chance we're going to need to deliver you early."

"How early?"

"Well, it depends on how things go. We don't want your placenta to detach, so we're going to monitor you very closely to make sure that doesn't happen. And I'm going to start you on a medication to help your baby's lungs mature early." The doctor patted her hand again and went out the door.

Gracie closed her eyes. Tears fell from the corners.

"Are you okay?" Katie asked.

"Yeah. I just..." The girl turned her head away.

"What is it, sweetie?"

"Why do I always hurt people I love?"

"The doctor said this wasn't your fault."

"I heard her. But they said that about my parents' death, too, and it's not the truth."

Katie's brow furrowed. "What do you mean, sweetie?"

Gracie made a gulping sound. "The night my parents had that wreck...I'd sneaked out of the house to go to a party." Gracie flung an arm over her face, hiding her eyes. A sob eked out from under it. "They were out looking for me when their car crashed."

"Oh, Gracie." In addition to grieving her parents, Gracie was drowning in guilt for their deaths. She must have been smothering under the weight of it all. Combined with the rape and the pregnancy, the poor girl was carrying an almost unimaginable burden.

Katie leaned down and folded Gracie into her arms. She felt Gracie's pain like a physical thing wedged in her chest. She wished she could take all the girl's hurts and bear them for her. "That doesn't make it your fault. It was a terrible accident, that's all. It's no one's fault."

"But if I hadn't sneaked out, they wouldn't have been in the car, and they wouldn't be dead."

Katie searched her heart for a way to comfort the girl. "You wouldn't have gone if you'd known what was going to happen. So many things are just beyond our control, Gracie."

"But it's my fault, because I didn't do the right thing."

"No one does the right thing all the time. All we can do is ask for forgiveness, let it go, and make better choices in the future." Katie stroked the girl's arm. "Do you think your parents would want you feeling miserable for the rest of your life?"

"No."

"What kind of life would they want for you and your baby?"

"A good one. A happy one."

"Well, then, honor their memory by trying to live like that."

Gracie drew a sob-wrenched breath. Katie found a tissue on the exam room counter and handed her one.

An orderly and a nurse came through the door, pushing a gurney. "We're going to take you to a room now, Gracie."

"Okay." Gracie reached for Katie's hand. "Will you come, too?"

Katie squeezed the girl's fingers, her eyes nearly as full as her heart. She blinked back her tears and smiled. "Absolutely."

Five hours later, Zack strode down the hall toward Gracie's room, only to nearly collide with Katie.

"Zack!" Her eyes flew open wide, then rapidly narrowed. "What are you doing here?"

"I caught a plane right after you called and told me what happened at school. I got your message that Gracie was at the hospital when I landed." He peered into her face. She looked exhausted and depleted, and her eyes were red, as if she'd been crying. "What's going on?"

As they walked to a bench at the end of the hall, Katie filled him in.

Zack leaned his head against the wall and closed his eyes, feeling like he'd eaten a batch of bad oysters. Holy crap—that poor kid! He opened his eyes. "I want to see her."

"She just fell asleep. That's why I left her room."

"Okay. I'll wait."

Katie rose from the bench. "Well, then, I'll give you some space."

The words cut into him like barbed wire. "Kate..."

She started to walk away. He grabbed her arm.

She turned and looked at him, her eyes guarded and wary, and then, there it was again—that miserable, sick, needy feeling, the same feeling he'd gotten in his gut when he'd seen Katie wearing her late husband's clothes. It wasn't like him to feel this way. He didn't want to feel this pathetic longing and yearning, like a friggin' homeless person gazing into a warm house. He liked his life separate and simple and clean and straightforward. No attachments, no obligations, no strings.

Except...all of a sudden, there were strings everywhere. Heartstrings, tying him to Gracie and Katie. He couldn't explain it and he didn't understand it, but he needed to be with them, needed to take care of them, needed them to need him.

He didn't know when or how it had happened. One minute he'd thought everything was normal, and the next, he was in alien territory. How the hell was he supposed to navigate? He didn't have a GPS or a map or a compass or even a friggin' clue.

No clue at all. Hell. He'd been miserable ever since he'd left. He'd tried to focus on work, but his mind kept wandering back to Katie. He started to call her a dozen times each day, then each time, he changed his mind. What good would it do? What was he going to say? He wasn't going to make a lot of promises he didn't know if he could keep or pin labels on emotions he didn't understand.

Still, he owed her some kind of explanation. Or did he? She'd probably be better off just thinking he was a total ass. Which he was, where she was concerned. He should just leave her alone.

But something about her wouldn't let him do that.

"Kate—I missed you."

"Not enough to pick up the phone, apparently."

"I didn't know what to say." He shoved his hands in his pockets. "I still don't."

"Well, then, I guess that says it all."

She started to walk away again. He fell in step beside her. "Where were you going?"

"To the house. I need to pick up my toothbrush and a few things. There's a recliner in Gracie's room I can sleep in."

"I'll stay, too."

"No need. Besides, there's nowhere for you to sleep."

Was she saying he'd just be in the way? His chin jutted out. "I'll just stay out here, in the hall. I'm not going to leave you two at a time like this."

To his relief, she didn't mount any further protest.

"I'll run get what you need. Just make me a list."

"I can probably name them on one hand." She lifted her hand and counted them off on her fingers. "Toothbrush, toothpaste, face soap, hairbrushes, the Game Boy, and the iPod."

He grinned. "That covers Gracie. How about you?"

"I don't really need anything aside from my toothbrush."

What about me? Do you need me?

Jeez, when had he turned into such a basket case? It wasn't like him to think crap like this.

What was happening to him? It was as if an alien had taken over his body. He'd always been independent, self-sufficient, detached, and aloof. He was a lone wolf, and he liked it that way.

So why the heck did being alone suddenly seem so lonely?

Katie slept in Gracie's hospital room for the next three nights and kept a nearly constant daytime vigil, as well. Whenever Zack would step into the room, she would leave.

Zack went to the boxing gym in Hammond and pounded on a punching bag, pretending it was the cretins at the high school, taking another few swipes at the A-hole who'd raped Gracie, and finally throwing a few punches at himself.

On the fourth morning, the doctor caught both Zack and Katie in the hallway outside Gracie's room. "I'm going to release Gracie today," she said. "She can get up to use the bathroom and take a quick shower, but other than that, she's to stay in bed. I don't want her climbing stairs or walking unnecessarily. And she'll need someone with her around the clock, because if she has any bleeding, she needs to get to the hospital immediately." The doctor looked at them. "It's not going to be easy for her. And it's not going to be easy for you, either."

Boy, that was the truth. And the way Katie was avoiding him was going to make it even harder. As the doctor walked away, Katie started to head back into Gracie's room. Zack touched her arm.

Katie froze, then slowly turned toward him. She blew a lock of hair out of her eyes, her expression exasperated. "What?"

Her clothes were rumpled, her hair was askew, and she had dark circles under her eyes. She was so beautiful it made his chest hurt. "Kate, this is ridiculous."

"I don't know what you're talking about."

"The way you're avoiding me."

"I'm just trying to give you space."

The way she said it, all emotionless and sarcasm-free, hurt worse than snarkiness ever could. He wished she were angry or indignant or at least snide. That would mean she still felt something for him.

"Kate, look—I blew it." He ran a hand down his face. "I'm sorry. I just don't know how to deal with emotional things."

"And whenever you don't know how to deal, you leave."

"It won't happen again." He looked at the floor. "I was wrong."

"No, you were right. We needed a breather."

His hands clenched and unclenched at his sides. "I've had enough of one."

"Well, I haven't."

He deserved that. It was only fair. He cleared his throat. "I've arranged my schedule so that I don't have to travel until after the baby is born."

"I'm sure that will mean a lot to Gracie. I'll try to stay out of your way."

"I don't want you to stay out of my way. I want us to go back to the way things were."

She looked at him. For a moment, he saw a depth and breadth of pain in her eyes that nearly stopped his heart. "There's no such thing as going back," she said softly.

He watched her disappear into Gracie's room, and he stood there, wondering if he had put that pain in her eyes or if it was all about Paul. He didn't even know which would make him feel worse.

CHAPTER TWENTY-EIGHT

Megan: What's it like being homeschooled?
Gracie: Pretty cool. Katie teaches social studies and biology, Annette teaches English and history, and Zack does trigonometry and chemistry. I'm also taking an art course online.
Megan: Do U still think your birth parents are hooking up?
Gracie: No. They had a fight or something. When Zack comes in the room, Katie leaves. It's really tense.

Katie opened the kitchen door, then bent and picked up the grocery bags she'd set down, pushing through the door backward. "That wind is something else! And the sky is practically black. It looks like we're in for one heck of a..." She turned around to find Zack sitting at the kitchen table, his laptop open. She immediately froze.

"I—I thought you were Annette. I mean, she was here with Gracie when I left, so..."

Zack's chair scraped against the hardwood floor. "I told her to go home before the storm hits."

"Oh."

He rose and came toward her. "Let me help with those." Before she could protest, he'd taken most of the bags from her arms.

Her mouth went dry. Ever since Gracie had come home from the hospital two weeks ago, Katie had tried to keep her physical distance from Zack. Just being in the same room with him unnerved her. She noticed things she had no business noticing—the way his chest rose and fell as he breathed, the swirl of his hair at his crown, the shadow on his shaved jaw.

"Any more bags in the car?"

"No. That's all."

He set the bags on the counter and started unloading them. He lifted the gallon of milk and headed to the refrigerator.

It was an ordinary activity, yet it held her riveted. She watched his pectoral muscles shift beneath the cotton of his blue polo shirt, watched the dusting of hair on his forearm catch the light, watched his hand curl around the handle of the plastic jug. Memories of those hands—the way his fingers moved across her skin, the way the little callus on the inside of his palm rasped the underside of her breast and the inside of her thigh—flashed through her mind, making her dizzy.

She swallowed hard and tried to act normal, whatever that was.

The silence was stilted. Painful. Stifling.

"How's Gracie?" she managed.

"Sleeping now. She was kind of grouchy."

"Can't blame her. Staying in bed all the time must be awful." Katie opened the pantry and put away a can of soup. "I'll put these away and then get out of your way."

He moved forward and lifted a bag of fresh peaches. "You know, you don't have to run off every time you see me."

Yes, I do. She silently removed a loaf of bread and put it in the breadbox.

"Gracie asked me why you were mad at me."

"What did you tell her?"

"That I acted like a jerk."

"At least you were honest."

He leaned against the counter and smiled. Oh, dear heavens—she'd forgotten about the wattage of his smile. It had a way of melting her.

"She wanted to know what I'd done that was so bad you couldn't forgive me."

"I forgive you," Katie said.

"You do?"

"Yeah. I just don't..."

There was that smile again, sneaking its way past her defenses. "Don't trust me?"

Her lips curved of their own volition, an automatic reaction to his grin. "Something like that."

"Is it really me?" His dimple winked at her. "Or is it yourself you don't trust?"

They were slipping into dangerous territory, back into flirtation zone, back into their old teasing ways of verbal foreplay. "Zack..." She meant his name to sound like a warning. It came out more like an invitation.

"Let me guess." His dimple deepened. "You're afraid

you're going to hurl yourself into my arms in a mad lather of passion."

She rolled her eyes. "Oh, please."

He moved closer. "I love it when you beg."

She grinned in spite of herself. "You were right about the first part. I'm afraid I'm going to hurl."

He laughed and moved still closer. "God, Kate—I've missed you."

His eyes were blue fathoms, twenty thousand leagues of ocean-deep feeling. The emotion in his gaze stole her breath. He might not be able to put his feelings into words, but she couldn't deny the message in his eyes. Her legs went weak.

He moved yet closer. His thighs wedged her against the kitchen counter. "I've missed you like crazy," he said. "I've missed you so much I can't think."

He was going to kiss her. She felt it coming, felt it like the storm brewing outside. She knew it was about to happen, and she did nothing to stop it.

His mouth lowered to hers. And then, God help her—she wound her arms around his neck and kissed him back, as if he were oxygen and she was coming up for air after a long, undersea dive.

"Don't mind me."

Katie dropped her arms. Her eyes flew open, and she saw Gracie standing in the doorway. One hand rested on her enormous belly, which was pushing her "I heart T-shirts" T-shirt to the outer limits of the cotton's stretchability.

"Gracie!" Katie pushed Zack away. "What are you doing up?"

"I woke up, and I had to go to the bathroom. And I heard you in here."

Katie turned toward the counter and pretended to need something in the cabinet above. "You know what the doctor said. You're supposed to stay in bed."

"Except when I go to the bathroom."

"Well, this isn't the bathroom."

"I know." She grinned. "It's not a bedroom, either."

"It—it's not what you think." She turned and looked to Zack for help. He grinned and shrugged. No help would be forthcoming from that quarter, she realized with frustration. "We haven't been—I mean, we're not..."

Gracie rolled her eyes, then waved as something caught her eye through the kitchen door. "Oh, look. Here comes Annette."

Katie turned as Annette let herself in the kitchen door. Annette's gaze locked on the girl, and she frowned, her eyes alarmed. "Gracie! What are you doing out of bed?"

"I got up to go to the bathroom, then I caught them snogging."

"Snogging?"

"Making out."

"Gracie, go to bed," Katie said.

"Okeydoke." She shuffled off to her room. "But it looked to me as if you two are the ones headed in that direction."

Zack scooped up his laptop. "Nice to see you, Annette. If you'll excuse me, I've got to print out a letter."

Coward. Katie telegraphed the word to him with narrowed eyes. He winked.

"Well!" Annette looked both flustered and amused.

"I came back for my glasses—I think I left them... Oh, there they are." She scooped them off the table.

Katie felt compelled to offer some kind of explanation. "What Gracie said... We weren't... I mean, we were just..."

Annette threw up her hands. "No need to explain. But, Katie, I want you to know... I mean, I don't know what your situation is, but if you were to be involved with Zack—or with someone else, for that matter... well, I want you to know that I'm all for it. Not that I think you're waiting for my approval or anything."

Katie's face heated. "Annette, I..."

"I just want to say that Paul would want you to be happy." Annette gathered up her keys. "Gotta run—the weather center is predicting this storm will be a bad one."

"Would you like to stay for dinner?" The thought of being alone with Zack suddenly seemed fraught with danger.

"Thanks, but no. Dave's cooked a pot roast."

"He cooks?" Paul used to say his dad was totally lost in the kitchen.

"It's a recently acquired skill." A soft, amused expression crossed her face. "He's got quite a few of those." She closed the door behind her, leaving Katie to wonder just what she meant.

CHAPTER TWENTY-NINE

The storm raged like a jilted lover. Lightning blazed, thunder roared, and rain pounded on the roof, as if demanding entry.

The memory of the storm that had destroyed her house less than two months earlier made Katie's nerves quiver. She tried to reason with the fear as she chopped a green pepper to add to the onions and garlic simmering on the stove. *Just because your house was hit doesn't mean Zack's will be. In fact, it makes it more unlikely. Lightning doesn't strike twice.*

Or did it? It certainly seemed to, where her heart was concerned. She'd had no intention of kissing Zack again, and yet she'd done exactly that.

She wasn't sure which had her more rattled—the storm or the fact that Zack was likely to walk through the garage door at any moment. Another rumble of thunder shook the house just as Zack stepped into the kitchen.

He inhaled appreciatively. "Mmm. Smells delicious."

"It's shrimp Creole. One of Gracie's favorites."

"Katie!" called Gracie from the other room. "Katie, come quick!"

The panicked edge to Gracie's voice turned Katie's blood to ice. Zack looked at her. They both dashed out of the kitchen, across the living room and to the bedroom.

Gracie sat on the edge of the bed, her face white. "I'm bleeding."

"How bad?" Katie asked.

"Like—like a heavy period. Maybe worse. "

"I'll call an ambulance." Zack grabbed the phone and dialed 911.

"Lie down." Katie plumped the pillow against the headboard and lifted her feet. Her heart thumped so hard it should have bruised her ribs. Outside, the rain was thumping down, too—hard, then harder.

The lights flickered, then went out.

"Oh, no!" The panic in Gracie's voice rose.

"It's okay, sweetie. We're going to take care of you. You need to stay calm for the baby."

"I'm scared."

I am, too. "It's going to be okay."

"How do you know?"

Because anything else is unimaginable. "Because it is. I just know."

Zack came into the room with a flashlight. Gracie looked like a pregnant ghost in the eery beam of light. "The ambulances are all tied up. We need to take her ourselves." He handed the flashlight to Katie. "I'll carry you to the car."

"I'm so scared." Gracie's teeth were chattering.

"That's natural. But it's going to be okay." He looked

at Katie. "Why don't you grab her blanket—we'll want to keep her warm."

As in avoiding shock. Oh, God—this was Katie's worst nightmare.

"It's too soon," Gracie said. "I'm not due yet."

"You're just three weeks early. It'll be okay," Katie said. "Are you feeling contractions?"

"No. I'm just bleeding."

Zack picked Gracie up as if she were a small sack of potatoes. Katie walked beside them, Gracie gripping her hand. "I'll sit with you in the back," Katie told her.

"I'm so...so...scared."

"It'll be okay. When I called the hospital, they said they were calling your doctor and she's going to meet us there," Zack said.

The storm made it virtually impossible to see. Zack backed the car out of the driveway. Gracie started to sob—deep, gut-wrenching, breath-stealing sobs.

"Let's do some deep-breathing exercises," Katie said.

"I—I can't."

"Yes, you can. Breathe in: one, two, three, four."

"I can't!" Gracie sobbed harder, verging on hysteria.

"Yes, you can," Katie said firmly. "Pretend you're counting your baby's toes and fingers: one, two, three, four, five. Come on. One, two, three, four, five. You can do this."

Rain thundered on the car, oceansful of rain, pouring out in blinding streams. Zack drove as fast as he dared. He could see the road only in split-second intervals. At one point, the water on the road was so deep he was afraid it was going to wash out the engine.

In the backseat, Katie counted and breathed with

Gracie, keeping the girl from giving in to panic. At last Zack pulled up to the ER entrance. He'd called ahead, and medical staff were waiting. Two men in blue scrubs opened the back door of the car, eased Gracie out, and placed her on a gurney.

Zack helped Katie out of the car. Her face was ashen. "Go with her," Zack urged. "I'll take care of the paperwork." He watched her take Gracie's hand and walk beside her as the EMTs wheeled the gurney through the electric doors.

Zack parked the car and headed inside to the ER waiting room, where he numbly gave the insurance information at the check-in window. He wasn't a praying man. He hadn't even thought he believed in God. But as the woman copied his insurance card, he closed his eyes and prayed anyway. *Please, God. Help Gracie. Help the baby.*

At long last, they let him into the back part of the ER, where he found Katie standing in the hall as Gracie was wheeled out of an examination room.

"They're taking her up to obstetrics. Dr. Greene is already scrubbing up for an emergency C-section," Katie said. "The placenta is detaching."

"The baby..." Zack was scared to ask.

"Her heartbeat's strong."

They were already wheeling Gracie away. "Katie— Zack—I want you with me," Gracie called, reaching out her hand.

"I'm sorry, but they can't come," the nurse told Gracie as the orderly pushed the gurney toward the elevator.

"But I want them there when the baby's born. They're my parents."

"Sorry, but we'll have to put you out completely. They'll be with you the minute you wake up."

With that, they wheeled her down the hall.

"Love you, Gracie!" Katie called after her.

The ER nurse's face was kind. "You can wait in the maternity waiting room on the third floor. We'll come and get you as soon as it's over."

CHAPTER THIRTY

A large family, armed with balloons and flowers and unwrapped boxes of cigars, filled the small waiting room. Katie selected a spot on a padded window bench across the room. Zack followed her to it and put his arm around her.

She was trembling. "She called us her parents."

"I heard." His hand moved up and down her arm. Her skin was soft and warm.

"I feel like a part of me is in there with her, as if I'll just die if she..."

His arm tightened. "She'll be fine. The baby, too."

"What if something's wrong with the baby?"

"Whatever happens, we'll deal with it."

"We?"

"Yeah. You and me and Gracie and the baby. We're a team."

Team. Why had he used that word, when what he really meant was family? Something about the F-word completely freaked him out.

A nurse came into the waiting room. Katie started to rise.

"Travers family?" the nurse said.

Katie slumped back on the bench.

"That's us," said a gray-haired woman holding a bouquet of balloons.

"Congratulations." The nurse smiled. "Amy just gave birth to an eight pound, eleven-ounce boy. Both mother and child are healthy and fine."

"A boy!"

Everyone was on their feet, hugging and clapping and cheering.

"The baby's father is in the nursery, helping clean the baby up and weigh him. You can see them through the nursery window down the hall to the right in just a couple of minutes."

One of the men clapped the other on the back. "Gotta go see Danny as a dad."

"Hope he holds on to his son better than he holds on to a football!"

The boisterous group ambled off, leaving the waiting room ominously quiet. Zack ran his hand up and down Katie's arm, wanting to reassure her.

She jumped to her feet as a woman in teal-colored scrubs rounded the corner. "Dr. Greene!"

The doctor smiled. "They're both fine. Gracie has a little girl, six pounds, three ounces. She's a little early, but her lungs are fully developed and she seems great. The pediatrician is checking her over and will tell you more."

"Oh, thank God." Katie clutched Zack's arm. "And Gracie's good?"

She nodded. "It was touch and go for a while there. Gracie was starting to hemorrhage. If you had been even a few minutes later..."

Katie's fingers dug into Zack's arm. "Thank God you drove fast."

"Thank God I didn't run off the road."

"Gracie will be coming around in a few moments," the doctor said. "You can go into the recovery room."

"Thank you," Katie breathed.

"Yes. Thank you." Zack shook the doctor's hand.

Katie grabbed Zack by both arms and bounced on her heels, her face aglow. "Did you hear? They're both fine."

"Yeah." Relief flooded through him. He gathered Katie in a tight hug, then lifted her off her feet and swung her around. He kissed her soundly on the lips as he set her down.

She smiled up at him. "I'll bet that's a first."

"What?"

"The first time you kissed a grandmother."

"Oh, wow. That's a concept."

"It's okay. I've never given a grandpa a full frontal kiss, either."

"We're grandparents." He shook his head. The reality of the situation was hard to absorb. "I'm still adjusting to the concept of being a father, much less a grandfather."

He'd missed out on so much. On a lifetime. Gracie's lifetime.

"Yeah, well, start adjusting, Grandpa." Katie poked his side. "Let's go see our daughter."

Our daughter. For some reason, the words hit him like a hammer, hard and heavy, each one abnormally weighted. *Our.* As in, not mine. Not yours. Ours.

Daughter. As in, the child we made together. As in, our living, breathing, commingled DNA, who has just given life to another generation.

He and Katie were connected in a profound, intense, physical way that would march forward through the years, stretching into the future beyond the span of their own lives.

No wonder he felt so connected to her. This must be how the tree felt to the soil, how the fish felt to the water, how the earth felt to the sun—bound by forces beyond mere wills and wants, beyond choice, beyond a false sense of separation.

He belonged to Katie, and Katie belonged to him. They were inextricably connected. Why hadn't he realized this sooner? He didn't know but now that he did, he had to do something about it.

"Here she is." The smiling blonde nurse pushed a pink bassinet into the hospital room.

Gracie struggled to sit up. The movement made her stomach throb and painfully jangled the two tubes in her arm, but she barely noticed. Finally, finally, she was going to get to hold her baby.

The nurse lifted the pink-wrapped bundle and placed it in Gracie's arms, avoiding the elbow with the taped needle and the tube. The baby was wrapped like a mummy. Gracie gazed down into a tiny red face.

Her heart tripped over its own beat, then dove, headfirst, into a sea of love. "Oh, my God!" She was holding a miracle—a pink, swollen-eyed little miracle. "Oh, my God!" It wasn't an exclamation; she was genuinely invoking the name of her Creator. This must be what people meant when they said they'd had a religious experience.

The baby screwed up her face and opened her little bud of a mouth. Gracie had never seen anything so amazing in all her life. "Oh, baby," she whispered. "Just look at you!"

The baby blinked puffy eyes and squinted at her. Gracie's heart, like the Grinch's on Christmas, grew three sizes.

"Am I holding her right?" she asked Katie.

"You're doing it perfectly."

"Look at her!"

Katie leaned forward. "She's gorgeous."

"Beautiful," Zack echoed.

Gracie looked up and saw tears tracking down Katie's cheeks. Zack's eyes looked suspiciously wet as well. Katie's hand sifted through Gracie's hair, soft and gentle. "I'm so proud of you, sweetheart."

Gracie looked at Zack. He nodded, his eyes tender and warm.

"Help me unwrap her," Gracie said to Katie. "I want to look at her. I want to count her fingers and toes."

Katie found the edge of the soft pink blanket swaddling the baby and gently untucked it.

"Oh, look at her little arms!" Gracie exclaimed as Katie pulled the blanket back. Chubby and fat, they appeared to have no elbows or wrists, just sweet little dimples. The baby gripped Gracie's finger. Wonder gripped Gracie's heart.

She lifted the baby's little fingers, one at a time. "One, two, three, four, five." Gracie shot a smile at Katie. "Just like I pictured on the drive here." Katie nodded, her eyes shining and wet. She drew back the blanket further, exposing the baby's little legs.

Gracie drank in the sight. Her baby had fat little legs, plump tiny feet, and cankles to the nth degree. Who would have guessed that cankles could be so completely adorable? Gracie counted the tiny toes, complete with rounded little toenails.

"She's a beauty." Zack's voice was oddly husky.

"Perfect," Katie muttered.

"Perfectly perfect. My miracle baby." Gracie's cheeks hurt, she was smiling so hard. "I'm going to name her Faith."

"Oh, honey!" Katie's eyes filled with tears. "That's beautiful."

"Great name," Zack agreed.

Her heart felt like a hot bath—full and bubbly and warm. *Thank you, God.* For the first time in her life, Gracie knew peace. And she knew, beyond a doubt, exactly whose child she was.

Several hours later, Zack paced the hall of the obstetrics ward outside Gracie's room, while the hospital's lactation specialist nurse consulted with Gracie. Some things about women were a total mystery, and breast-feeding was one of them. Gracie had wanted Katie to stay with her while the specialist showed her something called latching on.

He felt like he needed a specialist himself, because he wanted to latch on to Katie, and he didn't quite know how to do it. Katie was his steadying, stabilizing, life-giving force, and he needed her. He wanted her. He had to make her his.

He took another turn down the hall, impatient for Katie to come out. He had something to say to her, something to ask. Something momentous. The words had been there, swelling, heating, bubbling like lava in his heart for a while, and now they were ready to erupt.

The door opened. The lactation specialist came out, followed by Katie. Zack watched Katie take her hands and thank her.

"How did it go?" Zack asked.

"Great. They're both getting the hang of things. The baby's in the bassinet, sleeping. Gracie's going to try to get some sleep, too."

She smiled, but her eyes were wistful. "I never had a chance to do any of the stuff that Gracie's been doing. I didn't get to count her toes or nurse her or..." Her voice broke, then stopped.

Zack's chest felt as if it would crack, as if it couldn't contain all the emotions running through him. "I hate it so much that you had to give her up. And I hate it that you went through all this alone."

She lifted her shoulders. "I wasn't entirely alone. There were people from the adoption center."

"Yeah, but that's not the same as family."

Even as he said it, he realized how ironic it was. Hypocritical, even. Him, espousing the importance of family? All of his life, he'd told himself that relationships didn't matter, that connections were temporary and replaceable, that people pretended family was important so they didn't have to face the cold fact that everyone is really alone. And yet here he was, talking as if connections mattered.

Because they did. Good God—they did. All his loner bull—it was just that: bull. A way of dismissing something too painful to look at.

All his denial about how much relationships mattered—it was because they did. How much had he wanted a family, a real family, when he was a boy? A mother and a father who wanted him and loved him, who listened to him and talked to him and actually enjoyed being around him?

He'd wanted that more than anything in the world. And when he couldn't get it ... well, he'd pretended it just didn't matter. His life had turned into a great big exercise in denial.

What a fool. How could he not have seen what was so obvious? Families mattered. Families were the place where love was stronger than bad behavior, where forgiveness wasn't a single act, but a continuous choice.

He had to talk to Katie. The pressure built within him. "Want to go down and get a cup of coffee?"

"Sure."

They got in an elevator. Zack punched the halt button.

Katie looked at him, startled. "What are you doing?"

"The offer of coffee was just a way to get you alone."

The elevator alarm shrieked.

"I don't think a hospital elevator is the best place for a private conversation."

"Apparently not." He punched the open button. The elevator door slid open. He pulled her out. "Let's take the stairs."

The middle-aged nurse at the desk frowned at them as he led her out of the elevator and down the hall to the metal door under the red glowing EXIT sign.

Katie stepped through the door, and he followed her into the stairwell. The door closed behind them with a loud steel-on-steel bang.

He took her hand. "Kate—I've got to ask you something." It was hard to talk around the lump in his throat. "Will you marry me?"

Katie's mouth opened, then closed, her eyes so bright and hopeful it almost hurt to look in them.

"You know how we talked about being grandparents before we were ever parents? Well, this is a chance to be both. To help raise Gracie's baby together. To be a family. I know how important family is to you, and I feel so bad that I wasn't there for you when you had Gracie, and..."

Her expression changed. He couldn't say exactly what happened, but it was as if the light went out of her eyes.

He spoke faster, hoping to smooth things over. "I want to be there for you and Gracie and the baby. I want to marry you, Kate."

She gazed at him, her expression telling him nothing. "Don't do me any favors."

This wasn't going well. Not well at all. He dropped to one knee. "Kate, will you marry me?"

"No."

He stared up, startled by the word, equally startled by the curt way she'd said it. "No?"

"No way." She shook her head. "I refuse to marry you to create some kind of weirdly retro family unit."

"But..."

"You can be a father to Gracie and a father figure for her baby without making the ultimate sacrifice."

He frowned. Where the hell had that come from? "Who said anything about a sacrifice?"

"Zack, I know how you feel about commitment. The very mention of the L-word sent you running for the Vegas hills. Call me crazy, but that is not the behavior of a man I want to marry." She punched his chest with her finger. "You are not exactly ideal husband material, Ferguson."

A nerve worked in his jaw. "Look, I know I'm not Saint Paul, and maybe this isn't the proposal of your dreams, but we can make this work."

"*'We can make this work?'* That's supposed to convince me to marry you?" Her eyes blazed. "Well, here's a news flash, Zachary—marriage isn't supposed to be *work*."

She turned away and huffed down the stairs.

He leaned against the wall and blew out a harsh breath. If he lived to be a hundred and two, he would never understand what women wanted.

CHAPTER THIRTY-ONE

"Zack proposed?" Bev gripped the steering wheel of her Range Rover and stared at Katie. Katie had called Bev from the hospital and asked for a ride back to Zack's place to pick up some clothing and other things for Gracie, the baby, and herself. "And that's why you look mad as a wet hen? Because he *proposed*?"

"Well, yes. I mean, no. I mean, yes, he proposed." Katie sank against the headrest and closed her eyes. "But I didn't like the way he did it."

Bev's forehead creased like corrugated cardboard. "What? You wanted him to get down on one knee and he didn't?"

"Actually, he did."

"So what's the problem?" Bev looked at her as if she were the most ungrateful moron on the planet. "You didn't like what he said?"

"I didn't like what he *didn't* say." She gazed out the window. "He didn't say anything about love."

"Ah." Bev looked both ways as she pulled out of the

hospital parking lot. "You know, honey, lots of men have trouble verbalizing their feelings."

"Yeah," Katie said glumly. "Especially if they don't have any."

"You know better than that. That man is crazy about you."

"He was also crazy about Scarlett Johansson."

"He's been with you a lot longer than he was with her."

"And that's supposed to make me feel good?"

"Well, actually—yes. It would make me feel terrific, that's for sure. And come on, Katie. He asked you to *marry* him. A guy doesn't do that unless he's got strong feelings."

"Yeah. And those feelings are guilt and obligation."

Bev frowned. "I don't get it."

"He doesn't really want to marry me. He just thinks it's the right thing to do. He's all emotional from Gracie nearly losing and then having this baby, and he feels bad he wasn't there when I had Gracie, and he thinks the only way he can make things right is to marry me, because that's what he thinks he should have done when we were kids."

"Even if what you're saying is true—and I'm not sure I was even following all that, much less agreeing with it—none of this means he doesn't love you."

"I'm not sure Zack knows what love is." She knit her fingers together so hard they hurt. "He's never seen it up close. His parents' marriage was a nightmare."

"It's not like you had a great example from your family, either." Bev braked for a stop sign. "But you and Paul still managed to have a wonderful marriage."

That was true. Katie closed her eyes and rubbed her temple. "You know what the difference is? I wanted love and marriage. And I believed it was possible." She opened her eyes and stared at the light pole illuminated in the black night. "Zack never believed in it, and he never wanted it. And I don't want to marry a man who only wants to marry me because he thinks he should. If I marry again, it'll be to a guy who loves me with all his heart, a guy who can't wait to share his life with me, a guy who loves me as much as I love him."

She gazed out the window, her heart as dark as the rain-slicked street. "As much as I'd like him to be, I just don't think Zack is that guy."

CHAPTER THIRTY-TWO

Two days later, Zack cornered Katie in the hallway out-side Gracie's hospital room. His mouth was set in a hard, angry line. "We need to talk."

He took her arm and steered her down the hallway to a doorless supply closet. One wall was stacked with bed-pans and other creepy plastic receptacles. Another held folded hospital gowns, sheets, and towels. A mop sat in an industrial-style bucket, making the room reek of pine disinfectant. He loomed over her, his face like a storm cloud. "What the hell is going on?"

"What do you mean?"

"You asked me to stay at the hospital with Gracie today while you ran an errand."

A little tremor shot through her. For the last two days, she'd avoided Zack as much as possible. She'd spent the night in Gracie's room at the hospital, and she left when-ever he came to visit.

"While I was here, you moved all of Gracie's and your belongings out of my house."

"My house is nearly finished, so I thought it would be

best if Gracie and the baby and I adapt to the new normal as soon as possible." A normal that didn't include Zack as a day-to-day part of their lives.

"Why the hell didn't you tell me?"

"Maybe I was hoping to avoid a scene like this one."

His scowl darkened. "This isn't a scene. This is a conversation. But if you think a scene is called for, I can damn sure ramp things up for you. In fact, I'm ready to do just that, because the thought of you lining up movers and bringing them in behind my back really chafes my ass."

"I didn't line up movers. Bev and her husband helped me."

"Same thing. You planned things out and didn't tell me." He stepped closer. "What is the big idea?"

"It's *your* big idea. I'm just following your plan."

The furrows between his eyebrows deepened. "What the hell are you talking about?"

"Your plan. We'd share custody until Gracie had the baby and turned eighteen. Well, she's had the baby. She'll be eighteen in a few months. So I figured we might as well get things settled so that she doesn't have to move twice. She can simply bring the baby home."

"What's wrong with my place being home?"

"You and I have no reason to live together. And you'll soon be leaving Chartreuse."

"Who says?"

"That was the plan."

"I'm not going anywhere. Gracie just had her baby."

"She's going to be raising that baby for the next eighteen years, and you're going to be trotting all over kingdom come while she does it." Katie deliberately kept her voice calm and upbeat, as if she were explaining something to a small child. "We all might as well get accustomed to the new routine from the outset."

His scowl turned into a glower.

She forced what she hoped was a conciliatory smile. "You're welcome to pop in for visits whenever your schedule allows."

"My, that's big of you."

"I don't understand why you're upset." Katie used her best talking-to-a-sulky-kindergartner voice. "This was our arrangement."

"Initially, maybe. Before we started sleeping together."

"That didn't change anything."

"It damned sure did. I proposed to you, didn't I?"

"What do you want, a gold star? You proposed, yes, but you made absolutely no mention of love."

"Oh, for Pete's sake. If I haul out the abracadabra word, will that change things?"

"No. No, it won't." *Not at this point. Not when I know you don't mean it.* A lump formed in her throat. She willed herself to shove it down, to keep her voice calm and unemotional. "Zack, thank you for bringing Gracie into my life. Thanks for helping out after my house was ruined. Thank you for the"—she swallowed—"romantic interlude, too. It was very therapeutic."

His face was beyond a storm cloud. It was a tornado of fury. "You thought our *romantic interlude* was *therapeutic*?"

"Yes. It helped me move on."

A muscle worked in his jaw. "From the little scene I witnessed in your closet, it didn't help at all."

"What?"

"After you were so talkative in bed. I went up to your room later that day, and saw you sitting on the floor, wearing your dead husband's clothes and going through his things."

"I..."

He cut her off, his face hard as a steel trap. "You haven't moved on. You haven't moved an inch. You've simply moved back to your house—or should I say, to your rebuilt shrine."

Anger flashed through her, white-hot as lightning. There was no talking to this man—no point in trying to explain. Zack would never be able to fully commit to her, to give her the unconditional, full-hearted love she needed. He couldn't even listen to her!

"This conversation is over." Katie's arms went rigid at her sides. "I have nothing further to say to you. I will be polite to you in front of Gracie and everyone else. I will include you in birthday and holiday celebrations, and I will be civil and kind. But you and I have no reason to ever have any more conversations of a personal or romantic nature. Do you understand?"

"Oh, I understand, all right. I understand more than you know. I understand that nothing really personal ever happened between us, because there was always a third party in the room. Well, I leave you to him. I hope you two will be very happy together."

He was the most impossible, pigheaded, insensitive man she had ever encountered. She wanted to walk away, but he was closer to the door, so he walked out first.

It made her furious. It made her tremble with rage. It made her burst into tears after his back disappeared around the corner in the hallway.

• • •

Annette sat in Katie's new kitchen and watched her turn on the stove under the teakettle. "I understand you and Zack had a big argument at the hospital."

"Where did you hear that?"

"Nellie has her sources. Apparently you were overheard."

"Great, just great." Katie sank onto a barstool at the kitchen counter, her heart sinking with it.

"What's going on with you two, anyway? I heard Zack proposed."

Bev was the only person she'd told, and Bev knew how to keep a confidence. "How did you hear that?"

Annette lifted her shoulders. "Apparently someone coming down the stairs a couple of days earlier heard you talking in the stairwell."

Terrific. Were there no secrets in Chartreuse? "Does the whole town happen to know what kind of toilet tissue I prefer?"

Annette smiled. "That would be Charmin."

Katie stared at her.

"Just kidding. I happen to know because I once changed a roll at your house." She shifted, stretching her leg. "Seriously, Katie—Zack proposed and you refused?"

"He doesn't love me. The word didn't even come up. He's just trying to do what he thinks he should have done back when I had Gracie. And I'm not going to rope him into something that he'll resent in a year or two."

"But…"

Katie held up both hands. "I've already heard the 'people can change' speech so many times I know it by heart."

"Okay, okay. I'll spare you. But I do have two things to say, and I'd like for you to hear me out."

As if she had a choice. Suppressing a sigh, Katie nodded.

The teakettle started to rumble. "First of all, people sometimes reverse their opinions—even their most deeply held opinions. Take you, for example. You hated Chartreuse, and you vowed you'd never live here. Well, here you are."

"That's not the same."

"Isn't it? It's a strong belief you held as a teenager, based on your childhood experiences. As your own life experiences accumulated, your perspective changed. The things you wanted—and didn't want—changed. It happens to everyone. Zack is no exception."

It made sense on the surface, but Annette didn't know how deeply Zack was set in his ways.

"The second thing I have to say is, look at this from the man's perspective. Zack walks into your house, and the first things he sees are your wedding picture and Paul's ashes on the mantel. You move into his house, and you keep the ashes by your bedside and Paul's things in your closet."

"And you know this, how?"

"Gracie told me."

Of course. Every vestige of privacy had disappeared the moment Gracie moved in.

"Then you and he start a love affair, and one day he walks in and apparently sees you wearing Paul's shirt and going through his things," Annette continued. "How can he help but feel that he's competing with a dead man and coming in second?"

Katie's heart started to pound. "And this information came to you via..."

"Lulu. She heard the conversation you two had in the hospital closet."

The whole friggin' town knew every bit of her business. In fact, apparently they knew more of it than she did, and they were putting pieces together in ways that Katie hadn't.

The teakettle whistled. Katie got up and took it off the stove, glad to have a diversion.

"Zack thinks you'll never love him the way you loved Paul."

"And I won't," Katie said. Her eyes filled with unexpected tears. "But I could love him differently."

"You already do."

"I'm trying not to." A tear spilled down her cheek.

"But you do." Annette's eyes were kind and warm. "And honey, it's all right. Paul would want that for you."

"That's not the problem."

"Zack thinks it is."

"Well, he's wrong."

Annette put her hand over Katie's. "Maybe you're wrong about Zack, as well."

Annette's words rattled around in Katie's head for the next three days. Zack gave her a wide berth at the hospital, then, in typical Zack fashion, he left on a trip to Seattle two days after Gracie came home. He IM'd and texted and phoned Gracie several times a day, but Katie heard nothing.

She thought about calling him, then decided against it. He was the one who'd left—the one who hadn't seen fit to talk to her, to tell her his feelings, to sort things out. If he wanted to be with her, he'd have to prove it.

Besides, she'd already written him off. Now that little Faith was here, she had far more important things to do than wonder whether or not she'd been mistaken about Zack. Obviously she hadn't been. If he couldn't or wouldn't reach out to her, she was better off without him.

The only problem was, her heart wasn't buying it.

CHAPTER THIRTY-THREE

Zack stood on the porch of Katie's house three days later, clutching two bouquets of pink roses. Gracie opened the door, then broke into an ear-to-ear grin. "Zack!" She hugged his neck. Zack hugged her back, careful of her incision. She smelled like Oreos and baby powder. He handed her one of the bouquets.

"Thanks!" She smelled the flowers, then looked up and grinned. "You texted me just this morning, and you didn't say a thing about coming home. I thought you weren't due back for two more days."

"I know. I got homesick."

It was true. He'd never been homesick before, had never even really thought of a place as home, but all he could do now was think about Gracie and the baby and Katie.

Especially Katie. Gracie and he texted and Facebooked and IM'd several times a day, but he still hadn't heard from Katie. He'd told himself that the next move should be up to her. He should just leave her alone. If she wanted to be with him, she'd call.

But she hadn't. He'd pumped Gracie endlessly for information about her, and Gracie had fed him tidbits: Katie watched the baby during the day while she worked on lessons with Annette; Katie had fixed chicken fricassee for dinner; Katie had gone to her book-club meeting; the beauty-supply guy had the hots for Katie; Lulu was trying to fix Katie up with another porcelain-veneered loser.

And then the news had stopped. When Zack asked Gracie about Katie, he'd learned that Katie had seen one of the messages two days ago, and told Gracie to stop discussing her with Zack.

Surprisingly, Gracie had complied with the request.

Zack stepped into the foyer, took Gracie's hands, and held her at arm's length. "Just look at you, sweetheart! You're beautiful." Gracie's resemblance to Katie was more marked than ever. Her face was fresh-scrubbed, free of black eyeliner and nose jewelry. Her hair was spike-free and a normal-looking brown, a shade somewhere between his and Katie's. She wore jeans and a long red T-shirt. "You look so grown up."

Gracie shrugged. "Having a baby will do that, I guess."

"Gracie doesn't look like she just had a baby, does she?" Zack looked up to see Annette in the living room doorway, Dave beside her. "That's one of the blessings of being young—everything springs back fast."

Zack stepped forward and kissed the older woman on the cheek, then shook Dave's hand. "You both look terrific, too. There must be something in the water."

"It's not the water. It's the company," Dave said, looping his arm around Annette. The warmth in the smile they shared made Zack's chest ache. He turned to Gracie. "Where's the baby?"

"Sleeping. I just fed her and put her in her crib for her morning nap. She'll be up in about half an hour."

"I can't wait to see her. How are you feeling?"

"Good. My incision doesn't hurt too bad today. And get this—I got my ACT score from taking it last spring, and I got a 30! That's a really good score. Twenty-four is what's required for the Louisiana scholarship program."

"That's terrific." He cleared his throat. "How's Katie?"

They all looked at one another.

Zack's heart hitched. "What's the matter? Is she okay?"

"She's been pretty down since you left," Dave volunteered.

"Yeah," Gracie said. "She cries in her closet where she thinks I can't hear her."

"Yeah, I know. Into Paul's clothes." Zack hadn't realized he'd muttered it aloud until Annette shook her head.

"No," Annette said. "She gave all those away."

Zack looked at her. "She did?"

Annette nodded. "Weeks ago. We scattered his ashes, then Katie divided his clothes and donated them to a couple of charities. She gave the urn to Dave and me."

Holy cow. She'd been sorting through Paul's clothes to give them away? His heart felt like it had just sprouted wings. "Really?"

"Yeah," Dave said. "Didn't you notice she's not wearing her rings?"

He hadn't. It had completely skipped his notice.

Probably because he'd tried for so long to avoid noticing that Katie still wore them.

"She doesn't go in the closet to cry over Paul. She's crying over you, you moron." Gracie rolled her eyes.

The new wings fluttered. "What?"

"She loves you."

Dave shook his head. "I don't understand what went on between you two."

"I proposed, that's what went on."

"You must have done an awfully crummy job of it," Gracie said.

Zack shoved his hands into his pants pockets. It *had* been pretty lame. "Yeah, well, I came back to take another stab at it."

"Really?" Gracie's face lit up. So did Annette's.

"Yeah. I've got an engagement ring in my pocket."

"Oh, that's so cool!" Gracie jumped up and down. "Can I see?"

"Later," Annette told her. She turned to Zack, her face all schoolteacher-ish and serious. "A woman needs to hear that she's loved. Katie thinks you don't believe in love."

Zack looked at Gracie. This really wasn't something he wanted to discuss in front of his daughter. He cleared his throat. "I, uh, have an aversion to saying empty words."

"*Love* isn't an empty word," Annette said. "It's the fullest word in the English language. And it's a verb, as well as a noun."

"Yeah," Dave said. "It's not about stardust and floaty feelings—at least, not entirely. It means you're willing to do whatever it takes. It means you'll be there through bad times as well as good. It means you'll admit it when you're wrong and you'll come back even though you get ticked off. It's a choice you make, day in and day out, despite the circumstances and how you feel at the moment. It means this person is your best friend and the keeper of the biggest part of your heart."

"Wow." Gracie stared at Dave, her eyes wide. "That was beautiful."

Annette gazed at Dave, a soft smile on her lips. "Yes, it was."

"Maybe I should write that down," Zack said. "Where is Katie now?"

Dave, Annette, and Gracie said the same thing at the same time. "Uh-oh."

Zack's chest tightened. "Uh-oh, what? Where is she?"

The three of them exchanged looks. "On her way to Italy," Dave finally said.

"*Italy?*"

"Yes. Her friend Emma called and asked her to come do her hair for her TV special," Annette said. "It's being taped day after tomorrow. She's been pretty down lately, so we offered to stay with Gracie and Faith so she could go."

Gracie nodded. "I played the guilt card. She didn't want to leave me and the baby, but I told her I'd feel guilty if she missed this opportunity. Besides, she'll just be gone five days."

Five days seemed like a lifetime. Zack's shoulders drooped.

"She might still be at the salon," Gracie offered. "She was going by to pack up her curling iron and rollers and stuff."

It was worth a shot. Zack turned toward the door. "I'll try to catch her. Do me a favor—call her and see if you can detain her. But don't tell her I'm in town."

Bev was waiting by the door of the Curl Up 'N Dye when Zack pulled up to the curb, parking behind a pink panel truck sporting the name "Color Me Gorgeous Beauty Supplies." She bustled forward as he climbed out of his Volvo. "Katie left for the airport just before Annette called. She accidentally left her cell phone at her workstation."

"Oh, great."

"Annette told us that you're going to propose." Bev rubbed her hands together and bounced on the balls of her feet, her thin frame vibrating with excitement. Five other women poured out of the salon, all grinning like monkeys. He recognized Rachel the manicurist, Josie Pringle, and Lulu, whose red hair was wrapped in perm rods. A large pink-faced woman had foil wrapped around her head, the retired librarian's hair was wound up in giant pink rollers, and a woman he didn't recognize wore rolled-up pants with weird purple spacers between her toes. Behind them ambled a beer-bellied balding man wearing a navy shirt with a "Color Me Gorgeous" logo on the pocket. He unlocked the back of the panel truck.

"I called Joe with the police department and asked him to stop her for you," Bev continued breathlessly.

Being stopped by the police was not likely to put Katie in the most romantic mood. "That's not necessary" Zack said. "I'll catch her at the airport, or..."

"Joe's already got her stopped."

Zack climbed into his car and drove like a desperado.

Three miles out of town, he saw flashing lights at the side of the road. He braked behind the police car, opened his door, and climbed out.

Katie stood with her hands on her hips, her back toward him. She wore a pink polka-dotted sweater set, black pants, and ballet flats. She looked both adorable and pissed off. "Joe, you've checked my registration, my license, my insurance, and my inspection sticker," Katie was saying. "You've known me all my life, so I don't believe you really need to see any further identification. I don't think it's even legal for you to stop me, since we're out of the city limits. So quit fooling around and give me back my license. You're going to make me miss my plane."

The officer scratched his wispy thatch of hair and shifted his stance uneasily. "I, uh, have orders to detain you."

"Orders from whom?" Katie demanded.

"Actually, that would be from me," called a woman's voice.

Zack turned to see Bev climbing out of the passenger side of the pink Color Me Gorgeous van, her hand sheepishly raised. The other women from the salon were scooting out, rollers and all, to stand on the shoulder of the road.

"Hi, y'all," called Lulu, merrily waving. "Don't mind us. We're just here to watch."

Katie's eyes locked on Zack. They immediately turned wary. "What are you doing here? What the heck is going on?"

He drew a deep breath. "This isn't how I planned it, but…"

A semi roared by, stirring up a wave of dust. Some of it landed in his mouth, making it hard to swallow. He swallowed anyway.

"...I love you, Kate."

She stared at him. Her eyes narrowed. "You don't believe in love."

"That was before."

"Before what?"

"Before you changed my mind."

She put her hands on her hips, her eyes skeptical. "Just how did I perform this miracle?"

"You made me miserable."

The women behind them laughed. Lulu's titter carried over the whine of a passing motorbike.

"Not exactly a shining endorsement," Katie said dryly.

"Maybe not," Zack said, "but it's a real one." He took her arm and pulled her away from the crowd, which was growing by the minute. A dozen old people were piling out of the Sunnyside Assisted-Living Villa van, Nellie climbed out of an old PT Cruiser with a camera, and the other police officers on the Chartreuse police force had joined the crowd of spectators. "Kate, the day you said all that stuff, I made plans to move my headquarters to Chartreuse. I went up to your room to tell you, then I saw you in the closet with Paul's stuff, and...well, I thought you weren't over him."

"I was getting rid of his clothes."

"I know. Annette told me."

"Annette?"

"I went by your house just now. I talked to Annette and Dave and Gracie." He looked up, and saw them climbing out of Annette's sedan. Gracie paused to get the baby out of the car seat in the back. He pulled Katie farther away.

"Kate—I want to be with you. I want to share my life with you. I want to see what you look like when you're old and gray."

"I will never be gray, not as long as I can get my hands on a bottle of hair dye."

"See? Now that right there—that mouth you've got on you—I love that about you."

She smiled. The tightness in his chest uncoiled a little.

"I didn't want to fall in love with you, Kate. Believe me, I did my best not to."

"Once again, your silver tongue is just enchanting me."

He took her hands. "The truth is, I didn't want to be second-best. I thought you were still in love with Paul. I thought you could never care about anyone the way you cared about him."

The guarded look faded. She met his gaze, full on and open. "Oh, Zack—my feelings for you are just as deep. Love doesn't get used up like a bottle of shampoo. It stretches out your heart so you can hold even more of it."

Zack stepped closer, looped a strand of her hair around his finger, and grinned. "Kate Landers Charmaine, did you just admit that you love me?"

"I…" She looked down, her cheeks flaming, then looked up. "Yeah. I guess I did."

Gravel bit into his knee as he knelt, but he felt no pain. "I love you, too. I want to marry you and spend the rest of my life with you." He reached into his pocket and pulled out a ring—a four-carat, brilliant-cut solitaire set in platinum, with diamond baguettes paving each side.

"He's got a ring!" Lulu exclaimed. Oohs and ahhs arose from the onlookers, who crowded in for a better view. "And, oh, my—it looks like a doozy!"

Zack continued, undeterred, seeing only Katie's face. "Kate, I want to live with you and make more babies with you and see your face the first thing in the morning and the last thing at night. I love you." His dimple flashed as he smiled. "In case you didn't catch that, I love you. I, Zack Ferguson, love you, Kate Landers Charmaine. I. Love. You. So... will you marry me?"

"Yes," Katie said, her eyes shining and bright as the Louisiana sun. "Yes, I will."

He rose to his feet, pulled her close, and kissed her, oblivious to the applause of the crowd or the roar of another passing eighteen-wheeler or the cloud of dust swirling around them. He had found his one and only, his everything and more, and her arms were both heaven and home.

THE DISH

Where authors give you the inside scoop!

♥ ♥ ♥ ♥ ♥ ♥ ♥ ♥ ♥ ♥ ♥ ♥ ♥ ♥ ♥ ♥

From the desk of Paula Quinn

Dear Reader,

While doing research for LAIRD OF THE MIST, I fell in love with Clan MacGregor. Their staunch resolve to overcome trials and countless tribulations during a three-hundred-year proscription earned them a very special place in my heart. So when I was given the chance to write a brand-new series featuring Callum and Kate MacGregor's grown children, I was ecstatic.

The first of my new four-book series, RAVISHED BY A HIGHLANDER (available now), stars Robert MacGregor, whom you met briefly in A HIGHLANDER NEVER SURRENDERS. He was a babe then, and things haven't changed. He's still a babe, but in an entirely different way!

My favorite type of hero is a rogue who can sweep a lady off her feet with a slant of his lips. Or a cool, unsmiling brute with a soft spot no one sees but his woman. Rob was neither of those men when I began writing his story. He was more. I didn't think I could love a character I created as much as I loved his father, but I was wrong, and I'm not ashamed to say it.

Rob isn't careless with women's hearts. His smile isn't reckless but a bit awkward. It's about the only thing he *hasn't* practiced every day of his life. Born to fill his father's boots as chief and protector of his clan, Rob takes life and the duties that come with his birthright seriously. He's uncompromising in his loyalty to his kin and unrelenting in his beliefs. He's a warrior who is confident in the skill of his arm, but not rash in drawing his sword. However, once it's out, someone's head is going to roll. Yes, he's tall and handsome, with dark curls and eyes the color of sunset against a summer blue loch, but his beauty can best be seen in his devotion to those he loves.

He is . . . exactly what a lady needs in her life if an entire Dutch fleet is on her tail.

I'll tell you a little about Davina Montgomery, the lass who not only softens Rob's staunch heart, but comes to claim it in her delicate fingers. But I won't tell you too much, because I don't want to reveal the secret that has taken everyone she's ever loved away from her. She came to me filled with sorrow, chained by duty, and in need of things so very basic, yet always beyond her reach: safety, and the love of someone who would never betray her or abandon her to danger.

I saw Rob through Davina's eyes the moment he plucked her from the flames of her burning abbey. A hero: capable, courageous, and hot as hell.

We both knew Rob was perfect for her, and for the first time, I saw hope in Davina's eyes—and her beauty can best be seen when she looks at him.

Travel back to the Scottish Highlands with Rob and Davina and discover what happens when duty and desire collide. And I love to hear from readers, so please visit me at www.paulaquinn.com.

Enjoy!

Paula Quinn

♥ ♥ ♥ ♥ ♥ ♥ ♥ ♥ ♥ ♥ ♥ ♥ ♥ ♥ ♥ ♥

From the desk of R. C. Ryan

Dear Reader,

Are you as intrigued by family dynamics as I am? I know that, having written a number of family sagas, I've been forced to confront a lot of family drama. But fiction mirrors real life. And in the real world, there's nothing more complicated or more dramatic than our individual relationships with the different members of our families.

We read a lot about mother–daughter and father–son relationships, not to mention sibling rivalry. Psychologists tell us life paths are often determined by birth order. And yet there are always exceptions to the rule— the child of poverty who builds a financial empire. The man with a learning disability who lifts himself to the ranks of genius. The girl who loses a leg and goes on to run marathons.

And so, while I'm fascinated with family dynamics, and our so-called place in the universe, I'm even more intrigued by those who refuse to fit into any mold. Instead, by the sheer force of their determination, they rise above society's rules to become something rare and wonderful. Whether they climb Mount Everest or never leave the neighborhood where they were born, they live each day to the fullest. And whether they change the world or just change one life, they defy the experts and prove wrong those who believe a life's course is predetermined.

In MONTANA DESTINY, the second book in my Fool's Gold series, Wyatt McCord returns to the Lost Nugget Ranch after years of living life on the edge, only to lose his heart to the fiercely independent Marilee Trainor, a loner who has broken a few rules of her own. These two, who searched the world over for a place to belong, will laugh, love, and fight often, while being forced to dig deep within themselves to survive.

I hope you enjoy watching Wyatt and Marilee take charge of their lives and forge their own destinies.

R. C. Ryan

www.ryanlangan.com

♥ ♥ ♥ ♥ ♥ ♥ ♥ ♥ ♥ ♥ ♥ ♥ ♥ ♥ ♥

From the desk of Robin Wells

Dear Reader,

"So, Robin—what's your latest book about?"

I get that question a lot, and I always find it difficult to answer. I usually start off by describing the plot in varying degrees of detail. Here's the short version:

STILL THE ONE is the story of Katie Charmaine, a hairdresser in Chartreuse, Louisiana—the same colorful small town where my previous book, BETWEEN THE SHEETS, took place. Katie lost her husband in Iraq, and she thinks she'll never love again. But when her first love, Zack Ferguson, returns, she feels the same irresistible attraction that stole her heart at seventeen. To Katie's shock, he's accompanied by the teenage daughter Katie gave up for adoption at birth. The daughter, Gracie, has a major attitude, a smart mouth—and is now pregnant herself.

The medium-length version adds: Gracie's adoptive parents were killed in a car accident, and when she discovers her birth parents' identities, she locates Zack first. She wants him to declare her an emancipated minor and give her a nice wad of cash. Instead, Zack takes Gracie to Chartreuse, where he and Katie share custody until Gracie turns eighteen.

The long version gives still more detail: Zack and Katie experience the ups and downs of parenting a difficult teenager, while rediscovering the love that initially drew them together. Can they forgive each other for their past mistakes? Can Zack overcome his commitment-phobic ways? Can Katie get beyond her feelings of disloyalty to her late husband and her fear of opening her heart again? Can Gracie let go of her anger and open her heart to Katie?

The long version still doesn't fully cover everything that happens, but then, a book is much more than a plot. So I also answer the "what's your book about?" question by citing the following themes present in STILL THE ONE:

Romance. There's nothing like the heady feeling of falling in love, and nothing worse than believing you're falling alone.

Family. This book is about some of the ways that families shape us, for better and for worse.

Grief. Love doesn't die, even though people do. How do we get past the feeling that loving someone else is disloyal to the deceased? How do we ever find the courage to care that deeply again, knowing how much it hurts to lose someone you love?

Mistakes. Teenagers aren't known for making wise choices, but adults don't always make the best decisions, either. Regardless of age, we all can get lost in the moment, make incorrect assumptions, repeat a destructive pattern, or neglect to say something that needs to be said.

Blessings. Sometimes mistakes that have haunted us for years can turn out to be life's biggest blessings.

Forgiveness. How do we let go of hurts—especially big, bad ones? Once we've been hurt by someone, can we ever fully trust that person again?

And last but not least, **Love.** If I had to give a single answer to what my book is about, this would be it. I believe that love has the power to heal and redeem and transform anyone and any situation, no matter how hopeless it may seem, and that's the major underlying theme of this novel—and all my novels, come to think of it. I hope you'll drop by my website, www.robinwells.com, to see a short video about the book, read an excerpt from my next novel, and/or let me know your thoughts. I love to hear from readers, and I can be reached at my website or at P.O. Box 303, Mandeville, LA 70470.

Here's hoping your life will be filled with love, laughter, and lots of good books!

Robin Wells

Want to know more about romances at
Grand Central Publishing and Forever?
Get the scoop online!

GRAND CENTRAL PUBLISHING'S
ROMANCE HOMEPAGE

Visit us at www.hachettebookgroup.com/romance
for all the latest news, reviews, and chapter excerpts!

NEW AND UPCOMING TITLES

Each month we feature our new titles
and reader favorites.

CONTESTS AND GIVEAWAYS

We give away galleys, autographed copies,
and all kinds of fun stuff.

AUTHOR INFO

You'll find bios, articles, and links to personal
websites for all your favorite authors—and
so much more!

THE BUZZ

Sign up for our monthly romance newsletter,
and be the first to read all about it!